A MONUMENT TO EVIL

There on a broad open knoll above the sea it stood, like some dreadful beast of wood and stone. It leered out obscenely at him, seeming to squat proudly in a cacophony of twisted lines, great asymmetrical blocks of stone and angling, leaping spires of deepest black.

Scott's eyes ran unbelievingly over those grim, absurd contours.

Overwhelming all other features, though, was the central tower standing over forty feet tall. At the very top of this tower, just under the triangular, shingled roof, was a great round portal, an unfathomable eye that gazed out into the misty, unreasoning depths of the ocean. And atop the conical roof, something hunched and squatted—something of deepest black stone veined in spidery red.

At such a height its exact features were difficult to determine, but Scott could feel that its form was bestial and unholy, canine and glaring, an unhallowed avenger and an enemy of all that was sane and good. It was the crowning glory of the anomalous, blasphemous house—its final horror.

We will send you a free catalog on request. Any titles not in your local book store can be purchased by mail. Send the price of the book plus 50 cents shipping charge to Leisure Books, P.O. Box 270, Norwalk, Connecticut 06852.

Titles currently in print are available for industrial and sales promotion at reduced rates. Address inquiries to Nordon Publications, Inc., Two Park Avenue, New York, New York 10016, Attention: Premium Sales Department.

BLACK

James Tarab

A LEISU

Published

Nordon P
Two Park
New York

Copyright

All rights
Printed in

LEISURE BOOKS •

1

Harry had gotten up on the wrong side of bed that morning. Literally. They had been redecorating the apartment, and everything was just where it shouldn't be, with the result that Harry had smashed his toe into an end table that belonged somewhere in the living room. Curses and assorted profanities notwithstanding, the table had not disintegrated into its primal atoms, and Harry's toe would continue to ache throughout the morning.

Grace had given him little comfort about this tragedy, but at least she had not tried to stem the stream of expletives either. He had to give his wife credit there. She wasn't the sympathetic type, but she didn't care much what the neighbors said either. It was this massive indifference that made life with her tolerable.

This plus the important services she performed after a listless fashion produced a sort of grudging gratitude in Harry. She cooked tolerably, washed and darned the clothes on a semi-regular basis, kept house and was even known to become amorous once or twice a month. That she did all these things with such a plodding matter-of-factness would have disturbed a more romantic character, but Harry never had cut much of a dashing figure, even in more youthful days. Going on fifty, he was hardly Don Quixote and knew it. His life was lived in endless routine, the dull comfort of monotony.

He had just sat down to an uninspiring looking breakfast of cereal and poached egg—another one of Grace's enforced diets—when the call came. He could hear her droning monotonously out in the hall. Yes, he's here. Yes, she'd get him. He shook his head resignedly. What would it be today? Another burglary? Some kid starting his own auto part store with stolen hubcaps? A two bit pusher with an ounce of grass in his pants?

He pushed himself away from the table almost gratefully. They only called like this if they needed him for something, and that meant he could stop at Dunkin' Donuts on his way down. The inside of his mouth went wet with anticipation.

He took the phone from Grace's hand and muttered a hello into the mouthpiece. A woman's nasal voice hissed back at him.

"Sergeant Oronski? This is dispatch. We have a report of vandalism at St. Mark's Church, 718 Wennemac. Squad already present. Please investigate."

Just like that. Clipped, precise. No hi, how are ya or isn't the weather nice. He hated that board. She must of seen too many episodes of *Adam-12*.

"There's a squad there already? Why the hell give it to me then? Uniform can handle a simple vandalism?" There was annoyance in his voice, but he cringed when he heard the woman's next words.

"Lieutenant Elliot said to call you on it."

There it was. He should have known instantly. Frank Elliot just loved to give him the real "plums." Some little punk throws a rock through a stained glass window . . . big time crime. Send the second-ranking detective in the department to find him and slap his wrist. The glamorous life of a cop. "I'll get right on it," Harry replied and hung up the phone. Women's Lib had left him pretty much unscathed until the department had hired that broad.

He threw on the first tie he came across, kissed Grace perfunctorily and made his way downstairs to the cobalt-blue Plymouth, unmarked but also so unadorned as to signal "cop" from a mile away. It was a cloudy, dull gray morning which fit his mood just fine. Toe hurt, no breakfast, a stupid vandalism, Elliot. A litany of despair.

He turned the car at Ester and headed north. The streets of Oak Grove: broad and domed with majestic elms, oaks and maples. On either side the street was graced by large, gracious Victorian homes that bespoke pride, money and culture. It was a beautiful town, he reminded himself. But that thought contested with images of hot coffee and chocolate-covered donuts and, yes, a vague feeling of disquiet about this assignment. He wasn't Catholic, but he had been to St. Mark's for a wedding once. A beautiful church and a damn shame if some little monster had defaced it. He had an idea what should be done with these kids when you found them, but it was hardly acceptable by modern standards of penology. Too bad.

At the last moment he swerved hard to make the corner at Fairfax. Screw the donuts. As much as he wanted them, he'd better get right over to St. Mark's if Elliot was involved in this. All the bloody bastard wanted was one excuse, one slipup on his part . . . .

He guided the Plymouth to a stop in front of St. Mark's. The building was an excellent example of miniature gothic, rendered in highly polished limestone and redolent with flying buttresses and gargoyles. It was a church done in the old way, a reflection of a time when a man still thought he could buy his way into heaven with generous donations. Nowadays it was hard to find a man who even believed in heaven.

His stomach sunk several inches into the steering wheel, but Harry managed to push his way out of the car, his thoughts momentarily turning to Grace's frequent admonitions about his weight, heart attacks, life insurance and other similarly cheerful matters. But then he saw the trio standing on the front steps of the church; the two uniformed patrolmen and the black-cassocked priest. This wasn't going to be too distasteful—he hoped.

He recognized one of the uniformed cops. It was Danny Clark, young but not a know-it-all. Harry knew his father, Sam. It was good, somehow, to see a familiar face. The priest's face, fiftyish, hawklike and scowling, looked like it had just finished inspecting the list of truant parishoners. "Hiya Danny," Harry said hopefully.

"Hello, Sergeant." He motioned to the priest. "This is Monsignor Kratschke. Monsignor, this is Sergeant Oronski." His hand flapped back toward Harry.

Harry nodded his head but didn't offer his hand. Ordinarily it would seem proper to shake a priest's hand, even on professional business. Sort of a gesture of respect—police work necessitated so much of the impersonal, the "keep the citizen in his place" attitude—but the priest's look warned him off. It seemed safer facing Danny Clark. "Why'd they call me in on this, Danny? You guys can handle a simple little vandalism."

He regreted the words almost immediately. "Simple? Simple?" exploded the priest, his face going scarlet. "Look first and then judge it simple if you can!"

"We asked for a detective to be sent over, Sergeant," Danny Clark said quietly. "We, we didn't know how to handle this." The young man looked embarrassed.

Harry looked at each of them in turn, a little awed by the powerful expressions on each of their faces: the priest shocked and outraged, Danny Clark almost humiliated, the other patrolmen puzzled and distant. "We'd better take a look."

The priest opened the door and led them into the vestibule, which was low and dark, but here Harry could see the multi-toned hues of stained glass, the unusual blue-painted dome above the chancel, the elaborately carven altar railing and high-backed oak pews.

But slowly his glance settled on something else, something on the center aisle which ran all the way from the vestibule to the distant altar railing in the very front of the church. An irregular, rusty stain that congealed here and there into still liquid pools of blackish red. It was grisly and incongruent: blood on that brightly polished expanse of Florentine marble—and never for instant did Harry suspect he was in the presence of a miracle. The blood of Christ did not spring to mind. No, something darker and alien flitted in the dim recesses of his consciousness for a moment before it was swallowed by the starker, safer image of some monstrous little kid with a bucket of paint in his hands.

But this wasn't paint. Harry's life as a cop wasn't right out of the movies by any means, but he had seen blood before. Knew it. Could feel it. He took a few steps down the aisle while carefully avoiding the wide crimson swath. Bending over, he put his fingers gingerly into a small pool of the stuff. All doubts were gone.

He looked back at the others. They remained in the vestibule, as if he must undergo this himself, like some obscene initiation. He straightened and moved forward, his girth rubbing against the polished oak pews as he moved to avoid the awful stains and pools. Unconsciously he averted his eyes from the altar, almost as if he knew what to expect next. But he finally came to the carven altar rail, and his gaze came up from the floor and onto the white marble altar just ahead of him. He looked and he blinked and he felt for a moment like the little kid who'd stumbled upon something dark and shameful and who wanted to hide more than anything else.

But it was there in front of him, and he could almost feel the eyes of the others behind him, riveting into his back, measuring his reaction to the shocking scene before him. Harry was not what you would call a religious man, but the sense of revulsion he felt now was more complex than mere disgust at the sight of the thing on the altar. It could only be described as a sense of outrage and defilement, a powerful emotion that transcended the ludicrous theatricality of the dead animal with the inverted crucifix sunk into its belly.

It was a sheep. A large, fat sheep. Harry couldn't remember if he'd even ever seen a real live sheep before. He'd seen more of blood than these plump, neutral looking creatures. He looked at it, and the animal stirred no familiar emotions whatsoever. He had to remember where he was again, before he could feel anything at all.

"The sheep is the traditional symbol of Christ," came the words from behind him.

Harry jumped at the sound of the priest's voice. This thing had spooked him more than he'd care to admit. "What, what's that, Father, er, Monsignor?" Harry inquired nervously as the priest joined him by the altar railing. He wished the damn cleric had worn louder shoes.

"What I mean is that whoever did this was certainly aware of the religious symbolism. This is not just some grisly prank, Sergeant." His voice choked a little, and his eyes filled with water. "I—I mean, would practical jokers go to all the bother of getting a sheep?"

Harry shook his head ruefully. "Yeah, some kids would, Monsignor."

"Kids? Why do you say kids? How do you know children did this?"

"I don't, Monsignor, but it's usually kids in cases like this. Who else?"

"I told you," the priest said with irritation, "someone who knows the religious connotation of this, someone with a grievance against the church."

"This particular church or you mean the Catholic Church in general, Monsignor?"

"How do I know? I just opened the church this morning like I do every morning, and I find—this. How do I know?" The priest's voice was rising now in anger and baffled irritation. It echoed from the high reaches of ceiling and rafter above, and it sounded out of place in this sacred building.

Harry hadn't been to church in twenty years save for an infrequent wedding or baptism. "You're probably right, Monsignor. Seems like a lot of bother for practical jokers as sheep aren't exactly plentiful around these parts. Not unsheared like this or else I'd be thinking that maybe it was from a wholesale meat house in Chicago."

Harry looked at the priest carefully. He was deadly pale. "Listen, I know is is hard on you, Monsignor, but any help you can give us . . . any reason why somebody would do this, no matter how farfetched it may seem—"

"A symbolic act," the priest's voice droned, spent of all feeling, "to slay the body of Christ, I would guess."

"You mean like witchcraft, black masses and that kind of thing?" Harry watched a lot of late movies.

The priest's voice trembled a little. "It would be lunacy, of course, but that is a possibility. Churches have been known to suffer such things before."

Harry looked toward the large, crudely fashioned cross. It was common, pre-cut lumber, maybe a two-by-four, and came to a wicked taper, though you couldn't see the point which was imbedded deep in the unfortunate animal's belly. He looked up above the altar at the crucifix suspended there. Two objects, roughly the same but a whole world of meaning and intention apart.

"Can I go on the altar for a closer look, Monsignor. I mean, is it permitted?"

The priest shrugged. "These days in the church almost anything is permitted," he said wearily. He leaned over and unlatched the double doors in the altar railing. Harry looked back at the patrolmen who were still lingering by the vestibule and motioned them forward. Police were used to taking charge. It was foreign to the type to hang back, but something like this could make the best cop reluctant.

Harry moved his considerable bulk across the intervening floor and up four stairs to the altar. He was standing right over the carcass now and could see clotted blood clinging to the protruding edge of the cross. A pool of it lingered under the animal's body, and some had spilled over the edge of the altar and run in grotesque rivulets to the floor below. Christopher Lee and Boris Karloff sprang unbidden to mind, and Harry felt a twinge of guilt at such trivial images when the sacred function of this place struck home again. But he couldn't afford to overlook even the trivial; there might be something to it in this case.

"You notice it's the top part of the cross the animal

was impaled on, Monsignor. It would have been easier to sharpen the longer, bottom part of the cross, I'd think."

"So?" The priest's voice didn't betray much interest.

"The cross is inverted. Isn't that a symbol for devil worshippers, satanists and that sort of thing?"

"I believe it is in popular fiction, Sergeant. I don't know if there are any *real* satanists or devil worshippers."

"Hmmn. Looks like there might be," Harry said matter-of-factly. Who the hell else could be this sick? Oh, kids could be awfully vicious, but they wouldn't have this kind of imagination. They were content with throwing rocks through stained glass windows or heaving bags of shit onto the front door. This was of another order.

Harry heard the two patrolmen approaching, their footsteps ringing hollowly on the marble floor. "Danny, why don't you get the lab boys over here. No one's been hurt, but I think this is a special situation." He looked at the other man's nameplate. "Carmin, maybe you'd better stand outside for awhile and make sure no one gets in."

The priest waved his hand. "Lab boys? What's this?"

"Modern science, Monsignor. They might be able to come up with some clue as to who did this to your church."

"This church has suffered enough indignities, Sergeant. It is a sacred place. I don't want your 'lab boys' pawing around all over it."

"I can't see how it would do any more harm, Monsignor. It's standard procedure and might be the only way to make an arrest or make one stick if we find the maniac or maniacs who did this."

The priest looked searchingly at him for a moment. His face seemed tired and old. All the Christian wrath was gone, and hawklike features seemed to sag in resignation. "Very well. But your men . . . they'll remove this monstrosity when they're done? I can't bear to touch it."

"Certainly they will." Harry snapped his fingers lightly, and the two officers moved off. "Now, just a few questions, Monsignor. Please. Then you can leave this to us."

The cleric nodded weary assent.

"When did you discover all this?" Harry asked as he removed a small notebook and pen from his pocket.

"About six this morning. I told the others—"

"Once more for me, please."

"Yes, surely. You need to know, too. About six . . . I came about six."

"Why?"

"Oh, to open for mass, of course. I do every morning."

"Same time every morning?"

"Yes. Mass is at six-thirty every day."

"Did you hear anything during the night, Monsignor? Any unusual sounds at all?"

"No. I slept very soundly. Had strange dreams though. But I can't remember what—"

"Anything else? What time did you lock the church last night?"

"At eight. Then I went back to the rectory and read until nine, said my office until nine-thirty when I went to bed. If only I'd awakened. If only I could have caught whoever commited this, this blasphemy." The wrath was coming back into his voice.

"I'm sure you're better off for not having surprised whoever did this, Monsignor."

"I imagine, but all the same . . ."

"Monsignor, if you locked the church, how did anyone get in? I'll look around shortly, but if you noticed a broken window or a —"

The priest hesitated before he spoke. "I—I never did it before. Know I didn't. I left, somehow, the side door off the sacristy unlocked, I guess. At least it was open this morning when I came over from the rectory."

"The building right next door?"

"Yes. I imagine that makes me responsible for—for this then."

13

Harry saw the slight tremor pass through the priest's body again. He was taking the guilt upon himself. "No, not really. They may have picked the lock. But look, they would have gotten in one way or another, Monsignor. Obviously, they were determined."

"Sergeant, I—I can't take anymore of this. Thirty years. I've been at this church, the last ten as pastor. I've watched a whole generation grow and die in this town. I've tended the wealthy and the poor, the good and the bad. Sometimes I wonder if I've done anything that makes any difference to them, affected them at all. But never have I seen anything like this, Sergeant. I'll take a hundred bored faces at mass, a thousand monotonous confessions of petty sins to this any day."

Harry went to take the man's arm but drew back. He wasn't at ease in such surroundings, couldn't behave as he might have liked. "Go back to the rectory now, Monsignor. I'll call if I need you. Trust us to treat your church with respect. I'll make sure of it."

"Thank you," the priest said simply, all the flame gone out of him again. He turned without another word and slowly made his way off the altar. Harry noticed that he hobbled slightly, his limbs twisted by arthritis. Looking at all this he was suddenly certain that Monsignor Kratschke's reward would have to be a heavenly one. He didn't envy the priest in the least.

Danny Clark was hurrying up the front aisle. "I called in for the lab boys," he called out from a little distance.

Harry held up his hand as if for a discreet silence. He turned and watched the black cassock disappear through a door off to his left. Danny Clark made his way onto the altar, and Harry's voice was low and hushed as he spoke. "Danny, make sure this place is cleaned up after lab is through. Do it yourself if you have to. I don't want to hear that this place was left looking like a goddamn butcher shop. Got me?"

The younger man nodded assent.

"You checked the point of entry?"

"Yeah, Sergeant. That door off to your left then up

the flight of stairs. No sign of forced entry that we could see."

Harry made as if to move off. Clark's voice stopped him., "Sergeant, who'd want to do something like this?"

For a moment he wanted to say something grim, something about wait until he saw someone's entrails splattered all over the street by a shotgun blast. That boyish, innocent face seemed to beg for it somehow, but Harry knew he just wanted to punch somebody's fucking lights out for this godawful mess. "I don't know, Clark," he said. "All I know is that I'd sure like to get him off the streets."

He turned and walked off the altar then, walking around the altar railing to the small door where the priest had just exited moments before. It opened on a dimly lit passage that moved in one direction toward the sacristy and another up a flight of stairs to a door leading outside. This latter door was flanked by two small windows, each maybe twelve inches by twelve.

Harry puffed his way up the short flight of stairs and bent to examine the glass panes. Both were undamaged. The putty was old and dry, and there was no sign of wood shavings on the sill or floor. Nobody had tampered with these windows, though it wouldn't have done them much good if they had. Too small for much more than a hand to go through.

Next he scrutinized the lock on the door from the inside then opened it to look at the outside. Kneeling, he carefully noted the area around the keyhole. There were none of the tell-tale scratches that betrayed the use of a lockpick. The door itself was firmly moored in the surrounding wood, and the edge of the door and the area around the hinges showed no signs of splintered wood or shavings. No signs of forced entry that he could see.

He stepped outside into the cool morning air. It was a relief to be out of the church. An air of unreality had begun to seep into the proceedings inside, and now he was grateful to be in more mundane and familiar territory again. He scouted around the perimeter of the building as he mused about the events inside. Any windows that opened and closed were set too high to be reached excepting by a very long ladder. It had rained hard the day before, and the ground was soft, but there were no indentations or footprints in the ground. Ultimately he circled the whole building twice in vain pursuit of some clue or bit of information until he again came back to the little side door leading to the sacristy.

He had just decided to leave and head down to the department when he spotted it gleaming dully in the grass a little to the right of the sacristy door. It was a circular bronze ring, no bigger around than a fifty-cent piece. It opened slightly in one place so that it could be slipped through or around something, and it looked like nothing so much as a drapery ring—an old-fashioned one made of sculptured solid metal. Harry got down on hands and knees and combed the ground. Ah! There it was.

He raised it aloft in triumph: a simple piece of torn cloth, an inch or two of fabric design. What that design signified was unclear, as it was only a fragment of some far greater piece of workmanship. One piece out of a whole jigsaw puzzle. But no matter. He'd give it to the lab boys, and sometimes they could do things just this side of miraculous.

Wrapping the ring and fabric in his handkerchief, he placed them in his pocket. It was probably nothing, but at the moment it was job to a detective's heart. He started to walk around the building again but this time detoured toward his car. It would be another long day and an even longer evening, but at least this one had started out a little differently. He had mixed feelings about such a start, but, the possibility of a tiny triumph in his pocket, he had to admit that any change—even this—was needed. Ordinarily there was hardly anything, good or bad, to alter the monotony of his hours and days.

2

She guided the car around the corner at Elmsworth and headed east. It was one of her favorite streets in town and she used it frequently on her way home from work. One of many favorite streets. She loved this town, loved its stately, turn-of-the-century ambience. Oak Grove was a haven for her—a small oasis perched on the far western edge of Chicago's city limits.

She was one of those people who couldn't believe or accept what the world was turning into: a world full of mass production and plastic veneer, housing developments and treeless streets, artificial plants and cultivated indifference, stainless steel kitchens, and indoor-outdoor carpeting. A world where disco dancing seemed to be becoming the highest form of cultural expression. She hated all of it.

Coming to the corner of Scanlon Avenue her eyes passed fleetingly over the familiar contours of the vast vertical upthrust of house that dominated that corner. A huge old Queen Anne style home, it was a virtual maze of spires, gables, octagonal and circular bays, and projecting wings. Her eye caught a glint of sunlight projecting like diamond ray off the massive circular beveled glass window that crowned the center of the second floor, and from there her gaze was drawn to dormers, to masonry set upon timber set upon shingle, to the elaborately carved design set into the central pediment crowning the massive front porch.

The pretentious audacity of the house never failed to amaze her. The great wealth that must have built it, the kind of age that would invest the time and quality to construct it, the culture that would embrace it—all these things were a wonder to her. This town and its graceful old buildings, wide tree-lined boulevards and seeming abundance of tottering, cheerful little old ladies all gave her a sense of stability, of certainty that was missing in the rest of her life. It was home.

The next corner brought a different response, in the shape of one of those long, low Frank Lloyd Wright houses that the town was justly famous for. All stucco, wood trim, low-hipped roof, wide eaves, long rectangular chimney, banded art glass windows, it seemed to hug the very ground it was set upon as if an extension of the soil beneath. Clean, austere, geometrical it bespoke purity and simplicity—a whole different frame of mind than that which had spawned the great Victorian dwellings.

And to Barb it was equally engrossing in a different way, speaking silently or spaciousness and unpretentious grace, of thought and concern with the quality of human life. Another age. Houses that had been built seventy to a hundred years ago when Oak Grove had first become a sanctuary to those enterprising capitalists and entepreneurs who were making their mark in the first heyday of Chicago's rising commercial star. A lost age. And with what was it being replaced?

She hated her job. Hated the noise, the grime, the crowds that she suffered every day on her way down to Chicago's Loop, the vast central business section of the city. Hated the dull, everlasting routine of typing and filing and the total lack of creativity or independence such a job forced upon her. Hated the vast, leering monolith skyscrapers that dwarfed her. Hated the everlasting struggle, competition, greed and babble of the colossal city.

She would begin to unwind on the train ride home, but it wasn't until she would get into her car at the train station and begin her leisurely ride through the streets of Oak Grove that she would really feel that "letting go" she so treasured. How could *place* make such a difference? Did she really have so little inner resource that she was both that sensitive and vulnerable to her environment? God, she'd be walking an emotional tightrope all her life. What she'd give for a little continuing sense of stability in her life, a little equilibrium.

But how to find it amidst all the dreams and discontent? Sometimes she felt as though the very ground beneath her feet was in reality a shifting, treacherous sea. Sometimes her mind would disconnect from things around her, and the sly pull of the ethereal would lull and seduce her into a misty, undifferentiating oblivion of half-formed images and broken dreams. And sometimes there would be the fear. Fear of her own inner loneliness. And then she'd wake to the numbing banality of it all again, and as common and shabby as it all seemed, there was a strangeness to it too, a certain alien quality to her life as if she knew there had to be something more, that something was missing.

Of friends and even acquaintances there were few. By choice. She was too diffident, too insular to let others approach very often, and when she did it seemed that invariably she was disappointed. Cardboard values and insignificant interests. She'd rather be alone.

Men approached her often, of course. Even in her shyness and lack of self-confidence she knew that she was pretty: tall and leggy, full-busted, long brown hair, deep, limpid, doelike eyes. She knew she was the type to inspire both protectiveness and lust in a man. Unfortunately, this had proved too often to be a deadly combination in her life. Her beauty and her vulnerability would spur passion in a man, and afterwards his sense of protectiveness wouldn't let him forgive himself. Invariably he would end up treating her like a little sister then, or he would succumb to his baser instincts in order to submerge his guilt, thereby effectively deciding to use her for what he could. Or so it seemed. Either way she lost and retreated further into herself.

But finally something good had happened. Six months ago she'd met Scott, and an instant liking had turned—very swiftly for her—into deep affection and then love. Often she would analyze this new found, no, this first-found love of hers. He was rugged, handsome, outdoorsy. She liked that. He was personable and communicative yet hardly brash or aggressive. She liked that too. He was sensitive to her needs and her interests, as unconventional as they often seemed to others. But mostly she liked—no, respected—his underlying confidence. He had talked once or twice about his early life, and she knew it had been as rough as her own. Still, it hadn't beaten him down or made him shy away from life. Oh, he was somewhat reticent on the surface of things, he had an innate form of reserve, but it wasn't aloofness or coldness that was intended to shut you out. If you cared to penetrate the veneer, you'd find that underneath he was approachable.

What's more, he was an adult. At twenty-five years of age she had met so many men her own age and older, but they were men who seemed like boys. Childish, trifling, aimless and wanting only to be pampered. Unwilling to take responsibility for themselves or others. Confused and discontented, like herself, but in an uncaring, destructive way.

The alternative was the business type, as she liked to call them. Aggressive, seemingly strong, independent, resourceful. She suspected they were a good deal less strong than they appeared beneath the facade, but in any event they were untouchable emotionally, hopelessly walled off, as if by design. Aloof and intractable when you got beyond superficial mannerisms, they had no real sense of commitment. They only wanted to put you in a little box and take you out for special occasions: parties, lonely nights, moments of self-doubt. Otherwise, they wanted only to be left alone. So she did.

But after six months Scott's strength and sensitivity seemed to still be real. Maybe it was the rugged childhood he'd had on a southern Indiana farm with only a grandmother to raise him. Maybe it was two years combat duty in Viet Nam. Maybe it was in his genes or his astrological sign. She loved to calculate the possibilities and the alternatives. It satisfied her penchant for analysis, and it let her pleasantly daydream about him too, thereby satisfying simultaneously both of the contradictory directions her mind would usually take. She was glad for his presence in her life.

Then there was Daddy, the other great love and concern in her life. A gray-haired hulk of a man, his most distinguishing features were his intelligence, his iron will and his love for his only daughter. Of this last she was certain, more certain than of anything else in her life. Undemonstrative, even stern with others, he had nothing but glowing love for her, and try as she had to change as the years passed, apparently he would always be "Daddy" to her.

They took care of each other. She still lived at home, doing the cooking, cleaning and laundry, and he lavished her with every kind of attention and praise. A feminist might have thought it a somewhat exploitative relationship in a practical sense, but it would never have occured to her to justify it in any way. She paid no rent, and her father often treated her to dinner or a new dress or some other need. But she didn't balance the books on their relationship in any way.

Besides, he genuinely appreciated it. His look of pleasure upon first seeing and smelling the pot roast she had prepared for them last night had been nothing short of sublime. His beloved pot roast. It was the closest she ever saw him to veneration, eating pot roast with pan-fried carrots and whole potatoes. Seeing it, he had let out a war hoop and run down to the cellar to break open a bottle of his good burgundy—too good, in fact, for pot roast, she thought—and he had spent the whole meal merrily reminiscing about World War II and his less-than-horrible experiences as a medical orderly in an army WAC battalion headquarters in Lancashire, England. So it was with manpower shortages during the war, unlucky bloke that he was, that he was forced to spend the duration of conflict tending to the medical needs of 500 women. He was one of eleven men in the whole camp out on the isolated English countryside far from raiding German planes or any other real danger—except all those women.

She laughed again as she remembered some of those outrageous stories—outrageous and racy, he was never one to pamper her too much—and turned the car onto Farrington Place, her street. She looked at her watch. It was quarter past six, and she could picture him pacing in his den even now, his enormous appetite already building to feverish proportions. But she loved his joy of good food and drink; it made rushing right home from work to cook so much easier.

From out of a series of substantial homes, she picked out the ivy-covered, half-timbered Tudor that she called home. It was too big for the two of them, but her mother had wanted, had insisted on having that home. Even after she had died that dark, ugly death, he had kept it. Maybe as a memorial. Even now, twelve years later, she knew that her mother's hold over her father was still a strong and unhealthy one. It was one of life's great mysteries to her; how such a good, upright man could have such an enduring hunger for the darkness that had been her mother.

She guided the Mustang into the driveway behind her father's Buick. Getting out, she felt the warm September breeze billow about the hem of her skirt as if to lift her and carry her along. Autumn was her favorite season, and soon the leaves would be turning scarlet and golden. It was a time of peace and wistful melancholy for her, and she and Scott had planned a camping trip up to the Wisconsin peninsula for later in the month. Her mind went out to that trip often during the last few weeks of stultifying daily routine in the office. It was to be her hedge against the overpowering discontent of too many miserable days of confinement in the offices of the E.B. Walker Company.

She opened the front door and stepped into the relative coolness of the house. "Daddy, I'm home." she called out lightly. There was no answer from the dim interior of the house. He must be out in back, she thought. Dropping her purse on the hall table, she bounded up the stairs towards her room. Dresses were fine for work, but she was at home in her blue jeans and a t-shirt. So attired she would then feel sufficiently inspired to put on one whale of a meal for the two of them, though he would probably be disappointed that it wouldn't be pot roast again. For Dr. Richard Brennan pot roast every night would probably be nirvana.

As she moved down the hallway, she passed her father's room. An idle sideways glance made her stop short. There on the bed lay her father's long body. One hand was thrown over his eyes, and he appeared to be asleep. "Daddy?" she said softly, and his body seemed to jump a little on the bed. Quickly the hand was retracted, and the man's surprised, almost frightened gaze shot out at her from the bed.

"Daddy, did I startle you? I'm sorry. Were you sleeping?" The strength of his sudden reaction took her aback.

"Barb. It's you," he said and paused for what seemed like a long time. Into the rugged contours of his face was etched a slight but perceptible look of concern. "I—I'm sorry, Barbara. I was just . . . laying down for awhile until you got home." His voice seemed to trail off here as if he were forgetting something.

She knew him. Something was wrong. She also knew that if something was wrong he'd deny it, but she'd ask anyway. "C'mon now, Pop. What's up? IRS suing you for back taxes?"

He smiled somewhat ruefully. "No, nothing's the matter. I was just a little tired, that's all."

She knew it wasn't like him to take a nap, though he had slowed down some since he'd given up his practice last year, but the indefinable sense of worry playing even now around his features was unmistakable to someone who knew his moods so well. "Daddy, I'll be glad to listen—"

"It's nothing I've told you," he interrupted, irritation edging around the words as he spoke them. "Now, leave it alone."

"I'm sorry. It's just that I worry when you seem worried."

She could see him soften then at her apparent hurt and concern. "I'm sorry I snapped at you, sugar. Really, I'm fine. How was your day?"

She looked at him, knowing he was changing the subject, but what was the use. Stubborn Irishman. "The same as usual," she said. "Boring."

"Barb, I've told you to quit that job and go back to college if you want. My treat." he said with a little exasperation.

"But I don't want to go back to college. I've been there. It's a lot of aimless misfits and overpampered teenagers looking for something to do. At least in the business world they know what they want."

"Then another job."

"Oh, Daddy. That'd be the ninth job in three years. No one will hire me soon with the work record I'm getting."

"Maybe you'll get it right next time."

She couldn't repress a laugh. "Very funny. I suppose it amuses you that you'll probably end up supporting me for the rest of my life?"

"If I have to."

"Ach, you aggravate me," she said in a mock vexation. "You know darn well that I'm a weak sister. You'll have to start a whole new practice just to support all my fancy habits and lack of ambition."

"You're not always happy with your life, I know that, but you're no weak sister either." he said with mild reproach.

She decided to try to open the lines of communication to draw him out. "Thanks for that, but sometimes I think I was *born* strange. From the time I can remember anything at all, I knew I was disatisfied. I didn't want what other little kids wanted, but I didn't know what I wanted. I was always dreaming, always restless, just like—" She cut herself off, suddenly realizing that she was getting into painful territory, the one subject he always took great pains to avoid.

But not tonight. "Say it—like your mother," he intoned flatly. "Never content, always wanting more, never wanting what she had. Yes, you're like her in that way only without the nastiness."

She was stung. These last words sounded hurtful—as if they were intended that way. And he never brought up the subject of Barb's mother, never even acknowledged it if someone else should happen to mention it. It was a dead issue suddenly come to life again.

"Daddy," she protested, "that sounds unfair. I know I'm confused sometimes and I want unconventional things out of life, but I'm hardly like Mother."

He pushed himself up off the bed rather quickly and moved over to the window, seemingly avoiding her gaze. There was a long silence as he toyed with the drapery and stared outside. He would never be the one to break the silence, and she sensed that he was gripped by some inscrutable but definite anger.

"Don't shut me out. We always talk our problems through."

Silence. The fingers moving rapidly over the edge of the drape.

"Why won't you talk to me? What made you bring up Mother? You haven't done that in years."

"Forget it." his voice was sharp now. Silence again. "What's for dinner?" at length.

She sighed. "There are some minute steaks in the frig I'll broil. That and a salad and some frozen brussels sprouts, I guess."

He kept looking out the window, the muscles in his jaw alternately clenching and unclenching.

Desperation. "Though hardly pot roast," she said hopefully.

He turned and looked at her intently from across the room. "What did you think about your mother, Barb? About the way she died?"

It took her a while to answer. Such a question from him was unprecedented. Even if Barb had ever wanted to talk about her mother, she was sure he would never have allowed it. And discussing her death? She felt like the world had suddenly turned over on its side. "I—I don't know. I was only thirteen when she died."

"Thirteen is old enough to have feelings and opinions," he said softly but forcefully, as if trying to control some raging inner struggle. His voice was measured, but his brow trembled imperceptibly as he said it.

"Oh, all right. I hated her. Hated everything she was and did. Hated her for what she did to you and to me and everybody around her. Yes, I hated her—my own mother!"

"No pity for the sick?" he said softly and sardonically.

A torrent was rushing out of her now, and she couldn't stem it. "No, no pity. You know I'm not a hard person, but there's no pity in me for someone who was that hateful, that deliberately cruel and twisted. I wouldn't lift a finger to this day to save her from falling into hell itself."

"That's not good for a girl to feel that way about her mother."

"She's dead!" Barb nearly shrieked.

His voice was still calm, but she could feel the underlying tension in the words. "Yes, she's dead. But you came from her body. Her blood flows through your veins as well as my own. Maybe more so."

"What's that supposed to mean?" The tears were beginning to well up behind her eyes.

"Did it ever occur to you that you might be like her or will become like her? I'm a doctor, and I know it's possible. Some abberation in the gene pool."

"God, I can't believe what I'm hearing!" she yelled and clapped her hand to her cheek. "It's like something out of a novel, what you're saying. Stop it. Please stop it!"

"Have you ever thought about it?" he bellowed and moved across the floor at her.

She cowed instinctively. He had never acted like this before, and she didn't know what to expect now. She felt his arm go around her shoulder and his massive hand bit into her arm. "Daddy, why are you doing this?" she mewed as she felt his other hand force her head slowly up and back until her eyes were forced to meet his.

They were narrow now, and she wouldn't have believed they could look so cold and appraising, that he could hold her so helpless like this. He seemed to hold her and stare at her face for a long time, and she stood motionless, not daring to speak. But finally the dark words tumbled out of his mouth, and it was then that she began to sob and cry in long wrenching heaves of her body. It would be a long time before she would forget those words or their impact. "I never noticed it before," he said in deadly tones, "Never noticed how much you look like your mother."

3

Willie Malone was king of the corner. None of the street-wise dudes messed with Willie. He was six feet tall and 240 pounds of the proverbial solid muscle. This fact combined with the perpetual scowl he wore were enough to scare away any pretenders to the throne.

Willie enjoyed his local status. To him the whole world was bounded by Laramie and Winston Boulevard to east and west, and by Chicago Boulevard and Water Street to north and south. This is where he spent his nights. This is where he spent his life and was king, the thirty or forty square block area of Chicago immediately adjacent Oak Grove.

Willie had no real place to call home and prided himself on living by his wits, but he never strayed from the comforting continuity of his miniature domain. Here he was the boss, so there wasn't any other place that he recognized being real. Here everybody gave him respect, because if there's one thing the ghetto respects it's force or the threat of force. Willie got a lot of mileage out of that story how he'd taken down Big Leon right in the street one Fourth of July . . . Big Leon, the former pro football tackle . . . Big Leon, *former* king of the hill.

Hell. Now he could stay anywhere he liked. There were plenty of rabbits that couldn't stand up to a man, so he stayed with the rabbits. Sometimes he slept in the back of Amos's barber shop. Sometimes at Tony the pimp's place—Tony liked to have a little muscle around sometimes. And there was always "Lucky" Eddie's, the two bit pusher. But Eddie wasn't so lucky. He'd been pinched three times in the last six months, and Willie didn't like to park himself there too often.

Yeah, everything was going down real good lately, and he had life by the tail. Fact was, things were even getting better. He stood to make a hundred bucks tonight for just a few hours work. Crazy white woman. He'd thought she was a little goofy just bein' where she was. Weren't white ladies supposed to be scared of big, ugly niggers? Shit. Don't we rape the pretty ones and settle for mugging the old and ugly ones? Course, some of the brothers weren't too discriminating: they'd rape and mug all of them. But Willie knew that if he ever raped anyone it would be a young pretty white fox. If you gotta chance to take a rap, better get your money's worth.

But he couldn't imagine even the worst-off brother taking on this fat old bat. She'd walked right up to him and looked him in the eye until he yelled. "Boo!" Then he'd laughed, and they all laughed, all the brothers who were basking in his reflected glory in front of Skinny Al's Saloon. But she had just stood there looking up at him and somehow looking like she was looking down.

"What you want, lady?" he finally asked her peevishly. "You look like you're lookin' at some monkey in the zoo." With this he jumped up and down, scratched his armpit and made small grunting noises. Black Power was out these days. It was more fashionable to be a nigger, to mock your own blackness while all the time you knew it was Whitey you were laughing at.

Gales of laughter broke from the four or five brothers standing around Willie. One of them said, "Right on, Willie," and he felt good, felt very much like the king of the corner in that moment. An audience made your triumphs so much better.

"When you have stopped laughing, I would like to offer you $100.00," came the woman's nonplussed reply. Willie decided she was a foreign lady—she talked a little funny, and she sure don't know enough about the ghetto not to walk around in it. Yes, sir. Not your typical white woman at all. They'd just drive by, eyes frozen forward, doors locked, pretending not to hear your jeers and whistles and obscene compliments. Even the old ones avoided your look, but not this one.

"Lady, I like you. I'll take your $100.00," replied Willie with feigned seriousness. There was a titter behind him, and he couldn't help but smile a little himself.

"You will work for it. Three or four hours maybe. Come to this address at nine o'clock tonight. No earlier. No later. Simple moving work. Easy for a man like you." With that she had handed him a piece of paper, turned on her heel and walked stiffly away.

"Well, look like ol' Willie's gonna make a hunnert the hard way," proffered one of the blacks with an obscene cackle.

"You mean he's gonna have to make it hard to collect the hundred," offered another. "Willie's gonna have to rip off a piece of that dry, tough old white meat for his money. Who else gonna pay that kinda money?"

They started to laugh again then, their bodies twisting in mirth. But they were prepared to stop in an instant if Willie showed any signs of being unappreciative of this kind of humor at his expense. But Willie was absorbed in something else. He held the scrap of paper in his hand tentatively, a worried frown covering his broad, scarred face. The address was over in Oak Grove where he didn't know the turf. It was alien land where muscle and black skin still counted but not in the same way. He could still inspire fear—even in Oak Grove—but he couldn't feel half so comfortable in backing it up—not over in Whitey's world. He'd have to think this one over, but $100.00 was worth thinking over.

So he passed the rest of the day in places like Skinny Al's and Hickory Pit. He even paid a visit to Reverend Richard T. Davis's Christ the Savior Evangelical Church. He wasn't getting religious, mind you, but he wanted to find Doris, and Doris liked to sit around and talk to the preacher. Doris had big tits, and every so often she liked to get it on with the king of the corner. But today he couldn't find her, and it was probably just as well. Charlie Spikes had said something about her gettin' the clap.

Besides, he was preoccupied. All day it was nagging at the back of his mind. Should he go or not? The woman hadn't been kidding—you don't go into the ghetto to jive the head monkey, even if you're some crazy white woman. No, the offer had been real. But there were a lot of intangibles if he did, and there was a lost hundred if he didn't. Willie didn't have to make such major decisions very often.

About eight o'clock he had decided to go. He thought about taking a few brothers along, just in case. But that might mean splitting the hundred, and he decided against it. He'd have to borrow some wheels of course, but that'd be no problem. But if the old bat really did have somethin' on her mind besides his moving some stuff, well she could just forget it. He'd never be that hard up. Matter of fact, he could just hear the ring of laughter in his head, as he thought about some of the boys talking about Willie's "white meat." Bastards! Can't let up even a little.

It was a windy fall night. The first of October. Dark, scudding outlines of cloud raced through the sky in pursuit of some aimless oblivion. The moon was a pale, lonely crescent angling forlornly up toward the heavens, and a bitter autumn chill was still in the air. Times like this Willie longed a little for Mississippi. Times like this it was easy to remember all the good things about the South and to forget the bad. If he'd ever really thought about it, he wold have shuddered. He'd already found nigger heaven, and there wasn't no use in tradin' down.

But already he'd forsaken the outer perimeters of paradise, as he guided the old Oldsmobile down Water Street past Winston Boulevard and into Oak Grove proper. Already he had to exercise caution, to curb his natural enthusiasms and take on a bit of that hunted look common to blacks outside their own realm of influence. Already *he* was looking straight ahead without realizing it.

Row after row of apartment buildings and small storefronts glided by. It was a Tuesday night, and the small businesses that were the town's commercial lifeblood were closed, so no neon shed its harsh glare on Willie's furtive journey. Only the old-fashioned incandescent street lamps sent their feeble glow onto the street, and they barely overpowered the dim illumination of the thin wedge of moon. The town council had discussed installing the far more powerful mercury vapor lights, but the purists, the aesthetecists and the die-hard Oak Grove lovers raised such a fuss that the council tabled the resolution. These new lights turned night into day in the most grotesque way, casting a lurid half-light over everything—stealing the power of the night to cast magical mysterious shadows over the town and its inhabitants. But it would surprise no one when the council passed the tabled resolution a few months later. Passed it unanimously. By then the dark wasn't so comforting.

When Willie was almost at Oak Grove Avenue, he turned into a gas station to get directions. He'd spotted one of the brothers pumping gas, and in a land of strangers that was a welcome sight. "Hey man, how do I get to Fair Tree?" Willie yelled out the car window.

"Fair Tree? Go back on Water Street four blocks then make a left." the other one shouted back.

"How about the seven-hundred block?"

"Seven blocks up."

"Thanks," Willie called out. "You jive ass nigger," he chuckled under his breath.

Willie turned the Olds around and headed eastbound again on Water Street. Here and there he spotted people strolling along the sidewalk. Ain't like my neighborhood, he thought with perverse satisfaction. It'd take somebody like me to go walkin' around my neighborhood late at night.

Counting four blocks, he turned at Fair Tree and proceeded north. Quickly the apartment buildings gave way to huge old homes that seemed to loom up at you over the sidewalk and into the street. He chuckled again and said out loud, "Watch out, you people. Willie Malone's comin' to dinner." He laughed noisily at the absurdity of it and laughed at what he considered to be his keen and ironic sense of humor and, in truth, laughed a little out of nervousness. Here he had no reputation to maintain, no brothers to impress, and he could be a little more himself, which was a good deal less tough then he seemed to be.

Oh, he could handle himself all right, but he knew that he was really a good deal more shiftless than he really was mean. Mean meant survive where he came from, and it wasn't much different in Chicago. People'd lean on you as much as you let 'em, and Willie had learned a long, long time ago not to let 'em. But he only really came on hard when it was necessary, and there was no other way out.

He remembered stories his father had used to tell about dodging the Klan back in the 20's. But that had never made Willie feel especially political. Black Power was just a way of puttin' ripoff artists with the same skin as you in big, fancy offices with impressive sounding names. Names like the Afro-American Peace and Benevolence Association—there was one of those down on Laramie.

Black, white, pink, yellow—they'd all steal from you if you let 'em. That's why Willie liked to keep on the move, why he avoided puttin' down any roots. A rollin' stone gathers no leeches. He chuckled to himself again, noted that he was on the seven-hundred block of Fair Tree. He pulled the Olds over to the curb and looked around. Shit. These houses were somethin' else!

He looked at his watch, saw it was eight-fifty and decided he better get moving. It wouldn't hurt to be a few minutes early when a fast hundred was at stake, but the damn street lights were so dim it might take him ten minutes just to make out the house numbers on these big old barns.

He got out and stretched his thick body like a cat. The address on the piece of paper was 714 Fair Tree, and that oughta be right in the middle of the block. He looked at the house directly in front of him. It was a mammoth frame place that looked as big as an apartment building. It was all windows and corners and roof and seemed to spread out all over the lot like it wanted to engulf the trees and shrubs that were wild and overgrown and seemed determined to shield the house partly from view. A sole dim light burned in one of the downstairs windows, muted by a thick length of curtain.

Tentatively, he took a few cautious steps up the long sidewalk leading to the house. He craned his neck looking for a street number, but the exterior of the house was shrouded in darkness. He took a few more steps forward while hoping some old lady wouldn't decide to look out her window just then, see Willie and call the cops.

As he moved forward, he thought he saw something move in the shadows on the huge verandah that girdled the front and near the side of the house like some big boat. He stopped. There was definitely a figure on the verandah, and now it was moving toward him. One huge fist instinctively came together. He only hoped there was no goddamn dog.

"Good evening," the accented voice wafted out to him in the darkness. "I trust you had no difficulties in finding us."

Willie breathed a sigh of relief. It was the woman who had approached him this afternoon.

"Nope. No problem." He hoped it sounded casual enough.

"Fine. Then follow me."

He loped up the verandah steps which creaked ominously under his weight. As he gained the top step, he saw the rather frumpy outline of the woman ahead of him. It was almost reassuring in the surrounding blackness. She turned and walked a few steps to the massive front door. Opening it, a flood of murky yellow light illuminated the porch. She turned to face him, and in the light he could see her eyes. They looked hard and cunning and suddenly he was dubious again about the whole thing. But this was a woman, not a man. What could she do, if he didn't want to? And she smiled broadly when she said, "Please. Come into our house." He followed her in and instinctively swung the massive wooden door shut behind him. It closed with a merciless thud.

4

"Pull!"

The tiny gray disc sprung up into the vaster tract of slate-gray sky above him. Quickly, smoothly he brought the long line of the barrel around in front of him and followed the trajectory of the clay target as it peeked in and out and in between the scudding clouds. Carefully his finger tightened around the trigger, and there was a sudden pop as his body felt the 12-gauge recoil into his shoulder. Far above him tiny fragments and shards of clay scattered into the surrounding vault of leaden sky.

"Christ almighty!" Lenny whined. "That's nineteen in a row, you bastard. Don't you ever miss?"

"Not hardly, pardner," drawled Larry slowly. "That thar's the meanest, toughest sonafabith in the whole corral."

"Okay Gabby Hayes, let's see you shoot now," Lenny said skeptically to the bearded Larry. "You're always talking that country hokum; let's see you shoot, Andy Jackson."

"Ah wish you'd decide who ah'm supposed to be," Larry drawled in supreme exaggeration of his Texas dialect. "Ah mean, it gits confusin' what with me bein' all these great Southern heroes in your admirin' eyes."

Lenny just shook his head mournfully and signalled Scott to step off the firing line. Larry took his place and immediately went into his Ed Norton impression: cracking the knuckles, rolling the arms, twisting the shoulders back and forth—anything to infuriate the efficient, methodical Lenny Hahn.

"I'm not going to fall for it," Lenny mumbled to Scott. "What would that guy do if he didn't have me to bait all the time? I mean I was all ready to re-up for another year's duty in Nam just so I wouldn't have to come back to the States with that guy."

Scott smiled but something deep inside of him jumped a little at the sound of Larry's Remington going off. It was still there. He could shoot two hundred rounds himself and never feel a thing, but just let somebody else start popping away and he'd get nervous. He wondered if he'd ever get Viet Nam out of his system, those nights on search and destroy missions . . . the black-clad Cong snipers with their infra-red scopes . . . the thought that any minute it might be you with the hollow-point bullet twisting and careening through your body.

"Hey, what's getting into Dave?" Lenny asked absently while watching Larry shoot. "This is the third week in a row he hasn't come with us."

"Think his wife is giving him trouble," Scott replied. "She keeps telling him to grow up and realize that he isn't one of the boys anymore."

"Marriage and friendship. Mortal enemies—at least from a woman's point of view."

"Oh I don't know about that, Lenny. It doesn't have to be that way."

"Says who? You? You're practically married yourself. You've been taking out Barb for, what, four or five months now?"

"About six."

"Practically a lifetime for you, Lothario."

"Yeah, and about a lifetime away from having to ask when I can go out with my friends, too."

"Ouch. That one hurt. Take it easy on us poor married guys—we've got enough problems already."

"Hey Bozo, your turn," Larry called as he stepped back from the firing line and motioned to Lenny to take his next round of shots. "I'm goin' to the car and get me a jolt."

"No wonder he's got half a brain—drinking that

hillbilly piss," Lenny said, referring to Larry's penchant for grain alcohol. "I wish he wouldn't drink that stuff when we're shooting."

"Hell, you know Larry," Scott replied with a smile, "he can drink a gallon of anti-freeze and never feel a thing."

Lenny shrugged and walked to the firing line, leaving Scott alone with his thoughts. Quick. Catch it. Yep, there it was, like some infernal, eternal itch she sprang into his mind. Damn it to hell. His life had been so much his own for a long time now. And now along came a spider in the form of ethereal, lovely and somewhat abstracted Barbara Brennan.

He hadn't ever realized how secondary women had become in his life until Barb had come alone. Women. Those light, frothy, silken, wispish things that he had been so enamored of since his teens. Then they had been girls, but they hadn't seemed to have changed in the last few years—maybe even since he'd returned home from the war—and unconsciously he had begun to treat them like a pleasant but unessential point of interest in his life.

Almost two years of combat duty, of not knowing from minute to minute whether you were going to live, changes you in some very profound ways. It wasn't the "live for today" attitude popularized in war movies. No, that would have just made him more of a womanizer. Perhaps the constant fear of death had made him more aware of life's gifts, so that he didn't want to waste them on trivial pursuits and shallow relationships. Instinctively but gradually he had begun to avoid the casual associations, the hit-and-run affairs. Even his circle of friends had diminished until it was confined basically to these men who had fought beside him and shared his deepest experiences for two years.

Then Barb had come along, and she was definitely different. Fragile like fine bone china, vulnerable yet possessed of an underlying strength of character that only she doubted. A girl who wasn't afraid to go backpacking in the wilderness with you. A girl who could freely admit that she had some old-fashioned but oddly pleasing inhibitions about things. A girl who was sensitive to life and love and couldn't separate the two.

"Your turn again, Blue Eyes." Scott looked around to see Larry standing a few feet to his side. "Looks like you got a bad case of the 'thinks'."

"Beg your pardon?"

"The 'thinks'. That's when you think too much. Then you get the 'thinks'."

"Something terribly wrong with thinking?" Scott inquired.

"Why you know there is. I'm always tellin' you that, but you're too busy thinkin' to pay any attention. I'll tell you again, thinkin' ain't no good for a man. It clutters up his head and interferes with the important things—like drinkin'."

Lenny stepped back and joined them. He looked quizzically at Larry and said, "You know, if this was a movie, right about now the narrator would be voicing in to say how you're really not what you seem to be, that you've got an IQ of 180 and were a Rhodes Scholar, but is isn't and you aren't, you fucking ignorant hillbilly."

"It's hard to believe you two really like each other sometimes," Scott felt obliged to say. "I mean, Larry will be into his 'Jew Boy' routine any minute now, and one of these days we're going to turn these guns on one another . . ."

"You shut up now, Blue Eyes." Larry's eyes were lighting up with the devil now. It wasn't often that he could draw Scott into one of his elaborately contrived confrontations. "You wouldn't be fair game. It would be too plumb easy to lay you out, boy."

"Why? Am I too waspish?"

"Waspish! Shit, man. You are pure, unadulterated Establishment. You're so fucking straight your clothes don't even wrinkle."

"Oh, oh. At last the stinging barb of your satirical sword is turned on me. Woe is me."

Larry began to jump up and down like a jack rabbit and applaud. "Fightin' back! Fightin' back! Hey, Blue

Eyes, I didn't know you had it in you, you bein' the strong silent type and all that."

"You know your problem, Larry? You're too subtle," said Scott. He laughed then, and they all laughed until they came close and clapped each other on the back. That's the way these "disputes" always ended. They made sure of it. Otherwise, there would be no telling when somebody might take something seriously that was only meant in fun. They had come too far together to risk that.

They spent the rest of the day in a country bar about thirty miles west of Oak Grove. Out in Du Page County it began to become farm country again, land where there was room to shoot skeet and do a little hunting if you could bribe the farmer whose property you wanted to stomp through. Dull land. Flat land. But open.

Larry and Dave—when he was along—liked to drink a little too much on these obligatory outings, but it was seldom that anything got out of hand, thanks mostly to the "sober twins" as Larry liked to call Lenny and Scott. Neither enjoyed the booze that much; both took a silent pride in always "keeping their wits about them." But it never interfered with the good times. They were all too close to need alcohol to make them comfortable with each other. A year and a half in one of the worst combat areas in Viet Nam together can do that for a man. It can make you feel what's on another man's mind before he even says it.

So they talked. Talked about the season's upcoming fortunes for the Bears. Talked about their jobs and their wives or girls and a whole lot of other things that were commonplace and, no doubt, boring to any outside listener who might have overheard. But they felt no need to speculate on the ultimate, cosmic implications of this or that. They weren't scholars, and the experience they had shared together, the pain and fright and misery they had lived through together, had taught each and all of them a respect and a satisfaction with the small things, the ephemeral pleasures. All had become aware how much life is a day to day proposition—a retractable gift. The lien might be called in any time.

But he knew he'd never be comfortable in the role of a hedonist, so he lived by his instincts. When he and his friends had finally parted company, he was grateful for the solitude. Right now all he was looking forward to was a tub of hot suds while thinking about absolutely nothing at all. Larry had been wrong. He only thought too much part of the time; other times he didn't think at all. Maybe he'd call Barb later, and they could go out to dinner, or maybe he'd stay at home, eat a can of tuna and sleep out on the roof tonight. Right now he'd keep his options open.

He pulled the Chevy into the alley behind the sprawling old apartment building just as the sun disappeared behind the roof of the house across the street. The venerable old red-brick building, the vast, spreading elms along the boulevard—it all looked so mellow in the growing dusk. Gone were his complaints about squeaking stairs and leaky pipes and quarrulous old people—gone in the sudden ephemeral glow of well-being that seemed to suffuse the sky and all under its dominion. Oh, great. Now he was beginning to think like her, his loony, mystical girl friend. Abstraction must be contagious, he chuckled to himself.

He met Mrs. Packwood on his way up the stairs. She was a tiny, eternally cheerful old widow of many years. Her exact age she kept secret with more than a little apparent mystery, much as if to imply that you would never believe her real age if she told you. She reminded him of his own grandmother: dwarf-like and indomitable. Grandma had run the family farm and raised him for a full eighteen years after his grandpa had died, and she lived on to an even ninety. He had never heard her issue one complaint in all the years that he'd known her, and though he had been nineteen years old at the time of her funeral he'd cried at the loss of the steel-willed, cantankerously funny old woman.

Mrs. Packwood served a similar purpose for him now. She was a beacon too. Once or twice a week he would stop up to her third floor apartment for coffee and rolls and listen to her chatter amiably about nothing in particular. She had so little company, and she wasn't like some of the other oldsters in the building: She hadn't let the years and the disappointments and the forgotten dreams wear her down.

"How are you today, Mrs. Packwood?"

She smiled graciously, her small wrinkled features contorting into an elfin grin. "Oh, fine. Just fine, young man." She never remembered his name. "And how about yourself? You look a little . . . you look a little thoughtful today."

"That's funny. That's the second time I've been told that today. Maybe I ought to ask you the same question. Is there something wrong with looking thoughtful, Mrs. Packwood?"

"Wrong?" she chuckled. "Oh, I should say not—not when you're young at any rate. It gets to be a little too much effort when you're my age, though."

"Well, your answer was better—more thoughtful anyway—than the last one I got. I'll bet that you're as thoughtful as the rest of us."

The old lady simply laughed and continued on down the hall. He could still hear her laughter as he came to his apartment door. Let me grow old like that, he made a silent wish.

He fit his key into the lock and opened the door. Streaks of late afternoon sunlight glimmered in through the windows and threw rich shades of sepia over the dim contents of the apartment. The pleasant and familiar mustiness of aged wood and old carpeting wafted up to greet him. The smell of long and good years. If he ever bought a home, it would have to be like this shabby old building, the air of gentle memories clinging to its very wood and stone.

Crossing over to the window, he unlatched it and swung it inward. He stood there and looked out at the great, gnarled oak tree that sheltered one corner of the side yard. A slight breeze turned through the branches, and the early autumn leaves whistled a restless tune. His mind turned to Barb again, and the thought occurred to him that somehow the night reminded him of her. Beautiful, elusive, with some underlying silent mystery about it, the night seemed to beckon you into the gentle unknown much as Barb beckoned to his still too self-protective soul. Maybe it had been the war that made him fearful of committing himself to any responsibility beyond the immediate ones that keep you busy only from one minute to the next, that insure your survival into the next moment of time.

But committing yourself to a woman, even short of marriage, implied a future of some sort, and he realized that maybe that proverbial Hollywood wisdom was applicable to him after all. Maybe he was just living for the day, the war having shattered his capacity for sustaining anything important in his life. Maybe he was just trying to make each individual day more of a heightened experience.

He sighed and turned away from the window. Sitting down on the couch, he began to undo the long laces of his boots. He was no psychologist, no philosopher. Fathoming such labyrinth layers of his inner self was beyond him and alien to his temperament. Besides, he was losing the battle. More and more he caught himself thinking about that future—that future with her. He lay back against the couch and closed his eyes. A smile began to cross his face. He decided then to take the money and run.

5

Harry got the call at a little after seven in the morning. It was from Frank Elliot, chief of detectives, and that automatically meant bad news. "Harry, get over to 636 Lincoln Boulevard pronto. A couple of squads are already there."

"What's up Frank?" mumbled Harry sleepily.

"Some lady just called the station to complain that someone cut her sister's throat."

"Very funny, Frank."

"For real, Harry. Get on over there right away."

"Well, what are you doing at the station at—" Harry looked at his watch—"at seven in the morning?"

"I'm not at the station. I'm home in bed. They called me."

"And you called me." Harry grumbled sorrowfully.

"Let me have your report as soon as you get into the station, Harry." There was a click on the line.

Harry hung up the phone and headed for the bathroom. Wasn't it just the other day he was lamenting the fact that nothing ever happened in this town? Well, things were turning around in a hurry. First that unfortunate business at St. Mark's and now a murder.

"What's the matter, Harry?" came Grace's nasal voice from the bedroom. "Who's calling so early?"

"Lieutenant Elliot." He made the reply as succinct as possible.

"But you're not due for another two hours. Can't they get someone else to do it?"

He had heard this question many times before. Too many. "Go back to bed," he said and kicked the bathroom door shut with his foot. Ten minutes later he was speeding down Winter on his way to Lincoln Boulevard. His hair wasn't combed, he had toothpaste on his upper lip, and he had put on a plaid shirt with a light gray sportcoat. But he was the law. That was always some consolation at times like this. No matter how sleepy he might look, no matter what kind of ass he might make of himself, he could always hide behind the dignity of the law.

Besides, it was patrolmen who were supposed to look neat and well-groomed. Detectives—at least the good ones—were supposed to be rumpled and rough looking. Or so Harry reasoned.

At seven-forty he pulled up in front of the apartment building of 636 Lincoln Boulevard. Two squads, the police emergency ambulance and medical examiner Bill Tolson's black Buick with the CB antenna were already parked in front. The building was one of those blocklong seventy or eighty-unit jobs that had sprung up like wildfire in the 30's when the rest of the world was still in a Depression and Oak Grove was growing in spite of it. Harry got out of the car and walked into a narrow courtyard that was studded with many doors leading to different sections of apartments. There was a small crowd of people gathered in front of one door, and Harry headed in that directio;n—there were always buzzards around any corpse.

Pushing his way through the crowd and into the inner vestibule of the building, he saw two uniformed officers standing guard. Nothing could foul up an investigation like civilians milling around the scene of the crime and maybe lifting a few souvenirs of the latest massacre. Sometimes he felt more sympathy for the crooks.

"Morning, sergeant," said one of the patrolmen. "It's up in 3-A."

Great, thought Harry. I would get a third floor one.

Huffing and panting his way up the three flights, his stomach alternately swelling and contracting like some vast balloon, he eventually arrived at the top landing and saw the open apartment door. Inside were members of the paramedic team and another patrolman. Stepping inside, he also saw Bill Tolson and another uniformed man standing in one corner of the room, their backs slightly bent as they looked down on a diminutive, wrinkled old crone sitting in a battered rocking chair. It was a bizarre sight, the old woman rocking back and forth like some runaway hobby horse, an air of vacant desperation impelling every lunge forward and back. Her face was an expressionless mask, a distant look glazing over the old, tired eyes. In any other situation it might have been almost comical.

"Bill," Harry called.

Bill Tolson turned around and walked over quickly. "Christ, Bill, Since when are you the first man on the spot?" asked Harry.

"Since I live two blocks away and since Frank Elliot starts calling me at seven in the morning. We don't get many homicides in this town."

"Yeah, thank the Lord." Harry replied. "It's been awhile."

"The body is in the kitchen, Harry. Come on, I'll show you the way."

They went down a narrow corridor past two open bedrooms. Before he could even see the whole of the tiny kitchen, Harry could see the blood. The stark whiteness of the cooking area just intensified the impression of gore. White plaster walls, white stove and refrigerator and old-fashioned white porcelain sink. All were stained by enormous quantities of blood. In the middle of the kitchen floor lay a tiny crumpled figure, face down in a pool of red.

"Oh, Jesus Lord," Harry said softly.

"Emma Johnson, age sixty-seven," Tolson flatly intoned in his professional manner.

"How'd you find that out? The other one?"

"Yes, it's her sister. They lived here together. Been in the same apartment for twenty-three years."

"What's your end of it say."

"Not much until I get her on a table downtown. But I can give you the basics. Her throat has been slashed.

Slashed from end to end with a very sharp broad-bladed knife. Judging from the angle of the wound, I'd guess that the attack was from the back by somebody who was considerably taller than her."

"That'd leave the sister out, I guess," said Harry. "Unless she did it from a ladder."

"Are you serious? You think the sister could have done this?"

"I can't afford *not* to think anything, Bill."

"Yeah, but Jesus. That'd have to be . . . just ghastly." Tolson sounded incredulous.

"You mean this isn't, Bill? Tell me something. You examined the body, right?"

"After a fashion. I told you. I'll have to get her . . . I mean *it* downtown."

"Yeah, but you handled the body, didn't you."

"Well, sure. But it was all within procedure—"

"That's not what I mean Bill. You handled the body, examined her throat, yet you let her fall back face down into the pool of blood. Doesn't that strike you as ghastly?"

"I'm just doing my job, Harry. Lab boys will be here any minute. They have to take photos, make mock ups—you know the routine. I've got to leave things just as they were."

"Yeah, I know the routine. And I know my routine too. If it strikes you as ghastly, so be it. I'm like the old comedian: I've only got one routine, but it's all I've got, even if it's awful."

"I'm sorry Harry. I didn't mean—"

Harry waved his hand. "No, Bill, don't be. Something like this isn't calculated to bring out the best in either of us."

Harry took another look at a kitchen gone insane and turned around. He went back up the hall into the small living room where a patrolman still watched over the madly rocking old lady. Going over to where she sat, he squatted down right in front of the tiny woman's line of sight.

But the eyes were vacant, staring, listless. They clearly

said: Nobody home. And the body just kept up its rocking race to an aimless oblivion. She had found a measure of safety and comfort somewhere deep inside herself, and there was probably little to be gained from trying to make contact. But it was Harry's job to try. He could only try to do it without seeming like the world's biggest asshole.

"Miss Johnson?" he paused and waited. "Miss Johnson, can you hear me? Can you talk to me for a minute?"

Bill Tolson had followed Harry back into the living room. "I don't think it will be much use, Harry," he said from somewhere in back of the detective. "She blabbered quite a bit when the boys first got here, but she's in shock now and probably won't be talking for quite awhile."

Harry sighed and heaved himself to his feet. He turned to one of the medics. "Okay, get her over to the hospital. But I want to know the minute she's fit to talk."

The medic nodded, and Harry turned to Tolson again. "Haven't seen anything like this in the town since '67. That business at the hotel."

"Yes, I remember. Too well. I did the autopsy."

"Anything else you can tell me, Bill? Anything to give me a lead?"

"Not really. She obviously put up quite a fight. It wasn't easy or there wouldn't be so much blood over the whole goddamn kitchen. It's amazing what even an old lady can do when her life's at stake."

"Yeah. But she didn't do enough. Any chance that any of that blood is the murderer's?"

"Could be. Lab boys will be here any minute. We'll check it out."

"And the other one," Harry said motioning at the old lady who was being placed on a stretcher by the medics, "any sign of blood on her?"

"No. None." Tolson replied with a touch of emphasis.

"Nonetheless, I want the whole place checked out

from top to bottom including the garbage cans downstairs and the incinerator, if there is any." He turned to the patrolman who was standing by. "You make sure that gets done. I'm going to have another look at that kitchen."

He had to steel himself to go in there again. It always seemed more than a little obscene that they had to leave the victim untouched until the medical team was through. If anything should be personal, it should be your own demise—especially under circumstances like these. Harry surveyed the kitchen from outside the entranceway. He could just see two dotty old ladies puttering around in there. Who'd think such a common place would be the site of a murder? But, then, he was getting overly ironical. Most murders take place in just such commonplace situations.

He noted the door leading out to the back landing and rear stairs of the building. Mostly for delivery men, but anybody had access to it. No protection except for the back door, and he solemnly noted the pane of broken glass in the door's window. Could have been broken in the struggle, of course. Or the sister might have broken it on purpose to make it look like an intruder. Unlikely though. After twenty-three years people get too used to one another. Even if you hate the other one, you get too accustomed to the company and support. It was sort of like him and Grace, he thought mournfully. And he hadn't thought of killing her—yet.

A commotion in the living room told him that the lab boys had arrived. He took one last look at the pathetic, shrunken figure on the floor and turned to leave. "I'll be downstairs," he said on his way out the door. "Let me know the minute you find out anything."

The trip down was a good deal easier. Approaching the two patrolmen by the door he said, "Get all these people outside out of here. Then we'll have to start knocking on doors. Somebody must have seen something around here."

He noticed that one of them was looking at his sport shirt and then his coat. The patrolman grinned. Silently

Harry sighed to himself. It was going to be a long day for Lieutenant Columbo.

6

Scott was barely out of the car when he saw Barb bounding down the front stairs of the house to meet him. Usually she waited, ladylike, until he was at the door, but she seemed impelled by a particular urgency tonight. "What's up?" he called out, sensing her haste.

She ran quickly across the lawn and around the side of his car, smiling as she reached out for him. "Just glad to see you," she said breathlessly as she slipped her arms around him, hungering for a kiss.

Their lips met briefly in a familiar sweet embrace. "Goodness, my princess is getting uncommonly bold." he said wryly while still holding her. "It's not like you to be so demonstrative in public—especially right in your father's front yard."

Her head tilted back a ways, and a frown came over her face. Looking up at the large house she said, "Oh, that wouldn't bother him—at least it wouldn't have in the past. Recently, I'm not so sure."

"What? He's started to object to me already? Is it because I haven't offered to make an 'honest woman' out of his daughter yet?"

He laughed as he said it, but she looked at him earnestly. "Why Scott, that's the first time you've ever mentioned the subject, I do believe—about anybody."

He recoiled a little. "Yeah, and probably the last. Don't get any ideas."

She looked vaguely hurt for an instant but smiled a moment later., "No, I don't want to scare you, Scott.

You're my only leg to stand on right now," she said, looking toward the house again.

He knew something was wrong by her look and the tone of her voice. "What's wrong, Babs?" he asked softly.

"Wrong? Oh, nothing." She seemed to hesitate. "No, that's not fair. I can't be like him—can't block myself off."

"Who? Your dad?"

She nodded assent. "Come on. Let's go for a ride, and I'll tell you about it."

They got in the battered old Chevy then and rode silently for awhile. He sensed something serious was bothering her and that it was difficult for her. He decided to let it wait until she brought it up again. He turned the car on Winston Boulevard and headed south, driving some ways before she said anything.

"Where you going?" she asked absent-mindedly.

"I thought I'd get on the expressway and head down to the lake."

"No, Scott. I don't want to go into Chicago. Let's just drive around town."

"Around Oak Grove?"

"Yes. It's beautiful."

He turned the car right and headed back into the heart of town. She sighed slightly and looked out the window, silent again. He almost said something but waited again. He knew she talked when she was ready.

"Scott, how big is Oak Grove?" she asked at length.

"What?"

"How many people live here?"

"God, I don't know. About 60,000, I think. Why?"

"Hmmn. Just wondering. It seems so big sometimes, like part of Chicago. Other times it seems like some little town out in the country."

"Little town in the country," he snorted. "Hardly. Not with all the blacks moving in from the west side of the city. It's starting to look like the ghetto over by Winston Boulevard."

She looked at him appraisingly. "I never knew you

were prejudiced."

"Did I say I was prejudiced?"

"People never say that they're prejudiced. They just act it."

"You should hear Larry talk sometime," he countered, "if you think that people never say that they're predjudiced."

She laughed lightly. "Yes, I must admit that Larry might be an exception."

"Hoo boy, is he the exception." Scott chuckled. "Wouldn't be surprised if he was a member of the Klan."

"But seriously, Scott. They've been moving in from the west side of the city for two or three years now, and the town hasn't fallen down or anything."

"No, it hasn't fallen down, Barb, but it certainly hasn't made the town any better. Look what's happened to the West Side in the last ten years. That used to be all middle-class Jewish and Polish neighborhoods. Now it's black, and every fourth or fifth house along Laramie is boarded over and abandoned, every business has its windows chained and gated at night and you don't dare walk the streets alone once it's dark. It never used to be that way. Are you telling me that's just coincidental?"

She hesitated. "Well, no. The blacks themselves admit they've got a problem with crime and—"

"Yeah, and before you know it, it will be Oak Grove's problem too. Oh, not up on the north end of town for awhile where you live. That's all $150,000 houses and lily white, but the south end of town is practically half apartment buildings. They're moving in there in droves."

"So what?"

"So, a girl nearly got raped in my alley two weeks ago at night. They haven't caught him, but she said he was black. Luckily, she screamed and somebody yelled bloody murder out their window. The bastard took off."

"Oh, Scott. One attempted rape and you're going to blame a whole race?"

"Shit. Forget it!" he said sourly. "It's gonna be one of those liberal-conservative things where I come off looking like Ghengis Khan. Mr. Insensitive to the Plight of Underprivileged Minorities."

"Maybe you are."

"Maybe. But just maybe you aren't the only one who cares for this town. You've lived here all your life, and I've only been here six years, but that doesn't mean I can't object to the changes for the worse I'm beginning to see all around me—that is, over on my side of town, the poor side."

"You mean middle class, Scott. And upper middle at that. A few apartment buildings don't make the South Side a federal works project. As for you caring about this town too, I know you do, but you don't realize something. Thirty years ago *you* wouldn't have been allowed in this town. You're the one who would've been discriminated against."

"What?"

"You were raised Catholic, weren't you?"

"Sure, but I haven't gone to mass in—"

"Doesn't matter. No Jews or Catholics were allowed. The realtors, city government, even the police conspired to keep them out. You think this town is Waspish now, well back then it was virtually aristocratic, the last bastion of values that went out of fashion with Louis XIV."

He looked a little perplexed. "That was different—that was mindless prejudice based on fear of an unknown culture—"

"Oh, Scott. Catholics have been in this country practically since the Mayflower—way before blacks. Bigotry is the same everywhere and in every age. Only the faces change."

"Thanks for the history lesson," he said grumpily. "But I still haven't changed my mind. I haven't had the benefit of a college education."

She sighed. "Scott, I'm no sociologist, and I only had a year and a half of college. Every time we have a disagreement, you say you haven't been to college. It's not like I discount everything you say because you haven't been to college. I know you're sensitive about your lack of education but—"

"I could care less about college," he said defensively. "The average professor probably couldn't even saw a two-by-four straight for all the books in the world."

Her mood was bad enough already. Some hurtful comment about the working class hero lingered momentarily at the tip of her tongue, but she restrained it with an effort. "Scott, let's not fight. Please? I'm not trying to argue with you. It's just that I've felt like a misfit, an outcast nearly my whole life. I can't help it that I can feel what it must be like for other outcasts because of my own experiences."

"You, the girl born with the silver spoon in her mouth?" he said, a trifle irritation still in his voice.

She laughed ruefully. "Oh, yeah. It's so convenient to dismiss me as just another spoiled rich kid, isn't it? Father is a doctor. Lives in a big, expensive house. All the earmarks of a pampered, happy life, eh?"

"I'm sorry, Barb." he said regretfully and reached out for her.

She moved away quickly but looked at him, her eyes full of tears. "No, I don't want sympathy. I don't want to be patronized just because you think I'm sensitive and don't know how good I've really got it. And maybe you're right. Maybe all we should expect is food and shelter out of life. Maybe to hope for happiness is stupid and unfair!"

He pulled the car over to the curb and moved quickly over to her side of the car. Enfolding her in his arms, he felt her resist for a moment, then surrender. "What the hell is the matter with you tonight, Barb? I'm sorry about the racial thing. I didn't mean to sound like I was—"

She squeezed him tightly, her voice quavering as she interrupted. "It's not that, Scott. It's—it's Daddy. Oh, I shouldn't talk about it—it's family," she said and hesitated.

He cupped her chin in his hand and smiled at her.

"Hey, I'm family. Or just about. Besides, you said you'd tell me. Out with it."

She squeezed him again but was silent.

"I'm not trying to be nosy, but you might feel better if you talked it out. I know how close you and your old man are; you need someone comparably close to hash it out with. Pardon my, how do you say it, presumption, but I think I'm the only person nearby now who qualifies."

She sniffled and smiled weakly, the tears subsiding. "Yeah, I guess you're right."

"So tell me."

She sighed. "We've always been so close. We talk over everything together, but the last few days it's like I've got the plague."

"How so? What'd you do?"

"I didn't do anything—not that I know of. I just came home the other day and he started raging about mother. Ever since that he's hardly talked to me. He's totally distant—from me, from everything."

"Your mother is dead, Barb. I mean that's what you always told me."

"She is. Twelve years dead."

"So what's he bugged about?"

"God if I know, Scott."

"This doesn't make any sense at all."

She looked at him for a long moment, as if deciding on something. Finally, she said, "I've never told you about it. There was no reason to. But, you see, my mother was a strange person. God knows. No, strange doesn't say it at all. She was a devil."

"You're going to have to explain that."

"I don't know if anyone can explain my mother."

"Try, Babs. So far I feel like I'm in the 'Twilight Zone.'"

She laughed a little. "You see, even we college girls can screw up our explanations." She took in a big breath. "All right, here goes. My father met my mother at some big party thirty years ago. Met her and fell hard, instantly I guess. I can see why, Scott . . . She was beautiful, all curves and dark, mysterious eyes, and she was magnetic too. I was too young to know it at the time, but my relatives have talked to me about her in the past—trying to help me understand."

"Understand what?" he interrupted.

"Understand her and how she could be the way she was. Not that they really knew anymore than the rest of us. Anyhow, they told me that she had a funny effect on men. It was like she was more than merely beautiful. I know that sounds strange, but that's how it was told to me. They said that there hardly seemed to be a man alive that could resist making a play for her. There was some underlying unapproachability to her that made all men want to have her."

"Including your father?"

"Especially my father. He was determined to marry her, though there was plenty of competition, I guess. Why she accepted his proposal no one seems to know. Everybody says that she never loved him—that she never loved anybody besides herself. Maybe it was because he was a doctor and was starting to make good money. She was always greedy, always wanted more of everything. She nearly bankrupted Daddy. She was the one who insisted he buy that huge house we live in, even though it was way too big.

"But I guess she wanted it for her parties. Daddy's always been sort of a loner, but he suffered through her parties constantly. Even I suffered through them."

"How so? You must have been kind of young at the time."

"I was. Nine or ten. I'd be upstairs in bed, but the noise would be tremendous—so bad that the police used to come sometimes."

"Noisy parties? Your dad? I don't believe it. He doesn't seem the rowdy type."

"Oh, he must have gone through hell. Even at that age I could tell. She used to demand that he invite his relatives and all the important people they knew and all the important people he was beginning to know from his practice, which was getting more and more successful.

Then she'd go and invite all these incredible lowlifes she knew from God know's where. They'd come to one of mother's parties and begin mingling with half the cream of Oak Grove and Chicago society, and before an hour went by there was a fight or half of Daddy's guests had left outraged and insulted. Five or six parties and fewer and fewer people would come until finally it was all lowlifes—these absolutely bizarre people mother dug up from somewhere. Even Daddy's parents and brothers wouldn't come anymore—they'd objected violently to the marriage in the first place."

"Why? Was your mother that crude? I know your grandparents are wealthy—high society and all that."

"Crude? No, actually she was enormously sophisticated, I guess. Well educated too. My Aunt Mae told me once that mother could talk to and charm anyone she wanted to, and that she did want to. She hungered for social recognition and acceptance. But at the same time, something dark and hidden in her wanted to shock, outrage and hurt everybody she came into contact with. It was like she had a split personality. Matter of fact some of the psychiatrists really did think she was a clinical case of split personality."

"Psychiatrists?"

"That wasn't until near the end." Barb's voice began to tremble. "It wasn't until her drinking—she'd always been a near alcoholic—had gotten out of hand completely and she had to be confined. In an asylum. A raving thing, I guess. I don't know, I was never allowed to see her, and I never heard about it until years later. I still don't know much, just that she died raving in some mental institution. Daddy will never talk about it. Never."

"It's hard to figure," Scott said softly. "Your father seems so solid, so middle of the road, so *formidable* to put up with that kind of thing."

"He is, Scott. Daddy's never taken abuse from anybody, even when it was to his advantage to do so. But with mother it was like a fatal fascination. He and his own mother hardly spoke to each other for three or four years after the marriage, and they'd always been very close. But Daddy wouldn't listen to any criticism of her from anybody for years, even with all she put him through—and that included a lot, Scott. Alcohol, drugs, sex."

"Sex?"

She blushed a deep scarlet and struggled for words. "I—I told you . . . every man seemed to want her. Apparently she wanted every man who wanted her, or almost. Nymphomania was another one of her favorite tricks."

"Jesus, your father didn't know?"

"Oh, he knew. The way she flaunted it, he couldn't help but know. I used to hear him yelling at her at night and her teasing and taunting him back. I was too young to know what it was really about, but I could tell she had a way of driving him near to the edge and then bringing him back. Somehow, though God knows how she did it with his temper. Daddy broke some man's jaw once. But in all the years they were married, I don't think he ever laid hands on her once."

"And they stayed married? He put up with all that?"

"He loved her. He put up with it all. It meant constant emotional pain to him, public humiliation, lost friendships, near bankruptcy despite all the money he made and all his family had given him, but he stuck it through to the end. I can still remember that rainy day at the cemetery even now: Daddy's whole side of the family there acting properly sympathetic but secretly relieved, the total absence of anybody there from Mother's side of the family—if she had any; that was one of the things Daddy's parents objected to about her—and Daddy standing there by the gravesite looking so thin and worn, the tears streaming down his cheeks. I'll never forget it until my dying day."

Scott reached for her again and gripped her tightly, his hands caressing her shoulders lightly. "I'm sorry, Babs. It must have been awful for both of you."

She chuckled mirthlessly. "Bad? Yes, you might say so. Worse on Daddy. He loved her. I didn't. She would never give me the chance. I remember once when I was nine or ten, oh Christ—" she broke it off, the tears welling up in her eyes again.

"Hey, hey. Stop it," he said soothingly and stroked her hair. "Don't go on if you don't want to. It'll wait."

Her body spasmed slightly, and her voice was a tremor as she replied. "No, I've got to go on now. You see, all my life the one person who has been close enough to me wouldn't talk about it. But now I've got you, and now is the right time, and now I know that I've got to talk about it."

He was silent, feeling her pain. Her voice choked again as she continued. "I was nine or ten and mother called me in one morning to her dressing room. I remember, she was putting on makeup and with no warning or reason she just told me very matter-of-factly that—that she didn't love me, that she'd never loved me and that no one ever would. I remember crying then and her smile—that awful, hateful smile—as she told me that I had been an accident, a blight on her life that she despised and that she'd just come back from some doctor who made sure there'd never be another accident. I didn't know what she meant at the time. Years later I discovered that her two-week 'vacation' about that time had really been a hysterectomy, but it didn't matter. All I really heard was those hateful words: that she didn't love me, that she despised me." She stopped, her body heaving for breath.

He went to stop her from saying anymore, but words tumbled forth before he could say anything. "But Scott, I needed to love her. I didn't—she wouldn't let me—but I needed to. Any little girl needs a mother to love."

He wanted to nod agreement, to say that little boys need a mother's love too, and a father's. He had had neither, though grandma had done much to make up for the lack of both. Deep inside, though, he realized the situation wasn't the same as having an actively malignant parent as Barb apparently had. What that had done to her sense of self-worth was probably incalculable. He didn't know what to say.

"I'm sorry, Scott." she said after a long pause, her voice low and drained. "I shouldn't be burdening you with all this. It's just that you and Daddy are the only people in my life that I'm truly close to, and now he's just withdrawn from me. When he does say anything, it almost sounds accusatory. And the worst of it is, I don't know what he's upset about. I don't know why mother has suddenly surfaced as a topic of debate after twelve years of total non-existence in our lives. I don't know why he's alternating between avoiding me and almost, well, blaming me for something I don't know."

"Give it some time. That's all I can suggest, Barb," he said skeptically. In truth, there wasn't much he felt he could say or do that would make a difference.

She smiled and leaned back against the seat. It was a look of resignation and weariness. Worry and tears had worn her out for now. He drew her over and into the crook of his shoulder, reassuring her with his very presence. For a long time they were silent until he said, "Barb, I don't know what to say except that I'm sorry for your pain and that . . . I love you. You make my life better. You make me feel whole."

He could feel her squeezing him silently in grateful response. "Maybe we should get away for that weekend real soon," she said softly. "A weekend in the woods might be just the thing I need."

"We both need," he countered. "I get a little frazzled too, you know."

She smiled and looked at him. "Yes, I know. I can have that effect on a man."

He grinned and she laughed, and they settled back again into the seats, staying silently together there for a long time while the night grew silently around them.

7

Tommy Watson hadn't slept very well last night. For once his mother had been right: Ten year old boys shouldn't watch horror movies just before going to bed, because the nightmare had been a lot worse than the movie but in a different way. He had seen plenty of horror movies before, and some were pretty scary, but he never let his mother know—or else that would be it for Boris Karloff and Bela Lugosi. He would just lay there in his bed with his eyes open, carefully watching all the corners of the room. Once or twice he had seen a movie that was really bad—just like a nightmare—and he had kept the light on his dresser table on all night.

But the movie last night hadn't been bad at all. He had actually seen it before, so he knew what to expect all along. Besides, wolfmen didn't scare him much anyway, and when his mother had kissed him goodnight, turned out the lights and closed his door, he had hardly been scared at all. Oh, the shadows that clung about the sides of the room may have been a little more ominous than usual, but sleep came pretty fast anyway. Tomorrow was Saturday, and he'd be going on that Scout pack trip, so he'd made up his mind that he better be well rested. He could be rather stern with himself when he needed to be.

But the movie must have been a lot scarier than he'd thought, because when the nightmare came, it was the most awful ever. And the worst part was that it had seemed so real—not like those crazy dreams where you're floating upside down in purple space with some awful ghoul or goblin chasing you. Those were bad, and when you woke up you might spend the rest of the night with the lamp on, but next morning you knew it was just a dream and by school you'd forgotten all about it. But this one had been different.

He dreamed that he had awakened some time in the night and was watching the shadow flit about the wall opposite his bed. Shadows that came from the street light outside his window, peeking spectrally around the edges of the window shade. Dreams often started like this. Sometimes he really did wake up in the night and lie there watching the shadows until, eventually, he fell back into slumber. He would have thought he was awake last night except then the nightmare *really* started.

It started as a simple tapping coming from outside the bedroom window. He heard it clearly because his bedroom was on the ground floor immediately adjacent to the sidewalk, and street noises easily intruded. And as he listened the tapping sound seemed to be getting nearer and louder, until he finally got up to go to the window and see what the noise was. Pulling back the shade, he had a clear and unobstructed view of the sidewalk and street beyond for some distance in one direction, and the street lamp cast a pale, bleak visibility over the immediate area. It was all gloom beyond the dim circle of light, and Tommy remembered looking intently but seeing nothing save a few wind scattered leaves whistling along the sidewalk. But his room was on a corner of the house; he could only see the sidewalk running east, not south, as it angled around the house.

And the tapping persisted and grew louder—a heavy, hollow sound. He was just about to go back to bed when he spotted something out of the corner of his eye. Coming around the blind side of the walk was an outline, a moving figure. But it was already past Tommy's line of forward sight by the time he'd really noticed it, a small, bent figure that was wrapped from head to toe in some kind of dark, billowing cloth. Slowly, laboriously it moved away from him into the shadows

63

beyond the light, but Tommy could clearly make out the long pole or stick it carried with it—a pole with which it seemed to alternately lean and tap the sidewalk in a regular rhythm as it hobbled along and out of sight. That was when he had made the mistake. Wanting to see what the strange heap of moving cloth looked like from the front, Tommy had tapped sharply once or twice on the window pane.

Slowly the figure came to a standstill, almost as if hidden wheels and gears needed time to stop operating. It seemed to pause and become very still for a long while, as if listening, and everything became motionless as Tommy waited. He was just about to rap at the window pane again when the figure turned around.

That was horrible enough, and Tommy knew then that it was a nightmare, and he wished he'd wake up. But gradually the figure began to move toward him, and Tommy just froze. It came closer and closer in what seemed like an eternity of time, until that face was pressed nearly against the window and was staring right in at Tommy, and all he could see was something that looked incredibly old and dried out and had two dark flames for eyes.

He tried to scream and wake himself up, but nothing would come out. He just stood there, in his dream, frozen with fear, his body shaking spasmodically, as it seemed those withered and ancient lips parted in a ghastly, rotten-toothed smile of satisfaction and something had talked to him and said that he would do just fine and that someone would be coming for him . . . coming soon. He tried to scream again, but something had caught hold of him like an invisible hand, and he just remembered standing there helplessly until he woke up the next morning feeling exhausted and scared again.

The dawning light of day and the familiar bustle of common activity were not to have their customary effect. Even his mother commented on how quiet he was at breakfast.

The Scout pack trip went on as planned, but somehow there was little fun in it. The woods looked a little somber and frightening, even with all those other kids and adults around. It wasn't until late afternoon that he began to unknot and feel a little better. Boyish thoughts filtered back into his mind like welcome friends, and he even played with some of the other boys with animation and interest. But as nightfall approached, something dark and furtive stole back into his heart, and the shadows of evening lay heavy upon him.

About nine o'clock the adults came around to help the boys into their pup bents and sleeping bags. Tonight they would sleep out in the open under the stars. Most of those small boys thought it a great adventure and marvelous fun. They were growing up fast, and they didn't have to be scared of anything. Especially when adults were around. There was some hushed talking for awhile. David Hackins screamed once when a cricket landed on his face, but soon everything was still except for the dull murmur of forest noises. Like the campfire that was gradually dying into embers, the consciousness of little boys was fast being enfolded in delicious slumber. All save one. One little boy lay awake long into the night, he was determined not to go to sleep.

8

Willie didn't wake up until sometime after three o'clock that afternoon. He had crashed at Rufus White's place, and that was about the noisiest digs in town. But Willie hadn't heard a thing: not the party, not the kids, not even Rufus's screamin' old lady. No, Willie had been stone cold out. He usually had to down a whole fifth before he got that bad, but he hadn't . . . or had he?

Willie really didn't remember much about last night or even the last few days. His life was usually pretty much a day to day thing. Catch as catch can. The monotonous events of one day comfortably blending into the non-events of the next. But lately it was different. Everything was kind of blurred and hazy. Memories fuzzy. Perceptions altered. Maybe he needed a vacation—a week or two down on Western Avenue. He chuckled mirthlessly to himself.

He seemed to remember lying in bed yesterday—all day. The intervening hours between darkness and dawn were gone, missing, nonexistent. But he vaguely remembered the day, remembered feeling tired and weak, and he hadn't wanted to get up at all. And catfish. He remembered catfish. He'd been a small boy again, and he'd gone down to the Tombigbee with his father to catch catfish.

Oh, his daddy had liked to fish. Fishin' and talkin' were the two things he'd been best at. He'd even talked to little Willie a lot; he didn't save it all for the adults like a lot of other grownups. Together they used to go down to the river and fish in the hot, moist afternoon sun. Together, Willie would lie against a tree and lazily watch his bobber move up and down in the rushing muddy waters of the Tombigbee and listen to his father talk.

He talked about everything: Huntin' coons and possum. How to cook chicken. What makes a carburetor work. The stars in the sky. The swamp man that sometimes you could see on the night of the full moon. Ladies dresses and trips to Jackson City. But mostly he talked about France.

Willie's father had been in France in World War I, and boy had he been a conversation piece. It was a story just how he had gotten drafted and survived in an all-white platoon from the Deep South. That was a story he'd tell at least once a month. But France—and Paris—he'd tell that one every day to anybody who'd listen.

Those French women had gone nuts over him, to hear him tell it. Had gone crazy over his black skin—for once it was an asset. Willie could tell his father left a lot out of his stories about France when he was tellin' them to Willie, but he didn't mind. They were good anyway.

France was a lot different than Mississippi. In France you could drink wine with every meal, and nobody'd ever say anything about it. The food was sort of rich and saucy, but you could eat three times a day for a year and never have the same thing twice. Everything was different and just plain fine. The French women had told him that it had been a lot better before the war, but he didn't see how it could be. Where else could you laze around the whole day without feelin' ashamed and being called a shiftless nigger?

Yeah, it had been hard coming back to the States, hard to go back to Mississippi, but that was all he knew. He had a place there. He was accepted. But that acceptance had a lot of "ifs" about it, a lot of traps and uncertainties, but it was better than some place else where he didn't know what to expect at all.

Willie always knew that secretly his father had regretted coming back to Mississippi, that he would have liked to stay in his wonderful France, but that he knew he didn't belong there. He was just an oddity admired for his oddness by a people who were bored by everything that was conventional—who made it a point of life to court the unusual.

So Willie's old man was smart. He came home, stayed outa trouble and just stayed in Mississippi, fishin' and talkin' and once a month going into Jackson City for his relief and VA checks. He had just smiled and shook his head when Willie had finally told him that he was going to leave and go up North. He never did let Willie bring him up either, just stayed there in the squalor and the humiliation even after Momma was gone and Betty and Martha had gone away to Little Rock and Shreveport to live . . . the memory slipped away.

Willie rolled over, his thoughts running out on his brain as if it were a sieve. He couldn't keep anything in there lately except for a few jumbled thoughts and half-impressions. Yet, something definite, almost tangible, hung on in there. Something hid and burned at the back of his brain like an itch you can't scratch. He knew it was there—constantly. But when he reached for it, it was gone.

And he was sleepy too. Sleep rolled over him like a fog. Maybe he was sick; he was too tired to tell. He knew he had slept most of the last few days away, but he didn't know about the nights. Sleep must have been deeper then, because he had no memories of the night at all, just dreams. Or what seemed like dreams. Dim images of night memory occasionally drifted through his mind, but they were quickly extinguished by the languor or by the dull flame that seemed to constantly burn at the back of his head.

He would have to be getting up soon—one of these days. He was king of the corner, and you can't vacate your post for loo long . . . always pretenders to the throne . . . damn niggers . . . mother fuck, he hated being a nigger sometimes. Othertimes, rollin', rollin' along on a cloud. He was rollin' around on a cloud. It got dizzy once in a while, but it was soft and comfortable. No more worries, no more fret, the bogeyman's gonna get you yet.

He laughed hollowly and rolled over, his head hanging off the side of the mattress. Fucking shit! There it was again. Trying to get in. What was he trying to remember!? What the hell was keeping it out!? That burning . . . burning in his brain. *That* was keeping it out—filling his head with so much pain that he couldn't think or remember. Suddenly he coughed dryly and his insides heaved and convulsed until his gut exploded and he threw up all over the floor and the side of the bed.

It was there now. He felt something dry and useless and hateful in him at that moment, and his legs curled up instinctively close under his chin. Slowly his body began to rock back and forth in the compulsive rhythm of misery. The burning in his head became greater, and he shut his eyes on a sordid, ugly world. A tear formed gradually at one corner, there was a whimper, and Willie's powerful big body arched and spasmed once before it hit the mattress with a dead and lifeless weight.

9

"Hello, Harry. See you're doing some work for a change."

Harry looked up from the clutter of papers that made his desk look like a federal disaster area. It was Bill Tolson. "Goddamn reports," he muttered. "All in triplicate—everything has to be a goddamn triplicate. It makes up 95% of my fucking time."

"Looks like you're the man for the job," Tolson replied while gazing sceptically at the litter on Harry's desk. "If ever there's a paper shortage—" he left the thought incomplete purposely, then smiled.

"Yeh, it's rare that I get anything really interesting to do—like cut up stiffs," said Harry sourly.

"You always were malicious, Harry."

"Okay, what's up, Bill? You don't usually come down here on a social call."

"Thought I'd drop the report on the Johnson thing off."

"Well, you can sure tell it's a small town. Where else do you get the coroner's report delivered personally—and by the coroner himself. Want a spotlight, Bill?"

"Well, I thought I'd fill you in on the details, but if you want to wade through it yourself—"

"Oh, no you don't. You're a captive audience now. Sit down. I'll get you a cup of coffee."

Harry rose with surprising quickness out of the chair. Could it be that all this action lately was reviving his tired spirit and renewing his enthusiasm for a job that had become more and more an endless round of investigation into petty and pointless crimes? "You know Bill," he called over his shoulder, "I handled one other murder case. The Dominic business ten years ago at the hotel, and that wasn't like I really handled it myself. Those gangland slayings draw more cops than you'd think could be alive. There was state cops, Chicago cops, the feds . . . Christ, I got lost in the shuffle."

"Yes, I remember that one, Harry. Who could forget those shotgun wounds? What a mess. But you handled it well, Harry."

"Yeh? Well thanks, but I never found out anything. You never do in those things; even the fed were stymied. But if I had," his voice became a little wistful, "well, I was up for promotion and it was my big chance to impress, what with the papers and the TV and everything. But nothing ever came of it, and zap!—there went my chances."

"Just more papers to fill out," Bill said consolingly. He could tell that Harry was in a mood—one that could easily by pushed over the line into bitterness. He had gotten some bad breaks, like being made the scapegoat in that Dominic case with the result that an outsider with less experience had gotten Harry's promotion to chief of detectives. Not that it was such a big job: Oak Grove only had five detectives. But it had kicked the man's pride, and it had effectively negated any chances for future promotion.

"Well, this one's got the old adrenalin pumping again, Doc," said Harry with barely forced enthusiasm. "I've been chasing kids for too long. Somehow, arresting some punk for stealing hubcaps or buying a nickel bag ain't my idea of being a cop. But this—this is something worth the aggravation."

"Harry! You sound positively delighted that the old lady was killed, you shocking scoundrel. I wouldn't be surprised if you did it yourself just to stir up some excitement." Tolson laughed.

"Well, if I did it, you can be sure of one thing."

"What's that?"

"I'll find some way to pin the rap on Frank Elliot." The rancor was showing through loud and clear now.

Tolson decided he'd better change the subject. "Let me run over this autopsy report with you."

Harry came back balancing two cups of coffee. Both were overfull, and some had spilled over onto Harry's hand and cuff. "Okay, give it to me simple."

Tolson removed some papers from his briefcase. Putting on his glasses, he immediately assumed a professional air. More like a doctor, a pillar of society and all that, thought Harry. "All right, Harry. Straight and simple. There were no signs of significant rigor mortis or decomposition . . . Analysis of blood and fluid lividity suggests that the time of death was about six-thirty in the morning. The fact that the death was instantaneous throws a considerable amount of uncertainty on this conclusion, but I'd doubt that the death could have been before six o'clock."

"But your hunch is closer to six-thirty."

"Right."

"The sister called to report the murder at six forty-seven according to the station's automatic monitor. That would hardly give her time to cover her tracks."

"Probably not. But there's no way she could have, Harry. The direction and the inclination of the wounds on the throat tell us two things. One, the killer was right-handed. While I was talking to the sister the morning of the murder—you know, before she went virtually catatonic—I saw her pick up an old photograph of her and her sister. She picked it up with her left hand."

"You should have been the detective, Bill. But that's hardly proof."

"No, but I'll bet you'll find out the old lady is left-handed if you check."

"I'll do that."

"You probably don't have to, Harry. Point number two. The inclination of the wounds or, more acurately, the wound indicates that it was inflicted from behind and by somebody about a foot taller than the victim. I told you that at the apartment, of course, but now I'm sure of it."

"Yeah, that would seem to leave out the sister," admitted Harry.

"The lab report also indicates that some of the blood they found had spattered in such a way to suggest that it issued from a source five to five and one-half feet above the floor. The victim was five foot three, so we can assume that she was slashed while standing up, and that nullifies our only other possible conclusion: that she was forced to lie on the floor, the knife was placed under her chin and then drawn across and upwards. No, the killer was a good deal taller than she was."

"I was just going over the lab report when you came in," said Harry a trifle defensively. "The position of the body suggested a fall."

"Right. There were small bruises on the knees and one elbow that suggest a fall. But they might have occurred during the struggle or at the moment of death when the body fell to the floor."

"Well, I never really suspected the old lady anyways, but you've got to cover all bases. But come on, Bill. Is that all you've got?"

"No, Harry. I've been saving my *piece de resistance* till now. You see, the victim had a good deal of skin under your nails: Negroid skin. I also found Negroid hair follicles. She must have put up a real fight."

"Great," replied Harry. "That narrows it down to one-tenth of all the people in the country and about half of all the people in Chicago."

"How about one-tenth with type AB blood?"

"What? You're kidding. That's only about five percent of the population, isn't it?"

"Closer to four. The old lady was type O, so we know the blood had to be the murderer's."

"Hot dog for you, Bill. We find a suspect, and it's an open and shut case. But that isn't going to help me find anyone, Bill. It doesn't give me any idea where to look."

"Well, you've got to do *some* work on your own, Harry. How about the lab report? I've only read the section relevant to my autopsy."

"Naw. They vacuumed up some tobacco. Neither of the sisters smoked, and they never had any visitors except deliverymen. It could be something, but right now it just tells me that our man probably smoked Marlboros."

"Maybe he's a black cowboy." laughed Tolson.

"Oh, Christ. Stick to medicine, Doc. You've been sniffing too much embalming fluid or something."

"That's for morticians, Harry. Anything else?"

"Yeah, some suede fibers. He was probably wearing a suede coat or vest."

"Fancy. Well, listen Harry, I've got to get going. Oh, there's one other thing that might interest you. The murder weapon. From the depth and angle of the wound—its irregular depth, actually—I'd say the knife had a curved blade."

"Curved?"

"Like a scimitar. Only this was a knife."

"Yeah," returned Harry absent-mindedly. "Thanks Bill."

Tolson left, and Harry put one hand to his head, rubbing wearily. Shit. He had about as much to go on as the guy looking for the needle in the haystack. Maybe if he could line up every big nigger from here to Cleveland and give 'em blood tests, he could narrow it down to a couple thousand suspects. All he could do now is ask the FBI and the prison bureau to run the blood type info through their computers. It was worth a chance, but he didn't expect that would lead to anything. No, his best bet was the sister. She'd had two days to recover from the shock, and it was about time he was talking to her.

Harry got up and got his coat then headed down to the car. It was only five blocks to the hospital, and in ten minutes he was arguing with the receptionist. Ten minutes and a thousand disjointed thoughts and jumbled impressions later. Ten minutes in an infinity of routines and mild indigestion. Ten minutes less in the meandering, always vaguely frightening course of life.

"I'm sorry, sir. You'll need the doctor's permission to see the patient. She's under police protection, so I can't give you the room number."

"I *am* the police, goddamn it." He flipped open his badge.

"I'm sorry, you'll still need the doctor's permission."

"Will you page him, please?" Harry asked with aggravation. He wondered if Columbo had these kinds of problems.

"Dr. Forster isn't due until two, sir. If you'd care to wait—"

"No." Harry replied somewhere midway between a tone of resignation and a snarl. "I'll come back later."

As he stalked through the lobby, he contented himself with thinking how much he'd like to put that nurse in one of her own hospital beds. But what was the use? No one gave the cops any respect these days, and if you decked everyone who had it coming, you'd end up a full time pugilist.

What was important now was getting a line on whoever had murdered Emma Johnson. The neighbors had been no help. It had been too early in the morning, and neighbors never see anything even when they see something—not in a murder, at any rate.

But several things were clear already. The murderer had escaped down the back service stairway as evidenced by bloody shoe prints on the top few stairs. But the prints were partial and incomplete. Nothing could be inferred from them, because they hadn't been heel prints. Sometimes you can make something of those. The method of entry had been crude and obvious. The murderer had merely broken a pane of glass in the kitchen door and unlocked it from the inside. The murder had obviously taken place in the kitchen itself, and it had not occurred without a struggle. But beyond these few meager facts, Harry had little to go on.

But, Christ, you'd think somebody would have seen something. Harry and four patrolmen had covered two square blocks, and that area was virtually all apartments. No one had seen a thing, not even a motorist or a delivery truck driver. Saturday at six-thirty in the morning the streets were pretty empty. No, not much hope in that direction, but you couldn't just wait around and hope that somebody might call the station to ask if there were any recent murders they might have been witness to. You had to dig up your own leads, but sometimes your chances were worse than your chances of discovering buried treasure in your own back yard.

He headed the car downtown again, his brain churning with a multitude of possibilities and an equal number of discards. He'd almost forgotten that this job could be more than exasperating, that there could be more to do than fill out reports and interrogate fifteen year old bicycle thieves.

He parked the car behind the city hall. Police headquarters were still in the massive old three story building along with about thirty other city departments, and Christ were they crowded. He'd be more than grateful when they finished the new building. Hopefully it would have an elevator, and he wouldn't have to climb all those stairs. Another year of this, and it would be the cardiac ward for certain.

He walked by communications and gazed grumpily at the prim, neat policewoman behind the glass. Damn broad. She had a voice like a chainsaw. He started upstairs to his second floor office.

"Oh, sergeant. Sergeant Oronski."

"Yes." he turned slowly back toward the glass. The hawk-like face was looking directly at him.

"Lieutenant Elliot wants to see you right away. He's with the D.A. in the third floor conference room."

"All the way up there?"

"Yes, sergeant. Lieutenant Elliot said the climb would do you good." She smiled sweetly, but he could see the disapproval, the slight scorn, behind it. She was so neat, so trim.

"Bastard," he mumbled under his breath as he began the long ascent.

10

October 31st. Halloween. A night when the most precious and lovely little girl can work the most marvelous transformations and suddenly become a fiendish, gruesome old hag replete with long pointed hat, warts on her nose and a most incongruous but sinister broom in her tiny hands.

One might think that the satchel she carried contains all the tools of her trade; eye of newt, frog's skin, henbane and the like. Would you really be surprised if the contents were a bit more commonplace? There's more of marshmallow than witches' weed; chocolate is found to the virtual exclusion of deadly nightshade. Even apples are not likely to be of the poisonous variety. Little girls—even on Halloween—stay mostly little girls.

Halloween. A night when the most innocent, cherubic little boy is stirred by a love of the horrible and mysterious, and the costume of crypt and graveyard works the most frightful changes. Little boys are suddenly to be feared. They howl and they moan chillingly, their small faces transmuted into masks of shivering terror. What matter that their stature is still a bit diminutive for a monster.

On this night the world is no longer so big that it can resist their onslaught. The proof is in the tribute of terror paid to them: the surfeit of good things they carry in their bags as implied testimony to the mortal dread with which all adults view their coming. Only the youngest don't realize that it's a game, but for all of them it's a very good game. Little boys—even on Halloween—stay mostly little boys.

Tonight starts like most other Halloween nights in Oak Grove. It is a cool, cloudless evening. An intermittent wind springs up, swirling ghost clouds of dead and whispering leaves about, then subsides again. A pale gibbous moon hangs dubiously over the whole scene, casting a reluctant and baleful light on the almost barren limbs of trees that writhe beckoningly in the invisible grip of the wind. The street lights are dim and only add to the atmosphere of murky gloom.

Priscilla Hansen and Jenny Ritter hurried along the sidewalk in a state of half-fright. Two older boys had just jumped out from behind a tree and scared them, and Jenny and Priscilla had screamed and squealed and run off to the noise of laughter which was both delighted and derisive. They continued to run long after their fright had left them—they ran for the excitement of it all and in embarrassment and anger for being so scared, if only for a moment. After all, Priscilla was all of nine, and Jenny was almost ten. Too old to be scared by that sort of thing.

Jenny finally realized that they had run a long way, almost down to Ridgedale Park which was a good nine or ten blocks from their homes. They had been given strict orders to stay within four blocks of home, but here they were. Other children were scarce down here. The big, dark park flanked one side of the street for over two blocks before it ran into Ridgedale, and St. Peter's Episcopal Church. They were immersed in a small oasis of emptiness in the very heart of the town's residential center.

Jenny looked at the dark park and then over to the massive lightlessness of St. Peter's. A block ahead of them numerous cars sped down the main thoroughfare of Ridgedale. A block behind them the familiar line of houses and their welcome lights began again on the opposite side of the street. But here and now she felt quite alone and a little bit frightened. "We'd better go back," she whispered softly to Priscilla.

Priscilla lifted the fright mask off her head almost as if she were trying to banish any potential fears of the night by giving up the game: I'm not gonna play this Halloween any more, so don't scare me! She turned around in silent response to Jenny's words, and together the two suddenly quiet girls began to head back up the street to more familiar surroundings. There they would feel secure again and could once again resume their reign of terror.

Stepping out of the dark shadows of the park and coming toward them was the figure of an adult. At least it looked larger, like an adult, but it was dressed for Halloween. If Jenny or Pris had seen that figure in the day, they might have sniggered and laughed, but it was the night now and it was Halloween.

Something long and black covered the body and trailed down all the way to the ground. It was even drawn up around and over the head, so nothing of the person's features could be seen. And the dark-robed figure walked with something long and thin in one hand. A rod or a pole of some kind. Tap, tap, tap went the pole against the sidewalk. A hollow, rhythmic cadence as the figure alternately leaned on the great stick and pushed itself slowly forward. Lamely. With an effort.

Jenny giggled nervously and whispered something to Pris. Maybe it was Sister Theresa, their mean old study hall teacher. Pris giggled too, but the sound just sort of gurgled in her throat. The figure inched nearer, looming blacker and stranger with every step.

Instinctively they began to cross the street to avoid it. Like a lame shadow, the figure moved to meet their move. They stopped on the parkway, unsure of what to do. Silently, inexorably the black figure moved closer, and the tapping grew louder until it seemed to swell up all around them and swallow the night. Hypnotized by the hollow, ringing sound. It pealed like bells now, like the bells of St. Peter's high above them. Fascinated, frightened, they gathered up their senses too late. A long, bony, incredibly gnarled hand reached out from between the heavy folds of black and seized Priscilla

Hansen by her long strawberry hair. She screamed then, a small, high sound that wouldn't carry very far. A sound that was quickly lost in the choking, stifled gasp that broke from her as that grim hand slid caressingly down her face to her throat.

Jenny had just stood there for a moment. Shocked. Her mind quickly evaluating a panic of alternatives. As her presence of mind returned she looked up into the face that was set in the folds of the dark cowl. She stared into the eyes of the thing that held her friend so cruelly in a merciless grip. It was an old face, so very, very old—a face of centuries past and a thousand remembered evils. Age hung from those bones like some inconceivable horror. And the eyes drew her. All that was still alive in any real way in that face was found in those eyes, and they were hellish and remorseless. If she had been older and more discerning, she would have noted how grotesque amusement danced in those eyes and mingled with a hostility that knew no bounds or limits. All that was carnal and bestial could be found there, lingering behind a mask of ultimate detachment that was possibly the coldest horror of all.

Jenny didn't try to scream or struggle. She just turned and began running up the street, her life saved by the fact that the nightmare come to life had only two arms and all the while had kept its grip on the long pole with which it had tapped the sidewalk. Jenny ran. She ran a full nine blocks to her home where she collapsed into the arms of her mother, her fragile body heaving in spasms of terror and pain. Jenny Ritter wouldn't speak that night or for three days after, but long before she could finally tell what she had seen, Priscilla Hansen's parents knew that their daughter hadn't returned home. When Jenny came out of shock on the third day, Priscilla Hansen hadn't been found.

But such news travels slowly, and the screams of a child on Halloween, even when heard, are not likely to arouse much attention. So it is not surprising that the round of trick or treating continued for several more hours that night. Oak Grove was oblivious, wrapped in the perpetual slumber of her gracious way of life.

A mile and a half to the south of Ridgedale Park the Grischik twins were busy soaping the windows of old lady Bishop's house. She never went anywhere, the old cripple, but every Halloween she turned off the lights and pretended not to be home just so she could save a few lousy dollars on candy money. Well, this year she was going to have to spend it anyway—on window washers. Maybe Jerry and Billy would do it themselves. They'd come over tomorrow after school and ring that big bell above the front door. They'd bet old lady Bishop would come running then, like she always did when somebody was just trying to have some fun. She'd peer out at them and ask what they wanted in that petulant, whiny voice of hers, and they'd reply, oh so nicely, how they'd noticed her windows had been soaped, and would she like them washed for, oh, maybe ten dollars. Would serve her right.

They were laughing quietly now as they moved around to the side of the house. They'd streaked those big front windows that looked out on the front porch real good, but now they had an even better target, that big round window by the weeping willow tree. Jerry would have to give Billy a boost up if he was going to reach it, but the tree would provide plenty of cover if someone should happen to walk by on the sidewalk out front. Besides, it would only take a minute or two and then they'd be off. Tricks were a lot more fun than treats anyway by the time you reach twelve and thirteen.

But someone had decided to play a trick on them instead. Jerry was just about to give Billy a boost when right out of the air it seemed to appear beside them, barely distinguishable from the surrounding night. It couldn't have been more than fifteen feet away, but Jerry still had a hard time trying to figure out what it was. Like a tall black outline of some kind, blacker than the night around it. Half surprised and half curious, he let go of Billy's foot and just stared at it as it seemed to hover and float a foot or two above the ground.

Whatever it was, it was about seven feet high and

kind of thin and shapeless, like a big, flat billowy blanket of blackness. No arms or legs or features but two pinpoints of glowing red where its face should have been.

"What's the matter? Why'd you stop?" asked Billy. He looked at his older brother and saw his stare and then looked in the direction of his brother's gaze.

Right away Billy was scared; he nearly yelled. But Jerry was known far and wide as a bold and bratty little kid who didn't scare easily. "Shit!" he exclaimed with precocious vulgarity. "That ain't nothing but cardboard and an old blanket or something with a couple pen lights for eyes!" It was a quick and courageous analysis, but wrong.

Jerry rushed at the thing just about the moment when Billy first wailed his fright. He stetched out his hands ready to pull down the crude approximation of a monster or whatever it was old lady Bishop had rigged up and yell in triumph at his conquest. He was only a few feet from the shapeless, undulating curtain of black when he saw those two phony red eyes again. Only this close they didn't look so phony. They looked deep, almost bottomless, and kind of empty. They blazed and swelled with a soulless ghost light of unnatural red. They sparkled and sucked you in, a whole maze of color dancing behind and around the edges of that primary throb of pulsing scarlet. They grew hot and cold before him, they menaced and invited. He couldn't have stopped if he had wanted to; something held him fast in his very soul.

He ran right into the thing, and right away he felt tingly and sort of wet or filmy. It was all very insubstantial, very intangible—not like running into a real person at all. For just an instant Jerry thought he had been right, that it was just a big piece of blanket or papier mache. He wanted to laugh, to laugh at the poor joke and his own momentary fright, but he didn't. Something sticky and binding seemed to be closing all around him. The lights in the sky and the street seemed to dim, and he felt his body go numb a little. Then there was a voice, though he didn't really hear any words. Don't struggle. Don't struggle, it said again and again. All over soon . . . Just let it happen. Don't struggle. Don't struggle.

He thought he must be dreaming, because he was suddenly terrified for no reason. No, there was a reason, but he didn't know what it was . . . couldn't figure . . . his body was beginning to feel oily . . . very strange . . . not at all right.

Then it all changed again, and in an instant his world became a vast dark cavern whose walls were the black depths of a starless infinity, but his own body felt as if it were tightly wedged and contorted as if imprisoned in a tiny box where there was no air or room for movement. He began to cry and struggle then, to hurl himself against the invisible confines of his prison, but there was nothing to struggle against. The last thing he remembered doing was calling for Billy and hearing his words and pleas just sort of echo back at him and be swallowed up in the maw of darkness that surrounded him.

As for Billy, he never heard, nor would he have answered anyway. At first he had watched his brother flail and fight the night air, his arms clawing at the nothingness while his torso twisted and writhed in agony on the ground. Billy saw nothing; there was nothing to see. Only the hint of a darker bit of night that hovered a few feet above Jerry's thrashing body and a dull speck of pulsing red that now ebbed and went out. Billy watched, open-mouthed. Then he turned and ran.

It would be a strange night all over the town. A very strange night. At least fifteen people called the police to register vague, sometimes embarrassed, complaints. The next day the phone lines were busy with calls from neighbors to neighbors and friends to friends. Nobody knew exactly what they had seen it seemed, yet everybody knew they had seen something. And most of them certainly weren't telling, weren't going to expose themselves to public ridicule by calling the cops or the newspapers.

And what had they seen? One woman had looked out her window just after ten o'clock thinking she had heard a noise close to the house, perhaps a late tricker—the treaters and little toddlers would all be home and in bed by now. Well, if he thought he were going to soap her windows or string toilet paper all over the yard . . .

She saw several small children—it looked like a pack of them—scuttle with incredible speed across the front of her lawn and down the alleyway out of sight. All dressed in black and . . . funny looking. Too squat and broad for real children, normal children. Yet she distinctly remembered seeing several of their faces—childrens' faces. One had seemed to grin at her as it fled across the wall—a leering canine grin, and the woman had the recollection of long teeth. But somehow it was so fleeting and illusory. A vivid impression, but had it happened at all?

She called four friends. None had seen or heard anything out of the ordinary. She would call one more. What? She had? Thank God! She needn't doubt her sanity anymore—not unless they were both going round the bend.

Yes, they had seemed strange, almost as if there had been something grotesque and hideous about them, something unnatural. And had she noticed that they had seemed, well, almost transparent? Yes, it does sound silly, but they had moved so fast. You hardly saw them, and they were gone. It was pretty hard to say anything for certain.

A bad night. The screwball calls the police just recorded and dismissed—God knows there were enough of them. Was the whole town on a drinking jag? But some calls they couldn't so easily dispose of, and they'd have to be looked into. Angry parents calling to complain that their children were in hysterics because of the antics of some sadistic practical jokers. One child was even missing and her friend hospitalized for shock. Well, the town was changing, no doubt about it. A new element was coming in, and it surprised no one that even children could suffer the consequences of "socioeconomic dislocation." When somebody has a grudge against the world, it doesn't seem to matter who he takes it out on. Last year it had been razor blades in some of the kid's apples. This year it was apparently going to be elaborately staged frights and—God forbid—maybe a kidnapping.

11

Hilda Higgins locked her car and began the long trek to her apartment. The apartment had been a steal at $190.00 a month, but this walk always bothered her. It could be raining or snowing as often as the weather was good, and that wasn't the worst of it. Things just weren't safe like they used to be, and she got home too late at night to be walking around alone in the empty streets.

But that was one of the problems with this town that you didn't see from the outside. Lovely old apartments, sure. Cheap rent, sure. But try to find a parking space that wasn't ten blocks away. You couldn't do it, because the city didn't allow overnight parking on the streets and there wasn't a garage space to be had at almost any price. Not her price, at any rate. Not on a hundred and a half a week.

She shouldn't have to do it. She shouldn't have to work from noon to nine every day then have to come home and walk two long blocks and up three flights of stairs. She was fifty-five years old, and it wasn't right.

Besides, the town was changing. Everybody knew it. Coloreds were moving in, and it wasn't such a hot place to live any more despite all the publicity the town put out for itself. It wasn't safe to walk the streets anymore. Dotty Moore had been mugged only a month ago near the hospital, and even though it hadn't been a colored then . . . well, when thing start to go bad, everything else just sort of falls in line. She patted her purse for reassurance, her fingers searching through the leather for the comforting outline of the tear gas pen she'd sent away for.

The railroad viaduct was coming up pretty fast now. She always hated walking underneath that damn thing. So dark. If anybody was going to try to get you.... She gripped her purse a little tighter and determinedly set into the tunnel, holding her breath all the way. Once she was through there, the pilgrimage to safety became easier: just a long block and a half down Geddert Avenue to her building, and the way was pretty well lit.

She noticed how her feet crunched against the dry fallen leaves that littered the sidewalk and lawns all around her. It was kind of a nice sound, definite and reassuring, because it distracted her from the surrounding silence of the night. But when she thought about it for a moment, she decided that it only reminded her of how alone she was, even here in the heart of town. She increased her pace a little, as she thought reluctantly about all the obvious and unobvious dangers that possibly awaited her.

After all, there had been that article in the *Tribune* just the other day about that Johnson woman being murdered only eight or nine blocks away, so there was no reason to feel guilty about being paranoid. That was the only way you ever found out if anything really bad happened in this town: You read it in the Chicago newspapers. That miserable *Oak Tree*—that was an in-town publication if there ever was one. To judge by the *Oak Tree*, the worst thing to ever happen in Oak Grove was the Dutch elm disease. Hell. She might as well live in Chicago; you weren't safe anywhere.

A car drove by, and again she had ambivalent feelings. It was nice to know that somebody was around in case you needed help, but who'd stop to help these days? What's worse, who's to say that the occupants of the car are the friendly ones? Murderers and muggers had to have some way of getting around too. Shit. She was just scaring herself. Better to think of something else—anything else. She began counting the street light poles as she walked. There were nine of them between the railroad viaduct and her front door. She had just passed the third.

Boy, what a day it had been. The customers were usually bastards, but today had been the pits. One jerk had sent back his hamburger three times, because when he said medium rare he meant medium rare. The manager told her to dump it on his head the third time if she wanted, and brother, she had wanted. But he had exhausted his list of complaints by that time and accepted this last slab of ground beef on a bun without so much as a whimper of protest. It was hamburger number two recycled, and apparently it had gotten rarer on its last trip to the kitchen. And then there had been the old lady who had lost control of her bladder in the middle of a vanilla shake. Luckily she had been in a back booth, but that fact hadn't made it any easier or more pleasant for Hilda to clean up.

She passed the sixth pole and looked behind her. Not a soul in sight. That could be good or bad. Slowly her mind returned to the financially unrewarding rigors of the day. She'd only made twenty dollars in tips today. With her salary that came to under $25.00. All the aggravation for that! She didn't know what she'd do if the Ford ever gave out, but it was still going strong after 115,000 miles.

If only she could find a job in one of those fancy places in downtown Chicago where the girls bring home two or three hundred a week easy. But for those places you had to be young and pretty or at least middle-aged and classy. She couldn't fit any of those criteria, and what was worse, she knew it.

Light pole number eight. She could see her building a little ways up and to the left, and something that had been knotted in her stomach let go—she could run it from here if she had to. She might not be any gazelle, but if it came down to it . . .

She felt a sudden breeze sweep out of the south and brush cooly across her face. The weather the last couple of weeks had been just incredible. As tired as she was, she would have sat out on the porch for a while tonight—if she had had a porch. Coming to the front walk, she opened her purse and fumbled for her keys. As usual, they eluded her in the maze of things she kept there. Her hand chanced across the sleek metallic contours of the tear gas pen, and she smiled a smile of satisfaction, almost hoping some bastard would try to grab her once.

Finally she found the key ring and jiggled it noisily once or twice. Anything to drive off the evil spirits, she laughed to herself. Entering the vestibule, Hilda listened to her stiff heels ring hollowly on the terrazzo floor, as she crossed the inner door and unlocked it. The sound of home. Haven. The door felt heavy and solid in her grip, and she started to feel a little silly about her fears as she began the long climb to her apartment.

She paused to catch her breath outside the door before putting the key in the lock, wishing all the time that she could afford a building with an elevator. Hell. She couldn't even afford air conditioning. She sighed as she turned the key, the tumblers stiffly rolling to open the door to her little oasis. Once inside, she reached for the light switch on the wall, her nostrils reacting uncomfortably to the unaccustomed thickness of the air. Damn it was stuffy. Better open a window right away, she thought as the light sprang to cheerless life overhead.

But she closed and dead bolted the door first and then removed her coat, idly throwing it over the sofa. Oh, her poor dogs. She plopped down gratefully into the old easy chair next to the sofa and removed her shoes. One of these days she'd go and see that foot doctor no matter what it cost and get her corns and bunions taken care of properly. She was tired of hacking away at them with a safety razor. She was tired of so much.

But for now she would soak them for at least an hour before they began to stop aching and burning. Sometimes they ached so much that she forgot that the rest of her ached too. Fifty-five years old and on her feet all day. It wasn't right. So went her perpetual litany of despair.

That stuffiness, it was too much to ignore. She sniffed tentatively. It smelled almost like gas. She prayed she hadn't left the stove on, or the pilot light hadn't gone off again. Sometimes she still lost sleep thinking about that. It might not be the worst way to meet your maker, but she wasn't quite ready to go yet, thank you, even if sometimes she did feel like giving up the ghost.

With an effort she pushed her ample frame up and out of the chair and angled it out of the living room and down the dim hallway toward the kitchen. The doorway to the tiny cooking area was a black void ahead of her, and she stopped as she reached the kitchen entrance. The gas smell was almost overpowering now, and she decided that she'd better not turn on the kitchen light. One little spark might blow the whole place up.

She stepped through the dark portal and moved cautiously in the direction of the stove, the hiss of escaping gas growing louder with her every step. How the hell could she have done that? She hadn't used the stove this morning. Her outstretched hand came into contact with the knobs that controlled the flow of gas to the burners. Two were twisted all the way on, but no blue flame shot upward, illuminating the dark. She coughed and hastily turned them off, puzzlement overcoming her fatigued mind and spirit. Was she going senile?

But it took only a moment for her puzzlement to be transformed into fear. Glancing at a tiny glimmer of light, her eyes fell on the kitchen door that led to the back landing outside. A small beam of moonlight was seeping through the curtain etching in diamond-light relief the jagged edges of glass where one of the window panes had been broken.

Hilda's eyes then darted through the glass and out to the landing. But no hint of light broke from the other side of the landing where Mrs. Lambert's kitchen window was usually lit up. There would be no help there—no sense in screaming. Panic seized her as she tried to weigh her alternatives in a tiny shard of time. But something happened before she could resolve her crisis. Something was suddenly at her out of the corner of the kitchen, something that moved swiftly like a vengeful shadow of the night.

She tried to scream then, but it was too late. The looming shadowy figure became all too real and substantial as it swiftly circled around her and caught her by the throat from behind. She was a large, strong woman but abruptly she felt the powerful arm around her pull, and she was jerked backwards and up, her feet suddenly leaving the floor. The only physical sensation was the brutal pressure at her throat, the long length of muscled arm cutting cruelly into her windpipe and stopping all flow of air to her lungs. The rest of her just dangled helplessly off the floor, like some big rag doll caught on a string.

But the need for air overcame her shock and her terror, as lungs began to heave and contort desperately in their search for oxygen. Her whole body began to twitch like some great worm on a pin, and she lunged forward in a hopeless attempt to bring her feet back to the ground. It should have been easy for a 160-pound woman, but the grip around her neck and throat was so incredibly strong. At first terror had brought with it the strength of fear and the overwhelming desire to survive, but now a deeper and a grimmer terror had set in, and Hilda Higgins began to go numb with the fear and the exhaustion of a lost struggle.

A burning sensation that was unimaginable began to well up in her chest, and she felt the blind rush of hysteria, the onset of death. But in some deep and remote corner of her mind a memory sought to intrude. A fragment of information was vainly attempting to push past the pain and the panic and into the light of consciousness. What was it? Could it be important now? Could anything be important now? She waited for her life to rush before her eyes like in the movies. In the end it was better to give up the hopeless struggle, to surrender to the inevitable. Then there would be no more pain: not the excruciating agony in her lungs or the duller and slower but equally killing pain in too many lonely nights and useless days. When there is no choice, death is best.

But wait. That insistent fragment, that graceless and inopportune message was still insisting on getting through—if only she'd listen. Slowly she became aware, aware that she still clutched something in her hand, in a viselike, instinctive grip. It was her purse! She had been so tired she'd even forgotten to put down her purse, and in it was her salvation: the tear gas pen!

Frantically she managed to raise her arm and with the other hand fumbled at the clasp. Open, damn it! Open! She felt something that seemed a million miles away move in her hand, and the tiny clasp gave way. She reached with desperate haste into the inner contours of the bag, her fingers clawing through the bewildering maze of junk she kept there, all the while searching for the sleek, metallic outline of the pen.

She made an ironic promise to herself in that last few moments of consciousness. She promised herself that if she ever got out of this one alive, she'd have the neatest, tidiest purse ever for the rest of her days. Still the fingers searched. Her brain began to cloud over as the last vestiges of vital oxygen in her lungs began to evaporate, but those fingers possessed the dexterity of a sculptor. She had pushed by her wallet and the compact case and her rosary when they finally closed on the thin contours of the tear gas device.

Just then she felt the attacker subtly alter his position, but her only thought was the pen. She had just began to pull it up from the purse when suddenly her head was snapped back, and something thin and cold was laid against her throat. She was still trying to aim the thing backwards over her shoulder, as she felt the first stream of something warm and liquid begin to spurt from her in a torrent of death.

12

Barb lay in Scott's arms feeling protected. Their lovemaking had maintained that delicate balance between passion and tenderness that silently said, I want you but I also care for you. You're desirable but not expendable. This is the only way she had ever been able to surrender herself to a man.

He also sensed the magic that had sprung up between them. His mind drifted back to their first night together, to his worries about the little old ladies in neighboring apartments and the noise they were making, to Barb's look of vulnerability and shy expectancy as he had slowly undressed her, to the fire and gentleness of their lovemaking.

Strangely, he had thought of St. Paul that night—St. Paul and the Bible classes that Grandma had forced him to attend every Sunday. The venerable saint had warned of the pleasures of the flesh, had warned that the path of God was not through the appetites, but then, in that moment, he thought he might even dispute with St. Paul. He knew little of the spirit, but something had awoke inside of him then and cried out in hunger, gratitude, and love, and the clay of their bodies had mingled and merged for awhile in a oneness seldom felt. It had been sublime, and to Scott it was sufficient height of spiritual pretension. Nothing in him craved for more.

Barb shifted her position slightly, and he could feel her light kiss on his chest. "This feels so nice," she purred and hugged him close. "Sometimes afterwards is even nicer than during."

He smiled. Another one of her quizzical expressions.

When she talked this way he knew that she was usually somewhere else, her mind climbing the clouds in search of mystery and magic. Only a small part of her remained, just enough to reassure him of his importance.

"Hey, bubblehead," he said softly, "you off on one of those flights of mystical fancy of yours?"

"Mmmn?" she returned absent-mindedly.

"You know, grabbing hold of the wisdom of starry gulfs and limitless voids and all that."

She laughed a little. "What do you mean?"

"Oh, I don't know. I guess. It's just that I've never met anyone who can tune out the world so fast for so long. Sometimes it gets lonesome being with you all by myself."

"Silly," she said and hugged him again. "But Scott, I'm sorry. Did I tune out on you?"

"No, not really. You were getting ready to, though. That comment about after and during sort of warned me."

She laughed again, knowing what he meant. Sometimes they'd be in the middle of a conversation about something interesting or vital when all of a sudden she'd begin to drift off, not saying anything more for ten or fifteen minutes. The most surprising thing was that most of the time he let her get away with it.

But now it was different. She wasn't retreating into one of those nebulous, incharted landscapes of that inner mind of hers—she was just remembering. And the memory, half formed as it was, called out to be shared. "I was just thinking, Scott. Thinking about this dream I had last night. That's all."

"Yeah? Was it sexy?" he said, playfully tweaking her nipple.

She giggled and twisted away. "Pervert," she said scornfully. "That's all you think about."

"Me and every other man on the planet."

"No." she replied emphatically. "You're hardly like every other man on the planet—a fact for which I am eternally grateful."

"And me too. But what about this dream? Was it sexy?"

"Oh, cut it out," she laughed and gently slapped his wrist. "You must think you're irresistible. Well, forget it. It wasn't. Actually, it was strange. It would have been a lot stranger if it hadn't been for what's been going on the last few days with Daddy, though."

"How do you mean?"

She sighed slightly. "Well, it had to do with Mother—with her and Daddy actually. It was so weird. I dreamt I was at their wedding, Scott, that I was at their wedding."

"That is strange unless, of course, you were a little, how shall I say, premature."

"Rat. You're a rat. But actually, I was hardly that. They were married five years before I came along, and even then Mother didn't want me, I guess. At least that's what I remember her telling me over and over again. She didn't want any children, but she especially didn't want me."

He was pleased to see that she could be more detached about this subject now, days before it had reduced her to tears. "Unhappy people like to make other people unhappy, too," he countered reassuringly.

"No. She didn't want me. Her every action said that distinctly. Besides, Aunt Mae, Daddy's sister, used to talk to her sometimes. She tried to keep the whole marriage from blowing sky high for Daddy's sake, though everybody else in the family hoped it *would* for Daddy's sake. Anyhow, she told me a few years ago that mother had hated the thought of having children, even though Daddy wanted them badly. But I remember Aunt Mae saying for some reason that she especially hated, even seemed afraid of, having the first one for some reason. It took five years before I came along, and even then Mother said I was—well, I told you."

"Best damn accident I ever met," he said matter-of-factly.

Her elbow nudged him playfully in the ribs. "Quiet.

You're spoiling my dream."

"Beg pardon, m'lady."

"Rat." she replied hastily. "But it was strange, Scott. There I was in this huge, dark cathedral with Mother and Daddy in their wedding outfits facing the altar. I couldn't see the priest—I could hardly see the altar. Everything was sort of misty around me, and the two of them standing in front of me were all that stood out clearly.

"I remember—remembered in the dream itself—that it was impossible that I was at my parent's marriage, as if part of me were awake and conscious. Even when I heard the priest's voice—I heard it but couldn't see him—say, 'Do you, Richard Brennan, take this woman, Rennata Glaeston, for your lawfully wedded wife?,' I knew it was a dream. Somehow, part of me was detached from it all, was just looking at it. Until—" her voice drifted off for a moment."Until I sensed the other one behind me." These last words sounded foreboding the way she said them.

"The other one?" Scott asked.

"Yes. I think I remember my father putting the ring on my mother's hand, but instead of kissing him she turned around toward me. I thought for a moment she was looking at me, but then I realized she was looking beyond me to some point in back of me.

"It was then that I felt the other presence behind me. It was then that I stopped remembering it was only a dream and got frightened. I tried to turn, Scott, tried to turn around and see who or what it was even though the idea seemed frightening for some reason.

"But I couldn't move. It was like I was frozen there, and all the while I became more and more frightened by the thought of what was there behind me. Something hideous and evil. Everything else faded except the feeling of that presence behind me. Then I woke up. Woke in a cold sweat and feeling like I'd just been put through some sort of giant wringer."

She stopped and looked at him for a moment. "You

think I'm nuts?" she asked, trying to make it sound flippant.

"It does sound a little Freudian, Babs, but I'm not the one to ask about that. It also sounds perfectly normal after what you've been through lately."

"Normal? I guess so. Guilt or something. I could feel my mother, even in the dream, not wanting me just like in real life. But the uncanny thing, Scott, the really awful thing was the utter certainty that whatever that terrible thing was—*it wanted me*."

He felt her shudder a little and squeezed her protectively. "It was a dream, Barb."

She shook her head in affirmation, as if trying to make it so.

He laughed, "You loon. How did I ever get a girlfriend who listens to Bach, reads philosophy and dreams crazy dreams? Me, the last one of the illiterates."

Her mood lightened perceptibly. "Illiterate? No, hardly. Not well read exactly but you've got a curiosity about things that I like. You look closely at things. I noticed it last week when we went to the art fair. Even the things you didn't like, you looked at and examined. I could see the wheels turning. You just need to educate your tastes a little more."

"Why do you think I'm taking you out?" he countered. "It's cheaper than an art appreciation course."

She went to tickle him in revenge, but he grabbed her firmly by both her wrists. His grip was tender, but she could feel the strength behind it. She loved the feel of his lean, sinewy body against her. Slowly she moved her still-imprisoned hand around until it came into contact with the sloping curve of his bicep. Her fingers traced its contours gently until he gradually released her wrists. "You get all this muscle from just being a carpenter?" she asked softly.

"Muscle? This? I'm no Charles Atlas, Barb."

"No, I wouldn't want you all beefy and puffy like

those bodybuilders. They look like big, overstuffed sausages. You—well, you're just right."

"Must be all that tennis you've been making me play."

"That's just to introduce you to how we in the upper crust live." She feigned haughtiness and laughed.

He looked at her intently for a moment and her eyes went slightly serious again. "Feel better?" he asked.

She nodded. "Yes. Much. It helps to talk about some things—even when they're silly."

"They're not silly at all. You've always been very close to your father, and now something has temporarily affected that closeness. I'm sure it's only a passing difficulty, but in the meanwhile, it's serious."

"Thanks," she said and hugged him closer. "I'll try not to dream anymore."

"Not necessary. Just dream sexy dreams—about me."

"I love you." Her eyes were as soft as a fawn's as she said it. Her eyes were full of a warm, sad tenderness. He felt a stirring deep within his loins, and he pulled her closer yet. She came to him willingly, and their bodies rolled and entwined, his mouth coming to the soft tip of her breast.

His hands explored her then, as if for the first time, and felt only velvet. At first she wrapped her fingers around his neck, touseling the soft curls there, but soon she just lay back in a gesture of total submission. His lips moved again, down to the satin of her stomach, probing, tasting, adoring. She whimpered, and her body began to rock with an age-old rhythm, the music of abandonment. Male and female locked in one embrace. The cosmic polarities come together in the dance of life and love.

Time was a fleeting shadow as they embraced in eternity. There was no world or reason beyond the iron of Scott's thrusting body. She lay open and willing to him, her body like the flower that encloses upon itself in the night's chill, drawing its sweet fragrance in to its very center. Scott reveled in that softness, the liquid warmth of her core. His hunger was engulfed by the vast suctioning of her body and spirit. Finally, his fire was quenched in the certainty of her love.

13

Tommy Watson tossed in his bed. He hadn't been sleeping at all well lately. Even his mother was beginning to watch him and worry over him all the time, as he seemed to get more and more tired and nervous. But Tommy insisted that he felt just fine. His appetite had decreased markedly, and he jumped at any sudden sound or movement but he felt just fine.

He had started taking naps on his own in the afternoons. He would get home from school about three-thirty and go right up to his room and lie down. His mother had told Tommy's father about this, and he had had a long talk with the boy. But Tommy only insisted that he was tired because he played so hard at recess, and Tommy's father could only shrug his shoulders stoically. You couldn't force the boy to admit that he was ill. They puzzled about it and they talked about it but neither parent could arrive at any satisfactory conclusion for the boy's behavior.

Neither of them could be expected to know that Tommy slept in the afternoon because he was afraid to sleep at night. The nights weren't good anymore. He should never had watched that old movie. Then he might not have had that nightmare that had scared him so much. Only he wasn't sure it was a nightmare, and it had seemed to become more and more real to him as the time elapsed between that night two weeks ago and every night since. And he had this feeling of *waiting* he couldn't get rid of or understand. He kept waiting,

waiting for something to happen, and he felt that something was waiting for him too.

One afternoon he had rummaged around in the attic, until he had found grandma's old crucifix. It had hung over her bed for years: a big wooden thing etched in silver. Now he kept it under his pillow at night but was careful to hide it each morning under his dresser. All he needed now was his mother finding it and asking him a lot of unanswerable questions. But it comforted him somehow. His mother had told him that the Lord would protect you from anything, no matter how bad, and it was the only defense he could think of against his nameless terror.

School had been going badly since that night. He seldom forgot the shadows that plagued his mind, and his teachers were starting to call on him regularly, knowing he wouldn't be prepared. And Eddie Sutter had leapt out at him the other day from behind a bush, and Tommy had wanted to kill him in his fright and anger and had socked him in the stomach.

Tommy's inexplicable fears were sufficient to cause him to spend the better part of each night in sleepless turmoil. Often he would just lie there staring at the walls. Often he would get up and creep to the window upon hearing some vague noise outside. It would take all his courage to peel back that window shade and look out into the night, but having done it he would feel better for a while. No apparitions of the night had come back to haunt him again.

About three or four in the morning he would usually manage to fall asleep, but it wasn't enough rest for a small boy. In two weeks he had grown noticeably thinner, his complexion had become pale and pasty, and his eyes had come to resemble sunken hollows. At ten he looked almost eighty. This so alarmed his mother that finally she insisted on calling Dr. Blackburn and making an appointment for Tommy which he suffered out in silence. The doctor had asked him what was the matter, and Tommy diplomatically admitted that sometimes he didn't sleep too well. A mild sedative was presribed, and the physician told his mother to discourage the afternoon naps. Great, thought Tommy. She *would* have to mention the naps. Now I'll never get any sleep.

But he did. The pills worked. He struggled against them for a night or two but soon grew used to the feeling of being comfortably tired again. By the fourth night he dropped off a half hour or so after his head had hit the pillow, and his body's need for slumber consumed him as he slept peacefully for several nights.

But soon the nightmares began. All the distortions of time and space, all the implausibilities of dream were present, but that made them no less terrifying. For a few nights he had had his standard ones: He was looking down the old well when all the monsters floated up and began chasing him and the one where he was floating upside down in outer space and being chased by something bug-eyed from another planet. These were bad, but they weren't nearly as bad as when he began dreaming about the apparition he had seen at the window that night. That one recalled a fright he'd rather forget, and soon he was sleeping with the light on the dresser again.

But sometimes his mother got up in the night to use the bathroom, and she would see the light under his door. He pretended to be asleep when she came into the room, and she would just shut off the light and go back to bed, a look of puzzlement on her face. It was hard, but after that he would leave the light off. Above all else he dreaded his parents' questions. How could he, a ten-year-old boy, explain to them his fears of something old and terrible that haunted the night . . . of something or someone clothed in a long, dark garment that covered it from head to toe . . . of something evil and malevolent that seemed to be followed by something shadowy and monstrous that was even worse.

14

Harry had been talking to George Stavich when the call came in. George had been investigating the kidnapping of a little girl on Halloween, and the story he had gotten from the only witness, another little girl, had been pretty bizarre. But Harry had more important things to think about now. There had been another murder.

He was on his way immediately. Elliot had only taken time to tell him that it was a woman and that it was the same MO as the Emma Johnson murder: The woman's throat had been slashed from ear to ear. It was disgusting, but a tiny part of him was secretly pleased—he was sorry to admit. He had been getting nowhere on the Johnson case, the sister had been no help at all once he'd finally gotten to talk to her, and Elliot was starting to get on his back about it. But if this was the same fellow, this time he might have left a clue, though that could be a worse problem. It might be a psychopath.

He pulled up in front of the building at 311 South Bryan, a large yellow brick affair. It was only about nine or ten blocks from where Emma Johnson had been killed, but then Oak Grove wasn't all that big either. Why couldn't the creep have gone a mile or two east into Chicago? One more murder would hardly be noticed there.

He noted the squad cars, some with lights still flashing, as he got out of his car. Three of them. And a crowd. Shit. Must be fifty people out front. Fifty goddamn morbid vultures. "Coming through. Watch out. Coming through," he said brusquely as he pushed his way though the throng of onlookers. He noted the patrolman outside. It was Danny Clark.

"Hi, Sergeant. Haven't seen you since up at St. Mark's. Any news on that business yet?"

"Nope. Nothing at all, Danny. This Johnson case has sort of taken precedence." He liked Danny Clark. The young man was respectful, referring to him as "Sergeant." Such formality tended to be overlooked in small town departments, but Harry wasn't so self-assured these days that it wasn't appreciated.

"That's too bad, Sergeant. By the way, the lab boys and the doc aren't here yet."

"Tolson's going to be on the scene on this one, too?"

"Yes, sir. Lieutenant Elliot requested it."

"It figures," he said grumpily. "What apartment am I looking for?"

"One-B, Sergeant."

There was some small consolation: having only one floor to climb. He trudged slowly up the steps. Inside there were several patrolmen already present. Upon seeing Harry, one of them approached him. "The body is in the kitchen. Plenty of blood in there."

"Hello. How are ya?" Harry said and walked down the corridor to the kitchen. Sometimes, lately, he wished he were a shoe salesman.

The kitchen was like an instant replay of the last one. Lying face down in a vast pool of blood was the form of a large woman. The only major difference was that this time blood wasn't smeared all over the place. It had been a much tidier homicide.

He looked at the back door, seeing what he had expected: One of the window panes was missing from the door, jagged pieces of glass scattered across the floor below. Someone had broken in and lured or trapped the woman in her kitchen. Then he'd murdered her. Simple and awfully ugly.

Harry walked back into the living room. "Who reported this?" he asked one of the patrolmen.

"Lady across the hall. Raney's with her now."

Harry stepped across the hall and knocked on the door of apartment 1-A. A patrolman quickly answered it, and Harry looked past him to the frail, fiftyish woman sitting on the couch. Her eyes were tearful, but they were also scared. She had that hunted look about her that people—especially women—get when they witness a tragedy that hits too close to home. "How is she?" Harry asked the patrolman.

"Pretty shaken up, but she's coherent enough. Her name is Ida Lambert, and she's just come home from her daughter's in Wheaton about nine this morning. Says she went out on the back landing and noticed a broken window pane in her neighbor's door. She looked inside and, well, the rest is pretty obvious."

"What's the name of the deceased?"

"Hilda Higgins."

"Did this one go inside?"

"No, she was pretty definite about that. She said she 'ran like hell out of there.' "

"Thanks, Raney. I'll take it from here." The patrolman nodded, and Harry waited for him to leave. He walked over to the couch and sat down opposite the woman who was softly weeping, her eyes to the floor.

"Miss Lambert? I'm Sergeant Harry Oronski of the Oak Grove police. May I ask you a few questions?" He tried to find the middle line between sounding solicitous and official.

She looked up slowly but seemed composed in spite of her tears. "It's Mrs. Lambert, Sergeant. I'm a widow," she said mildly.

"Sorry, ma'am. I know that you must be very upset by this, this tragedy, but it would be most helpful if I could ask you a few questions."

"I understand, Sergeant. Go right ahead."

"Thank you ma'am. I'll try to be as short and to the point as possible, so please don't think that I'm being insensitive to your feelings."

"No, that's all right. I know you have your job to do."

"Thank you. Now, first, I'd like to ask you how well you knew the deceased."

"How well? Oh, not very well, I'm afraid. We had coffee on occasion, but we weren't really friends. She was kind of a private person—worked hard and seemed kind of worn out by the end of the day."

"You mentioned her work. Do you know where she worked?"

"Some restaurant over on Farrington, I think. I don't recall the name."

"That's all right. Now, how about her personal life? Do you know anything about her family or friends?"

"She had a sister in Pittsburgh, I think. Pittsburgh or some suburb. Both her parents are dead, I know."

"How about friends?"

"I don't know. I don't think so. She never mentioned any, and I never saw anyone in the apartment."

"Oh, then you would sometimes visit her in the apartment?" Harry asked casually.

"Only for coffee. Like I said."

"That's right, you did. Well, how about a boyfriend or male companion, Mrs. Lambert?"

The woman paused and smiled to herself. "I doubt it. She was kind of rough, and like I said, she was a private person. I never saw her with anyone."

"Mrs. Lambert, do you know of any relatives in the area that we could notify of the death?"

"No. Just the sister in Pittsburgh."

Harry scribbled down his notes quickly. The woman's replies were admirably succinct, but he could tell that that was her nature: independent, self-reliant, matter-of-fact. Her tears were probably motivated more out of her own fright than out of sentimentality or grief for Hilda Higgins.

Mrs. Lambert, do you know of any enemies the deceased might've had? Perhaps a petty grievance or a jealousy somebody might have felt for her? This is important, so think carefully and take your time."

The woman answered immediately. "No. She wasn't the type to talk much or confide, so I doubt whether I would have known even if there had been something. Like I said, she was a little gruff at times, but she didn't seem like the type to have any real enemies."

"All right. Now, as close as you can tell, what time did you find the body?"

The woman gulped, and the veneer of quiet composure seemed to crack a bit. "Well, it—it must have been about nine-fifteen."

"Why nine-fifteen?"

"Well, I got home about nine, looked through yesterday's mail and put a pot of coffee on. Then I went out on the back landing to see if the laundryman had been there yet. But he—"

"This laundryman," interrupted Harry, "does he come every Monday morning?"

"Yes. Always."

"About what time?"

"Oh, anywhere between eight and ten. If I'm not home, he just leaves it on the landing."

"What's the name of the laundry?"

"The name? Well, it's—funny, I've done business with them for eleven years, and I can't seem to remember the name."

"Take your time, Mrs. Lambert."

"Oh, of course. It's the West Suburban Laundry Company."

Harry noted the name in his pad. "Did the deceased have her laundry done by West Suburban?"

"No. She liked to do it herself. She always used to complain how tough it was to do the laundry at the end of the day, but sure as anything no one else was going to wash her clothes."

Harry thought of Grace. She could care less either way, and sometimes he was lucky to get a clean shirt at all. "How about other deliverymen?" he asked. "You know, grocery, florists, and the like."

"I don't think she got any regular deliveries. We used to talk about that. Stores that deliver charge too much—especially the grocery stores. Everything is marked up 50 percent. No, we both did our own shopping."

"Together?"

"Only coffee," she returned a bit snidely. This was one sharp lady.

"All right, Mrs. Lambert. Now I want you to think carefully here. When you looked inside the door, what did you do next?"

The woman's voice began to rise a little as she said, "I could make out the—the body on the floor. I could see it through the curtain. I think I took a step back then looked in again. I just couldn't believe it."

"Did you at any time attempt to enter the apartment?"

"Are you kidding?" she replied shrilly. "With that broken glass and what looked like blood all over the floor? Hell, I ran so fast into my own place and locked the door, it would have made your head spin."

"You suspected foul play then?"

"Well, wouldn't you, Sergeant?"

Harry smiled. "Yes, ma'am. I would imagine so." He could see the woman's lips quiver and sensed that she was starting to lose control. "Just one more question, Mrs. Lambert. Can you think of anything that might be of assistance to us in this investigation? Anything, no matter how small or insignificant it might appear to be."

"This investigation—you're talking about a murder investigation, aren't you?"

"We can't rule it out, ma'am." Harry said, trying to sound noncommital.

For a moment a real look of regret and anguish passed over the woman's essentially stolid features. "I wish I could help you, Sergeant. It's a pity when a harmless woman isn't safe in her own home. It's a sin and a shame, but for the life of me I can't think of one thing that could help you other than what I've already said."

"Here's my card, Ma'am. If you think of anything at all, please call me—night or day. And thank you for your cooperation."

Harry left her there looking small and alone. In some

ways she was worse off than Hilda Higgins. At least for Hilda the fear was over. Stepping across the landing, his thoughts quickly turned back to the necessities at hand. The lab technicians were already in 1-B, dusting for fingerprints, photographing the corpse and making diagrams of the scene and the body's position on the floor. The place looked like a convention site or, more accurately, a funeral.

Bill Tolson emerged from the corridor leading to the kitchen. "Beat you again, Harry."

"Sorry, Doc. Not this time. I was here a half hour ago. Been next door talking to the witness."

"It's just as well. Now I don't have a reputation to uphold anymore." He smiled rather grimly.

"How's it look, Bill?"

"I'll have to get her downtown to be sure—I know I always say that, but it's true. Anyways, from here it looks like the same deal as the last one, even down to the kitchen. Throat is cut in the same way from behind, and the weapon was probably the same or similar."

"And what does that suggest to you, Doc?"

"Either some connection between this one and the Johnson murder or, worse yet, a psychopath."

"Exactly. It's just what I'm afraid of. You know damn well, Bill, that we never catch the crazies—or hardly ever. If you do it's only after they've already done in a dozen or more people. There are never any proper leads or connections in these things, no apparent motivation—nothing concrete to go on. You just gotta hope you get lucky."

"Did you ask the witness if this one had known the Johnson dame?"

"She wasn't a direct witness. And no I didn't ask. Thought I'd save it. But I don't think we're going to find any connection. I think we've got a crazy on our hands."

Art Evans, one of the lab team members, came into the room. He nodded a hello to Harry. "Whatya got, Art?" Harry asked hopefully.

"Not much. No blood on the broken glass in the door

as far as we can tell here, and the outside landing seems clear of any residual traces. Dave's taking prints right now, but nothing looks promising. Found some traces of the woman's clothing and hair, but they'll have to go downtown for analysis."

Harry turned to one of the officers still lingering in the living room. "Check upstairs and see if any other neighbors heard or saw something. Something about—say, Bill. When did this thing take place?"

"Can't say for sure right now, Harry. Sometime last night."

Harry turned back to the patrolman. "Just ask if anybody saw *anything*. If we've got to, we'll canvas the whole neighborhood again." The officer groaned but went out. Harry turned to Tolson again. "Bill, get me something this time. Get me something or Elliot will have my shirt," Harry said morosely. "I don't think we've had a goddamn double murder in the town's whole history."

"It's not really a double, Harry."

"May as well be. The press will make them sound that way, if we give them half a chance. I'm gonna stick around until those creeps get here. If there's any way I can make these two murders sound totally unrelated, you can believe I will."

The phone rang, and one of the patrolmen picked it up. "Yeah," Tolson opined philosophically, "I don't envy you that task. If word gets out, our illustrious city fathers will be furious, and if you don't let the word out reporters will be knocking down the walls at headquarters. Win or lose."

"Sergeant," came the patrolman's voice, "it's Lieutenant Elliot. He wants to speak to you right away."

Harry suddenly felt like Prometheus chained to the rock. The raven was just about to start picking at his liver.

15

He was just about to hang up when someone finally answered. The voice on the other end was familiar but tentative. "Hello? Who is it?"

He laughed into the mouthpiece. "You sound like you're expecting the Internal Revenue Service."

Silence.

"Barb? Is that you?"

"Yes—it's me."

"What's the matter? You sound upset."

"Nothing, Scott. What is it."

"What is it? Now what's that supposed to mean? I told you I'd call tonight."

"Oh, that's right. I'm sorry." Her voice sounded hollow and distant, the conversation mechanical.

"Something's the matter. Did you have another row with your old man?"

"No. No, everything's all right."

"It doesn't sound like it."

"I'm just tired, Scott."

"I'm sorry, hon, but maybe it's just as well. Lenny called. He's having car trouble and wants me to come over and help him."

"So?"

"Jesus Christ, you're good for a guy's ego. Didn't you remember that I was supposed to come over tonight and take you for a walk or something?"

"No, I forgot. I'm sorry." Barb sounded light years away.

"What the hell's the matter? Do you want me to come over anyways? I can tell Lenny to call Larry, though that'd nearly kill him to ask Larry to help."

Her voice rose a little. "No, Scott. Go ahead and help Lenny. I want to get to bed early."

"Are you sure?"

She sounded a little irritated. "Yes, I'm sure."

Bitch, he thought. No, that wasn't fair. She'd been going through something lately. "Barb, I don't want to frighten you, but don't take the walk without me tonight, okay?"

"Why not?" her voice was dull and inflectionless.

"Well, I don't want to sound like one of those little old ladies in town, but there have been some weird things going on. I mean, you know, about the two murders and the kidnapping of that little girl on Halloween. That's reason enough to stay indoors."

"All right. I'll stay inside tonight."

"Good. It's just that the town is a little loony right now. I've been hearing all sorts of crazy things. Everybody's imagination is working overtime, and they're dreaming up—"

"What sort of crazy things?" Her voice seemed more animated now.

"What?"

"Scott—" she began but the word seemed to choke in her throat and her voice trailed off for what seemed like ages. "Scott, do you think that the police—I mean with all that's going on, would they think someone was crazy who called them about—oh, what's the use!" she said desperately.

Suddenly, for no good reason, he felt panic somewhere deep inside of him. It was an intution, born of the fear and hopelessness in her voice in response to his recounting of the recent events in the town. "Barb, what the hell is the matter, and, goddamnit, don't tell me 'nothing!' "

There was a long pause on the other end, as if she were mentally weighing and balancing the alternatives.

"I want to tell you Scott." Her voice was plaintive. "I've got to tell somebody."

"Me. Tell me."

"Daddy told me not to dare mention it."

"Yeah, and it's obviously ripping you apart inside, Barb. Frankly, from what you've told me lately, your father is acting a little strange himself. He might just be going around the bend like some of the other people in this town."

"We've been getting phone calls, Scott."

"What? Phone calls? What kind of phone calls?"

"Some lady. She sounds foreign. German or something. Daddy had got them all until the last one when I answered the phone. She asked to speak to him, but he had me listen in on the extension. Oh, it's so hard to piece it all together. It's about my mother and about what's going on here in town and—"

"Do you mean these murders or the little girl's kidnapping?"

"I—I'm not sure." Her voice was halting, sorrowful. "Maybe. Oh, Scott! For thirteen years my mother was a constant anguish and humiliation to Daddy. I knew she had left scars on him, but I thought it was all over when she died. But now she's still hurting him. She's dead and she's still hurting him."

He felt impelled by a sudden urgency. "Barb, you've got to explain this from the beginning. Please, tell me everything, so I can figure out—"

"Scott, we may be going away."

"What? Where? Why, for God's sake?"

"He says he won't be blackmailed with his own pain anymore, Scott, and I can't just stand by and see it happen to him."

"Barb, listen to me. If something's going on that has anything to do with these murders—"

"Scott, there's nothing definite we could give the police. It's just these telephone calls—this awful sounding woman talking about Mother and all the terrible things that will be happening in town."

"*Will be?*"

He could hear her draw breath in sharply. "Well, yes. She said there will be more, if—"

"If what, for Chrissakes."

"If I, if—oh, I don't know!" her voice was flooded with tears now, and he could feel her anguish even through the wire of the phone in his hand.

"Barb, I'm coming right over."

"Oh, no! For God's sake no!"

"Why not, dammit. You need me."

"Because he'd never speak to me again. He told me last night, everybody always thought he was the strong one in his family. So capable and commanding. But he told me that those years with Mother nearly drove him insane, that the only thing that kept him normal was the thought of becoming like her. He lost all his friends, he was estranged from his family, the other doctors at the hospital used to ridicule him behind his back. Now to have all that dredged up again, even if it's only in association with some complete nut—he might as well pack his bags and move out of this town forever. All he needs to push him over the edge, I'm afraid, is to read his name in some newspaper in connection with Mother and some goddamn murders!"

"Barb, how the hell can your mother who has been dead for twelve years have anything to do with—"

"Daddy's coming up the stairs!" The tears had stopped; the voice was low and urgent.

"Barb, you can't hang up on me now."

"I have to. I can't let Daddy hear any of this."

"But Barb—"

"Please, oh if you love me, please don't say anything about this to anyone."

"Will you call me later?"

"Maybe. I'll try."

"No maybes, Barb. Promise me you'll call or I'll come right over there—"

There was a click, and the line went dead.

Scott began pacing nervously around his small apartment, his mind alive with a thousand doubts, fears and questions. What was going on? What should he do? Could he really do anything? He thought of calling her again but desisted with an effort. He went to the frig and pulled out a beer. Three beers later his mind still tumbled with thought.

What could he do: call the police and tell them his girlfriend had been getting funny phone calls about her dead mother? With the present mentality in town they would either think it was perfectly normal or laugh him off the line. Besides, it sounded like Barb and her father were all set to deny anything. And there was the risk of losing her over something that really might not be any of his business.

But Christ. Weren't we talking about some bizarre connection with the murders of two women and a child's kidnapping? Could he ignore that? Or was it all in her mind? How could she be involved, her or her father, the respectable doctor? That was silly of course. Being a doctor and watching football on the weekends didn't make you immune to criminal connections, but somehow it seemed so unlikely for that stolid, insular man. As for any involvement on Barb's part—it was silly even to think of it.

The whole thing was silly. Yet, this girl was in a panic about it. She'd been growing more and more apprehensive over the past couple of weeks. Something obviously was going on, but where the key to the puzzle was to be found was beyond him. Only one thing was certain: something out of the ordinary was going on. Whether it was real or, God forbid, only in Barb's mind, about all he could do was wait.

But he wouldn't wait too long. She needed somebody now to help, somebody who stood outside of the situation. In many ways she was terribly vulnerable with no one to lean on except her father. Now, her father seemed to be withdrawing that support. Damn if he'd let her go it alone.

Finally he lay down on his bed, the thoughts beginning to run out of his brain. Concern turned inevitably to fatigue. He killed off another beer. Shit, Lenny. He'd forgotten to call Lenny. The poor schmuck had probably called Larry by now. Oh, the abuse he'd take in exchange for a little mechanical expertise.

He dozed fitfully, restless dreams troubling his sleep. He woke feeling clammy and washed out. He looked at his watch. It was after eleven. He looked at the phone, wrestling with himself. Finally, he decided. Picking it up, he dialed Barb's number. He let it ring a long time, but there was no answer.

16

Mary Watson had gotten up at her usual time to prepare her husband Joe's breakfast. Everyday seven o'clock. Her life was a never varying routine on this theme. Even weekends had their own singular procedures that had to be observed, but at least they were different rituals than those she so scrupulously observed Monday through Friday. Oh, she craved a little change now and then, but everything was pretty much stuck in one groove, and any real change would have been disconcerting.

This day started like all the others. She got up, put on her house coat and went to the bathroom to brush her teeth. Going down the hall, she would pause at the front door, step outside and get the morning paper. It would be neatly laid out on the breakfast table when Joe came in. Breakfast itself called for little imagination or culinary flair. There would be cold cereal and milk, juice, coffee and bacon and eggs. No deviation was allowed beyond the occasional substitution for ham or sausage for the bacon. Joe knew what he liked.

About seven-twenty he would amble sleepily into the breakfast room, kiss her lightly on the cheek and settle into his Cheerios and the sports section. Few words would pass between them, and Mary would sit across the table staring absently into the folds of newsprint that confronted her or out the kitchen window into the backyard. Instinctively her body would rise from time to time to refill his coffee cup or get some more toast or butter, but her mind would be elsewhere in some distant fog of halfmemory or vague dream.

Then if Tommy wasn't in the kitchen by quarter to eight, she would go to the end of the hall and call for him to get up. Then she would trudge back to the kitchen to start the morning's second breakfast. Usually Tommy never had to be called, but lately he had been sleeping late. Once or twice, she'd even had to go into his room and shake him vigorously into wakefulness. Something was wrong with the boy; she had the discomforting feeling that something different was taking place in her life. The boy seemed furtive and anxious lately and hadn't been sleeping well until she took him to the doctor, yet he refused to admit that anything was the matter.

Well, he always had been a close-mouthed little kid—like his father. Sometimes she wondered about the kid part too. But it wasn't any use to try and press the boy for information. Sometimes she felt that her son was stronger and more determined than herself in many ways. He seemed to know just what he wanted and didn't want—again like his father. She wasn't like that at all, or she never would have gotten into this mess.

But this morning it was already ten minutes to eight, and there was no sign of Tommy yet. She went to the end of the hall and called his name once or twice. There was no answer. "Tommy," she called again. "Tommy, if you're awake answer me." Damn kid, she thought crossly. What does he expect when he stays up half the night? She dreaded his next report card what with his walking around like a zombie all day.

Wearily she began to walk down the hall toward Tommy's room. She opened the boy's door and looked sharply in the direction of his bed. Tommy wasn't there. Her gaze quickly turned toward the window as she felt the cold blast of late autumn air rush past her. The window was open, and the screen had been pulled up and slightly out of its runners. A sizeable space intervened between the sill and the bottom edge of the window—plenty of room for one small boy to get through.

"Joe!" she screamed hoarsely. "Joe, come here!"

Surprisingly, Joe recognized the note of terror in her voice and arrived in the bedroom rather quickly for a man of phlegmatic temperament. Noting the window, he turned sharply back into the hall and bellowed for Tommy at the top of his lungs. Maybe he was somewhere in the house. Maybe he had just opened the window for whatever strange little kid's idea had gotten into him. So many days of monotonous regularity and sameness had passed through Joe's life, he had little reason to suspect anything dramatic now. But he did. Instinctively he realized that something was wrong. The smell of trouble was in the air.

"I'll go outside and look for him. You call the police." He was a man suddenly come alive.

"The police? Oh, Joe! Why the police?" Mary asked frantically.

"Because something might have happened to him. We can't take any chances."

"Oh no, Joe. You don't think he ran away?"

"Hell, why would he go through a window to run away? He could go through the front door and do that."

His reply had been frantic and ill-considered. He saw the look of fright and pain on his wife's face at those words, and he softened and put his arm around her protectively. "Don't worry, Mary. I'm sure he's all right, but we really should call the police as a precaution. Tell you what, you let me call them. I'll look for Tommy after. He's probably just down the street somewhere."

But the damage had been done. With lurid and awful images running through her brain Mary broke into tears, but went for the phone in the hall anyhow. Joe stood there looking after her. He promised himself if this was some goofy stunt on the kid's part, he wouldn't be able to sit down for a week. But something deep inside told him different. Tommy hadn't been right for weeks.

The police were there quickly. A squad arrived just as Joe came around the corner from his round the block search for Tommy. He had called the boy's name loudly at least a dozen times, but there had been no answer—not even an irate neighbor. He realized that it had been a futile gesture from the start, but when you don't know what to do, you have to do something—anything to relieve the terror that is beginning to grow and work inside you.

Joe led the two patrolmen into the house; Mary stood in the hallway, her face gone ashen and her hands clenched together until the knuckles showed white. The sense of routine that had become so central to their lives became an intolerable length of time as the police methodically embarked on their own routine. There were questions to be asked—many questions—then one of the officers suggested that he and Joe search the house and grounds for any sign of the boy. The other patrolman asked Mary to show him the boy's room and the window that had been found open.

The two parents set off then on their appointed tasks, their panic alleviated somewhat by the cool professionalism of the policemen. But not far from the surface lurked a fear that could not be allayed. It was more than a parent's fear over a missing son; it was the recognition that somehow the boy had known or expected something, that something had been wrong for weeks, and this was merely the culmination of it. Guilt vied heavily with their alarm.

The day was to pass in a monotony of apprehension. Joe called the plant and said he wouldn't be into work that day. After the two policemen had departed armed with photographs and descriptions of the boy, Joe went out to the garage to continue working on the old Ford he had been restoring. It was his one recreation, and he had to do something to keep from going crazy. He was worried about the kid—sure. As fathers went, he was about as responsible and attentive as most, but he thought the kid would turn up despite his fears. Even after other policemen had come and taken fingerprints from around the window sill and had poured plastic or something into some footprints under Tommy's window, Joe couldn't accept the possibility of kidnapping. He made only $18,000 a year and had no real enemies to speak of; who would want to kidnap his kid? Perhaps the boy really had run off, but that just didn't add up. At the urging of the police they had checked his dresser and closet and even the refrigerator. No clothes were gone, his jacket still hung in the closet and no food was missing. If he had run away, it was a spontaneous decision and a cold one, judging by today's temperatures.

Inside the house Mary fretted. She didn't have her husband's ability to carry on with the day's work in spite of disaster. She kept her resentments under tight rein, but the strains of the morning were making her docility increasingly difficult. Why wasn't he in here with her? Why wasn't he comforting her for once, staying with her for once? Even when they were together, they were apart; the boy had been the one common bond, and now he was gone. It was almost as if his disappearance had severed the last important tie in only a few hours time. No, that wasn't fair exactly. Joe would have been out in the garage working on that damn car even if Tommy were home safe. Whatever they had once had, if anything, was gone forever.

The phone rang, and her heart leapt. It was the police but they had called only to say they had notified Tommy's school of his disappearance. Patrol cars were looking for him all over the city, the Chicago and Suburban authorities had been notified too, and the report taken that morning had been turned over to a detective. That was all. It was scant satisfaction, like breakfast for a dying man. No one knows what a mother feels in such moments except another mother, and you didn't have to dote over a child's every move to qualify for the gut instincts that go with the breed. They told you when something was really wrong, and they were infallible. Mary Watson was essentially a worn and timid woman, but on this day she knew hopelessness for the first time.

The morning wore on into the afternoon, and the afternoon gave way to the evening. Mary had napped for an hour in the afternoon but had gained little rest.

Joe had taken a long walk, supposedly to look for Tommy, but in reality it was intended as a means of getting away from the situation. His actions seemed to suggest that he thought it was a problem that had a definite location, a tangible bearing which he could avoid by moving a few blocks in another direction. But he came back home in an hour or two, the burden of doubt and fear still laying heavily upon him.

They ate a silent meal together that evening. This was nothing unusual for Joe: He seldom contributed much to the conversation. Mary, however, was accustomed to trying to keep up a steady flow of talk at the dinner table. She seemed to think that she could overcome the massive silence between them by herself, that a steady torrent of words could prevent them both from realizing the utter poverty of their relationship. Probably she suffered from a school girl's apprehension of silence, a feeling that moments without conversation were necessarily awkward ones.

After dinner he would go his way, and she would go hers. Instinctively they maintained a discreet distance from one another, her slender hopes baffled and his need for solitude all the greater. Joe's need had little to do with the need for mystical contemplation. It was the need of a man who wishes to shut out a world that to him is only a grim reminder of his failure to achieve what he wants from life. She might join him later in the den, and together they would stare absently at the television. But there would be no reaching or contact—she would not have to talk now, because the mindless babble from the television would take care of the awkward moments, would protect from the silence, the silence that might make them aware of how useless it all was.

Some implied fatalism prevented them from calling the police to inquire if there was any news about Tommy. They hadn't even notified family or friends. This whole day was weighing on them like some secret shame. It was as if Tommy's disappearance symbolized the state of their relationship: Something had fled them long ago. It was a betrayal. The boy had given them a shared goal and interest, and now he had left. His action had exposed their nakedness.

As the day passed into night both were coming to feel that the boy had left on his own part. As the night wore on this suspicion began a subtle transformation into resentment. Even Mary's maternal instincts began to give way before these disquieting thoughts. The boy was becoming a natural scapegoat, and after this life would be hell.

But the phone rang at nine-thirty, and they both rushed to it in sudden anticipation. It was the police. A squad car would be by for them in five or ten minutes. Had they found the boy—some trace of the boy? Well, yes. Possibly. They shouldn't get their hopes up much. In fact, they might better prepare themselves for a shock. The voice on the other end seemed halting and embarrassed. Despite Mary's pleas for more information, it rang off quickly. Now they had only to wait a little while longer.

Two solemn-faced officers arrived at the house five minutes later. One of them quietly asked Joe and Mary to accompany them to the squad car. The ride took only minutes, but the pointed silence in the car made it seem like forever. They watched familiar streets and buildings pass by as the car moved up into the far north end of town. Ahead of them they noted many cars, some with the flashing mars light weirdly illuminating the darkness in baleful alternating winks of crimson brightness. Large groups of people were milling on the sidewalk and lawns just outside the perimeter of squad cars, while several uniformed policemen held them back.

Mary felt a knot beginning to form in her stomach as the police vehicle passed through the cordon of cars and onlookers. Looking down the block, she saw squad cars had sealed off the other end of the street. Then she looked at Joe who had gone pale, the veins in the side of his neck standing out in sharp contradistinction to the white pallor of his flesh.

The car suddenly turned into an alleyway that ran behind the large garage of a big brick house on the corner. In the alley were squad and two unmarked cars that had the tell-tale leanness of police vehicles. Several patrolmen and what were obviously detectives stood by. All of them looked in the direction of the approaching car.

The surroundings, the looks on the faces of the police, the whole feel of the place told them instantly what to expect. Joe looked at Mary and reached for her hand. Mary fought to hold down the hysteria that was struggling to get out of some deep inner recess of her heart and soul. Neither of them were aware of the argument that abruptly ensued between those policemen or of the shamed, almost tender expression of the detective who finally came forward to meet them.

Everything had become a blur, an awful fear and certainty as they were led around the side of the garage to the large pile of dead leaves that had been raked there. They looked then, and for a long while neither of them really saw or believed. But inevitably they had to admit to what was there, and only the shock, the numbing idiot absurdity of it, saved them from an anguish that was unendurable.

Half immersed in the soft swell of dull reds and browns and yellows lay the figure of the small boy, a figure made almost unrecognizable by the great gory rending of bone and flesh that passed from the top of the forehead almost to the groin. The blood that had rushed forward to meet this life ending assault was dried and caked about the body and clothes, but it eventually disappeared as its substance became one with those myriad leafy reminders of an autumn now slowly winding down to an end.

17

The *Tribune* article had broken yesterday morning, and Frank Elliot had spent this morning castigating his detectives in something less than gentlemanly language. In the past month the town had seen three murders and two kidnappings. Both kidnappings had involved children as had one of the murders. The other two murders had involved elderly ladies. They were the worst, most panic producing of all crimes, and Oak Grove had never seen anything remotely like it in all its one hundred and fifty year history. And now the goddamn Chicago *Tribune* had let the whole world know about it in a front-page spread.

The police switchboard had received hundreds of calls already from anxious and angry citizens. The mayor had called, the chief of police had been summonded peremptorily back from his vacation in Maine and the D.A. was having fits. Even the Chicago police were calling, and all the flack was eventually ending up on the head of Frank Elliot, boy-wonder detective.

But Frank Elliot wasn't about to let his job and reputation as a cop go up in smoke—not without taking a few heads with him, at any rate. Naturally, he had saved his choicest invective for Harry who was in charge of the homicide investigation of the two women and Vic Borman who was handling the kidnappings and the murder of the Watson boy. Comments about the relative abilities and ancestry of the two detectives notwithstanding, he had screamed and barked at all of them. From now on they would start working sixteen-hour shifts, and if that didn't work they wouldn't go home at all until this mess was cleared up. Mess singular because he only believed that bad luck came in threes, and the Watson deal made four, so he was inclined to believe that there was a connection between all of them. Bastards. Crumbs. He'd be watching every move they made, so they better be good ones. There wasn't any goddamn police union yet, and they might just remember that he had all of them by the balls. If he went down, they went down.

Linanchi was taken off robbery and put on homicide with Harry; Corson was removed from the "dope detail" to help Vic Borman. Let the little bastards run around and smoke pot and shoot up for awhile. The town would survive that, but to listen to everybody else the town was just this side of Armageddon over these murders and kidnappings. Something like this would have been just a matter of course in Chicago, scant few blocks away. But this was Oak Grove, middle America's idea of paradise, haven to the old, stomping ground of the rich. In a town of seventy thousand this was disaster.

Harry had bitterly resented Elliot's verbal abuse, but he felt just helpless enough about his own investigations to resist blowing his stack. Emma Johnson and Hilda Higgins. There was no apparent suspect or motive, no murder weapon had been found and the pathologist's and lab technician's reports had been equally unenlightening beyond a few general conclusions. In both cases he knew he was looking for a black, probably a big one, but that was little enough to go on. And that was all.

Well, not quite all. He had gone to see the sister again. She was back in the same apartment, a new set of dead bolts and safety chains on front and rear doors. When he had pressed the downstairs buzzer in the lobby, a tremulous voice containing more than a little fear and suspicion had answered. Vainly he had tried to establish some connection between Hilda Higgins and Emma Johnson with the sister. He never really expected any. The man killed for the sport of it or out of some twisted mental abberation, picking his victims at random. In doing so, he deprived Harry of at least half the investigative tools usually afforded him.

But that hadn't been all. They had talked and somehow the woman had blurted out that she *had* seen the killer after all, despite her earlier assertions to the contrary. Tearfully she told her story: how she had laboriously dragged her arthritic body from the bed and pulled it down the hallway to the kitchen just in time to see the huge Negro drop her sister's spent and bleeding body to the floor like an empty sack or discarded plaything.

He had looked right at her then, looked at her in the dim light of the kitchen with glazed and hateful eyes, but he had made no move toward her. Instead he had turned and run out the back door, his clothes smeared and soaked with the sign of his crime. Janet Johnson didn't know why he hadn't killed her too, but that face would be forever imprinted indelibly on her mind.

So Harry had come out of it with something after all—a sketch by the police artist. Right now that was where all his hopes lay. He hadn't been as lucky with the Hilda Higgins murder. No witnesses could be found, but the striking similarities between the two murders suggested that the same killer was responsible for both. This time the lab report, surprisingly enough, had failed to come up with any clear evidence linking the two crimes, but Bill Tolson's report made it clear that the wounds were almost indentical in both cases. As far as Harry was concerned, find the murderer of Emma Johnson, and you find the murderer of Hilda Higgins. There was no doubt.

The sketch had been distributed to local departments already, cross referenced with FBI composites and sent to the Bureau of Prisons and all Illinois mental institutions. You usually had a fair chance of success with all that going for you, but this time Harry had drawn a blank. That was the problem in finding the psychos, even when you had a good description. Often they lived perfectly normal lives for years, but then something inside would suddenly snap, and they'd go on a spree without so much as a traffic citation to their name. Sometimes you had to almost hope that they'd keep killing or raping or maiming until you accumulated enough evidence to find them and put them away. That's the point when you suspected you were in a fundamentally rotten business, and wished you were a toothpaste salesman or a librarian instead of a cop.

But every man in the department had a copy of that sketch with him now. If that big ugly nigger came within a mile of the town, he'd be hauled in for sure. The same with he Chicago cops on the West Side. The black ghetto stretched for a good twenty-five blocks east of Winston Boulevard, and the chances were that he was coming out of this area, if he didn't live in Oak Grove. The chances of finding him in his own territory were slim, but it was the kind of chance that kept a cop's odds from being something less than zero.

As for the town itself, Oak Grove was a little too big and cosmopolitan for people to start congregating at the general store in order to chew over the local tragedies. It wasn't some tiny rural hamlet where everybody knew everyone else's business. No, when a crisis hits a town the size of Oak Grove, it's got to be something major, and then everybody just retreats: inside themselves and behind locked doors and windows. Already he had talked to two patrolmen who were coming off the night shift. They had said that the town had looked so empty during the night that it was frightening. Not a soul on the sidewalks after seven and darn few cars too. The only sign of life was an indiscernable one. The telephone lines must have virtually hummed as neighbors called neighbors, boyfriends called girlfriends and nearly everybody called the police. They had investigated about five or six times the normal prowler calls, a sure sign of paranoia and approaching panic. It was as if everybody was peeking out from behind drawn shades and closed drapes, frightened and furtive eyes searching the night for omens of evil.

Of course, the town wasn't actually hysterical yet, but there were signs that it could happen. The city comptroller, George Middleton, was active in the Little Theater, the town's local repertory group. Currently they were presenting a revival of "South Pacific" and had been playing to full houses for two weeks. But last night the theater had been only one-third full, and George had complained to the mayor who had complained to the chief of police who had complained to Frank Elliot who had yelled at Harry. There were certain things you just didn't let happen; making George Middleton play before a small audience was one of them.

Yesterday had also been Thursday, and the merchants stayed open late on Thursday evenings. But the new mall had been empty as a desert despite a cool, clear night. Gordon Lisster, the chairman of the Chamber of Commerce, had been besieged all morning by complaints from furious merchants. Naturally, he too had called the mayor. Couldn't anything be done to make this town safe to shop in? Hell, the city was still paying off the mall, and the merchants were still screaming about the assessments. The screaming would get a lot worse if people stopped shopping in the town altogether.

Word had also filtered down that the Park District board was calling a meeting for tomorrow night. Several members apparently favored canceling all nighttime activities until these crimes were stopped or solved. It probably wouldn't be long before the school board met either. Attendance in the adult education classes at local high schools was bound to suffer. No, the approaching panic wasn't obvious, but if you had a line tapped into the heart of the city, you could see the danger signals already. Paradise was beginning to betray its warts.

All their other work had gone to hell. The robbery of that big house on Cumberland Drive, the filling station stickup on Winston Boulevard and that nasty business at St. Mark's—all that had gone by the wayside. The wheels of minor justice were grinding to a halt; petty larceny, dope dealing and God knows what else would have a free hand for awhile as the department concentrated all of its resources on the kidnapping and murders. No crimes except rape stirred up people like those two, and the worst kinds of both involved helpless young children and helpless old ladies. Then there was the spector of the black man. Inevitably the papers had discovered that the suspected murderer in two of the cases was a Negro. That really appealed to primal fears. Another murder or kidnapping and this town would go topsy-turvy for sure.

Harry only hoped that the publicity now that it was out would have some unforeseen advantage. Perhaps somebody might remember something that had seemed perfectly innocent or innocuous at the time. Perhaps a reluctant witness might come forward. Until then it was just routine. Circulate the sketch as widely as possible and hope. Try to determine a motive, if any. Try and dig up a connection between the murdered women and even the two children. It was like working a jigsaw puzzle; you just had to find how the pieces fit together. Until then all you could do was try to keep the lid on. He thought of the Watson boy and the details surrounding his death. Boy, if that one ever got out the town would become an armed camp. It was bad enough that the idiot Elliot had ordered the child's parents brought right to the scene to make an identification. He wasn't gonna miss a trick, regardless of how much it hurt someone.

The day wore miserably on, and Harry felt like a school kid again. It was bad enough working these hours, but goddamn Elliot had called him five times—five fucking times—just to see what Harry was doing on the case at that moment. He had nearly shit when Harry had told him he'd ordered police protection for Janet Johnson now that he knew she had been an eyewitness to one of the murders. The blood type and other lab evidence would be enough to hang the bastard if they ever caught him; they didn't need Janet Johnson as a witness. Why the hell was Harry wasting needed manpower on protection when even the uniformed men were working around the clock on the case?

The heartless crumb. He could care less about the old lady. And what if the killer came back to do the only known witness? For once Harry had blown his cork. He threatened to go right to the mayor, to call the newspapers if necessary if Elliot ordered the detail taken off Janet Johnson. Elliot, naturally, had backed down, but he left Harry with the distinct impression that there would be a reckoning later. Shit. But Harry was too tired to care.

It was about four-thirty when the phone rang. Harry just looked at the instrument in its cradle, silently cursing it, but then he picked it up with all the stoic resignation he could muster. "Oronski here," he said gingerly.

"Hello? This is Bob Nichols," came a rather high-pitched voice ove the phone. "I'm with the city sanitation department. I called the switchboard, and they transferred me to you."

La-de-da thought Harry. Somebody's probably stealing garbage now. "What about Mr. Nichols?" he asked.

"Well, I'm in charge of the city sanitation crews. One of my men just brought me in something I thought you might be interested in. It's a suede jacket—a jacket with blood all over it."

"What?" Harry exploded and sat up in his chair.

"Yeah, one sleeve is just covered with it. Of course, I could be wrong. It's all dried, and it could be something else. Sure looks like blood though."

"Mr. Nichols," Harry said urgently, "where did you get this jacket?"

"Well, one of our trucks has been out of commission for several weeks. Bad hydraulic pump. Had to send all the way to Toledo for the part. Anyways, the truck's just been sitting there waiting for that pump. It made a pickup one morning and just wouldn't work when we got it back to the yard."

Harry had been impatiently drumming his fingers on the desk when he heard "Monday." He practically shouted into the phone. "Monday, did you say Monday? What Monday?"

"Well, I don't remember exactly," came the squeaky voice.

"Can you look it up or something?"

"Sure. Hold on a minute."

This could be too good to be true. You had to hope for a break in these things, and this could be it. Come on, goddamnit. Get back on the phone!

"Hello?"

'Yes. Yes," Harry repeated impatiently.

"I've got it here. It was Monday the fourteenth. It's been sitting here ever since the fourteenth because of that bad lift gate. The smell got so bad I had some men clean out the refuse by hand this morning."

"And is that how you found the jacket?" asked Harry;.

"Yes. One of the men noticed it and thought it looked suspicious."

"Mr. Nichols, can you tell me where that truck made pickups on the fourteenth?"

"Sure. Hold on another minute." Again there was a pause on the line. Harry felt his stomach going up and down like a roller coaster ride. Thank God for bad hydraulic pumps, he said silently to himself.

"Here it is," the voice was back. "That truck starts its route right at Water Street and Illinois Avenue, goes south down Illinois to Douglas, comes back up Douglas to Maple, then back south on Orchard to Lincoln Boulevard where it goes East on Lincoln past Tyler to—"

"Hold it. Does it service the six hundred block of Lincoln?"

"Sure. It goes right by there. It would be rather inefficient—"

"Okay, I understand." Harry cut him off again. "Were there any other pickups before Saturday morning, the twelfth?"

"Nope. Pickups always on Monday morning."

"Where are you now, Mr. Nichols?"

"At the yard. You know, down on Taft Avenue."

"And you've got the coat?"

"Sure do. It's right here in the office with me."

"Don't let it out of your sight. I'll be there in fifteen minutes." Harry hung up the phone. He jumped up and quickly slipped on his coat. Goddamn if this didn't look like that break, that bit of luck that made for successful police work. The coat might turn out to have no connection with the murderer at all, but that would have to be a real bitch of a coincidence. The lab report had definitely said suede particles on the body of Emma Johnson.

He was at the incinerator yard in ten minutes still wondering how their fine-tooth-comb search could have missed such an obvious piece of evidence. They had gone through every garbage can for nearly two square blocks. No doubt some jerk uniformed man was worried about getting his hands soiled. He wondered how many pieces of evidence were lost that way.

Bob Nichols was a small, fiftyish, nondescript looking man who seemed inordinately proud as he handed Harry the stained and bloody jacket. After weeks of mingling with banana peels, coffee grounds, stewed tomatoes, chicken bones, furniture polish, and used Kleenex there probably wasn't much that the lab boys would be able to do with it. The jacket was a total litter of contending sights and smells.

But the blood was unmistakable. It had probably taken a long while to dry to its present state. One arm, the left one, was stiffened into a dull brownish-red color. The fabric had the brittle coarseness of dried blood and hung away at an angle in grotesque distinction from the rest of the coat.

With great distaste Harry carefully turned the coat in his hands examining it for any signs of who its owner might have been. Putting his hand into the pockets, he found nothing there at all except a few traces of tobacco that clung to the pocket seam when he turned it inside out. Lab boys could check to see if it was Marlboro tobacco, but that fact would be only of circumstantial value. He needed some clue to the killer's identity, not his smoking habits.

He looked at the discolored suede again. Splotches of dried blood were everywhere, but the sleeve looked like it had been dipped in the stuff. It was a large coat too. Size forty-six or forty-eight. Some big dude. How the old lady had put up such a struggle was beyond his comprehension. Sometimes it was incredible what people could do.

Next he turned the coat inside out to better examine the lining, though the blood-stiffened arm resisted all such attempts mightily. It was perspiration stained under the armpits, and there was a small grayish stain near the beltline—probably from the garbage. Not much there . . . . But wait a minute! A gleam of metal had caught his eye. Turning the coat over again, he looked down near the waist in the back of the jacket's lining and saw it. Clinging in serene indifference to the lining was a safety pin and attached to that pin was a tag. He looked closer. Yes. It was clearly a cleaning tag—a numbered cleaning tag. Harry let out a whoop of joy.

18

Willie was at a back table in Uncle Sly's Tavern when J.D. came in. Willie was working on his fourth double whiskey, the searing burn of it unclouding his mind. These alcohol fogs were consuming more and more of his time these days, but as the hours he spent with a bottle grew, so did his need for forgetfulness.

J.D. spotted Willie after a minute of anxious peering through the dimness and smoke. He was a tall, scarecrow-skinny, rather improbable looking man: large eyes, prominent cheekbones, and great ponderous ears. In distinction to, or perhaps in reaction to his comical appearance, he was prone to take life seriously and view it cautiously. Seeing Willie, he hurried over to join him in his isolated outpost at the back of the bar. He stood there for a minute over Willie, all eyes and excitement.

"Hey man, where you been?" he complained in a voice that was both whining and challenging. "I been lookin' all over town for you."

Willie looked up at him, a slight whimsical smile playing at the corner of his lips. "So whatya want, brother? You found me now."

"Ada went to go clean up your room this morning." He said it like an accusation.

"Why?" returned Willie, the smile shifting slightly to a sneer.

"Why? Why? What kind of place you think I live in? You've been holed up in that room for goin' on two weeks now. It's gettin' to be a rat's nest!"

J.D. reminded Willie of a rooster, all strut and noise, or of one of those little dogs Willie hated so much—excitable, nervous, jumpy, ready to bark at anything but quick to hide under the bed when you make any noise back at them. "Shut up and sit down," mumbled Willie disgustedly.

"Shut up? Shut up? You tellin' me to shut up?" J.D.'s voice was rising several octaves as he indulged his propensity for repetition. "Hey man, I been boardin' you for nothing and my old lady's gettin' plenty sore about that." His voice was getting louder and a couple of men in the back of the bar began to look back at them. A snarl rose in Willie's throat as his hand shot out and grabbed J.D. by the coat. Effortlessly he pulled J.D. down into the chair next to him where the stringbean man instantly become cowed. There was no telling what Willie might do—he had one big reputation for being mean.

But Willie's temper quickly subsided. His energy outlays cost him dearly these days, and he avoided any kind of stenuous activity when he could. His eyes began to glaze over, and he looked down into the empty shot glass as he rolled it back and forth between his huge hands.

J.D. just sat there silently, but finally spoke up in a quiet and supplicating voice. "Willie, Ada was changin' the sheets and cleanin' up—you know how Ada does everything like it was for the Olympics or somethin'. Well, she looked under your bed an' found an old sweat shirt all bunched up with a pair of pants. She was goin' to wash 'em for you 'til she noticed they were full of blood."

Some part of him began to listen to J.D.'s words and decided it should pay attention. "Yeah. Got into a little hassle last week with a couple of dudes. Got a little messy."

"Messy? My God, what'd you do, stab somebody?" inquired J.D. in a hoarse whisper that was almost worse than his yelling.

Willie looked at him sharply. "Whatya saying? You

throwin' me out on the street?''

"Hey man. It's not me. Ada is scared. She's scared you might get us in trouble or somethin'."

"You cockroach," Willie intoned flatly and let his fist drop a foot to the table. J.D. looked like a moth caught on a stick. His whole body twitched and jerked as he resisted the urge to jump up and run.

"Hold on, Willie. Hold on," he said placatingly. "It don't have to be tonight or even tomorrow maybe. Maybe if you could just give me a good story to give Ada—"

"Shit! Whatya gotta go tellin' her *any* story for, man? Who runs your fuckin' family anyhow?" Willie's tone was so scathing and his contempt so obvious that J.D. looked down to the floor. "Shit, you tomfool. I can stay anywhere. I'll be outta your crummy apartment by tomorrow."

J.D. was relieved but tried not to look it. "You know we're always glad to have you."

"One thing, J.D.," Willie said, his voice low and menacing. "You and Ada didn't see nothin'. You didn't see no blood or nothin' or there's gonna be big trouble goin' down for everybody concerned." He said the words with a threatening tone he didn't even feel. Something from deep inside of him seemed to push up and say the words for him, but their effect was obvious. J.D.'s eyes got even bigger, and he licked nervously at his lips.

He started to protest, to make a token effort to maintain whatever manly pride he had, but Willie suddenly grabbed him by the wrist and began to squeeze into bone and flesh until he thought he was going to scream. He didn't hold out long. He began to bob and nod his head up and down in quick, convulsive bursts until Willie finally relaxed the pressure, and J.D. let a long involuntary sigh escape from between his teeth. "Now get outa here, roach," Willie growled scornfully, and J.D. was up and on his way out the front door faster than a rabbit. Willie looked after him for a moment then laughed soulessly. J.D. was just another in a long line of ghetto rats living out their lives as if they were men. Willie had all the respect for them that he had for the vermin that lived in drain pipes and dank, dark corners.

He lurched to his feet and began a slow weave toward the door: his altercation with J.D. had ruined Uncle Sly's for him for the rest of this day. He stepped outside into the leaden gray of the early afternoon. A biting November chill was in the air, and the wind seemed to gust at Willie with an unrelenting and spiteful fury. He hated this kind of weather—had never adjusted to the cold or the winter. The winter always brought back memories of Mississippi where you could be outdoors nearly all the time, where you didn't have to spend half the year indoors or wishing you were indoors.

But he'd been feeling awful for weeks; that had to have something to do with it. Something had been crawlin' around in him for a long time and it probably needed a doctor. But he hated doctors—had hated them since he'd needed those rabies shots as a kid. Those long needles in the belly had been bad enough, but he'd gotten so sick he'd nearly died. Now sometimes he thought he was going to die again when the waves of weakness and nausea came over him, but they would always pass, and he would feel all right except for the washed out feeling that was always with him now.

Willie started walking aimlessly down the street, with no real destination impelling his slow, somewhat unsteady movements. As he walked on, his thoughts came to absorb him to the exclusion of his surroundings. Always at the back of his mind was that gnawing doubt, the hazy memory he was trying to focus and bring into consciousness. Sometimes he felt that the memory he was groping for became clear when he dreamed. Sometimes he had snatches of it upon waking, but the moment he tried to capture the fragment, it fled.

Other times he would wake up in a cold sweat, his heart beating a mile a minute. Those times he didn't remember anything except feeling scared—scared for no real reason at all. Once he'd even awakened to screaming—his own. That had been embarrassing because all of Rufus White's family had rushed in to stare at him, Big Willie, screaming like a little kid and sitting there in bed, the covers clutched around him for reassurance. He had gotten out of there the next day, and he wouldn't forget the strange look Rufus's old lady gave him as he left: like he was some insect crawling out the door that she was afraid to step on but all too glad to see go.

But once or twice he had caught snatches of it. Strange scenes had drifted momentarily before his eyes then vanished. It had happened once when he was enfolded in the mysterious depths of a bottle of rum and another time when he was in that semi-conscious state of torpor just between sleep and wakefulness where all our half-thoughts become lost forever. Both times it should have become a lost thought, a forgotten image, but he had been struggling so long to bring the gnawing thing at the back of his brain into the light that his mind had clutched at the brief, nebulous impressions in the same way that a famished animal attacks a piece of meat.

It was all dim and seemed incredibly distant. There was a fog wrapped around everything, but he seemed to remember the fancy room with all the books . . . the peculiar burning smell and the feeling of drifting . . . drifting . . . moving toward and away something at the same time. Only this and the two dark eyes that had seared like hot pokers into his own, making everything inside go limp and useless. And words—vague, hardly remembered words said slowly and carefully like a prayer. That was all. That was all he could remember, and it made no sense at all.

His mind drifted back to his surroundings for a moment, and he realized that he had been walking for a long time. He was getting close to Winston Boulevard, and that was the virtual end of his turf. On the other side of the street lay Oak Grove, and for some unknown reason, the very idea of the town loomed up his mind as a place that was ominous and forbidding. He turned at the nearest side street running south and parallel to Winston. He'd take it for a block, then turn east again toward Laramie.

But he realized that the walk was making him feel better. He hadn't done anything but lie around and booze it for so long that his body was beginning to feel like jelly. Some of the old strength and energy seemed to be pumping through his veins again, and he silently promised himself that he'd made a point of getting more exercise in the future. Maybe it'd help drive away some of this feeling of cold.

As he turned east, he remembered that tonight was the night that Hotshot Johnny was finally going to get his comeuppance against Rufus's younger brother, Wendell. Johnny was one good man with a cue, but his mouth was bigger than he was good, and tonight Wendell was going to prove it. Too bad. Hotshot Johnny had been dodging Wendell for months; if he hadn't gotten so all fired skunked at Uncle Sly's last night the match still wouldn't be on. But he had, and his mouth had started flappin', and money had been put down, and Hotshot Johnny didn't dare back out now. Willie wasn't going to miss that one for nothin'.

Shit. There were a lot of things to do, if you just wanted to look for them. He'd been sitting on his duff for too long now—had let everything slide for weeks. Hadn't even picked up his cleaning for two weeks. But sometimes he just didn't know what happened to the days anymore, and the nights were worse. Sometimes they were a total blank altogether. Well, shit. He had been sick. He had an excuse.

But that was gonna stop. Already his steps had become steadier and more purposeful as the long walk in the autumn chill stripped the alcohol out of his blood. The booze could do that to a man—even a mountain of a man like Willie—and you weren't going to keep on bein' king of the corner for too long if you got wasted all the time.

At first he hardly noticed the woman walking on the other side of the street. Willie was caught up in thinking about his mental and physical rehabilitation. His mood had taken a sudden turn toward the optimistic. When you see the end of the tunnel, you're all the more grateful for the light, and Willie was feeling good at the moment—feeling like life was coming back on his side.

She was a white woman. Average-sized and wrapped in a heavy cloth coat, she looked both a little bit harried and furtive as she moved swiftly along the walk. Funny. You didn't see many white women walking alone this close to Central anymore. Alien territory. You could almost see the fear clinging to them as they tried to look unconcerned and above it all. This one wasn't bringing it off much better than the rest.

Already his mind was beginning to cloud over. Already the rehabilitation of Willie Malone was becoming a thing of the past as jumbled thoughts and unbidden sensations began to rush into his head. Somehow the sight of the lone woman was triggering those same dim memories and confused feelings that he had just a few moments before resolved to let become things of the unlamented past. A small churning sensation began to work in the pit of his stomach, and he felt his knees go a little weak.

Willie stopped for a moment and leaned heavily against a tree. What was going on? He could feel the dimly familiar, hateful burning at the back of his brain begin again. He could feel it grow and swell from a tiny, distant, always-present flame into an unknowing blaze of havoc and destruction. At its heart were two cold and merciless eyes whose icy malevolence were the heart of that fire. Fire and ice. Opposites made one. Hate and indifference. Smiling vengeance and a million wrongs suddenly righted. His mind swam with a multitude of thoughts that came so fast that they were inseparable from one another, but instinctively, unknowingly, he put his hand into his jacket pocket and felt something long, hard and cruelly cold there. He felt it curve to a wicked, needle sharp point that had embedded itself into the lining of his chest.

Willie was hardly aware of it, but he turned around and slowly began to walk in the opposite direction, toward the now distant and retreating figure of the lone woman. Despite the fact that it was only a little after noon, the streets were singularly empty, and as Willie lengthened his strides and began to catch up with the woman, some protective instinct vaguely informed him that they were alone, the woman and he. Alone in the vast sprawl of dilapidated apartment buildings and shabby two-story homes. During the nighttime hours, the ghetto would come alive, but now they were surrounded by the vacant eyes of the dismal, crumbling buildings and the soulless emptiness of the streets. Only this.

Willie trudged on mindlessly, his body moving swiftly now but with the stiffened, automatic gait of a robot. If anybody had seen him, they might have wondered about the way his body moved, about the blank stare of those eyes. But the streets were still, and as he now approached Winston Boulevard once again, it would make no difference. Winston Boulevard was a main artery and connected to the expressway, and only the continual hum of automobiles intruded on the still-serene grace of the elegant but decaying old brownstones that lined either side of that block. Automobile drivers would take no note of the slight irregularities in movement of one lone black man. Willie walked on.

Ahead of him he could now see the woman clearly, his feeling of dislocation gone. The sharp edge of certainty had replaced the doubt until each step he took became more purposeful. Now the litheness and power had returned to his body like some gift that had long been withheld, and Willie's eyes narrowed with the look of the hunt. Every sense was sharp and ready, and the hunger in him was like a fever. He had to struggle to slow his pace as the woman paused for the traffic light at Winston Boulevard, but soon she was on her way again, moving briskly and obliviously into the heart of Oak Grove.

She felt comfortable again as the shabbiness and decay of the west-side ghetto gave way to the neatly trimmed lawns and sparkling paint of Oak Grove. She couldn't believe the difference a few blocks could make: One side of Winston looked like a bombed out city while this side . . .

She felt the tension letting go. Oh, she had read all the newspaper accounts about what was happening in her town, but it was daylight now and that all happened at night. Besides, the warm, comforting embrace of stately Victorian homes and placid old red-brick apartment buildings was beginning to lull her vague fears. This town would be good for a long time yet.

Her train of thought broke sharply with the crack of the small stick on the walk behind her. She was aware of rapid footsteps now, and quickly she looked back over her shoulder and saw something large and menacing hurtle at her with insane fury. All she remembered after that was crashing into the sidewalk under its weight, a mask of horror and hatred leering into her face.

19

It had happened again, in broad daylight a block from one of the busiest streets in town. When Harry got the news, he slammed his fist into the desk in disgust. Another murder was awful enough, but why another murder now? Why now, when he was so close to finding his man?

He looked down at the spreading pile of notepapers in his desk. Phone numbers. An infinity of phone numbers. He had spent the whole morning calling every cleaning store within a radius of twenty miles, and if that didn't work he would extend the radius to thirty miles. Sooner or later he would hit the one that was using a number series equivalent to the one on the tag of the suede jacket. If only the tag had had the cleaner's name on it, he might have wrapped this up already, and someone else would not have died. If only he could find the right one now, he might prevent another killing.

But what was he going on about? Did he really expect that this nut was going to murder at Harry's convenience? That he would wait a couple of days for Harry to catch up with him? Shit. That had been his whole problem all through life: He could never understand or accept it when things didn't go by the script, could never cope with the injustice of reality. Frank Elliot had gotten *his* job—that hadn't been just. He'd married a damn fine-looking woman twenty years ago, and look at the indifferent slob she'd turned into. That wasn't fair.

There was no justice, and he had become a cop—perhaps in pursuit of that elusive quality. He laughed at the irony of it all.

The mayor and the chief had come up personally this morning, had come up with Elliot, and the mayor had pointedly asked Harry just what the hell he was doing to find the bastard who was almost singlehandedly destroying the whole fucking town. He had said it as if it were Harry's fault that this psycho had picked Oak Grove as the target for his "escapades." Had said it as if Harry were the only goddamn cop in town.

Elliot had smiled at Harry's anger and embarrassment—already he was sticking the knife of his revenge in. He offered right there and then in front of Harry to take over the cases personally—to take them over now that he knew Harry had the key in the door. But Harry had spoken up in a hurry. He told the mayor and the chief about this piece of evidence, told them that he expected it to pay off momentarily, and Chief Anders had told him to keep working on the case. Elliot had scowled, and Harry had another small triumph. As soon as the three men had started to leave, Harry began dialing again.

He had already gone through the suburban book and was well into the Chicago West Yellow Pages when Vic Borman had walked in. He was beginning to look like a tired man, a beaten man. He had been getting no further in the kidnappings than Harry had been getting on the murders before the cleaning tag had shown up. "Whatya doing, Harry? If it isn't important, ring me dial-a-joke. I could use the laugh."

Harry looked up at him and almost felt sympathetic for the grouchy detective. Vic wasn't used to all this work. He liked to coast most of the time, and these sixteen-hour days obviously weren't agreeing with him. "No, Vickie, my boy. I'm in the midst of catching me a murderer."

Borman hardly reacted. "Glad somebody's catchin' something," he mumbled as he walked toward the coffee pot. "Think I'm catching a cold."

"You oughta be overjoyed you krauthead," Harry called after him. "I catch my guy, I might just be catching your guy at the same time."

Borman walked back toward Harry's desk. "Well, somebody better catch somebody. Do you know that my neighbors called a meeting of everybody on the block last night? Everybody but me, that is. They're going to organize a 'neighborhood protection association' or something like that. Marvelous. Bob Finster can't even clean out his gutters without falling off the fucking ladder, and now he wants to start walking around the neighborhood with a .30-.30."

"Yeah, I know," returned Harry woefully. "I talked to Leonard Frang over at Robinson's Sporting Goods yesterday. He told me he sold a .38 to some old lady who was seventy-nine years old—she had a gun card and everything. From what I hear, everybody in the whole goddamn town is buying shotguns, attack dogs—you name it."

"Shit," said Borman emphatically. "I gave Donna a Beretta to carry in her purse, and you know how jumpy she is. I just know I'm gonna come home some night, and she's gonna blow a hole in my face."

"What have you heard about this latest one, Vic? I just caught the tail end of it between everybody yelling at me."

Borman smiled sorrowfully at Harry. They had all been catching it, but he knew Frank Elliot had singled Harry out for the special treatment. "Two witnesses I hear, but all they saw was somebody running away. One was an old lady who couldn't even tell us what color the guy was—only that he looked big. The other was a nine-year-old girl who said the killer was black and that was all she could remember."

"Oh, they should make great witnesses for some goddamn defense attorney," Harry replied cynically.

"We'll have to shoot this fucker, if we ever catch him, Harry. The town's gonna demand it. People are going to want to string this guy up from a tree."

Harry shook his head slowly. "One in the afternoon and in broad daylight. I don't understand it. Here's a woman screaming her lungs out and nobody sees or does a bitching thing. It makes you wonder about our glorious populace."

"Hey, Harry. How come you weren't there? I mean, you're in charge of these homicides, and it was obviously the same creep."

Harry's hand flapped in a gesture of despair. "Who else? Glamor boy upstairs. He told me to stick on this lead, though any rookie cop could do this shit. I think he's getting ready to grab the credit, now that I found something."

"You mean that coat?"

"Yeah."

"Well Walsh said he'd be up later to brief you on it, though you've pretty much got the details now. I mean, even Elliot can only bend procedure so far. You should have been the one to be out there, Harry, not Walsh."

"Who needs it, Vic. I'm sick of blood and guts. All these years in the department, and I think I've drawn my gun twice. Never used it. I was getting so bored with chasing kids ripping off hub caps and smoking joints. About now, though, I'm ready for the kiddy patrol again."

"Yeah, and I'm ready for an eight-hour day again. Jesus, I think I'm gonna have a stroke if this keeps up much longer," said Borman with an audible sigh.

"Say, Vic, which way did the little girl say that big jig was running when he left the scene?"

"Toward Winston Boulevard. Hightailing it back to the slums."

"Yeah, I figured as much," Harry said laconically. "I wasted the whole damn morning calling these suburban stores. Maybe Elliot's right." He picked up the phone again and started to dial.

"What?" asked Borman.

"Nothing." Harry held up his hand, signally for silence. "Hello, Cassidy Cleaners? This is Sergeant

Harry Oronski of the Oak Grove police department calling. I'd like to talk to the owner or manager about a matter of urgency."

20

It was five days later that he decided to do something. True, she had said that she and her father might go away for a while in order to flee whatever strange events they had become embroiled in. But he hadn't liked the fact that no one had answered his call that same evening. Surely they wouldn't have decided to leave in the middle of the night. No, if this did have something to do with the terrible events that had overtaken Oak Grove, he couldn't afford merely to look for a facile or comforting answer. The worst possibilities had to be explored and the fact that no one had answered his frequent calls for five days hinted at the worst.

But what could he do? He'd already decided that calling the police on such flimsy suspicions was futile. Oh, they might jump at the chance to find a clue to what had been going on in this town, but more likely they would dismiss Scott as another one of the nuts the local population was producing lately. He didn't really feel right in implicating Barb or her father in such lurid events either—not after what Barb had told him about Dr. Brennan's unhappy past.

In the end he came to a plan of action. On Tuesday morning he opened the phone book and found the number for St. Anthony's Hospital where he knew Barb's father was still on the staff as as surgical consultant. A few discreet inquiries wouldn't hurt anything and just might help assuage the growing sense of alarm he was feeling. He dialed the number.

"St. Anthony's," the disembodied voice came through the earpiece.

"I'd like to talk to Dr. Richard Brennan, please."

"Hold on."

He sat and tapped the phone with one idle finger while waiting. Three days and it felt like three months. He was going the whole route, wasn't he? Little sleep, nervous, a knot of apprehension in his stomach—so this was love.

"Surgery. May I help you?"

"Yes, I hope so. I'm looking for Dr. Richard Brennan."

"Hold on."

The line went dead again, and once more he was alone with his thoughts . . . with the feeling of responsibility he had decided to take upon himself. No, his emotions were *forcing* him to take it on, and that wasn't exactly his style. Staying independent had usually meant staying happy in his scheme of things. But now, here he was putting his nose in where it probably didn't belong.

"Hello?"

"Yes," Scott replied.

"I'm sorry but Dr. Brennan isn't here today."

"Is he expected?"

"Just a minute, please." There was a slight pause then the faceless voice returned. "No, Dr. Brennan is not due on the floor today."

"I see. Can you tell me when he is due in?"

"No, I can't."

"Do you mean you don't know, or you won't tell me?"

"He's not on this week's duty roster, sir."

Sparkling conversation, thought Scott. "Can you connect me with anyone who can tell me where I can get ahold of the doctor?"

"Hold on."

Again there was the slight hiss of near-silence on the line, but soon another disembodied voice came on. "Personnel. Miss Wilkerson." It was a decidedly young and sexy voice which surprised Scott. He had begun to think that this hospital only employed spinsters and librarians by the sound of the dry, impersonal tones he had heard so far.

"Hello. I'm trying to contact a Dr. Richard Brennan who is employed with you. I already talked to someone in another department, and they referred me to you."

He expected the seemingly obligatory "hold on" but the girl replied immediately, "I'm sorry, but Dr. Brennan hasn't reported for duty since Friday, and we aren't allowed to give out home phone numbers."

"I've got his home phone number. I haven't been able to reach him there, and I'm concerned. Was he scheduled to be at the hospital at all the last few days?"

There was a pause then, "Yes. He was due on Friday, Saturday, and Monday, but he hasn't been in on any of those days."

"Didn't the hospital try to reach him?"

"Sir, I'm not certain that I should be discussing hospital procedure with you."

"Oh for God's sake, this could be extremely important!"

"Well, yes, we did try to contact Dr. Brennan, but we weren't successful."

"And the doctor left no word with you at all?"

"None. Say, who are you, if I may ask?"

"Thank you very much." Scott said and hung up. Now he was even more worried. Barb could be a little flaky at times, but he really doubted whether Dr. Brennan would leave town without attempting to contact the hospital either then or sometime since. Five days. It just didn't make sense. He picked up the phone again and dialed one of the numbers inscribed under the plastic disc on the middle of the dialer.

"Oak Grove Police. Officer Wiley."

"Hello, I'd like to talk to somebody about a missing persons report."

"You want to file one?"

"I don't know. I'd just like to talk to someone who could give me some information about filing one, I guess."

"Hold on," came the now familiar reply. Scott waited.

"Sergeant Rizzo. Can I help you?"

God, it's so programmed, thought Scott. "I hope so, Sergeant. Some friends of mine have been missing for several days, and I'm becoming a little concerned."

"How many days?"

"Since Friday."

"That's long enough. Where are these friends missing from?"

"Well, from their house. There hasn't been any answer there since at least Friday. I had a date with one of them," he decided to lie.

"How do you know that these people just aren't out of town, sir?"

"As I started to say, I had a date with one of the missing people, but she hasn't been home in days. Neither has the father. I just called his place of work, and he hasn't been there either. They don't know where he is."

The sergeant sounded bored. "You want to come down and fill out a report?"

"Then what do you do?"

"We check it out."

"How?"

"Maybe you'd like to enter the police academy to find that out."

Scott felt the anger rising up quickly but fought to subdue it. "Look, Sergeant, I've read all about the murders and kidnappings that have been going on in this town. Now maybe you think I'm overreacting, but two people have suddenly up and disappeared for no apparent reason. Now if I have to tell somebody that I think they've been murdered to get somebody to really do something, not just fill out a report—"

"Just a minute." The line went silent again. Sometimes he felt like he'd like to put the whole goddamn world on "hold"—permanently. Nobody gave a shit about anybody else; nobody wanted to be bothered.

A tired sounding voice came on the line. "Detective

Oronski. Can I help you?"

"You'll help me immensely, if you just don't put me on hold," said Scott resignedly.

There was a soft chuckle from the other end of the line. "You sound like a man after my own heart. Now what can I do for you?"

Scott proceeded to recount his concerns as briefly as possible—he could sense the detective was impatient with his story by the frequency of indifferent "uh-huhs." At length the detective interrupted him. "I can appreciate your concern Mr.—Mr.—What did you say your name was?"

"I didn't, but it's Scott."

"Scott what?"

"Scott Kearney."

"Well, Mr. Kearney, as I was saying, I can appreciate your concern, but I don't know why they switched this call up to me. This is a regular departmental matter, and not to sound indifferent, but I'm tied up with some important stuff right now."

Scott felt the surge of anger again. "Look, two people are missing. They might have been murdered for all you know. What the hell is more important than that?"

Silence for a moment. "Yeah, you're probably right, but the thing for you to do is come down here and fill out a missing person's report. We can't do a thing for you until then."

"All right." Scott replied passively. "Thanks a lot for your time."

He meant it scathingly but the other seemed to take no offense. "Sure, and don't worry. I'm sure that everything will turn out okay. You'd be surprised how many people disappear only to turn right up again a few days later." There was a click, then nothing, then a dial tone. Scott sat looking at the phone in his hand. As a means of communication it stank.

By now practical necessities intruded, and he had to get dressed and go to work. After all this run-around and indifference, he decided he'd better put off filing the missing person's report until tomorrow. Maybe he'd think of a better way, and by the sound of things it was hardly going to receive top priority anyway—not unless he told them what Barb had said, and he wasn't prepared to do that yet.

But he hated to let another day slide by and do nothing. He decided then that he would drive by Barb's house once more on the way to his job up in the Edgebrook area of north Chicago; otherwise he might start dreaming and worrying and put a two-penny nail through his thumb or do something equally disastrous. Who knows, maybe he'd drive by and find Dr. Brennan's car in the driveway, the house open and—the car! He'd never even checked to see if it was in the garage. Christ, some detective he'd make. No wonder the police had seemed impatient with his questioning of their procedures.

In ten minutes he was driving up Fairchild toward the Brennan residence. He thought of talking to the neighbors but decided against it. If all this turned out to be nothing, Dr. Brennan might resent his snooping. He was beginning to feel a little foolish already, but underneath that was a growing sense of foreboding that he couldn't shake. Perhaps it was just the combination of his love for Barb and the state the town was in, but something deep inside was spelling out a subtle but definite warning: Something is wrong.

He parked the car in front of the house and walked up to the front door. The house still looked like it was uninhabited; it had that certain air that houses get when they aren't being used. But he rang he bell and knocked for a long time before he gave up and started back around the driveway to the rear of the house. Going up to the garage, Scott saw a large side window and peered through its dirty panes into the dark inner recesses of the garage. Sure enough, Dr. Brennan's green Buick sat inside and next to it he could see the smaller outline of Barb's car. Damn it, he thought. Why didn't I check such an obvious place before?

But he knew it didn't prove anything. In an effort to get away quickly they might have flown somewhere—to some out-of-town relative's perhaps. And it was no use upbraiding himself either. It had taken time and an accumulated reserve of nervous apprehension to bring him to being such a snoop.

He looked toward the house. It was silent and still. He'd been crazy to do what he was thinking now. Logic told him not to. Something deeper and more persuasive impelled him onward. He crossed to the back door, which was set out of the neighbor's sight in a little breezeway. Wrapping his handkerchief around his hand, he hit a window pane in the door sharply, making sure to instantly withdraw his hand. The broken glass fell inward with a minimum of noise, and he set out to pick the few remaining jagged edges from the window frame. Then he stood on his toes, reached inside and down and just managed to get hold of the latch. It turned easily, and he complimented himself on his newfound skills as a housebreaker as the door swung open before him. But he hesitated a long moment before entering. He had killed people in a distant war, but this somehow seemed worse, this forcible entering of someone's house—even if for the best of reasons. He hesitated, but the thought of Barb forced him on.

The back door led to a small alcove immediately off the kitchen. He paused here and carefully listened. All he could hear was the faint ticking of the huge grandfather clock, like some patient sentinel, in the front hall, and that sound seemed intensified by the heavy silence of the house. Taking care to avoid the broken glass that lay on the floor, he walked up two steps and into the kitchen. Now that he was here, he realized that he wasn't certain exactly what he should do. He could hardly expect to find a note saying, "Dear Scott, in case you have broken in, we have gone on vacation. Love, Barb."

One thing was certain. If anybody was at home by some chance, he'd better announce his presence. Better to be taken for a crazy boyfriend than be shot as a prowler. "Hello," he called loudly. "Barb, Dr. Brennan? Is anybody home?" There was no answer, and as he walked through the kitchen, he noticed that there were no dirty dishes, no empty bottles or other signs of recent use.

Carefully he walked out of the kitchen and into the front hall, where the ticking of the great clock became louder and more ominous, like the steady measured rhythm of a single heartbeat. He went into the living room and the small den off the living room. Everything was neat and orderly, and there were no signs of recent use. He went back into the hallway and looked into the large formal dining room. Gads, it was a big house—too big for the two of them. But Barb had said that her father would never sell it: It had been her mother's greatest joy. He had bought it for her, and it was all that remained of her in his life now.

But the very size of the house seemed foreboding under these circumstances. He was here for no pleasant or hopeful reason, and the sooner he could leave the better. He dreaded the thought of going upstairs, but there was no other way.

He climbed the stairway cautiously, again calling out to insure his own safety should Dr. Brennan be lurking at the top with a pistol or something. If you invaded someone else's house, even for the best of reasons, you had to be prepared for anything. But he gained the top landing with no misadventure, and immediately his eyes were drawn to an open door on the left.

It was a bedroom, simply furnished with no signs of having been recently occupied. He stepped into the room and gazed quickly around, but nothing drew his eye. He was back in the hall when he first noticed it. The air was stuffy, which was to be expected if the house had been closed up for several days, but there was also another odor: slightly pungent and ripe smelling. He had smelled it before—in Viet Nam: the smell of the surgery, the smell of death.

He rushed now to the next room, all caution thrown aside. It was another bedroom, and by the looks of the furniture and appointments, a girl's room. The single bed was canopied, and the small writing desk and chair in one corner were singularly feminine in design and size. Hung neatly over one chair he noticed a cardigan sweater—the same sweater Barb had been wearing when he had last seen her over a week ago. Undoubtedly this was her room, and that fact reassured him some. By now he definitely expected to find the worst; not finding it in Barb's room provided some reason for hope.

Quickly he was out of the bedroom and further down the hall. The next room was a bedroom that had been converted into a study. A large desk and chair and bookshelves loaded with medical texts were the dominant features. He didn't go in but turned to face the doorway directly across the hall. The door was closed, but as he approached it he already knew. The charnel stench was stronger.

He hesitated but knew there was no alternative. Turning the handle, he slowly opened the door. A blast of stench and decay rushed out to meet him, and he backed up a few feet into the hall in sudden nausea and disgust. He could see that the room was dark. The shades were drawn and the window curtains were shut. Still, a tiny bit of light filtered around the edges of the window sill, and this was enough illumination for Scot to see the figure of the man draped across the bed. It faced away from him, and he was glad for that. A corpse of several days can do much to create doubts about the immortality of man.

Conquering his revulsion, he moved forward to the edge of the doorway where he had an unrestricted view of the room. Even in the gloom he could see that no other figure was to be found there, so he backed away and closed the door as he fought to hold his stomach down. Then his eyes fell on the bathroom at the end of the hall, and he hurried in its direction. This and the basement were the only two places he hadn't checked yet outside of closets and, maybe, an attic.

The bathroom was empty, and he rushed downstairs, nearly falling headlong down the basement steps in his haste and his fear. The basement was a labyrinth of smaller rooms and corners, of firewood and old bundled up newspapers, of boxes and trunks, but in less than five minutes he had scouted it thoroughly. Puzzled but grateful, he realized that Barb was not to be found in the house.

He trudged back upstairs and sat in the small den off the living room where he and Barb had often watched television together, his mind a maze of contradictory thoughts and feelings. Finally, he went back into the front hall and picked up the phone, dialing a number he had not yet forgotten. It rang twice and a voice answered, "Oak Grove Police. Officer Wiley."

"I—I talked to somebody awhile ago . . . a Detective Orsinki or Ornoski—"

"Oronski" the neutral sounding voice was chuckling now.

"Right. It was about an hour ago. Is he still in?"

"Hold on, I'll ring him."

Scott's hand tightened around the receiver as he put his mind to work on keeping his stomach in its customary place. For a moment even now he wondered if he was doing the right thing. Shit. Barb's father was dead, and she was missing. What else could he do? His stomach tried again to dislodge its contents.

"Oronski," the tired voice came on the line.

"Detective, this is Scott Kearney again. I talked to you earlier."

"I remember. And I remember telling you how to handle that. It's not my department. You get a homicide, then you call me back."

All the worry and sleeplessness caught up with him then. Momentarily he forgot that Barb was missing and that her father's decomposing corpse lay in a bedroom upstairs. Just now he wanted to strike back at all the faceless, uncaring people on the other end of the telephone and jobs and attitudes whose actions said, I don't give a fuck about you and your's. "Okay, Detective, we'll play it your way," he said with conscious irony. "Now mind you, I can't promise a homicide, but I sure as hell can supply a body."

21

Harry munched at the sandwich with no great conviction, biting at and around it as if it might strike back at him. He didn't like this eating in the car. He didn't like practically living in one either. That's what it felt like. Four days they had been watching the cleaners. Four days and no one had shown.

"Hey, Randolph," Harry said to the man sitting next to him, "you sure your guys aren't standing around with their badges hanging out or something?"

The other man looked at him. "If you mean, are we blowing it, the answer is no. Besides, you're the cop from the boonies—I'm supposed to be asking you that question."

"Oh, ho. The boonies, eh? Two miles away, you prick."

"I'm not talking about location, Oronski. I'm talking about know how."

"Excuse me while I puke," Harry replied with a grimace.

Randolph laughed. "It is a bite, isn't it?" he said more seriously. "I mean, for us it's just another bust, but for you it's probably a medal."

"No, it's more like my job," said Harry solemnly. "A couple more weeks, and they'll skin me alive."

"Well, no insult Harry, but it's no wonder with all the things that have been going on in your town lately. Lieutenant O'Reilly would have my ass by now, if all that had happened in my district. You're just lucky this old guy keeps records."

Harry thought about the old man who owned the cleaners. He did keep records—lots of very accurate records with names and their corresponding sales ticket numbers. The number Harry had found corresponded to a name, a Willie Malone. There were a lot of old tickets for a Willie Malone, but best of all there was a current one too. Cleaning to be picked up. Oh, come and get your cleaning, Willie Malone.

"Yeah, I never liked Greeks much before this," Harry said absentmindedly.

"Doesn't bother me," replied Randolph. "I'm strictly a Wasp myself."

"Shit, Dave. Do you realize how much effort I've put into this whole thing? I've done more work in the last three weeks than I've done in the last three years. I mean, I'm used to chasing bicycle thieves and investigating petty burglaries—this is way out of my league. If it hadn't been for that damn cleaning tag, I'd still be out there rooting around in the shit with nothing to show for it except blisters and aggravation."

"Yeah, instead of sitting in this lovely car here with me," chuckled Randolph.

"Well that ain't so hot either, Dave, but it sure beats wondering about my pension."

"Shit yes. Now you'll be a hero. Ticker tape parades, the whole bit."

"Naw, that's for you Chicago boys. You thrive on that. Besides, it's really your pinch. I'm just along for the ride. You know, sufferance of the Chicago Police Department and all that."

"Sure, Harry. You're Mister Humility, right? But listen, I still can't figure that this guy's got no arrest record, no record of mental illness—it doesn't add up."

"Christ, I checked with everybody in the whole godamned world. I checked with state, local, FBI, Treasury, Social Security. I checked with about fifteen different state mental health agencies from here to Alabama. I mean, everybody who goes crazy has to do it for a first time, right? Look at Speck and that Whitman fellow down in Texas. Nice normal fellows 'til one day they went bananas."

"I suppose so," said Randolph reluctantly, "but it gives me the creeps. I've got a wife and an eleven-year-old daughter at home, and the thought of these psychos on the street is enough to make you want to go home and lock the door and never come out again."

"Life in the big city," said Harry philosophically and he grinned.

"One Charlie A to One Charlie B, do you read me?" the voice came over the radio speaker.

Randolph leaned over and picked the mike up off the floor console. "One Charlie B here. What's up, Ray?"

"The old man just buzzed us. Someone's in the store trying to claim the cleaning for our boy."

"Who'd you see go in the store, Ray?"

"Two people in there now. Female Caucasian about forty, heavy, green coat and female Negro, thirties, thin, gray coat and hat."

"That's all?"

"Yep."

"And you're sure it's the signal. We don't wanna blow this stakeout too early. You know how fast good news travels in Shinetown."

"Nope, no mistake. He buzzed twice short and one long just like he was supposed to."

"I love those Greeks," Harry said eagerly.

"Okay Ray, you and Rodriguez get out and cover the front but first get on the pipe and tell those two Polish princes down the block to wake up and cover the back." Randolph looked over and saw Harry looking at him sceptically. "Sorry Harry. Just a figure of speech."

"Got you," came the voice over the radio again. "You two gonna make the grab?"

"Yeah, Ray. I figure my fat friend here from Oak Grove could use the exercise."

A soft chuckle rasped out of the receiver. "Roger, wilco, over and out."

"Cut it out,' Randolph said into the mike and put it

back in its cradle on the floor. He looked over at Harry, a gleam of delight in his eye.

"Very funny," moaned Harry. "But what's going on? It looks like our man didn't pick up his own cleaning."

"Yeah, but somebody did, and that somebody's gonna take us right to him."

They got out of the car and walked around the corner to the cleaners. It was a small building with a large glass front. Harry stepped aside and let Randolph go in first. As he entered, a slim black woman dressed in a gray cloth coat and carrying a thick bag of cleaning began to walk out of the store. Randolph stepped in front of her and proffered his badge. "We'd like to have a word with you, ma'am," he said politely.

Willie heard the front door close quietly. It was probably Ethel. He hoped she had picked up his cleaning for him; he had worn the few things he had around so long that they were beginning to stink. "Ethel,' he called out hoarsely from his bed. "Ethel, you bring my cleanin'?"

There was no answer. Damn woman, he thought grouchily. They all get their tails up after awhile. "Ethel, get your ass in here!" he shouted. He could hear the floor creak from somewhere near the kitchen, but again there was no response. He felt like getting up and cuffin' her one, but he felt too tired, too punk. Besides, his "host" might not like it, and even though Jimmy was a squirrel, there was no sense in alienating your provider if you could help it.

He rolled over onto his back with a weary moan; the fog in his brain rolled with him. Nothing was churning in there now. There was no burning, no insistence or pain. He had to take advantage of these respites, because they were fewer and further between. It was the only way he got any of his strength back . . . to lie here for hours and even days on end . . . to let the fever and the lust recede . . . the memories, so dim and terrible, recede.

He reached over to the nightstand and grabbed the bottle. His hand shook as he unscrewed the cap and took a long swig from the half-empty bottle. It burned and it seared as it went down, but it was a good pain, the type of pain that brings forgetfulness and sleep. He put the bottle to his lips again and drew another long pull of fire into his mouth, rolling it back and forth several times before swallowing. Then he lay there, arms outstretched, something working feebly at the back of his brain: something trying to get through, to tell him, to warn him—no! No more tricks. He wouldn't listen anymore. He'd shut it out this time. This time he'd beat whatever unseen force he was fighting against.

Yet, something was different this time—no commands, no merciless orders. It was a warning. Something was the matter. Danger. His clouded mind struggled to find the meaning, to translate hazy intuitions into thought.

The door flew open and crashed into the wall. Willie sat bolt upright, his eyes staring with fear and surprise. Before him were two men, one crouching, the other standing. Both were aiming revolvers at him. One of them began to talk then, to say something to him, but he couldn't make sense of the words. Already his brain was beginning to boil and bubble, to burn with an unholy light that blotted out all sensations and thoughts save one. He could see that one of them was shouting at him now, but he couldn't hear any better than before. Willie only heard one voice, only one command, only one insistence. Suddenly he felt the strength and the power flow back into him. Suddenly he was indestructible.

One of the men was beside the bed now, and a small part of him saw that there were several men in the room, all shouting angrily or looking grim and hateful. He looked up at the man standing beside the bed holding the revolver only inches away from his face. Then he moved. With lightning speed Willie's arm lashed out and caught the man's wrist. He pulled the man down on top of him. and together they sprawled and struggled on the bed until Willie had one hand around the man's throat, his mighty forearm already crushing into the windpipe with brutal strength.

Willie's other arm snaked under his pillow seeking something long and curved and cold there. He was dimly aware of the uproar in the room, the babble of many voices, but he was still really aware of only one thing: the need to hurt and destroy the lump of flesh that lay trapped in his arm.

But other hands and arms worked on him from behind in wrath and fury. He could feel their blows raining off his back and shoulders and head like small pellets of hail, but they hurt him little in the power that was his. And slowly his hand came to find it and draw around the smooth carved hilt. Others hands were there too now, but with a mighty jerking motion he wrenched his arm free and upward, there to hold the cruel, curved blade for a moment of triumph. Some mind, some will other than his own seemed to make him wait, to pause excruciatingly before the down stroke of steel, but that instant of hesitation was enough to rob him of victory. He felt a flash of sudden pain in his head as heavy metal hit bone and flesh, darkness quickly washed over him.

22

The police hadn't only been unsympathetic; they had been downright hostile. Seeming legions of them had gone out of their way to tell him off about his "stunt" and one of them had gone so far as to threaten to arrest him for breaking and entering. In the end, it was the stout detective he had talked to on the phone the other day who got him off the hook, telling them that it wasn't necessary to arrest someone who, after all, had benefitted them in the performance of their duties.

For that he was certainly grateful, but it did little to diminish his feeling that the police were a lot more concerned that he had invaded their private domain of privilege and responsibility than they were with the fate of Barb or her father. Even when the detective took him aside to explain that they were all a little uptight because of long hours and being constantly yelled at about the recent tragedies in town, Scott's resentment lingered. Even when the portly policeman seemed to be trying to be solicitous and pointed out that Scott could have implicated himself in a death and a possible kidnapping by his actions—at least from a legal point of view, as the detective explained it—he remained unmoved. He didn't like being browbeaten by authority, especially when he thought he was in the right.

And, as far as he was concerned, he was definitely in the right. The police were taking so much static over these recent crimes that they were paranoid about criticism or any indications that they weren't doing their job properly. But if he had waited for them to act, he had no doubt that he would still be in a complete state of limbo—and he would still know nothing about Barb's fate or her father's.

But what to do now? The detective had been considerate enough to inform him yesterday of the coroner's verdict: death due to heart failure. That, apparently, was a mixed blessing. The detective let him know that it was good news for Scott because it probably let him off the hook for any possible involvement in a criminal matter, but that it also reduced police urgency in searching for the girl now that foul play had been ruled out in her father's death. Oh, they would still be looking for her. They would put out bulletins and so forth, but with all that was going on in town they would have to treat it more like a conventional missing person's report. After all, she might have very well decided to go away for a few days on her own, not knowing the unhappy fate that would overtake her father later.

It was then that he almost decided to tell them about the conversation he had had with Barb—about her fears that somehow her and her father's lives were bing drawn into the terrible events that had overtaken the town in the last weeks. At least he might tell this detective—the only one of them who was trying to act human. Surely, they would have to make the search for Barb a priority then.

But he held off at the last moment. How would he explain it? Barb had only given him the vaguest information herself: something about phone calls from a foreign lady and a connection between Barb's long-dead mother and the grisly crimes that had taken place in the town. The police would probably think he was making it up just to get them to look harder for his girlfriend. He tried to put himself in the detective's place for a moment and had to admit that it all sounded hopelessly vague and unconvincing.

But beyond that, he realized he had no confidence in them. It had broken in the newspapers that they had caught the killer of the three women, but there was still nothing definite to connect him to the two kidnappings or the murder of the little boy. Maybe there was another maniac still on the loose out there. Why hadn't they caught him yet?

No, he was being unfair. He knew it. It took time for the best police work to catch up to a crime, and the Oak Grove police were catching up now, judging by the results. What it really amounted to was not wanting to leave Barb's fate in the hands of others who, no matter how competent or well-intentioned, didn't have the same level of personal involvement as he did. Besides, growing up nearly alone, except for Grandma's sparing influence, and two years of surviving combat in Viet Nam had taught him to fend for himself. He didn't feel so helpless, so the police weren't such a necessity.

Or so he told himself. He was long on guts but short on inspiration. Where could he start looking for her? The detective had told him that they'd been over the Brennan house with the proverbial fine-tooth comb and found no clue to Barb's possible whereabouts. They would put a photo out to other departments, interview neighbors and contact relatives, but that would all take time.

Time: He wasn't the panicky type by nature, so why did he feel there was so little time? Why did some inner necessity impel him forward with such haste? What was that about the wheels of justice grinding slowly? He couldn't wait that long.

It was by this line of reasoning—some would say wishful thinking—that he found himself by the back door of the Brennan house again, early that evening. He was letting instinct guide him now, or maybe it was his lack of any alternatives. But it seemed simpler this time. One sharp snap of his wrist, and his palm broke the thin strip of plywood the police had used to cover over the empty window frame in the door. Scott Kearney, accomplished housebreaker, was once more plying his trade.

Inside something seemed different immediately. He played the flashlight off the kitchen walls, heavy shadows reaching out for him. Nothing here seemed out of place. He hoped the police search had been as thorough as it had been orderly.

He stepped out into the front hall, carefully shielding the light so it couldn't be seen from the street. No use in taking chances: If the police caught him in here again, there was no telling what they'd think or do. Still, he sensed some intangible difference about the house from the other day, though the small arc of light did little to uncover it.

Then it dawned on him. He turned the flash onto the giant grandfather clock. It had stopped ticking. There had been no one to wind it, and it had run down, almost as if it had stopped in grief for its departed owner. In its place there was only the leaden, almost sinister silence of the house around him. It corresponded closely to the feeling that was coming to dominate his life these last few days: a shapeless, half-formed sense of loss and empty despair. The brooding silence of the house seemed like some kindred spirit to him now.

But he wasn't here to grieve. He was here to play maybe the only chance he had, however slim. He had realized days ago that he really knew less about Barb's life than he would have imagined after six months of dating her. Her basic insularity extended even to him, and she had never talked much about the private details of her own life.

And there was no one to turn to for advice or information about her either. He remembered her saying that her grandparents were dead now and that her two uncles and one aunt were, in some combination, dead, moved to the Eastern seaboard, and hospitalized for some long-term ailment. He had no vantage points, no mundane links to the daily fabric of her life at all.

Unless he could find some. He walked quietly upstairs to Barb's bedroom, listening all the way. He felt his instincts naturally on guard and wondered if even the most practiced thieves and burglars could ever get over their vague fear at being somewhere they shouldn't be. He knew he wouldn't.

He turned off the flashlight and walked over to the window, pulling closed the shade and drapes. Still, he didn't turn on the overhead light just in case some nosy neighbor might see a glimmer and call the police. Working by flashlight would be slower but safer.

He walked over to the small writing desk by the far wall. Inside was just about everything imaginable: old letters, high-school term papers and book reports, a college mid-term exam that had been graded B, a couple of Christmas cards with men's signatures, vacation brochures, job-training and vocational-guidance folders, scratch paper—everything but what he was looking for. Something pertinent. An address book or a letter with a relative's address. In all this junk you'd think there'd be something he thought unhappily to himself.

Next he went through her dresser and closet. Her clothes had a slightly sweet and fresh odor to them, and he thought wistfully about her for a moment. Carefully he checked each dress, blouse or pair of jeans. All he came up with was a receipt for a pair of shoes and an old grocery list. He sighed and went on, not believing the police had been through all this stuff and been so neat about it. Shit. He'd bet they hadn't done a thing except remove the body.

There was a small table with a drawer in it by her bed. He took the whole drawer out and emptied its few contents on the bed. It was then that he heard it. Switching off the flashlight immediately, he waited in darkness and listened.

The great silence of the house had amplified the sound of the door opening downstairs and brought it to his ears. He judged it to be the front door, and his first thought was that the police had returned for another look around. "Great," he moaned quietly. "Now they decide to do their job."

A dim hint of light wafted up the staircase and into

the hallway outside of Barb's room. Someone had obviously switched on the downstairs light in the hall. He only hoped they weren't coming up here. And if they were—should he try to hide in a closet or something or give himself up? If he was caught hiding, it might even look worse than it did now. Time compressed around him in an agony of indecision. He feared to even move in case he'd make some noise that might reveal his presence. Suddenly, his career as an amateur detective seemed an unwise choice.

But, then, a reprieve. It came in the form of a thin but unmistakable fragment of sound that penetrated the upper floor of the house in its note of anger and disgust. A voice: "Ach! Where did I put it?"

Even from this distance, he knew it was a woman's voice—low and guttural but definitely a woman's voice. That didn't exclude the cops, but it made it less likely. A lot less. Maybe it was an aunt, someone he could talk to and get some information about Barb from. But how did he approach her without scaring her half to death or compelling her to call the police herself? He had no business being here.

Then it hit him. The woman's voice—thickly accented, foreign sounding. Barb had said that the unknown woman on the phone had sounded foreign. Maybe she had no more business here than he did. Maybe she had less.

He crept out of the room and down the hall to the top of the staircase, thanking the solid construction of the house for the absence of any loud groans or squeaks that would give him away. From this vantage point he could see the front hall; he could see the light on and another light on in the adjoining living room that was just out of sight. But he could hear someone moving around in the room and after what seemed like hours but was probably only seconds, he heard the voice again.

This time it was clearer, the heavy accent unmistakable. "He will kill me for certain if I don't find it."

All doubts were gone. Whatever that meant, it indicated that the unknown woman was here for no good purpose, probably for something she'd failed to get on an earlier visit. Maybe it was something she was afraid the police would find, something that would incriminate her in Barb's disappearance or the death of her father. He felt less like a stranger in the house then.

He barely had time to duck back around the edge of the bannister as he saw the large, stout figure of the woman emerge from the living room, saw her head begin to turn in the direction of the upstairs landing where he stood. But he had moved into darkness and out of the line of sight quickly enough. There was no cry of shock or alarm from the hall below.

He listened. If he heard footsteps coming upstairs he would retreat into one of the bedrooms and into a closet. This was his chance, the sudden stroke of good fortune that had probably been his only chance all along. Even now the idea of hiding in a closet seemed comical to him, but it would provide time to think. Should he corner her and try to force information from her? Should he detain her and call the police?

He had no time to decide. The light snapped off downstairs and a moment later he heard the massive front door close with a thud. God! She was getting away. His one chance to find Barb, and she was getting away!

He raced down the stairs, nearly tripping and falling head over heels in the darkness. Never hesitating, he turned the corner into the kitchen and in seconds was at the back door again. By the time he was outside and around the front corner of the house, he could see the frumpy outline of the woman getting into a car parked a few houses down on the street.

But it was dark and difficult to see the car well in the dim glimmer of the street light a good twenty yards away. He felt helpless as he observed his own car where he had parked it at the end of the block so as not to arouse any curious neighbors. If he waited for her to leave, by the time he got to it, she'd be a mile away. If he started running for it now, she'd be sure to see him. If he could only see her license plate number.

But the old car began to pull away, before he could decide on what to do. It was halfway up the block, before he instinctively began running toward his own car, and it had already turned the corner before he'd reached it. Despair, utter total hopelessness, seized him then, and it was only the days of bafflement, frustration and anger that impelled him on. The old Chevy came to life, and he watched the trees and houses gradually gather speed around him as he moved up the block. At least he would try.

She had turned left, but he knew a half block down she had three choices: continue straight on Leona or turn north or south on Nageland. Would he still be able to see her, or would she be swallowed up forever into a night of everlasting remorse? As twice before that he remembered, both times in Viet Nam, hope turned to prayer.

But too many years of estrangement from his Creator had apparently been taken to account. Coming to Nageland, he saw no sign of another car. He pounded the steering wheel then, wanting to maim and hurt something—anything. Tiredness and confusion grappled with him, and the feeling of hopelessness increased until it was a dull ache in the pit of his stomach.

But he drove on, deciding who knows why to keep straight. Two blocks speeded by and another. He hoped he didn't crash into somebody at an intersection, but now was no time for caution. The old Chevy hit fifty as he threw hasty glances down side streets as they passed fleetingly by.

He hit the brakes, and the car squealed to a stop. Backing it up, he turned at the corner of Fair Tree and headed south. A block ahead of him or more he could make out tail lights—small, round amber-colored tail lights like those he had observed on the car the foreign woman had been driving. Hope was renewed, and he took in a great breath.

He slowed down as the intervening distance between

them diminished. No use in alarming her and ruining the whole pursuit. Still, he had to hurry, on the chance it might not be her. His life seemed filled with so many do-or-die decisions the last few days. He came to a stop sign just as she turned right at the next corner ahead. As the other car rounded the corner, it came fully under the nebulous glow of a street lamp. It was just enough illumination to definitely identify it as the same car—maybe an Olds or Pontiac from the 1950's. "What a relic," he whispered to himself happily. "You couldn't miss that thing in a parking lot full of cars."

He speeded up and was just in time to see the old car pull into one of the alleys than ran in back of all the big houses in this part of town. He guided the car around the corner and moved slowly up the block, though not so slowly as to attract attention to himself. As he moved past the alley he saw the old car pull into the third garage down. That was it!

He turned right at the next corner, suddenly elated. From here it would be simple. He would leave his car at the end of the block, hike back around down Fair Tree and find the third house from the corner. Then he would know where the mysterious lady apparently lived, and then he would know more—hopefully—about where to find Barb.

He had to restrain himself from running all the way. It wasn't worth attracting attention to himself now, and he knew that many nervous citizens still kept a wary lookout outdoors in this town at night. So, he walked, the cool autumn air bracing him as gaunt, almost barren tree limbs whistled ominously over and about him in the late evening breeze. He walked, his heart grown warm again in new found faith that all might end well after all, and he gave little thought to the perils that might still lie ahead.

But at last he came to it, and he felt the night chill creep into him a little then. Amidst a block of vast and stately Victorian homes, it was set far back on a huge, tree strewn lot and was probably the largest of all. Even in the near total darkness it leered out at him, a twisting, arching maze of wings, gables and bays that heaved themselves upward toward a distended and seemingly top-heavy third story where the house's bulk seemed intent on swallowing the very sky.

He looked at it for a long while. It was the kind of house that many would, no doubt, find magnificent and grand. But to him, under these conditions, it looked insolent and foreboding, with unkempt trees spreading their branches about aimlessly along great expanses of peeling board and batten and under long stretches of sagging eaves. The yard was piled with great undulating mounds of unraked leaves, and even in the blackness of night the house had about it the look and feel of neglect and decay.

He waited for a while under the protective cover of a maple tree in the parkway across the street from the vast, looming house. A few solitary leaves rattled above him; as if in warning, and he knew it wouldn't be safe to stay here long. But he had to decide what to do next. His mind was a jumble of conflicting feelings and thoughts as he saw a light go on in the darkened mass of the huge house. Moments later another light appeared from behind drawn shades on the second floor of the house, only to go off again almost immediately. This had to be it.

A long way down, he could see the headlights of a car approaching. He couldn't just stand here forever; everybody was still too suspicious around town. Setting off quickly across the street, he came to the curb before the house. Bending down, he could just make out the faded numbers painted on the curbing: 714. From here he walked down to the end of the block and around until he came to the alley. With a hasty glance in either direction, he made his way at a quick lope to the third garage. From here he could see the distant bulk of the house's rear looming grimly near. All was quiet save for the slight breeze pushing about the dead leaves in the yard. One look through a window set in the garage door and he was sure: It was the old car. Swiftly he made his way back to his own car and drove away into the embracing night.

23

Winds of time and endless change carried her down the long tunnel of oblivion. It was a dark and vaulted place, endlessly winding, and she was pushed along by some unseen force through the towering, mouldering gothic arches, past great broken windows through which no light could be seen and along cold and fetid passageways leading endlessly nowhere . . . nowhere.

She struggled to right herself in that twisting, turning labyrinth of dark corridors and endless spaces, but her body was prisoner as she floated and tumbled her way unceasingly through this grim and hopeless landscape of diseased and ruined magnificence. Sometimes she would just swoon and let herself be carried along by the unseen hands that guided her, but she found that to be hazardous because it was then that things lurking in the dim background would grow bolder and venture closer. Once she had opened her eyes only to look into a shapeless clot of darkness that hovered and undulated above her, its pale whitish lanterns of eyes greedily devouring her in their milkish horror. Once something had grabbed at her as she sped along through a particularly dark and dank stretch of what must have been a long and lightless tunnel. It had grabbed and nipped at her and panted in dog-like fashion, but she knew it was no dog. She knew that it was nothing the light would look upon with friendliness, for it was not meant by human eyes to be seen.

Then, at other times, nothing. The sudden aloneness, the all-encompassing sightlessness and soundlessness that, at first, was so comforting and peaceful. No strange and murky images intruded there. No frightening sights or sounds. There was just the cocoon, the thick, soft envelopment by nothingness where nothing was seen, felt, heard, nor smelled. Nothing. The quiet became so heavy that it was a noise unto itself. She could not move, could not speak, could only know the nothingness of which there is nothing to know. All was quiet; all was empty. The great void had surrounded her, captured her in its blank embrace.

But the comfort and serenity were short-lived. Emptiness is filling to too few. Silence soon becomes a shrieking cacophony of demon slur. The mind hungers. The body craves. She was entombed, buried in vast and cavernous palls of alien space where none would ever find her, where none would ever look. A breakneck of rocks, the cry of the lonely loon . . . the tangled limbs of the empty tree, the dull plop of fallen fruit . . . the soft blur of swift run clouds, the white froth of far flung and eternal sea . . . geese and choir boys, days and nights and the brooding church steeple—all were gone. In their place? The motionless limb, the shackled soul, the hidden spirit, the awful growing sickness of madness, death and despair.

The fiery gull wheels and turns overhead. Grim, black-robed strangers stalk from below. Woman is born of sea, and the heron stabs in the dark. All these things are vivid and have the lust of reality. The moment of contact is complete; it leaves only sorrow and the deep malaise of the soul no longer innocent. The spirit lives that has seen corruption grow and magnify until it is mountain and legion in one—until the whole universe shudders that it might spawn such a thing of blight.

Then, sweet winters of time laughing. Something that is the sum or essence of her comes back again into the sweetness and light. It dims and ebbs and flows . . . convoluted currents of form and time that bring her to a slow and uncertain new perception: wistful, drifting, seen from a distance but somehow more substantial.

Her eyes try to focus. Her mind tries to remember.

What seemed to be her moments of wakefulness were not determined by their apparent reality or coherence but by their banality. There is the impression that she is made to eat occasionally. More recognizable is the sensation of being forced to drink something steamy and pungent tasting. It was then that she would feel most alive. First, there would be the gradual seeping warmth stealing into her body until every muscle and bone was alive with it. This lazy, almost delicious feeling of heat would slowly build until it became a fever, a frenzy, a boiling, formless lust. Her mind would spin and reel with a thousand strange images; her body would burn with a thousand nameless and unsatisfied needs.

But gradually the fever would subside, the life would go out of her again, and she would be left feeling terribly helpless, cold and alone—the hollow clattering of her teeth sounding like some alien litany of destruction and despair. Then she would again slide down into the tunnel of eternal nothingness. Then she was a vacuum, an emptiness; she was an empty receptacle waiting only to be filled and too weak and lost to care how or with what she was filled. Anything was better than this formless, shapeless non-existence that knew no reason to continue.

So she waited for those infrequent moments of greater clarity when the gray room would take dim shape around her, when the shrill bleat of an automobile horn or the concentrated energy of rain falling on the roof above would bring her to recognition or when the stout, stolid form of the woman would appear before her with food or some of the hot, herbaceous broth. These were the moments of her existence, the fleeting specks of time when she clung to her identity and reason.

So there came a time when she seemed to wake from the endless oblivion, the gray room with the oddly sloping wall slowly taking form around her. She lay for a long time, motionless and not wishing any effort to push her back into the numbing clutch of mindless slumber. She lay there passively, and she fought to keep awake.

In some further passing moment she became aware of the presence. There was no sound, no movement to alert her, but it was there. It seemed to pull her from her misty oblivion, to grow and swell all around her. Elusive, intangible and yet overwhelmingly real, it struck at the center core of her with more immediacy than she could remember ever feeling. With languid effort she lolled her head to one side.

Dim shadow and splotches of amorphous light took shape before her. She could actually feel her brow furrow slightly as she strained her eyes to see. With infinite lassitude the sight took shape before her eyes.

There were folds of gray cloth that interpenetrated the gray walls of the room. From deep, billowing sleeves of it protruded two long and gnarled, spider-thin hands. One finger, snakelike, seemed to coil and unwind in beckoning to her.

Her eyes moved up to a face. It was a very old face. She looked blankly at it for a moment, trying to absorb meaning and significance from those features. Her faculties moved with torturous slowness, but gradually impressions began to seep past the fog of her mind and take hold. It was then that she first began to hunger for the sleep again.

It was a face that reeked of age, that was beyond all age. A face that spoke horribly of years and years and years of a life that had not been gracious or light: a mask dredged up from some insane and forgotten time when mankind's life on this planet was steeped in terrible hardship and awful mystery. Something rapine and vicious, something animal and infinitely cunning lay among those folds of tired and cracked skin and mouldering flesh. She felt her eyes blink in disbelief.

But there was no escaping that nightmare spectacle, indeed there was almost a fatal fascination in it for her, like the cobra with its prey. Her eyes moved over skin hanging loosely from sallow jowls. The great domed head was bumpy and hairless except for a few long, wild white strands that grew in aimless confusion about that mottled and craggy skull. The total impressions of that face was one of impossible age, of dry and barren skin covering an underlying rot that manifested itself in deeper yellowish patches that were found here and there in the spidery gullies and crevices of abused flesh.

But the eyes were the strangest and worse part of all. They danced and lived with an unholy energy that bespoke boundless youth, and in those deep, red-rimmed hollows lay a towering malignancy, a predatory and pitiless evil that smote her like a massive open hand. They were all cunning and dark lust—great pig eyes, smouldering with hatred.

They gleamed and changed before her, like some weird prism of feeling and color. Some lofty, Olympian detachment came into those twin hellish orbs until a demonic power filled the bottomless wells that hid ageless, immemorial secrets of life and time. She felt herself being swallowed by them, sucked up by their smoking, fatal fascination.

From somewhere deep inside she summoned a dim energy. It emerged as a bare whisper from her parched lips, but they were the first words she had spoke in aeons: "Who are you?"

Moments of vast silence. The great eyes slumbered. Whether the content or form of that reply was worse, she didn't know. It came as an awful gasp, a hideous wheezing croak of a sound welling out of that ancient throat: "Your grandfather."

She wanted to laugh at the insanity of it. She had known her grandfather too well . . .

The awful croaking voice anticipated her doubts. "Your *mother's* father."

It took a moment to register, but something from outside of her, some unseen force, seemed to be pushing images into her mind. She could feel the dull, clouded seat of her mind begin to open like a flower. Then she could see the ghostly pictures of her mother float before her mind's eye—her mother in that last moment of drunken, demented hopelessness raving like a wild beast against the white restraints that bound her. She could see the grave faces of nurses and doctors, looking solemn and caring not at all. She could see pain and despair in her father's tearful eyes—a pain that said: From this moment I am dead. She saw it all as if she had really been there.

Still, she thought the very idea. "Mother always said," she began but coughed a deep, liquid cough of dull pain, "said that . . . her parents had died . . . she had no family." Her wonder now was greater than the great lassitude that consumed her. .

Withered lips turned upward in a leering grin of lecherous and impossible evil, a macabre expression that betrayed yellowed and rotting teeth. "She would have had it so," the awful voice cackled obscenely, "for I was more than father to her." The hellish eyes here lit momentarily with a lustful rememberance that she could not bear. The meaning of those words were too evident to her, even in her present state.

"Who are you?" she said with as much volume and fury as her voice would carry. "Why am I here?" She felt the deep well of fear opening somewhere beneath her now.

"I am one who has sought and found power," he said matter-of-factly, as if his first answer to that question had never been stated. The voice was like a hideous barking now and then sibilant, like the hiss of a thousand adders. Always it was ugly. Every word breathed death upon a world of beauty and light. "You are here because you have been promised to me."

Her panic and anger had drained her in moments. She barely whispered, barely felt her reply. "Promised? How? Who?"

There was another crackle of awful glee. "Why, yoiur mother, child. She promised you before you were born, before you had taken seed in her, before your father had even known her. From the first you were promised to me."

She shook her head, not believing or fully comprehending. She struggled to find words, but her mind seemed a churning maelstrom of conflicting thoughts. And . . . the weakness was so great.

The withered old man who sat before her waited silently, for nearly an eternity. But then that harsh, guttural croaking started again, like some ghastly chorus of doom. "Yes, promised to me. As is fitting. In the great wheel of life, it was I who originated you, through your mother. Before you were ever conceived in her body through your father's agency, it was I who conceived of you in my mind. You, my beautiful child, may not understand or believe this, but it is important that you try . . . try, if your death is to have meaning to you."

She forced her voice to work. "My death? Oh, God this is some awful joke—no, a dream! It must be. You say you are my grandfather—"

He raised one gnarled hand aloft, the gray robe falling back from an impossibly thin and reedy arm. The fingers clutched the air like the convulsive grip of some great poisonous spider. "You will be quiet!" He spat the words at her, and the luminous eyes smouldered with an awful malevolence for a moment.

But they subsided, and the leering smile returned. "The herbs, my pet. You mustn't fight them. I have decreased the required dosage only long enough so that we can have this nice little talk. Soon you will be in slumber again. Soon you will be prepared."

She wanted to know what she was being prepared for, wanted to ask, but his eyes warned her not to.

"You see, my glorious child, it is difficult for me to speak, too. I am not used to using this voice much anymore, for I have no one to talk to except for the woman, and she is a woman, thankfully, of few words. So, let me do the talking for both of us. I will be brief."

He looked at her, capturing her eyes in his own. Everything about him was rotting, impossibly aged, dying. All except those eyes, and the light of life they contained was an unholy one. "You see, precious one," he began, "I have lived for a long while now. Great spans and ages of time have seen my breath, and I have cheated that jealous handmaiden of oblivion . . . cheated it with my mind." Here a throaty, awful chortling sound escaped that ancient throat. "Yes, my pet, though this body has long since wanted to slumber in the ground, my mind, which is me, would not let it be so. I have fought on."

He paused here, as if momentarily spent of energy. The domed skull shook from side to side sadly. "But each day it is a greater burden. Each rising sun finds more of my mind's energy drawn to the task of keeping this body alive, and it has been so for what to you has been a whole lifetime—and more." The voice was rising now, rising into a shrill, hissing crescendo. "Thirty years I have waited for you to come to the right time: the time when your mind and body would converge with the fathomless tides of the universe—the time of transformation!"

Energy born of desperation. She fought the dead weight of her body, the near paralysis of her vocal chords. "You insane old man!" she cried out. "I believe you are my mother's father, because she was insane, too. I believed she promised you something—me—for whatever stupid, crazy purpose you wanted. She was diseased. And you are, too!" She burst into tears here, a deep convulsive sobbing that stemmed from the innermost heart of her. Violently she jerked her head away from the awful sight before her and turned it toward a comfortung expanse of dull gray wall. How had she come to this? Was she ending, like her mother, dying in some horrid nightmare world of inner delusion and torment? Were the doctors and Daddy standing around her even now, looking grave and helpless? God, she needed help now! Wouldn't someone help free her from this nightmare?! "Daddy, help! Oh, Father, help me now!" she cried as best she could.

Something grabbed her wrist, and suddenly her hand lay in something dry and rough that felt like old parchment or the skin of a snake. Fearing to look, she forced her head around with a shudder. The terrible old man was standing beside her now, his long gnarled fingers, like withered roots, caressing her palm and the back of her hand. The thumb and little finger of that clawlike appendage circled around her wrist in an amazingly powerful grip—the grip of the spider clinging to its prey.

And as those hoary fingers continued rhythmically to rub and nuzzle and paw against the soft flesh of her hand, the terrible voice began again, this time soft and horridly purring in seeming reassurance. "No fear, my prized one. No fear. There is no one else to look after you now, but me, and you are too valuable to me to misplace." Here the awful chortling noise again, a sound of insane delight. "No one else, precious one. All gone. Your mother tried to resist my will and her promise, but I made her pay. Oh, yes. She paid dearly, and still you are mine. And your father that you call on for help? He too has paid for his interference. He was the unwitting agency of my will, so I wished to spare him, to give him free choice. But he wouldn't give you up either. He vowed to protect you, and we couldn't have that, could we? No, do not call for your father. I had Shalak, my trusty pet, pay him a visit. I'm afraid, and even now he lies stinking in the ground."

The wail that broke from her lips was the cry of the damned and uncaring. She tried to shut out the numbing, searing, portent of those words, but it was as if something more than that horrid voice carried them. It was as if they were being directly burned into her mind by a titanic and obscene will. There was no escape.

It started again. "Yes, fair one, there can be no opposition. For year's your mother sought to hide her origins from the world, as if ashamed of such a great legacy. But that suited my purposes, so it was let be. But, she tried to oppose me by refusing you birth, and, when you were finally born, she sought to protect you—not from love but opposition to me." His laugh was long and terrible, like some hideous cacophony of animal sound. "And look, my precious, at how it ended for her. So it ended for your father. I would have spared him, for it was his seed that brought you into the world.

But he would not give the gift, and his years of pain and humiliation at the hands of my daughter prevented him from seeking any help—help that would have been useless anyway. You see, fair one, it was he who dug his own grave."

She heard the slight, wheezing chuckle and turned to face him, conquering her tears and her loathing at the touch of his hand. Something deep inside of her had temporarily gone deadly calm—a calm born of hopeless despair at the loss of all she loved. "What are you going to do with me, then?"

The ancient figure dropped her hand and moved back a step or two. He was so thin, so insubstantial, like a scarecrow, all straw and bindings under the long, formless robe. Again she could see that it was only in the eyes that there was life. But no love dwelled there. Of this she was sure.

His reedy arms were suddenly aloft, as in supplication or exaltation. A thin, barely audible cackle broke from that dustly slash of a mouth, but quickly it was raised to a hollow, unearthly, piercing wail—a shrill, resounding dragon cry of glee and triumph. The walls of the room reverberated with it, and the universe seemed to swell and contract around her as the sheer volume and intensity of that beastly howl of foul ecstasy grew beyond all endurance. Her ears burned then with a thousand horrors and lamentations, her body and mind encompassing this sound of infinite suggestiveness bespeaking the furthest limits of joy, pain, hope and loss.

And then the gradual tapering off of that torturous, rending noise as the ancient shrunken chest convulsed and hoary lips greedily lapped at the air. But in her now was only loss and an infinite confusion. The words that tumbled out of that age-old throat and into her brain were only dimly recognized, to be resurrected later into a form of terrible portent and a malignancy that knew no mercy.

But it was not these strange elliptical mutterings and convoluted ramblings that brought her, finally, to the edge of near madness, because she understood little of it. No, it was the final assault of envenomed words that undid her, for the awful voice told her that she was to have a central place in this grand design, for she was the balance point, the fulcrum, and the crucible. Into her mind and body would flow and play forces of darkest potency and understanding. Into her very soul would descend the maelstrom of the dark side of life itself. It was to be a mass, a celebration, a convening, a gathering of enormous energy, a conflagration. Soon it would happen. She would be purified and made ready and soon it would be the night . . . the night of the Varleth. Then she would be abandoned and give up her life so gladly to the dark force that consumed her. The last thing she remembered before the darkness overtook her again was the sound of the scream in her own throat.

24

Willie awoke gradually, his mind rolling slowly together like so many loose cords that can only be reconnected slowly, one by one. He had been in a long corridor, an endless passage with many doors, but all had been shut against him until now. He remembered the feeling of having struggled to regain consciousness and the feeling of being entombed in his own body. Many thoughts contested for his attention in those first moments of wakefulness, but none were very clear.

He tried to move his body but found that he couldn't. A stabbing pain went through his head whenever he tried to turn it, and he quickly gave up trying to do anything at all. He lay there, barely conscious, trying to make out the vague sounds and motions around him, but his mind wouldn't cooperate. Thoughts would begin to form then quickly evaporated before he could make any sense of them. Once or twice he remembered seeing people with some clarity: a woman dressed all in white and a man who sat by his bed and talked to him. But these impressions just got jumbled and lost with the others.

Somehow Willie was aware that he was a prisoner, but in just what way he didn't know. It hurt so much to move, so he didn't try much. But the few times he did there was no result. He thought he could feel muscles strain and pull, but his body seemed somehow far away; and dissociated from the commands he gave it. This should have frightened him, but his brain was too busy with other things to pay any attention to the fears of his body. It was trying to put the pieces back together again.

Gradually, he became more aware of the people who would periodically appear, do something to him and disappear again. Sometimes he would will his eyes to open, and the blurred and indistinct silhouettes of men and women would loom above and around him; but inevitably the eyes would fall shut again, and the delicious darkness would overtake him. Occasionally, voices would also intrude, and sometimes he thought they were speaking about him. Only the heavy, harried looking man with the sagging jowls ever seemed to speak directly *to* him. He would listen when he felt up to it. He would strain to hear and understand, but all he could really hear were odd noises and unintelligible gibberish. Sleep was his only recourse and his only haven.

But even this refuge was a temporary one, because Willie began to dream: to relive the same horrid nightmares he had had before. There was the menacing slumped figure cloaked in black, and there was the thing that moved behind that figure, always in the shadows but somehow always getting nearer and closer. And there were the faces: empty-eyed and soulless faces of women that stared at him with accusation and malice—faces that were splattered with blood and gore and seemed to melt magically into his own. And always there was the burning. Even in his dreams, there was the burning and the lust at the back of his head that struggled to gnaw at and consume him. Sometimes he would wake in terror from one of these dreams, his body straining terribly to sit up, but still he could not move, and the pain in his head would become unbearable, persisting long after his struggles had ceased.

Once he woke to the sound of his own wild, terrified screams, and soon the dim faces were around him again, and he shouted at and pleaded with them. But he wasn't able to understand even his own words, and eventually he fell to whimpering softly in dumb self-pity.

It was aeons later that the end came. He had been sleeping restlessly, plagued by the dream of the horrid, menacing figure and its nightmare companion in the shadows, that crawling, bloated terror coming almost out of the misty blackness that mercifully surrounded it. It had seemed about to leap at him out of the darkness when he awoke with a violent start.

Willie looked around. His head throbbed dully, but he was fully aware of his surroundings for the first time. The room was dark, but he could see the baleful light of a full moon gleaming spectrally through the window. The curtains had not been drawn, and the milky light etched the contents of the room in a fine silver light. Moving his head slowly, he could see the empty bed next to him and the pulley devices attached to it. To his other side, there was a closed door, and next to his bed was a table with electrical equipment of some kind on it. The green and red lights winked and changed before his eyes like some grotesque toy. There was the smell of disinfectant about the room. There was the feeling of the slaughter house.

He went to raise his arm, but again there was no result. He tried to move his leg with similar lack of success. A sudden anger welled up in him then, and with a herculean effort he managed to raise his head up a few inches and stare forward down the white sheeted slope of his body. He was just able to discern the three darker bands that ran across the stark white of the sheet, before the wracking pain forced him to drop his head back to the pillow beneath him.

Bound! He was strapped and bound to the bed like some hog being readied for the butcher shop. He moaned softly then, a helpless animal caught in a trap, but he immediately fell to thinking about his situation. He realized that his mind was suddenly working again, that the thoughts were coming in orderly sequential series like they hadn't since before he could last remember. He was alive again—he had a chance again. Now the worst was over, because at least he could play the game.

Willie smiled. It was the smile of a man rescued from the desert, the smile of a man with a last minute reprieve from the electric chair. It was the smile of new hopes and future dreams. In the joy and satisfaction of that moment, Willie hardly heard the small scrabbling sound from the direction of the moonlit window. It was with an absent and unexpecting mind that he idly turned his bandaged head toward the odd rustling noise. He was just in time to see the front legs come through the window. Then the huge, bloated body, all shiny and inky black, came through the glass and plopped obscenely onto the floor and out of sight. It was the thing out of the shadows—the thing from his dreams!

Willie screamed with a volume and a pitch of pure terror. But he had screamed before, and the nurses were slow to respond this time around. By the time anybody got to the room, the horrid black eightlegged thing the size of a large dog had already climbed up the end of the bed, over his imprisoned body and onto the face of the helpless man where it seemed to lift and drop and pulse and quiver its grotesquely distended body for a long while. By the time the nurse finally opened the door and turned on the light, it had already gone back out through the window and into the depths of the night.

Harry woke to the insistent ringing of the phone at a little after one in the morning. He had been sleeping soundly for the first time in weeks, and he lay there for what seemed like a long time trying to convince himself not to answer it. Any call before morning was automatically bad news, and he had thought the bad news was over.

He looked over at Grace. She was sleeping soundly beside him, the covers pulled up around her ears. That woman. She would probably sleep through the Second Coming. But it didn't matter. Even if she had heard the phone, she would never get up and answer it. The call wasn't for her, after all.

Finally, he summoned up the will and the energy to stagger into the front hall. Dammit. Why hadn't he ever got a phone for the bedroom? It would be a hell of a lot more convenient when he got these midnight messages from Frank Elliot. Besides, he'd have the additional satisfaction of knowing that a phone in the bedroom would be bound to wake up Grace. That would be worth the extra expense by itself.

"Hello," he muttered sleepily as he plucked the noisy instrument from its cradle, "Oronski." He might as well sound official. It was no social call at this hour.

"Hello, this is Dr. Haffler from Oak Grove Hospital, Sergeant. I'm sorry to bother you so late—"

"Early," Harry corrected as he looked at his watch.

"Well, yes. Early," the voice chuckled on the other end. "But I thought you'd want to know. The patient that was brought in the other day, a William Malone—well, he passed away about an hour ago. You mentioned to me the other day when you were here that you wanted to be informed about any change in his condition."

"Yeah, well that certainly is a change, Doc." Harry grumbled. "What did he die from? I mean, I know he had a skull fracture, but you told me he was in no immediate danger, if I remember correctly."

"He wasn't. Not of dying at any rate. I can only speculate about any cause of death at this point, but it was apparently related to a hysterical condition of some sort."

"What do you mean 'hysterical,' Doctor?"

"Well, you know how he had screamed and struggled against the restraining straps sometimes. Apparently, he was screaming just before the nurse on duty found him. That type of extreme stress could have caused an embolism—he was already in pretty bad shape from that blow on the head. Ordinarily we would just sedate him, but this time we were too late."

"I understand, Doctor, and I appreciate your calling."

"That's quite all right. Gave me a chance to catch a quick smoke."

"Good enough—oh, say. Could you let me know what the official cause of death is once you find out?"

"Sure, I'll be glad to do that, Sergeant. Good night."

"Night," said Harry. "Thanks again."

Harry hung up, sighing as he went back into the kitchen only to reemerge in robe and slippers. No use in trying to sleep now. The call had gotten his blood boiling with this whole thing again, and there would be no real rest until he had it solved to his satisfaction. There were too many missing pieces.

Going into the living room, he sat down heavily at the desk. A small cassette recorder still sat on top of the great pile of dog-eared papers on the desk. He switched it on and listened to the hiss of the cassette as it spooled itself onto the reel. Suddenly it began: the long, frightening series of barbaric groans and moans—animal sounds, barely human, they were the auditory manifestations of human pain and confusion drawn to intolerable levels. Grace had shuddered visibly the first time he had played it, and left the room.

But he had played it again and again that night and every night since. Mostly there were only disjointed phrases and meaningless words interspersed with the awful inhuman sounds of misery. And those sounds and bleatings and terrible cries disturbed him more than he wanted to admit.

But something was wrong. Despite the fact that the case was all but officially closed, despite the fact that Janet Johnson had already identified a picture of Willie Malone, despite recovering the undoubted murder weapon itself in that dingy Chicago apartment where they had cornered the big black man, something was wrong. Something made him listen again and again to the insane ravings of this psychopath with a caved-in skull—a psychopath who even now was on his way to the morgue.

Harry rewound the tape and played it again. As he listened, he copied down the intelligible words that surfaced over and over in the almost forty-five minutes of babblings that he had recorded the second day of his attempted interrogation of the huge Negro. It would probably have to serve as his last will and testament, the sole legacy of a three time murderer.

But what to make of it? He looked at the hastily scrawled list before him: "fair tree," "just gonna move some boxes," "the burning eyes," "gave me the knife," "old, old man and the thing in the basement," and "didn't mean to . . . didn't want to do it" were constantly repeated in one form or another throughout the tape. Except for some adjectives that described great horror and revulsion, these were the only intelligible words he could hear. Harry had played with those words in his mind hundreds of times, turning them back and forth in every conceivable fashion; they still didn't make any sense. He couldn't tie them into the kidnappings or the murder of the little Watson boy in any logical way, and they were probably only the last ramblings of a demented mind.

So why did they bug him? Was he going to be like the guy in *Citizen Kane*, looking for "Rosebud" all his life? Elliot was all too willing to put the rap for the kidnappings and the child's murder on the dead black. That way he solved two cases at once. But what if there was still another crazy out there? What if a week or a month from now they found another child suddenly missing? And the little girl, she was still missing. What if she were alive somewhere, starving in a lonely cellar or attic? Harry had tried to talk to the killer even in his delirium in hopes of getting some information about the missing girl, but all he had done was continue to curse and moan and carry on like a totally demented soul.

But something told him that wasn't that was wrong. Some instinct that even lousy cops must get told him what Willie Malone hadn't had anything to do with the kidnappings or the murder of the Watson boy, that the disjointed ramblings of the black were important, but in some other way. If only he could find the key.

He looked once more at the sheet of paper before him. Fair tree, fair tree. That just had to be Fair Tree Street than ran north from Water Street up to North Avenue. None of the murders they pinned and Willie Malone had been within two miles of there, but the Watson boy had been found only three blocks west of

Fair Tree about six hundred north while the Ritter girl had been kidnapped four blocks east of Fair Tree and eight hundred north. Definitely a correlation by location in the two kidnappings, but then everybody expected there would be. Yes, superficially the dead man's ranting about Fair Tree would seem to link him to the abductions, except for one fact: He had murdered the three women on the *south* side of town; the kidnappings had occurred on the *north* side. That didn't fit the illogical pattern that psychos usually followed from start to finish. Each murder had involved a woman, each woman had been slashed from behind with a knife, apparently the same knife. There was a continuity, an orderly progression. But not with the others, the kidnappings. Even the crime itself was different.

But this speculation didn't help him figure out the real significance of Fair Tree Street, if any. And what about that bit about "moving boxes"? Moving what boxes and where? Moving boxes on Fair Tree . . . to Fair Tree? Harry had checked out Willie Malone's employment history, such as it was. There was no turn as a moving man, unless he'd done some free-lance work. Well, what else? Maybe he'd done some odd jobs for someone on Fair Tree. But for whom and when? And what the hell did "burning eyes" have to do with it all? He should just admit it: This was going nowhere fast. About the only definite thing he had was the knife—that very unusual knife with the engraved blade and the very ornate black wood handle that had been carved into the shape of a snake. It wasn't exactly your everyday, run-of-the-mill pocket knife, and the department had turned it over to some museum for identification. A big help. It was at least seven hundred and fifty years old, and the engravings on the blade were Egyptian hieroglyphics, but the knife wasn't particularly valuable in artistic or monetary terms. Harry was still waiting for the translation of the hieroglyphics. Now if he could just find a very old Egyptian who lived on Fair Tree . . .

He laughed at his own whimsicality. Shit. He should

have figured all this out by now—if indeed there was anything to figure out. Maybe he was just trying to find something that wasn't there. Maybe he really did want to enhance his reputation—to give Frank Elliot his comeuppance. He'd get a lot more sleep if he admitted to himself that the dead man's ravings had been just that: ravings. There was nothing rational or coherent about "burning eyes" and an "old man with a *thing* in the basement." Not unless they symbolized something else. Somthing that could be bound on Fair Tree? What could "burning eyes" represent? Street lights?

Hell. It was a lot easier chasing down the kids pushing nickel bags. A little action now and then was fine, but all this strain on his brain was an unaccustomed hardship. His natural mental indolence contested with his desire to see all the loose ends tied up. He sat there, his brain flirting with a thousand half-formed images and thoughts. Finally he came to a decision. Getting up, he turned off the living room light and quietly stole back into the bedroom. He was dressed in a matter of minutes, and soon he was creeping out into the cold night air like some nocturnal and furtive creature of prey.

25

"So, you're gonna call the police, right?"

Scott looked at the burly young man sitting across from him. "If I was sure of that, Dave, I wouldn't have asked you three over here."

Dave shook his head vigorously. "It's no good, Scott. I mean, God knows we all feel awful about your girl and her father, but it's a police matter, pure and simple. Frankly, I can't believe you've waited even a day. That time could make all the difference."

Scott looked at them all, trying to gauge their reactions. Dave was clearly the most skeptical, Lenny, as always, looked worried but willing, and Larry—well, he was always ready for anything. They had been through so much together in Viet Nam that he knew them all almost as well as he knew himself. There they had depended on their closeness as a group for their lives; he knew he had to appeal to those same instincts now if he was to get their help.

"Listen fellows," he began, "my first thought last night was to go right to the cops. I even started driving to the police station, but luckily I started thinking about it first. What was I going to tell them? I came up with some pretty disconcerting answers. First of all, I'd have to tell them I was back in Barb's house again—"

"You could just tell them you were driving by to check the place out, maybe hoping Barb had come back or something," Dave interrupted hopefully.

It was obvious Dave wanted no part of this. "Come on," Scott said with a little irritation seeping into his voice, "and tell them what: that I'd seen this lady—"

"Leaving the house," Dave continued for him. "Yeah, what business did some strange lady have in the house of someone who just died or disappeared? So, you followed her to this other place, and now you think the cops should check it out—you know, just in case it's got something to do with Barb's disappearance."

Lenny nodded ruefully. "It does sort of make sense, Scott. You wouldn't have to tell them you were in the house. Besides, what could they do to you, and you can't let the thought of some minor police charge stand in the way of finding Barb, can you?"

For a moment Scott hated Lenny or, rather, hated his logic. He had let precious hours slip by, all because of his reluctance to let the police do their job. "But what if the police raid the place or something and don't find anything? What if that woman has her, but is keeping her some place else? Then they know the police are onto them. Then we might never find her," he said with a feeling of growing helplessness.

"And what if we go in there, and don't find her?" Dave asked testily. "You think that won't tip them off? What's more, what if this lady's got nothing to do with Barb's disappearance. Then we're in a fine mess."

"We get in an' we get out." Larry entered the debate. "They'd never know who the hell we were. But if you're so all fired worried about that beautiful puss of your's bein' recognized, we could wear ski masks or somethin', Dave."

Scott looked across the room at Larry. His expression was earnest, a rarity for him. "Are you agreeing with me, buddy? I'm beginning to think I don't have a leg to stand on here."

"Shit! You sound like we're talkin' courtroom procedure. This is friendship—at least the way I see it," he said, looking hard at the other two men. "I mean it like this, you remember that little Vietnamese corporal at An Loc, the one who told us not to go through that village that the ARVN had shelled and bombed for about five days straight?"

"Yeah, sure," Lenny answered first.

"Well, then you must remember how everybody laughed, from fat ass Colonel Sims right down to the four of us. But all that little corporal could keep sayin' was, 'you don't go, Cong there, you my friends, you don't go.' You remember what happened next? We nearly got our butts wiped off the face of the earth. That fuckin' little corporal had a feelin' that wouldn't let go of him. Seems to me like ol' Blue Eyes here has got that same feelin' now."

Scott smiled gratefully. It took someone else to put it that way—he couldn't ask them to take such a risk himself, based on just an instinct—but he knew that was just the way it was. Some instinct, some gut level feeling told him that the only way he'd see Barb again was to handle this his way. Cops running all over, light, sirens—with what this town had been through lately, the situation seemed to call for a more unorthodox approach.

"It'll be just like one of those good ol' search and destroy missions we loved so much," drawled Larry, trying to lighten the heavy pall of doubt and gloom that pervaded the room.

"For Christ's sake," Dave complained, "you sound like you're looking forward to it—you and all that Texas shoot 'em up shit of yours. You sound like we'd be playing cops and robbers. Well, this isn't a war anymore. There are laws back here; we're not in the jungle anymore."

"Hey, Davey. I know I'm asking a lot. You don't have to go."

"It's just that I got a wife and kids now, buddy."

"I know," Scott said and tried to smile.

"You know I'd help you if there were no other way. Hell, I'd go anyways if it wasn't for my family."

"It's okay, Davey. Really."

"I still think you oughta call the police. You could get shot."

Scott smiled ruefully. His voice was low and measured. "I could have got shot lots of times, Dave. But listen, I might very well be nuts for not going straight to the cops with this, but it seems that virtually everything I've found out about so far is because I'm the one who found it out. The cops? They've got enough to handle already in this town with all that's been going on. That's not to say that they couldn't handle this, too, but I'm not too sure. I guess I'm just too used to doing things for myself—even crazy things like this. Still, I wouldn't know about Barb and her father yet if I'd let the police handle it—I'm pretty sure of that. And I'm dead sure I wouldn't know about this woman. No, if I got to go it alone, I'll do it. I'll do it again."

"Hey, Blue Eyes. You know I wouldn't miss all the fun," Larry said.

Scott smiled and turned toward Lenny. "And you, buddy? With or against?"

Lenny sighed audibly. "Christ almighty, there are a lot of holes: that story about the phone calls—it's crazy. But if it's true that means we could be involving ourselves in some rather heavy business, to say the least. After all, if there is some connection between Barb's disappearance and these murders and kidnappings—"

"Looks like it's against," Larry interrupted.

"Wait a minute. I didn't say that. I guess, well, I'm really arguing with myself. Hell, what I'm trying to say is that it's all cockeyed, and there are a hundred and one good reasons not to go. But—I will. I'll go for the same reasons Larry said and because I sure as hell won't let you go it alone. I only hope that you're right, that this woman is connected with it and, well, of course, that Barb is all right."

"That does it then. Dave? Thanks anyhow. No hard feelings, you know that."

Dave stood up and took Scott's hand, looking hard

into his eyes than downward. "I—I hope so, buddy. I sure do."

He turned and left without looking at the other two. They could hear his heavy tred and the slam of the door behind him.

"That sure makes me glad I'm not married," Larry drawled softly.

"You might wish you had been by the time this is over with," countered Lenny.

26

For aeons she swam in the corridor of nothingness. But gradually, inexorably, she was pulled back into dim consciousness—a feverish vortex of impressions and fantastic images that made her, as always, uncertain about the reality of any of it. There was only one certain test: Her waking moments were infinitely more terrifying and nightmarish than the long stretches of torpor and unconsciousness that beset her. She dreaded to come awake again, to lift the veil of nothingness.

But now she was aware of a strong, definitely physical sensation at her back. It was cold. Her back, buttocks and legs were pressed against something so very hard and cold. Her befuddled mind struggled to sort out its jumbled impressions. There was the darkness around her, the black, but it was not the all-embracing black of night. She could see the shadows as they clawed and clung at the dark, distant walls around her.

She could move only her head. Her arms and legs were pinioned to her side. No. That was not quite right. Gradually, she came to understand that her limbs were stretched out at an angle away from her body, that her legs were spread wide and her arms were almost in the pose of crucifixion. The sensations came slowly to her numbed brain, and they grew with a sickening lack of comprehension.

Tentatively, she arched her spine, partly to test the response of her body to her mind's commands and partly to get away from the numbing, searing cold that clung to the back of her body. Her mind was sluggish and disoriented, but her body seemed aware of every sensation, as if it had an intelligence of its own. The cold bit into her like some rabid, gnawing thing, and she squirmed miserably against the invisible bonds that held her.

But it was no use. Even her neck felt imprisoned, and soon she learned that all she could do was raise her head up three or four inches before something soft and sharp cut cruelly into her throat and forced her head back down onto the cold, hard surface beneath her. She was a fly caught in a web of doom.

From somewhere off to the right of her came movement and sound. She turned her head, and saw the thick form of a woman approaching her. Dressed in a long black robe, she walked stiffly and carried a golden bowl in both hands. Somehow she looked familiar, and for a moment Barb wanted to cry out to her for help. But then she remembered. Dim recollections of the woman feeding her came to form slowly in her mind. This one, she was an agent of the other. No help here.

The heavy, impassive woman reached her side and placed the bowl somewhere out of sight of her limited scope of vision. But already the hot pungency of its contents had assailed her nostrils. It was a smell that was somewhere between the sickish sweet and the malodorous, the flowery and the charnel. There was the cloying sweetness of flowers about it and the herbal and something more familiar—the noxious smell of human waste, sewers, and the grave.

"And how are you today?" came the gravelly, sardonic words from the woman above her. "Are we resting well?" Here there was a short, cruel laugh, and she knew that the woman shared much with the obscene old man.

"What's happening to me?" she managed to ask weakly. "Who are you?"

The woman's face now loomed directly over her. The eyes set in that broad, severe face were like nuggets of blank, black stone. "I am Ama Bloch, girl. It is I who have been tending you these past few days that you've been good enough to spend with us." Again the sardonic, mocking quality rang clearly through the flat, accented voice. She had the impression of a dull, indifferent cruelty when she looked into those coarse features.

"But what—why?" she managed to whisper, her thoughts rolling through her brain in confusion.

"Shush, girl," Ama Bloch said, her voice a mixture of false solicitude and anger. "It won't be long now. I have given you the herbs for sufficient time now. Yes, very special herbs. Very potent herbs. But now—another treat for you."

The woman smiled obscenely at her, one hand coming up into the air. Three stubby fingers were covered with something dark and thick and liquid. With a slight chuckle, the hand was lowered, and something wet and sticky crudely traced the outline of a small circle on the middle of her forehead. Down and touched again against the soft skin above her breasts. It was then that she knew she was naked.

"Different herbs, now, girl," the woman purred. "Herbs and other things. Things not so nice at all, I'm afraid."

"Please . . . no." Barb managed to mumble. "What—what are you doing to me?"

There was no answer. Again the clumsy fingers touched her, this time down low on the belly, probing into the defenseless secret of her vulva, along the rim of those pink wings and finally onto points on either side of her inner thighs. Something dark and sticky like molasses clung there like brittle, glutinous fingers that had a life of their own. Tiny, viscous movements began to reach her numbed brain almost instantly. The small, wet circle on her forehead seemed already to be stretching, growing, coming alive: a feeling of heat and something settling on her belly, a feeling of blood and an itching sensation running to her labia.

She pondered these sensations as best her foggy mind could. She became caught up momentarily in dissecting these feelings—it was a link with a world outside the nether world of inner nothingness where she had been so long confined. Then she noticed the movement above her again. Ama Bloch was standing above her with the golden bowl in her hands.

That condescending, mocking smile again. "You are about to experience the ultimate, girl. You won't understand it, but it will know you, full well. I will not wish you good fortune, for that would be overly ironic. I can only hope that you come to see the good of it before the end." With that the stout, robed figure turned slowly and walked away. Before she could martial up the will to say anything, the other's thick figure had been absorbed into the dark outside the dim ring of candlelight. Four sentinels of light stood in high brass candlestands above and around her. Her only link to the world of sight and sanity. She almost wished that they would go out, that the meaning they symbolized would be extinguished. A deep, hardly recognized part of her wished then that it would be over.

Eventually, another feeling came to dominate, an itch that covered her and infiltrated her loins with a growing warmth and need. The thick, viscous liquid covering her labia seemed to have an awful life of its own, and she felt it moving, or some property it gave off, moving. Moving into her vagina. Stretching and warming the delicate tissues there. Producing unbidden, unwanted feelings. Her buttocks traced a sudden involuntary motion on the cold surface beneath her.

And the spot on her forehead began to glow and grow. It was as if something small and writhing were burrowing into her skull. The impression of depth, of her skull and the mind beneath being an endless, bottomless well seemed to take shape in her thoughts. Something was drilling to that central cavity, to the core of her brain. It was intruding and invading her like some sticky wet worm. More and more, external reality—such as she could perceive it—began to fade. These impressions were gathered with detachment, with a laughing indifference; they were the mere playground of her eyes: eyes that now saw the black-clad woman return into the circle of sputtering light, big mannish hands carrying a large carven table, redolent of gargoyles, writhing figures and strange, terrible gods; eyes that saw another black-robed figure enter the uncertain, changing light: smaller, stooped, hideously withered and dome-skulled. Old. Immeasurably old and evil. But it made no difference now. Her imprisoned eyes looked out at that scene with sublime detachment, even as the gnarled and lame limbs of the ancient man were raised into an incomprehensible gesture of command and supplication. Imprisoned eyes watched passively as that terrible bent figure slowly circled about her and formed a large ring of gray powder poured from the large pouch in its hand.

Ama Bloch placed the carven table within the circle and stepped again beyond the sphere of light. The bent figure of the terrible man completed the circle of grayish dust, its snakelike contours just coming at four points to the bases of the huge brass candlestands, each fully six feet high. Then Ama Bloch returned into the light, something long and dark and thin clutched in one hand. But she did not step past the powdery substance and into the circle. She merely passed the long length of wood to the hobbled, withered old man. He made a gesture of dismissal then, and she was gone.

Gripping the dark-wooded staff, that tottering figure of centuries began to slowly move around and around the sandy-bordered circle, that hideous cracked and broken voice beginning to chant and groan in a grotesque and godless ululation. He moved slowly and lamely at first, but as that repetitive spiral continued, greater power and purpose almost visibly flowed into his movements. The nightmare figure circumscribed the outer edge of death grey ash and bent and turned and twisted in the performance of an unfathomable ritual.

Strange and barbaric words escaped his hoary old throat in a spitting, wild cacophony of sound. The ancient body turned and danced with amazing agility and purpose. Long, gnarled hands and arms were lifted in bony command upward, and rasping noises of insistence and urgency broke from that archaic throat.

Then it stopped. All motion, all movement suddenly ceased. The black clad figure was motionless before her. All was silence except for an occasional creak and groan of shifting wood and settling foundation. The back of the bent, black figure moved imperceptibly before her. Slowly, the ancient man began to turn. Again the awful, dark-flamed eyes were on her, boring into her mind and soul. Again she could feel the plundering search of those evil, hungering eyes. But this time there was no fear. The still growing, immensely cavernous source of her inner mind swallowed and absorbed the fear and hate that the archaic, wilted figure cast on her. She was absorbing everything . . . absorbing all. Her capacity to swallow up the world itself seemed to stretch and pull and distend to cosmic proportions.

She watched idly as thin, spindly arms stretched out, the long folds of flat black cloth falling back against the old man's shoulders. Dry, mottled arms with clawlike tendril fingers at their ends which grappled with the air. Deep, fire-rimmed eyes turned upward in a look of challenge and supplication. The high-domed skull reflected like a ghostly egg in the yellow-orange glow of the great candles.

Then suddenly the dry, cracked and feeble voice rang out with a power and clarity that was seemingly beyond the ability of those decrepit vocal chords. Words of power flowed in a voice no longer wavering or tremulous, and the ancient, dwarfish body arched itself and expanded as if in some prodigious inner effort to absorb the energy all around it, and he spoke: rich brocades of language, the timeless poetry of invocation.

"Thou who art, I come unbidden to the act of consecration.
I who have no nature born of ignorance.
I who have lessened myself to increase myself.
Thou, oh center and secret of the sun,
Thou, oh center and secret of the universe,

Thou, who plummets the depths of eternal night,
Thou oh majesty, thou who art alone,
I who stalk the fire within the fire,
I now invoke in the spirit of the force
That drives the world,
In the will of the inner Way,
To the seed of new life.
O star lost and not of this dusty sphere,
Kindle now in me the intents to which I aspire.
Move in me now the plower to achieve my purpose,
That I may penetrate the most holy mystery,
The shrine of life
In the center and secret of my sun.

The frail arms fell back to his side like the wings of a bird falling from the sky. The power ebbed and went out, and sunken cheeks and the white pallor of death again claimed those withered features. The time-rotted figure turned and walked back to the table, upon which she could dimly see various implements. There the staff now lay too, and the tottering, evil old man lifted it anew, its long darkness seeming serpentine in the eerie light.

There was a sharp rapping sound as one end of the staff was brought down upon the stone floor, as if to test its weight and potency. Then he was moving again, walking close to the great symmetrical stone where her body lay unmoving. She could see the color come back to those sallow cheeks, could see the great effort to summon strength and energy, and then the terrible voice reached out again, clear and bell-like in its aspiration:

Now do I consecrate this sap grown into form,
This length of wood,
This wonder-tree.
Now do I call down the power of ages to forge and fuse
The primal urgency into this staff.
Now do I invest it with sacred office,
With potency,
Earth-born, ethereal,

Sky and heaven bent.
Thing of two worlds you have become
Agent of mind and energy you have become.
Serve me well now.

He turned and walked to the edge of the powdered circle. Reaching the staff across that ring of ashen gray, the tip came to touch the small flame of the candle, and suddenly there was a spark and a flash of light as the thin tip of wood went alight with a blazing white effulgence of flame. There was a cackle of delight, and the black-robed figure heaved convulsively as it touched the brilliant bit of glow to the powdered circle beneath.

There was a sudden rushing sound as of wind, and the implosion of great forces as the dark abruptly went brilliant-hued and rainbow-bright for one briefest instant in an encompassing circle of color and warmth. But, like the flash of gunpowder, it was quickly gone, and in the place of that momentary kaleidoscope of multi-varied tints and primal white energy was a thick, seeping cloud of stifling, noxious fumes. Fumes that rose up in curious, curling tendrils of sullen, almost animate smoke that rose up like a blanket or wall from the ring of ash and did not disperse into broader clouds as it sought its height. The smell of it was herbal, stinging and repellent, and soon vast, acrid, billowing folds of the stuff hung low oppressively against the now-invisible ceiling.

She looked to her right where she could see that the ancient figure had drawn near to her again. But he seemed oblivious to her presence. The dreadful eyes were again upraised, full of lofty power and awe. And again he spoke.

Great Heavens, whose vast limits and expanses
No earthly man knows,
Primal parent, source and end of all
Forever turning around this dusty ball;
Mighty majestic hall
For you wandering ones,
Hear now my call.

*Hear now my summons
As I bid thee:
In all-time, in no-time,
In all-space, in no-space,
Come to me now with your hate.
Come to me now with your envy.
Come to me now with your lust.
Come to me now with all your potent troubles,
Your unquenchable desires.
Earthly, ethereal, whose all-possible names
None save my power can tame.*

The voice raised another octave, became shrill now instead of guttural. The upraised staff shook mightily in that horrid claw. The air itself had grown heavy with the smoke that curled in stinking, pungent wreathlets about them, and the atmosphere itself had become heavier, expectant.

*Abbadon, hear me.
Ye who draw eternal circles in your benighted
   night,
Come, attend to the North Point
In harmony and protection.
Bariel, return from thy furthest reaches
To attend on me.
Ye who everlastingly tread
The shores of the eternal Stygian Sea,
Come attend to the South Point
In harmony and protection.*

Something ponderous yet pulsing with hidden energy seemed to be forming, to be growing outside the circle. Something thick and dark and watchful. The clouds of choking smoke became hot and alive with it, and something of the very nature of that presence seeped into the circle with the shifting, ever changing patterns of gray, stifling smoke.

*Abrasar, oh mighty, bornless one,
Cast down your lightless light, your secret flame
And come unto me, for I promise you delight.
Attend to the East Point in harmony and protec-
   tion.*

Again the dark, serpentine length of wood pointed to the now vague outline of one of the brass held candles just outside the steaming circle. An unseen power seemed to flow darkly along the course of the rod and out into the nebulous mists beyond. There was a strange hollow scratching sound and then—could it be?—a sound that was not a sound. An unearthly momentary tittering, both immediate and star voids removed from this place. A horrible cosmic chuckle of delight. Thin, transparent, elusive, it rose in shrill thinness and was gone.

Mariodam, ye who ride the great winds,
The courses of space and time,
Come, complete the great square of energies.
Come and attend to the West Point
In harmony and protection.

The smoke billowed and rushed again. Cold and feverish winds, scents of sea and rich brown earth played about her as currents of alternately frigid and tropical atmosphere danced and weaved through the sluggish rings of fume. Something both light and infinitely weighty, capricious and cruel, boundless and ever the same through all eternities.

Now the voice was triumphant. It rang out gleefully with renewed strength, amplifying and resounding off the impenetrable wall of smoke that still grew around them into a suffocating fog of utter density. The figure of the terrifying old man wafted now in front of her, now lost, now seen again in the shifting currents of sickening herbal essences that lay all about and around her.

Glory to you from Eternal Tomb.
Glory to you of Winged Doom.
Glory to you from winds and seas unfurled.
Glory to you whose flame is unhurled.
Glory to thee in thy most blessed Unity.

She could see him turn away in the thick pall, the black of the long robe nearly lost in the wafts of gray cloud. She could see the dark form of the staff where he gripped it with an invisible hand. The voice was softer now, muted and once again harsh and gutteral as it seeped back at her through the vapors.

"Come child. Come closer. Do not step outside the circle." That voice, calm now, almost solicitous. Who was it addressing? She could not even move, much less step outside of the circle.

The words struck a dim chord of interest in her blackened brain. She strained upward against her bonds and attempted to peer through the clouds of smoke and mind that beset her. Something small and pale stepped out from somewhere behind her, something she could not have seen before. The small silhouette came into sight, and finally she could make it out: the figure of a naked child, perhaps ten or twelve years old. A girl.

A once pretty but now grotesque little girl. Her ribs jutted out cruelly from the thin layer of flesh that covered them. The eyes were dull and staring—vacuous, uncomprehending orbs that had no will or spirit to them anymore. Terror and starvation had driven out all hope, and her gaunt, tiny features looked horribly old in their hollowed, black-rimmed eyes and sunken cheeks.

"Come closer. Come closer to me," the ancient one's voice was soft now, purring.

The child moved forward again stiffly. Mindlessly. From her prison, she could see one of those parched, monstrous hands reach out and descend toward the girl's head, but the black expanse of robe and the swirling vapors obscured her sight.

There was a short sound, something between a laugh and a snarl, and the domed skull came alive in a leering look of anticipation. The words tumbled out like the hiss of some deadly viper. "The time is nigh. Tonight is the night of the Varleth, the Time of Changes, nineteen days before the winter solstice. It is now when all matter and form is most impermeable; it is now that the Dark Forces first have their season sway. And you . . . you lie on the altar of the Druids, tonight is your night and tonight is my night and tomorrow there will be one."

The deadly laugh and the eyes brighten in evil expectation. 'Now. Now will I rest my staff with you. I place it in your safekeeping. Let it rest upon the soft swell of your belly. Let it help serve to make the transition an easy one."

Something long and curiously cold was lain between her outstretched legs, its length traveling up her exposed stomach where the tip lay nudged against the underside of her breast. The horrid laugh broke in cracked gasps again from that depraved face, and she looked as he turned again, moving lamely toward the silent, solitary figure of the girl. Pausing by the hideous table, she saw him pick something up but could not discern what it was in the writhing smoke. Again that voice grew less tremulous, more certain and full again, as if speaking to itself in some vast cavern where its own sound would become lost in the endless spaces of limitless walls around. "Now it is to consecrate the circle itself, to protect and draw power. Now it is to bait the trap, to send out a signal of life and blood that will call unto us He that is necessary to our great work."

He moved to the girl and leaned stiffly downward. She was hoisted into those bony, fleshless arms as if she were a thing of straw or sand. Despite their great age and obvious infirmity, there was a strength in those limbs that was truly astounding. Still, that black bodied frame began to shake and waver unevenly as it held the child. For a moment it appeared that both might fall, but in an effort of monumental will and resolve, suddenly the child was thrust overhead, over the robed figure that held her aloft like some awful, living trophy—a human prize.

It was then that she awoke. It was then that she broke through the spell of drug that held her. Somehow the sight of a child so cruelly used struck a spark somewhere in the deepest reaches of her soul, and quickly she began to ascend from the black cavern within herself. She searched for and found her vocal chords, struggled fiercely to make her message known. Nothing seemed to work for a moment, but then something came together and she screamed a murderous sound of fury and warning full of hate for the evil, profane creature who held the child.

Whirling about with uncanny speed, he faced her while holding the child aloft. A look of insane fury burned in those eyes of hell. Contorting the nightmare face, a long wail, high and terrible, poured forth in a frenzy of hate and frustration. The child came crashing to the floor as she was flung down with demonic fury, landing on her hip in a crushing sound of loose bone and tortured flesh.

A plaintive cry of pain and fright issued from those small lips, and life and understanding once again flowed into those small, starved eyes. Barb cried out again. She yelled for the child to run, to crawl away, to do anything at all. Straining mightily against the invisible restraints that held her, she tried to sit up but only succeeded in cutting off the air to her lungs as the silken cords cut sharply into her windpipe. Her head hit the cold, iron-like surface beneath with a sharp pain, and she looked on helplessly at the horrible spectacle before her.

From somewhere beneath the folds of black cloth, something long and metal-looking appeared. In the dim, shifting vapors, Barb could barely make it out until it was already raised above the helpless child. There was a sudden thrusting, slashing movement, and Barb thought she heard a small sound—a whimper and that was all. Abruptly the old man was carrying the girl again, but now Barb could see with hideous clarity the long liquid swath that trailed behind the pale, lifeless body in a flood of crimson that dropped to the floor in grotesque splotches of red death.

And around that still smoking circle he went, while holding the girl face down above it. From her throat streamed a steady flow of lifeblood, the elixir of mortality. Down, down it cascaded in seemingly endless rivulets, there to mingle with the stinking, sulfurous chemicals and plants of the ashen ring. And in that moment when the great circle was sealed and completed in the spent life force of the child, something incomprehensible happened, for the vapor began to curl upward all deep red in some subtle alchemy of blood and wonder. And eyes—eyes a deeper and more violent red than the child's blood itself—could be seen staring in from outside the circle. Eyes that hugged close to the now all-but-invisible candlelight.

The ancient, tottering man held the frail, lifeless body aloft again for a moment, the few last drops of plundered red energy falling and collecting at his feet in a small ghastly pool. Then the thin envelope of flesh that had been the girl was discarded—heaved with one vast effort outside the circle where the eyes swirled in the foggy stench and darted with inhuman speed to the spot where the discarded lump of meat lay in silence.

"A prize! A tiny morsel of charming humankind for you but, alas, all spent. Nothing there to squirm and plead and give pleasure to the likes of you. Back! Back to your solemn posts, or there will be nothing left for you later to feed on, to dally with in your oh so delicate ways." A great peal of laughter sang out from the old man as he leaned forward at the edge of the circle like some great withered monkey that is taunting its prey. The disembodied eyes hovered there for a minute over the form of the girl. Then the ancient, obscene man turned and labored to drag his body toward the center of the circle—toward Barb who lay helplessly bound to the strange symmetrical stone.

Something dry that made her flesh crawl lightly touched her belly as it lifted the staff off of her and raised it overhead. Then, holding each end in a shrivelled hand, he began to turn round slowly in a circle.

"*Hassath Abahon*!" he called out as he turned.

The staff was brought down to the floor with a swift movement, its tip making a sharp, hollow ringing sound as it hit the floor beneath.

"*Neth Vayu. Neth Apas*!" he cried and turned the staff over to the horizontal, its length seeming to quiver now with a dark life of its own.

"*Aggram! Tra Ballatron*!" The voice yelled out in greater intensity, and one end of the staff was slowly brought around until its tip pointed to the small pool of blood several feet in front of the bent, black-robed figure.

"*Erem sabla viore.*" The staff made a strange looping circle in those grim hands, and the bent figure stepped forward to the foot of that reservoir of deep blackish red. The end or tip of the staff was brought slowly downward until it touched into the dark liquid, and the back of that horrid black-robed figure began to spasm and tremble as the tip of that long wooden staff began to trace some awful, inexplicable design, some curious, unfathomable geometrical shape, with the vile ink of the child's blood. Finally, the staff lifted again, and the spidery arms were lifted exultantly upward and outward.

And here the voice rang out into the darkness in a final gibberish, a wail of awful, supplicating sound. It was the voice of ultimate meaninglessness, the garbled vowels and consonants of primal chaos and despair, of no recognizable language. Of no wholly human throat did those noises proceed. Hard, gutteral, mindlessly dissonant, lost in a sea of discordant caterwaul that seemed to be without meaning or pattern.

And then the terrible sounds ended, and all was black and silent. A great still seemed to have descended—a pause in all sight and sound. Barb lay helplessly and waited, her eyes thrust upward into the darkness above. Waited. Waited for what? She could feel it in her bones, could sense the gathering presence.

It came. First as the growing smell, the seep of sewer that seemed to infiltrate the acrid odor of the burning circle. Subtly at first, it impinged on her sensitive nostrils in a smell more recognizable but even more unpleasant than the ubiquitous smoke. But it grew swiftly and suddenly was the overpowering stench of hell itself: the rotten, mouldering essence of a thousand opened coffins, the smell of eternal slime brewed of nature's putrescence, the core of all she discarded, all that was waste. It rushed at her, assaulted her in a hot breathy blast of abrupt, ultimate repugnance, as if some unseen barrier had given way and allowed the stench of ages to flood into the space around her.

But there was worse. Far worse. For the stench was only a precursor, an announcement of what was to come. It grew as a black clot above her. Her eyes filled with tears as her body tried desperately to reject the rankness around her, but still they saw through the haze of water and night . . . saw it begin to form above her, saw it wiggle and writhe, a black oozing cloud of ultimate darkness—darker even than the smoky black pitch all around her. And she could feel the sentience grow as the black ooze spread and congealed above her helpless body.

It was a thing dead from the moment of its hell-spawned inception, its noxious, idiot birth. Born to gibber and slaver and play in its ultimate inconsequence. Born to hunger and lust after destruction—the destruction of all that it could never understand, the destruction of all form and meaning and order. For it was Qlippoth, the force of primal chaos, the essential balancing factor to all that we hold to be sane and purposeful.

That is the way of the universe. There is order, so there must be disorder. There is meaning, so there must be meaninglessness. And Qlippoth was that balancing factor, the other side to the eternal, universal quest for equilibrium. The side of power used for no purpose save its own brutality, the side of desire that has no object, the side of action that follows no logic and has no purpose. It burst, this cosmic blight, into the world with inexplicable and conflicting feelings, as well as one might decipher those feelings. It had come from a place of infinite dark and was itself that darkness, from a place of eternal silence where nothing occurred and nothing ever was, where it gnawed at itself in mindless self-torture, where it could be eternally alone in its self-hate and meaninglessness.

But now it was here, summoned by the dark ritual link that surpassed its understanding. Now it had suddenly burst into the light of a dark far more brilliant and fearful than the ultimate black in which it lived and was. Thin cords of pulsating slime that were and were not began to separate from the main clot of black, began to form into rope arms that reached down hungrily for the helpless form of the woman beneath them. Arms of infinite softness and squishy, slimy wetness, the refuse, of nature's building blocks. Something cold and loathsome seemed to brush by her arm. Something widened and split in that formless mass of black above her and bubbled into the shifting shape of an obscene mouth that was alive with a million flailing tiny tentacles—each one ending in a long, cruel hook, a barb with which flesh could be torn and shredded and devoured in endless ages of enjoyment.

But all this Barb saw and withstood. Her mind—or a part of it—was still lingering somewhere in its innermost recesses, safely entombed in its own protective depths. Days of constant ingestion of the esoteric herbs had effectively removed her from the world around her, had made reality a thing to be noticed with abstraction and not much concern. It was only the emptiness she knew with any certainty. All the horrors and gibbering terrors she had witnessed—they were becoming less and less consquential as less and less could touch the inner sanctum of her mind. Her reaction to the plight of the little girl had been the last and meaningless scurrying of people and events and of things the waking mind does not want to comprehend.

But her mind was not waking: It was brooding, turning in on itself in an obsessive consuming of self, an ultimate preoccupation with its own isolation, its removal from all but its own benighted confines. And that was the only horror she could truly comprehend now: the ultimate loneliness of the self, the need to be part of the world, to live and work and suffer and die in concert with others. Too late she recognized her own ultimate frailty—the essential human frailty. Too late she realized her own necessities—the necessities of her species. Few did, if any. But all that mattered now was that she hadn't, and now she was left in all her human vulnerability, and that vulnerability was being used against her for some awful, inexplicable purpose.

And something winked and opened above her. Two dark orbs of greater black than the ultimate black that was the thing above her. Its eyes. The utter horror of it, for they revealed its essence, its soul. And the eddying shape quivered like some awful, sewerous jelly and began to flow downward toward her—toward and into her through the mind opening that stretched and yawned in her forehead.

She looked into its soul in that moment, that briefest instant of time, and knew the vast, cosmic emptiness of the thing—an emptiness, a deadness, an aloneness a billion universes of starless voids greater than her own. She knew that thing was flowing into her, mingling with her, becomine one with her in this instant that was becoming an eternity too mind and soul destroying to bear.

And she hung in the balance in that brief instant of time. The emptiness, the hopelessness and despair in her reached out to embrace that ultimate emptiness. But whatever remained of the spark—the low-burning flame of life and spirit—assailed her with its remaining feeble energy: *Anything but this*!

Something else moved above her, something bony and dry. She tried to focus her eyes, her senses, but her mind was too paralyzed now, too polarized by her infinite, imminent dilemma. Only the tiniest corner of consciousness registered external impressions: the dry, parched, leathery skin of a hand on her breast; the cold, stale breath at her cheek. Universes swam around her. Baffling, incomprehensible shadows and luminescent figures danced and played by her side.

Something hot-cold, night-day, lusting-dying began to seep into her, to bubble and ooze in acid invasion. Something that was not physical yet which created every physical torture imaginable as it bubbled into her brain. Her skull began to stretch and distend—to make room for the universes of emptiness that sought to lodge there. Another sensation intruded at the thin, tottering edge of her mind: something cold and hard pushing at the rim of her labia, intruding into the expectancy and the wetness that was there in spite of herself. Twin hungers, equally inexplicable.

But not equally awful. The heart, the essence, of that formless monstrosity, the utter alienness, brushed past her eyes and began the long, final descent into the tunnel of her mind. Ultimate stench, ultimate cold, ultimate hate, ultimate aloneness. All these things would be her. In the sudden flash of eternal choice, she knew the alternative. Now she could feel the steady push-pull in her belly, the familiar suction. The innermost reaches of her basic duality were being ravished, invaded and used. Something exploded in her head, and the black, mindlessly writhing tentacles reached to extinguish the tiny guttering flame of spirit and will. A shard of an instant of time away she faced the final horror.

She made the choice then.

27

The night was bitterly cold. A numbing wind beat down upon the town out of the north as if in inexplicable fury. The dry husks of the season's remaining leaves scurried madly over streets and lawns like tiny, furtive autumn ghosts whispering secrets in the night, and the great valuted dome of the night was alive with countless tiny diamonds of light secure in their remote majesty. All was suffused with the phantasmal luminescence of the moon, its soft, pale glow casting nature's touch of bleak and eldritch magic over the naked, writhing limbs of great trees and the silent shadows of looming houses.

It was one of those mysterious, melancholy-beautiful late autumn nights that was turning the last bend into winter. The remnants of nature's ethereal sorcery of the seasons was bellowing and gusting in defiance of winter's oncoming blanket of silence. The streets of Oak Grove were empty. No hearty souls trudged over the dancing, shifting carpet of leaves, their eyes and minds partaking of night secrets. Few cars had ventured onto those vacant corridors of concrete and stone, save the occasional squad car weaving its lonely vigil by and along the rows of shuttered windows and bolted doors of silent fortress houses.

So few, if any, eyes looked out at the car that pulled up to the curb late that wind-tossed evening. Few, if any, saw the three men emerge from the car and silently make their way up the street. Three men on a mission. Combat hardened. Apprehension and courage. Fear and adventure. They moved steadily onward until they came to a long line of empty bushes that bordered one end of a large property. Quickly they moved off the walk and out of the dim light of the street lamp, hugging close to the concealing line of bushes as they ran into the heart of the leaf strewn lot.

They didn't pause until they had skirted the whole southern edge of the property, cut across the back yard and up against the back end of the massive, silent house. Here they paused to catch their breaths and to examine their quarry from close quarters. Lightless, the tumbled, spreading, complex mass of board and glass and shingle stretched and yawned up before them like some great sullen beast of the night. It was brooding, watchful, patient, as it sheltered them in its expectant vastness.

Scott looked over to his partners. There were no recognizable emotions on their faces, though they must have been feeling something—excitement, concern, fear, something. But why did he feel this way? Why the undercurrent of dread, the mortal fear, mixed with all the more probable, less powerful emotional reactions? He had been through so much in Viet Nam, and he had grown to accept and ignore the fear, the cold, icy sweat of impending death. But here it was again, only somehow deeper, more unreasoning and terrifying—more hopeless in its feeling that he was facing something awful, some primal malignancy.

And why the compulsion, the certainty that he must come here to this mouldering old mansion? It ate at him night and day—this was the only way to help Barb, the only way to . . . what? Why did he really object so much to help of the police? Why was he so certain he had to go this one alone, or nearly alone? He looked to Lenny and Larry. Had he dragged them into this out of his own fear? If he was so damned determined to do this alone, shouldn't he really be doing it alone? Dim images of blackness and fright began to roll in his brain, and he fought them down with shuddering effort. "C'mon, Larry," he whispered softly. "There's the entrance to the basement. Let's check it out."

When they were all huddled in the small recessed landing outside the basement door, Scott turned on the flashlight. Even if someone were to pass through the rear alleyway, they would never see its feeble light. Larry removed a ring of keys from his pocket. "O master locksmith, do your thing," he said as he fitted the first key into the lock of the solid, heavy door.

"I still think we should cut the telephone wires," whispered Lenny.

"C'mon man," returned Larry softly. "If there's anybody here, and they really kidnapped Scott's lady—well, I don't think they're gonna be in any hurry to call the cops for help. Besides, it's too damned bright with that moon. I'd stick out like a sore thumb on top of that fuckin' telephone pole."

"Yeah, well, what if they didn't do it, and they decide to call the cops?" asked Lenny.

"You gettin' cold feet?" said Larry skeptically.

"No. I just don't think we should take any more chances than we have to take."

"Don't worry," said Scott while trying to sound reassuring. That's why we're going to split up once we get inside the house. I want to be in and out again in ten minutes at the most. It's got to be mighty big inside, but if we hustle—"

"Got it," said Larry as there was a click.

He stood up and turned the door knob slowly. It gave, but the door didn't open. "Damn. There's a bolt lock too."

"Can't you handle that?" asked Scott.

"Maybe. It depends on what kind. But it'll take too long. I'd rather try the back door."

"Yeah, but there's no porch or anything there to hide us," protested Lenny. "You use that flashlight out there, and there's a good chance somebody might see us."

"I won't need the flash. The moonlight oughta be enough."

"You certain?" asked Scott.

— 222 —

"Shit. I ain't certain about anything. All I can do is try," said Larry stoically.

"What if the back door has got a bolt lock too?" asked Lenny.

"Well, then I'd say we try the basement again., More protection from prying eyes."

"Let's go," said Scott.

The back door was reached by going up a flight of four steps from the ground. There was a small landing, but it wasn't enclosed. Larry quickly knelt and examined the lock. "Crap. Why don't they ever make doors with windows in these big old barns?" he said disgustedly.

"To keep guys like us out," said Lenny. "What's the matter?"

"Ah, it's an old lock. I ain't got any keys to even fit it. I'll have to pick it."

"Great," Lenny whispered. "With this fucking moon we might as well be working under stage lights."

"Not to worry," returned Larry. "It won't take long."

Scott looked back into the yard as a sudden gale of wind sent geat eddying sweeps of leaves up into the air around the yard. Still, everything seemed somehow very still. He glanced up at the house, at the maze of twisting corners and leaning overhangs. Was anybody there? What would they find, salvation or death? A big, empty house or unimaginable terror? Why this foreboding? His hand reached down and fingered the hard lump of metal under his jacket. At least he was prepared.

"Presto!" Larry called out almost too loudly. He put his hand to the door, and it creaked just slightly as it swung inward. "Service with a smile," he said and grinned at them back over his shoulder.

They paused there on the landing for a long moment, as if hesitating. Finally, Scott edged past Larry. It was his game, his responsibility to lead the way. "Well, gentlemen. This is it," he tried to say lightly, as if unconcerned. Switching on the flashlight, he stepped into the dark silence of the house.

Shalak was sorrowing in the only sorrow that she knew. She lived for one thing: to please the Master, but now the Master was gone. He had left her, gone and left Shalak to haunt the empty halls and rooms of the house alone by night and day.

Shalak avoided some parts of the house, even in her despair. Some parts had windows, windows with no drapes or shades or coverings over them. Windows that let the horrible, blinding light in. Shalak could not abide the light. She was a creature of the night: the night of the world and the night of the soul. Small lights she could stand for a little while, but big lights—they were her only fear and weakness.

So Shalak would trundle her ungainly body through the many rooms and corridors of the house, always looking, always searching, always vainly hoping that the Master would come back. After awhile, though, hope faded in her beast brain, and she mostly slept and dreamed in a corner of the basement behind the padlocked door. Occasionally, the old house would creak and groan around her as all old houses do. Then she would lift swiftly out of dream, all watchful attention and waiting.

The Master had told her to be on guard, to expect "guests." But she hadn't needed to be told, for her soul was the soul of the hunter, the beast of prey. Her one delight other than the Master's company was in those small tasks that he sometimes had given her—tasks admirably suited to her particular talents. She had grown rather thin and listless while waiting for something to happen in her black lair or the house above, but finally her patience was being rewarded. She pulsed and purred at the sound of voices and scrapings at the basement door, felt keen, bitter disappointment when it ended and had hope renewed upon hearing those same sounds at the back door upstairs.

Even now her simple beast brain boiled with the blood lust, and it was with a great effort that she calmed herself, trying to remember if the Master had given her any special instructions. No, she couldn't risk offending the Master. Once he had become angry with her, and she had burned and been torn apart and nearly ceased to be. The pain. The pain.

But even that wasn't as bad as the thought of his scorn or indifference to her. Shalak lived for the thought that he would come back; she lived for his few attentions, lived for the times he would come down here to her lair in the basement and stroke her shiny black back lovingly and call her his pet and his pride and she could spasm and undulate her squat body under his caresses. Those times he would sit there in an old rocker for precious moments, swaying back and forth, and she would lay by his side like some great black dog, moving her body in time with his movement, her uncluttered brain full of happiness and wonder.

At other times he had reached out for her with his mind, and then is when the communion between them became most complete, for she had been born from and out of that mind. He would instruct her, and she would listen, because it had been burned into her grim and simple nature from birth to listen to that voice, that mind alone. In nothing else did she invest any care, worry, or affection—nothing save the lust that was always in her: the lust to tear, to rip, to rend and destroy whatever the Master had not put his seal of protection upon.

But he was gone now, so she lived only for this latter need—her power to destroy. It was an illusion, this power. It was no more substantial than she was, no more substantial than the billowing of autumn smoke or the dark of night. But the power of illusion is still power: it shapes the span of most men's lives. Though Shalak didn't know this herself—her simple and incomplete nature was incapable of introspection or real deduction—her only real strength lay in a peculiar ability to touch men's minds somewhere deep and underneath in their soft, exposed underbellies of blind panic and fear. *He* had given her this power and had shaped and fashioned her from the potency of his own towering mind. She was merely a shadow, a reflection of that mind which had gained a measure of life of its own along with a certain deadly capacity for destruction.

But finally she was always his creature. He had even named her, Shalak, Breath of My Breath. Shalak the destroyer. Shalak who tears and grinds at herself in the root of darkness. Shalak who gnaws at the center of hateful oblivion. Shalak, creature of eternal night.

But now Shalak pined—she pined as the lover pines for the lost loved one. She was alone and unhappy, and such things as her are better met when they are reasonably content, if they must be met at all. So, imagine her delight on that late autumn night: lost and baffled affection transmuted into hateful fury with the rattling of a basement door.

She had been dozing in the closed corner of the basement, her long black legs curled up beneath her. She didn't really sleep, of course. Rather, she dreamed nebulous animal images of feral delight. She had been dreaming of the child—oh, how she had wanted the child—when she had heard the first tentative sound at the door. One small and suspicious eye had opened a bit at that sound. Then another. Eight flaccid legs slowly stretched then tensed with a shiver at knobby joints midway down their black, bony length. She listened, suddenly alert, her every sense awake in a carnal lust of expectation.

For a long while there was no other sound except the familiar creaking of the old house itself. The first pangs of disappointment had just set into her dark heart, and her squat, ovoid body had just settled back down to the floor when she heard the noise in the kitchen upstairs. She was up and scuttling across the floor of the root cellar with amazing speed. Coming to the closed door of the cellar, Shalak never paused. That low, trembling body passed right through the slabs of solid wood out into the black void of the basement itself. Never hesitating, she ran toward the northwest corner of that room, directly under the kitchen, there to wait silent and invisible among the ancient rafters of the ceiling.

To Shalak it felt like an eternity of waiting before anything happened. A subtle tremor, a tiny trembling that she could not restrain suggested a level of excitement as hideous as her intent. She was the hunter and knew that it was the hunter's place to be quiet and motionless as it baits the trap, but her brain was not her own. It bubbled and danced with the insane delirium of its creator. She waited, but she waited in a prodigality of joyous, rapacious appetite that would not be still.

And eventually her patience was rewarded. The sudden appearance of the flashlight beam from the stairway above signalled the end to her waiting. Still, it hurt. She squinted at the merciless brightness, but her black pulsating body finally became still. Her wrath became an altogether more cold and calculating thing, and Shalak became even a greater danger in the sudden caution of her murderous intention.

She waited. The light, the horrid light, slowly bobbed its way down the stairs, there to play about the room in an agony of blinding, confusing brilliance. Once a stray beam of light fleetingly fell across her suspended body, and she cringed and spasmed and nearly fell to the floor beneath, but the cursed light was gone before it could really hurt her.

Eventually, it moved to the great stone in the middle of the floor, the Master's precious stone. With her night eyes she could see the man behind the awful light, pawing at the Master's great altar, looking at it with the light. She felt his concentration go out toward the stone and felt him become less aware of the darkness around him. Slowly, silently she began to move across the rafters toward him, her eyes shut tight against the fearsome light.

She fell on him just as he was about to straighten up from his examination of the huge monolith. Her mandibles were at his throat before he could guess what had happened, and she clung to him as he screamed and twirled his body around in mad circles like some berserk toy. Her legs wrapped themselves around his face and neck and back, and he bellowed and writhed in agony as the flashlight dropped from his hand.

Finally, he fell—but not before another one had bounded suddenly down the stairs in response to the screams and cries of fear. Suddenly the light was upon her—another hellish flame of narrow, torturous illumination.

But she was running with the blood fever now, and she was in her own nest, the walls of black pressing around her in reassuring darkness. The light wasn't such a great one; she could abide it for a little while if she must. With preternatural swiftness, she was off the crumpled body and scampering grotesquely over the cool black floor at the other one who stood rigid and staring until it was too late. Two long, dark legs shot out and caught him by the ankles. He was down before he could do anything but give one short, strangled yell. Miraculously, he had managed to hang onto the flashlight, his last and only defense if he but knew it.

But he didn't know it. He swung at his attacker with the full force of the flashlight. It landed harmlessly against solid, leathery skin, the precious beam of light shining up and into the ceiling where it would do no good. Again he swung, this time from an angle where some of the light smote her for a second at close range. Shalak felt something go hideously hot and painful against her, and there was the smell of spoiled meat or decaying flesh.

But that had been his trump card. With the second collision against Shalak's hard outer skeleton, some tiny bit of wire or glass went wrong, and the light went out. All was black. All was as Shalak wanted it. She scuttled off the chest of the fallen man as he tried to rise and moved around quickly to his back where four thin but powerful legs grabbed his head and twisted with a sudden snap of bone and the grinding, rending sound of cartilage ground to mush. She played a long while with the grotesquely dangling head . . . bounced and rolled it like a child with a ball until finally it severed from the shoulders altogether. Suddenly she kicked it with one of those hard, powerful legs and watched the bloody sphere bounce away out of her sight.

She went to the other one again. Joyfully, she discovered that he wasn't quite dead yet. There was a little something left for sport, for her to wax even stronger upon. She inched close to his face. The two snapping mandibles reached out from the black basketball head and found their target. A short stabbing motion downward and she plucked the eyes out with neat, surgical precision. They dangled limply from the end of her mandibles before she dropped them and greedily lapped them into her mouth with a slight sucking sound.

But this one hadn't screamed at all. That had robbed her of a little pleasure and a little more strength, and now, unhappily, he was dead. The sport had lasted for so little time. She had been too eager and hadn't waited and dallied with them like she had the first one. That one had been the best.

But Shalak quickly sensed something now, and her body began to tremble in glee. Another one was in the house! Even now she could feel him racing through the house toward her. Even now she could taste his blood in her mouth. She needed only to wait for him to rush into her final embrace.

But Shalak didn't wait. She was up the wall and through the floor in a mere few second—up and into the long, dark main hallway of the house. She could hear the pounding steps already as the dim figure ran down the stairs from the upper stories and she could see the thin beam of terrible light illuminating his way. In the end this is all she really wanted: to kill and kill and kill still again. This one had the cursed light too, but this time she was better prepared for it. The other two had also had the awful lights, and she had triumphed. But the sport had gone too quickly. She promised herself that this one would take days to die. He would scream and beg for the end to be swift, but it would take days and days. Promised him. Promised herself. Days of it.

Torture and horror, and finally, death.

As Scott's foot touched the bottom step of the staircase, his mind was a jumble of thoughts and confusion. The house seemed empty. Indeed, it seemed as if it had never been used. Then there were the screams—screams like he had never heard even during the war. He had run down that flight of stairs as quickly as he had gone up cautiously moments before, the thin beam of flashlight nervously bouncing off dark, dusty wall and panelling all the way before him. But suddenly there was no more time for thought or confusion. Only panic and fear.

He felt his body go out from under him as it touched the flooring of the long hallway. Hurtling forward, he came to the floor with a sickening crash. But every sense was alert, and instinctively he rolled with the fall and up to his knees, shining the flashlight toward the base of the stairway. His other hand reached to his side, and the cold, hard steel of the pistol reflected grimly in the thin hint of light.

But what he saw by the foot of the stairs made him blink and quickly shake his head. Had the fall scrambled his brains? A new panic, a deeper more unreasoning fear began to take shape inside of him as the wispish chord of light vaguely illuminated the thing a few feet ahead of him.

It was there. Something that pulsed and undulated in eight-legged blackness. It was a monstrosity that had no rightful place on his planet—a thing out of a child's nightmare, the archetype of all of man's latent and unconscious fears. And slowly, with utter horror, he watched it began to waddle forward toward him.

He felt a grotesque and morbid fascination momentarily, hypnotized by the movement of many legs. It was almost on him when he aimed the pistol at the hideous thing. Fear pulled that trigger, pulled it eight times at a distance of only six or seven feet. That vast, empty hallway, a self-contained world from him now, went alive with spitting orange fire and the echoing thunder of the gun.

Each shot was like a new breath of life; each explosion was a blow for sanity and normality in a world suddenly gone mad. Acrid explosive smoke wafted up before his eyes and into his nostrils. His ears rang with the after shock of his assault. His eyes blinked over and over in an attempt to see beyond the ghostly after light of the orange spitting death. He struggled to view his fallen nightmare enemy.

But it was on him before he could even see it again. What would end any man's life was of little consequence to Shalak, and the deadly rain of bullets passed right through her ponderous body only to smash harmlessly into the staircase behind her. Only the explosions of light had hurt her, but she'd steeled herself to the numbing pain and scrabbled on toward her prey, managing to stay underneath the direct path of the flashlight beam.

And now she sensed her victory. He had hurt her with the awful light, but she was running with the blood fever now, and had forced herself to attack as best she could with the terrible light smoting and burning into her. Then those other lights, more brilliant and abrupt—like knives of white-hot iron. She had staggered and nearly fallen then, though the bullets hadn't even been felt. It was only the light that could hurt her, but now there would be no more misery: Two long, thin legs kicked out with murderous fury and hit an arm. The awful instrument flew out of his hand, hit the floor, and went out. Now the game was hers.

She trembled with delight as she heard him gasp. Four cold, hard arms wrapped around the middle of him and pulled the almost unprotesting body with a brutal wrench to the floor. She hesitated momentarily, relishing the deep moan of fear from beneath her. But soon she was moving with incredible, sticky speed, covering him with her many legs.

Scott screamed then, as his friends had screamed moments before him. Already he could feel tiny points of fire and pain erupt in him as something sharp and cold bit into the soft flesh of his neck. He could feel the cold, wet slickness of its belly against him, as it straddled him in a powerful, numbing embrace, as the many legs of the thing gripped and tore at him. He screamed, but not for help. Hope had left him by then, and that scream was only the wail of dumb animal pain and despair.

And Shalak strove to remember her promise to wait with this one. Lust and hate and anger—anger at the hurting lights—drove her on to the kill. She tried to remember her promise, but she was a creature of such little restraint. She clutched and unclutched her mandibles in a nervous litany of indecision, her prey helpless beneath her.

But then it was too late. From somewhere behind her came the hoarse and incredulous shout. From somewhere near the entrance to the kitchen at the back end of the long hallway came the powerful beam of light that suddenly found her shiny black back. She spasmed and wrenched hideously then, dim and horrible memories flooding her beast brain. She remembered the night the Master had sent her out to kill and the dull pain of the moon's baleful glow; she remembered the lights of the two in the basement, the spitting fire of the one beneath her—and now, this!

She turned with an inaudible snarl and made her way quickly off the body of the fallen one. Death! She would bring it to this other one first. Merciless pain far greater than any she had known. Pain! Great pain! She scuttled with murderous quickness over the polished wood floors toward this new adversary, and suddenly the light was off of her and somewhere behind her searching for her in the inky blackness that she was a part of herself.

Distance dwindled, and her speed increased. The hateful light bounced off the staircase somewhere to her right, not close enough to hurt her or slow her awful attack. Close. So close. Mandibles clenching. Razored claws scratching the floor as she loped with ungainly speed. Dark eyes full of ravening hate. So close. So deliciously close.

Then it hit her again in full fury. Like some great invisible hand, the powerful beam of light chanced upon her and stopped her dead in her tracks. It shook nervously about her body for a moment, as it shook in the hand of the one who was holding it. But it was enough.

Shalak began to shrink, and shrivel then. Too much light. Her obscene, bloated body arched and dropped, and it was only with a last, titanic effort that she was able to move uncertainly to her left and right into the wall of the hallway that had enclosed them both. Wafting up from the floor was a trail of malodorous vapors that clung to the air for seconds in pungent streamlets. After a long moment it was the only sign that the horrible, twitching anomaly had ever been present at all.

28

Harry pushed himself up from the battered armchair with an effort to answer the insistent ringing of the doorbell. Damnation, he thought. They would have to come during *All in the Family*. He punched at the buzzer on the wall and could hear the heavy tread of footsteps on the stairs before he got to the door. Opening it, he waited for the others to appear, glad it was them who had to fight the three flights of stairs. God, he was tired tonight. A tiredness that went right to the bone and the center of the soul.

A uniform came into view around the bannister, then the figure of a young man followed by another two uniforms. "Christ, did you call out the National Guard too?" Harry asked the first one.

"How's that, Sergeant?" asked the first patrolman.

"Never mind. Just turn the hardened criminal over to me, will ya?"

"Sure, Sarge. That's why we're bringing him."

Harry shook his head mournfully and signalled Scott inside. "Do you three want to wait outside in the hall with your guns drawn—I mean, in case he jumps me or something?"

"We're supposed to get back, Sarge, but if you want I can call—"

"Goodnight, gentlemen," Harry said and closed the door.

Harry turned and faced Scott. The young man looked solemn, weary. "Let me have your coat. It's been getting damn cold these last few days. But hell, what can you expect by November?"

The other didn't answer. "Here, come on into the living room. I was just watching the tube before you came. That damn Archie Bunker always gives me fits."

He signaled Scott to sit on the sofa across from his chair, which he did. He looked uneasy, a little sullen. Being locked up in jail for a night and a day could do that, though. "Can I get you a beer or a Coke or something?"

Scott just shook his head no. "Good, then I can sit down. I hate to have to try and get outa this chair once I'm in it. Springs are shot and, well, I'm not getting any thinner," he said, patting his swelling stomach affectionately.

Scott looked at him glumly. "Look, Sergeant, could we just get this over with? I want to go home and go to bed. I want to forget about you and your whole police department as soon as possible."

Harry's face flushed scarlet. "Listen, son. I can send you right back to the jug if you'd like. Maybe I could even still flag down those three fellows who brought you here."

"You've got no right to hold me," Scott said angrily.

"We've got every right! In case you don't know it, we can hold you on numerous charges: breaking and entering, illegal possession of firearms—why, in the mood this town is in now, we could just about blame you for World War II and make it stick."

Scott sat back against the couch, suddenly subdued. Thinking. Trying to organize his resentment into something coherent but, yet, fighting it. This was the last man he should be mad at.

"Let me tell you something," the portly detective continued, "I had to go directly to the chief about getting you released into my custody. My immediate boss, Frank Elliot, is so hopping mad at me that I'll bet he's sticking pins in some voodoo doll right now. I went out on a limb for you for sure, and right away you've got to treat me like some sort of creep just because I'm a cop.

He paused to get his breath, but Scott spoke up before he could speak again. "I'm sorry, Sergeant. Not just because of that but because of what you did for me last night."

Harry looked embarrassed. "Yeah, last night." his voice suddenly seemed far away, "That's why I want to talk to you—about last night."

His eyes met Scott's. He could see the concern there, the doubt and the deep underlying current of fear. The time when he talked, there was no tinge of authority or anger in his voice. "Look, you broke into a complete stranger's home, armed to the teeth,"—he held up his hand for silence—"for whatever good reason. The fact remains that you took the police's job on yourself with, well, disastrous results."

"Somebody had to do something."

Harry looked at him hard, but his voice was still carefully controlled. "With disastrous results. Your two friends were killed, and you barely got out alive yourself. No, I'm not an insensitive hambone, but you aren't going to make me stop by looking like a wounded cow. This has got to be said, and, dammit, you've got to try and really listen to me. You don't know what some people would like to do to you in this town."

Scott looked at him with sudden interest. Up until this time, he had felt like the persecuted one. Now who was going to be made to blame? "What do you mean?"

"I meant that there are two more dead bodies to account for in a very middle-class, respectable sort of town that is all of a sudden in two month's time chock full of dead bodies. I mean that the state's attorney, the town council, my boss and practically everybody who's got something to say about how this town is run is tired of taking flak from the newspapers, the citizens, their families . . . They thought they had somebody to take their revenge out on, but now he's dead. You aren't quite as good a suspect, you don't fit the stereotype they've conjured up as well as the black fellow did, but you'll suffice."

"You can't be serious?"

'Frank Elliot was seeking the D.A. this morning

about a charge of first degree murder."

"What?" Scott exploded. "I'm supposed to have broken into that old house just so I could murder my two best friends and then be attacked by that, that—"

"Hold it. Hold it. I was there, remember? I know damn well you didn't do it." He was trying to reassure, seeing the effect the mention of his two friends was having on the man.

"Then why didn't you tell them?"

Harry sighed and ran his hand over his face. A look of infinite weariness came into his eyes, and his voice was strained and low. "Tell them what? Tell them that I saw you attacked—and was attacked myself—by a hundred-and-fifty-pound spider? A lot of good I could do you then, me being in a straight-jacket and all."

Scott looked down at the floor for a long time, his shoulders hunched forward in resignation. "So how come I'm not in jail now?"

Harry struggled to his feet, the big arm chair finally letting go of its smothering embrace. He walked over to a near window, and pulled back the curtain. "Looks like snow," he said reflectively.

"How come?" Scott insisted.

The detective continued to look out the window. His voice echoed back at Scott off the windowpane. "Because I fought and scraped for you. I rushed the coroner's report through for one thing. Death by brain embolism and massive heart failure it said. That was it. Two bodies with no visible signs of violence. I told them they'd have a hard time making a murder rap stick—oh, not in this town now, maybe. But later—on appeal."

"I, I think you did enough—saving my life last night, I mean. Why go to bat for me?" Scott asked hopefully.

"Yeah, I'd like to think so too. It'd be a lot easier. I even tried. Only thing is, I couldn't get that goddamn *thing* out of my mind."

He could see the other shudder a little on the couch. "Could it have killed them?"

"I don't know. If it did, it's something right out of a bad movie. I mean, they must have been frightened to death by the thing. Shit. What am I apologing for? That thing was right out of a bad movie."

Scott moaned slightly. "Jesus, what's happened to my life?"

Harry turned and walked over to the couch, sitting heavily into the cushions next to Scott. "Same thing that's happened to the lives of a lot of people in this town apparently. It's gone topsy-turvy."

"What was that thing?" Scott almost yelled at him. Weeks of frustration and fear were at the verge of breaking him.

Harry looked at him intently, then spoke slowly. "This morning we had eighteen men over there, including crime lab from Oak Grove and Chicago, the coroner—all sorts of experts and that sort. Well, guess what? They went through that house from top to bottom—three times. They broke open locked doors, they even tore up some floor boards looking for some evidence of who had lived there, but they didn't find no goddamn hundred-and-fifty-pound walking nightmare."

"So? We imagined it? Is that what you're trying to say?"

"I might think so except for those two dead men in the basement—that goddamn screwy basement."

Scott fought to hold back the vile wrenching inside his body at the mention of Larry and Lenny. He was doing everything he could not to think of them now, just yet. He couldn't afford to now, and he'd have a whole lifetime ahead of him for regret. "I didn't see the basement. Didn't get a chance to."

Harry sensed his anguish. "Why don't you just listen for awhile? I've got a lot to fill you in on, and it'll be easier on you to just listen. You sure you don't want a beer?"

Scott shook his head vigorously. "If there's one time in my life I've got to stay sober—"

Harry couldn't repress a slight laugh. "Yeah, I can see what you mean. All right, just listen, but listen good, because a lot of work has gone into this, and it gets a little complicated."

"Go ahead. Tell me about the screwy basement." Scott said, a slight grin enlivening his features. Anything to keep his mind off the tragedy he had led two friends into.

"Jesus. That basement. After I got you out of there and over to the hospital to see if you were all right, I went back there with three squads."

"You left while someone might have still been there?" Scott interrupted. Even now he was still ready to distrust police procedure.

"I thought you were just gonna listen," Harry said with a little aggravation. "That just shows how screwed up you were. I called from my car and waited 'til we had men on the scene, so don't worry about any precious evidence getting away."

"They called it shock."

"What?"

"The doctors—they said I was in shock."

"Catatonia is more like it. Say, if you don't shut the fuck up, you'll never get to hear this."

"Sorry," Scott apologized.

"It's all right. I forgot: you think you're Inspector Clousseau. Yeah, well I went back there and went down to look at your—well, to look in the basement. The damn thing was painted black. I mean everything: doorknobs, floor, ceiling rafters, windows. A thick black paint on everything except . . . well, we were still trying to figure out what that other thing was until this afternoon."

"What other thing?"

"The stone. This big rectangular piece of what looked like marble or something. It was, oh, maybe eight feet long, four feet across, and about five feet high. That fucker must have weighed a couple of tons easy."

Scott was starting to feel a real interest welling up in him now, beginning to forget the blackness that his life had become. "Well, what was it?"

Harry was beginning to enjoy the drama of his presentation, despite the grim circumstances. It was so seldom that he got to play detective, to reconstruct the crime to an audience that wasn't yelling at him—like Frank Elliot always did. "We couldn't say—that is until we brought in some professor from the University of Chicago this afternoon. You see, there were all these funny little markings or inscriptions carved right into the thing. Like symbols or something. At any rate, he identified it as a Druid altar, something some ancient pagans who lived in Ireland used for sacrifices to their gods—that sort of thing."

Harry saw Scott go a little pale. "Of course, he said that today it would just be a curiosity piece or an archeological find. No Druids running around nowadays." He tried to sound reassuring. "But that was it. That basement was empty except for that big altar and a heating plant over in one corner and some tools and things in a padlocked cellar."

"But why paint a basement black or have an altar in it? It doesn't make sense."

"Nothing about that house makes sense. Hell, it's got sixteen rooms in it, and only three were furnished: a library downstairs and two bedrooms upstairs. The furniture was old and fancy. Very expensive. There was a big rosewood desk in that library and a Tiffany lamp and rows of all sorts of strange books: philosophy, occultism, books in foreign languages. The two bedrooms only had beds, dressers, a couple of chairs—the bare necessities. The rest of that whole damn house was empty, full of dust and cobwebs."

"Couldn't you find who lived there? That would tell you—"

"Way ahead of you," Harry said with a dismissive flourish. "Boy, you must really think we're incompetents. That's the first thing I tried to find out."

"No, it's not that. I'm just concerned. I told you—my girl."

"Well, we're concerned too, believe it or not. Like I said, I spent the whole day trying to find out who lived there—for reasons that go beyond you and your girlfriend."

"What do you mean, Sergeant?"

"Haven't you wondered how I just happened to show up there at the nick of time last night? Well, almost," he added, thinking of the two unfortunate men in the basement.

"Yes, I have. It took me a while, though. I was sort of out of it until this morning."

"Yeah, I know. Shock."

"How did you happen to be there?" Scott asked.

"It's a long story. It really is. Let's just say I was looking for a house on Fair Tree, because I thought it tied into some of the awful things that have been going on in this town. Looks now like I was right, too. Oh, some of the evidence is circumstantial, but it doesn't seem unreasonable to say that right at this moment I can tie that house into a murderer, a church desecration and possibly two kidnappings, including your girlfriend."

"Well, thanks for that much. At least she's still not just a 'missing person.'"

"She might be," cautioned Harry. "We've got nothing to tie her to the house directly, but with everything else that's been going on, it doesn't seem too unlikely that she was kidnapped."

"But by who?" Scott asked, desperation clinging to the edge of his voice.

"That, unfortunately, I'm not absolutely certain about yet, but I've got a pretty fair idea."

"For God's sake tell me," Scott implored him.

But Harry was enjoying playing detective. That and a more serious purpose impelled him forward in his methodical exposition. "No, one step at a time. You see, I was waiting outside that house when you three showed up last night. I'd been watching it for a good fifteen minutes from the street."

"What? We didn't see you—"

Harry looked hurt. "I'm not that obvious." he began.

"But how could you have let us go in there?" Scott

asked, his voice rising.

"Wait a minute. I didn't know who you were. It was dark. I certainly didn't know what you'd find in there. How could I?"

"Yeah, you're right. God, it's just that I'm looking for anything rational in all this. If you'd suspected that Barb was in there—"

"I suspected no such thing, I told you. I was there for other reasons. Actually, I had been looking for a house on Fair Tree—a house that had probably only been occupied recently. I must have driven up and down this street a dozen times the last few nights just trying to piece it all together, not knowing what to do other than check with the realtors and some of the moving companies. At first it seemed a dead end, but yesterday evening one of the local realtors called me back. They had slipped up, had sold a house on Fair Tree three months ago, but there'd been a change in personnel or something and they'd mislaid the files. Anyhow, it was that house: 714 Fair Tree. I got there just before you, but I sure as hell wasn't expecting you. One of the detectives who questioned you this morning told me how you said you'd found out about the place. Damn bit of good luck."

"Good luck? Yeah, great luck," Scott returned.

Harry looked at him hard for a moment, then reached over to put his cigar out in an ashtray on an end table. "We found so much weird stuff in that house, Scott," he said wearily. He was beginning to feel a bond with the younger man. "Did you read about that church desecration up at St. Mark's a couple months ago?"

"No, but I heard about it."

"Some maniac slaughtered a sheep on the altar. Probably carried the poor animal there in some cloth, a drapery actually."

"So?" He sensed the detective was making a point.

"So I found a drapery ring and a little fabric at the church. It might have been nothing, but it was a lead. The only one I had. Only it never panned out, not 'til last night. I found that same sort of drapery ring and fabric in the house on Fair Tree."

Scott knew he was trying to make a point beyond this. "So that tied together the house and the church desecration."

"Yeah, and that bothers me more than just the fact that that connects two different tragedies. I mean, that sort of connection is usually pure joy to a cop's heart." He seemed reluctant to go on.

"So what's eating you?" Scott asked with a little trepidation.

The detective hesitated. "I don't know. Maybe nothing. It just seems like all the troubles in this town started with that sheep being butchered on the church altar. Now I find the place where all these things have been going on here in town might have stemmed from in one way or another, and it's empty. Like it's all over. Like the ultimate organizer of a lot of seemingly unrelated crimes and crazy goings on just disappeared, never to be found or punished."

"Sergeant, you're beating around the bush. Give it to me straight."

Harry sighed. "What I'm trying to say is this, it started with some sort of hideous sacrifice, and it seems to have ended with some sort of sacrifice. Yes. That altar is one thing, but there's more. The lab boys went over this place, every inch of it. They didn't find much, believe me. There wasn't a single name on a piece of paper, not a label or a receipt—nothing to show us who lived here or where they might have gone. The place had been picked clean."

"So what the hell—"

Harry held up his hand for silence again. "They did find two things, though. One was a sort of circle of ash around that altar. Chemical analysis indicates that the unburned parts consisted of certain herbs and plant material, some common some not. Other than that there was only one other thing: dried human blood."

"Jesus," Scott intoned softly, his worst fears coming

to life again.

"They also found human hair samples in four different rooms. Chicago department did some newfangled protein analysis on it or something. Some strands were gray: from a woman between forty-five and sixty-years of age. Another sample was brown: a girl between about sixteen and twenty-five. Lastly a girl's again: blond, between seven and about twelve probably. None of it means anything in itself, but what does it suggest to you?"

"Me? You're asking me? I thought you didn't like my playing cop."

"Come on. Cut out the shit!"

"Okay. I'm sorry, I just didn't want to say what I thought—what I feared—that ma;ybe the second one was . . . was Barb."

Harry's face went grim. "All right. Here it is. This morning we dug up the dirt floor on the padlocked root cellar. It was just too inviting, what with the earth having been freshly turned and all. We found something in it—a body."

"Oh, God. No. Oh, no." Scott moaned.

"Hold it. What we found was a little girl's body. The little girl who had been kidnapped on Halloween here in town. She'd been slashed open from the breast bone to the crotch and then buried in the earth to rot. But before you start sounding too relieved—and I know that sounds morbid and insensitive—I want to tell you this: We found other hair samples that matched the length, color and protein composition of the girl in her twenties someplace else. We found several strands of it on that altar."

Harry didn't know whether Scott's silence was a sign of relief or further dread. But the young man was deathly pale, and Harry couldn't repress a pang of sympathy despite the present need for calculated, professional treatment oif this whole matter. Don't get personally involved. It was the first law of good police work, but Harry found himself getting involved anyway—maybe because he had seen and experienced something that made him doubt everything he had ever believed and Scott was his only link to that experience. "Don't get too pessimistic," he said reassuringly. "We've examined the grounds of that house all day, we've pulled up floorboards, we've looked everywhere, but there's no sign of your girlfriend. If she has been killed, God forbid, they might have dropped the body into a river or Lake Michigan or even buried it out in the country somewhere, but it's not likely. It's not likely they'd leave the body of one victim right in that house and go to greater trouble and risk to get rid of another."

"Yes, that seems to make sense," Scott began, the relief showing in his voice, "but I wonder if you can expect anything to make sense in all this. It's all been so crazy."

"I'm the one who should be thinking that; you're the one who is supposed to be optimistic," Harry cautioned. He didn't want the young man to despair, not before he'd presented all that he'd discovered.

"But is that it? I mean, all you know is she's gone but don't have any idea where?"

"No, I didn't exactly say that. I haven't just been twidling my thumbs, you know. Today I talked to some neighbors. Some of the people on the block didn't even know the house had been occupied, but a couple of local kids said they'd seen a woman going in and out who matches your description. They also saw her drive out of the alley in an old black car once."

"But that doesn't tell us where—"

"Just let me finish, Clousseau. Next I checked with the town water works, sanitation department, electrical utility company and so on. No bills had been issued yet but deposits had been left with the telephone and electric companies in the name of an Ama Bloch who gave her address as the house on Fair Tree. The deposits were covered with a check from a local bank, also in the name of this Ama Bloch. Unfortunately, the initial deposit was in cash. A check might have been traceable."

Scott was becoming anxious. The detective had been

working. Maybe he had found something out. "Can that name be traced?"

"I tried running it through social security and local credit checks. Nothing. IRS and FBI were blanks too. Finally, it was only the realtor who had any solid information. It seems that the house was sold as part of an estate, and the estate's lawyer still had all the paper work. The house was sold to a Jerold Weemes from Akron Ohio four months ago. It was—get this—paid for in cash. $240,000 was transferred from an Akron bank to cover the purchase, and the house was titled to this Jerold Weemes."

"Great. Then all you have to do is trace this Jerold Weemes in Akron."

Harry took a deep breath. "There is no Jerold Weemes. The money was put in an Akron bank, but only enough to cover the purchase of the house. It was deposited in cash, so there was no record of a transfer from another bank. The name and address were false. Jerold Weemes is an alias for some unknown person who exists only on paper."

Scott groaned. "Didn't the Akron bank question such a large deposit?"

Harry laughed. "You don't know much about banks, do you? Banks seldom question large cash deposits, my friend. It wouldn't be good business. No, the account was closed on deeding of the house. Whoever set this thing up was two things: smart and rich. Smart because he didn't take out a mortgage, thinking he could skip out on it later when he abandoned the house and rich because he could affort to pay $240,000 in cash."

"I don't understand the smart part," Scott said. "What difference does it make whether he took out a mortgage or not?"

"Simple," Harry replied. "A mortgage means paper work, credit checks, addresses. We'd have an easy trace then."

"I guess I'm not such a hot shot cop after all."

"Hey, I wasn't feeling so good either today. About all I was finding out was that none of the normal avenues were working. It's what we call negative lead in the police biz. I was beginning to think whoever had orchestrated this thing was one smart character—too smart for me. Then it hit me."

"What?" Scott was hoping for anything positive at this point.

Harry smiled. It was a sly smile of triumph. "Well, I'd called moving companies galore today—had four men on it, actually. I figured if the move into that old house was local, the companies would have records, and even if it was out-of-state some of the big companies cross reference records with local offices. Mostly they all told me it was impossible: They didn't keep those records or it would take a week to check or they didn't have the manpower. It was a nowhere idea, actually, but I was trying everything. It was then that I thought of that altar."

"The altar? What about it?" He wished the detective would get to the point.

"That altar must weigh two or three tons easy. I was sure it wasn't part of the estate left by the former owners—God, what a thing to buy with a new house, eh?—but I checked anyway. The point is, no goddamn moving company could have got that thing in to that basement."

Scott could feel the climax coming. He waited silently.

"So I went back to that house late this afternoon. You saw the entrance to that basement: that right-angle, low stairway and all. No way a bunch of moving men were gonna carry that thing down and around those steps, and they sure weren't gonna make it through the interior entrance and down a long flight of stairs. No, that hunk of rock was just too damned big and heavy."

"Jesus, I'm going in circles. So how did they get it in?"

"It was hard to see at first, what with that damn black paint over everything," Harry said quickly. He was getting excited too. "But I found it soon enough: a larger door frame cut into the surrounding wood. You see, the basement foundation was cement, naturally enough, but there was a large wooden understructure that helped support the porch upstairs. The basement door was set right into this."

"I'm a carpenter. I understand what you mean, but how would that—"

"If you keep quiet long enough I'll tell you. You see, somebody just sawed a larger door frame into the understructure, then fit it and nailed it back together, probably when they were done. You could still see the outline where the new frame had been cut. It was about nine feet across."

"Of course," Scott said excitedly. "They probably just rebraced it with some sort of two-by-four sectioning—like a whole new wall."

"But something like that takes skill, right? Your average moving man couldn't do it, could he?"

"No way," Scott replied.

"I didn't think so. I also figured they still couldn't carry that thing down a flight of winding stairs, that they must have slid it on skids or something. It was probably crated up, and they just slid it down into the basement."

"Yeah, it makes sense. But who did it? We still don't know who did it?"

"I think we do," Harry said and paused for effect. "I told you, I didn't think any normal moving company handled anything like that, but I called a friend of mine who is a dispatcher for North American. He agreed and said it was one of two choices: either some I'll try anything freelance types with a big truck or one of the so-called policy movers."

"What the hell is that?"

"That, my friend, is a rare bird. They only ship things like art masterpieces, valuable antiques, computers—all high-price items that come affixed with a huge insurance policy. They take big risks and get paid big money. There are four of them in the whole country, as far as my friend knew, but he said they would have the expertise to do something like I found done with that door frame. I don't mind telling you, for the first time today, I got excited. It could have been some local yokels with a truck who brought along a carpenter, but something told me no. Right away I called the first company. I told them who I was and that I wanted them to see if they had anything shipped to this town three to four months ago."

"I'm going to bust a gut," Scott complained.

"Getting there," Harry replied. "They said no dice. They didn't give out that info even to the cops without a court order. I didn't have time to argue just then—not 'til I'd exhausted my other possibilities—so I called the second company, a Surety Handlers in Baltimore. They were reluctant too, until I promised their traffic manager all sorts of bad publicity if he didn't help me. Bingo. It took him five minutes to find it: large crate containing 'archeological materials' was delivered to Oak Grove, to our house on Fair Tree, on August the sixteenth of this year. I asked him one more question and kept my fingers crossed: Did he have a point of origin?

"It was a silly question to ask a policy mover, I guess. Of course he did. The address where they picked up the crate was in a town called Inswich, Massachusetts, just a little ways north of Boston. The shipper's name was a Walter Garth Glaeston, and that's all the information they had."

"Glaeston?" Scott asked. "That name is familiar. I think I've heard it in conversations with—with . . . Jesus, now I remember. Barb said her mother's name was Glaeston—her maiden name that is."

"Bingo! That's it." Harry yelled so loud that Scott nearly jumped.

"No wonder she was so preoccupied with that stuff about her dead mother." Scott said, as if to himself. "It must be some relative."

"You got it," Harry returned excitedly. "Not only that, but it establishes a sound connection between the girl's disappearance and the possible perpetrator of a major felony. The FBI would raid that Inswich address today, if I gave them this information on the probability that your girl had been abducted and taken across state lines."

Scott could barely stay on the sofa: he felt like shouting, doing cartwheels—anything to express his relief. For the first time in what seemed aeons, a nightmare of despair was illuminated with hope. But looking at Harry, he could suddenly see that the detective was less than enthusiastic. "What's the matter?" he asked, suddenly cautious again.

"I don't know. Maybe I'm going nuts. I mean, I was as excited as you were a minute ago at the thought of catching up with these creeps. A two-month policeman's nightmare looked like it was ending, and I should be happy."

"So why aren't you?"

"Good question. I'm still thinking about it, but I know it's got something to do with professional pride—maybe you'd rather call it ego."

"I don't follow you. I kind of hate to admit it after some of he things I've said and done, but it seems to be that you've done a damn good job, Sergeant."

"Thanks. It's nice to hear somebody say so. But if it's true, that's all the more reason to be upset. You see, in my whole career as a cop in this town I had one chance to actually do something important and, yes, get some credit for it. All of a sudden the FBI was in on it, the state police, the governor's crime commission—everybody was trying to get a piece of this big gangland murder until everything got so balled up that the whole investigation fell apart."

"And you got blamed?"

"Well, no—not exactly. But it screwed up any chances I had for promotion, so I guess in a way I did get blamed even though the case was effectively out of my hands months before. But, most importantly, I've never been able to shake the feeling that if everybody had let me handle the case my way, it might have had a different outcome."

"That was that hotel murder down on Winston

Boulevard, wasn't it? I read about it."

Harry nodded assent. "Yeah, and now it seems like I've got another chance in my, how would you say, old age. I cracked this damn thing myself, at least the murders of those three women, and it looks like I may have almost managed to piece together the whole crazy jigsaw this town's become in the last three months." He paused here, and his eyes went hard. "It also looks like my boss may be getting ready to grab the credit too, if you can judge by the *Tribune* yesterday. They interviewed him, and it sounded like he's personally handled the thing from start to finish himself."

"So what are you saying?"

"I guess I'm saying a lot of things—I'm saying that I'm tired of being fucked over, I'm bugged by the idea of not following through something I've sweated over for two months to its conclusion, and I'm worried that somehow local cops or state cops or somebody up in Massachusetts could mess it up again, and then I'll never know the whole story about what's been happening in this town. You might not either."

"What does that mean? It's not like I don't care—I live in this town too—but I don't think I have the same stake in it you do."

"No, I'm sure you don't, excepting that it seems like your girlfriend is a part of some larger overall pattern of events. It's like a tapestry. Unravel one thread, and pretty soon the whole thing comes apart. Basically, it all means that if the police in Massachusetts blow it, she might be the one to regret it. Her and you."

"And to think you were lambasting me a little while ago for not doing things by proper police procedure," Scott said accusingly.

Harry looked sheepish. "I know. Crazy, huh? But it makes sense compared to the rest of this whole screwy business."

"Amen. So what do you want to do? You know I'll do anything to help find Barb. One way or the other," he said grimly.

Harry pushed himself off the sofa and went over to

an old roll top desk littered with a great mound of dog-eared papers. He picked up a small envelope and shook its contents toward Scott. "Two tickets on a 6:30 A.M. flight to Boston. If Frank Elliot finds out I've left town in the middle of this mess about that house on Fair Tree or that you've left town—even with me—hel'll have every justification for doing whatever he wants with me. Knowing him, I'd be looking in the want ads the same day for some job other than a cop. But the way I figure it is, we fly to Boston, rent a car and drive up to this Inswich. If we don't find anything, we can be back on a midnight flight to Chicago. If we do, well nobody will have any cause to rant and rave, because we'll be heroes."

Scott looked at him with wonder. "You'd be willing to do this?"

"Hey, it's not just for you. I told you, I got reasons, too."

Scott stood up and walked over to him. "You know, I owe you a lot. You probably saved my life last night, and whatever you say, I think you're doing this more for me than yourself. For my part, I've felt all my life that the really important things you've got to do yourself." He extended his hand toward the detective. "This may be the most important for me."

"Then you'll go?" Harry asked hopefully, accepting the hand in his own.

"Is the sky blue?" Scott said and smiled. It was the first time that a smile had felt like it should in what seemed like a long time.

29

The plane winged its way toward the ground through great swaths of sullen gray cloud that had lain heavily in the sky throughout the flight, piled and tumbled about like gigantic building blocks that obscured the distant landscapes below. It was one of those cheerless, forbidding winter days when nature conspires to evoke gloom in the souls of all her hapless subjects and all remnants of autumn's gentle nostalgia or summer's golden light are erased in the mists of seeming antiquity.

Such days are burdens, even to the most melancholy of hearts. There is the feeling of snow in the air—not that soft white blanket beloved of Thanksgiving and Christmas days but the wind-whipped variety that swirls in great frozen clouds out of the remote north bringing all of man's puny activities to a torturous end below. There is the portent of vicious winter storms, all frigid and icy with slate-gray skies. A time to be inside by a blazing fire. A time to remember other times.

Whether it was the specter of winter's icy lifelessness or something in the hearts and spirits of the people themselves, Scott noticed something odd in the eyes and faces of the passengers that surrounded him as he and Harry made their way out of the plane. There were many different types of people among that throng of crowding, huddling, hurrying bodies.

There were the rather tired and harried looking businessmen: gray flannel types with a vaguely hunted look about them—the mingled look of expectation, efficiency and a subtler, deeper impotency of the soul. And there were the women, some with children. The women were about evenly divided between those whose faces revealed only the sweet vacuousness of too many Thursdays doing the laundry and too many hours immersed in the soap operas and those whose features registered only relief that their sky ordeal was over, their fear and their feminine delight in their own helplessness finally ended. And then there were the soldiers, a sporadic few but studies in assumed casualness, each and every one. The young gods of war when war is not fashionable.

But the young, sultry girls seemed to relish the experience. They walked down the loading ramp in stately magnificence, twirling their heads with a sudden movement so that long, soft cascades of hair would fall at precisely the right angle across the sides of perfect, chiseled faces.

There was one elderly lady in a wheel chair. The flight attendants were carefully, gingerly easing her down the steps to the ground. Petulance and impatience dominated those worn features. She positively ached for something to complain about. She pulled the heavy mink coat closer around her with palsied, clutching hands. They treated her like the most fragile bone china.

Scott wondered how they could all look so lifeless, so insignificant. Empty animated husks wandering aimlessly through life in an uncomprehending search for their own oblivion. Spiritless. Second-hand ideals and petty desires. The bright mirror of life grown yellowish and waxy, cracked and chipped in innumerable places until the life it reflected was obscured in the mindlessness of convention and everlasting routine—until it became distorted in a legion's passing of life's mediocre moments and trivial perceptions.

He turned and looked at the figure walking beside him. Rumpled, wearing a dark shiny gray suit under a dark green overcoat with a stain on the collar. Fiftyish, balding, going on stout. It was hard to believe that he was going to share in this thing. It was hard to believe that he was joining his nightmare.

"Why don't you wait for the suitcases while I go pick up the car." Reality intruded unbidden.

Harry was looking at him searchingly, could see the dull vacuousness that had been growing in his eyes all throughout the flight. "Uh, okay," returned Scott hastily. "I'll meet you out front on the concourse."

He watched the detective move away from him, move tiredly with a forced determination. Here was another imponderable, that he and this man should be thrown together under such bizarre circumstances, that the detective should be willing to take such chances on his behalf. Still, he had admitted that it was in his own self-interest to go. He too had seemed self-absorbed during the flight, and little conversation had passed between them. They were operating almost as if some unspoken, implicit covenant were guiding and motivating them. Strong and silent, they were marching to their destiny, whatever that destiny might be.

Scott moved over toward the baggage area, moved again into the throng of scurrying, ant-like people who were pawing impatiently over the assorted leather satchels and suitcases that paraded by them to the tune of whirring gears and squeaking tracks. Soon he spotted his own small duffel bag and Harry's battered old black suitcase. He picked them up and tried to move out of the jostling crowd quickly. Whether it was the fact that they were intruding on the silence, the feeling of solemnity that was growing within him, or whether it was a resentment of their sheepishness, their unquestioning adherence to all the unspoken and unnecessary commandments of life, he suddenly hated them—he wanted to lash out at them. Something latent deep inside of him was surfacing in its full anti-social glory.

He carefully picked his way out of the small crowd and began walking toward the escalators that would carry him downstairs and out to the broad concourse where, hopefully, Harry would be waiting with a car. As he stepped onto the escalator, he noticed a girl walking away form him. She was tall, lithe, graceful. Her carriage suggested more of a cultivated sophistication than Barb's gait, but that same light and flowing quality was there. An easy grace. Movement and manner. Something indefinable but patently her own and something obvious to one who had grown to know those movements, to love those gestures. A bit of longing grew swiftly in his soul, took root and banished a little of the dust of despair.

The concourse was partly underground and shielded from the worst vagaries of the wind, but Scott was still thoroughly frozen by the time Harry pulled up in the plain dark brown Chevy. Scott got in quickly, heaving the duffel bag and suitcase onto the back seat. They were almost out of the city limits before either said anything.

Scott was referring to a map Harry had picked up with the car. "It looks like 1-A is your best route to Inswich."

"I'm already headed in that direction. Inswich is only about ten or fifteen miles northeast of here. It shouldn't take long at all."

"Well, Boston wasn't much to look at."

"The airport is on the outskirts," Harry said. "We bypassed the city almost completely."

"That's all right. I wasn't in the mood for sightseeing anyways," Scott replied, smiling grimly. "What'll we do when we get to Inswich?"

"Find a motel room, I imagine. Then we'll start looking for that address the moving company gave me. No reason to waste time."

Scott merely nodded and looked out the car window at the surrounding countryside. Even the distant urban sprawl of Boston itself had a different feel than Chicago. Buildings and highways looked the same. People looked the same. Trees looked the same. But some quality that was indefinably New England could be felt even here on the outlying border of the city. There was a change in atmosphere from Chicago and the Midwest: less electric, more stately and passive, older and more complex. Layers underneath. The feeling grew as they left Boston behind them and penetrated into the picturesque New England countryside. Roads began to twist and wind by white picket and stone fences, past proud but simple old white frame homes and along avenues lined by gnarled trees that seemed to whisper of antiquity. It was a countryside of nuance and soft, subtle impressions.

But both men became absorbed in the worlds of their own thoughts. Occasionally, Scott would glance in the detective's direction, but he was silent, his eyes focused forward toward the road. They were in Inswich before they had said barely another word to each other. Inswich, with its austere black-shuttered houses dating as far back as the late seventeenth century. Inswich, fabled only after Salem for its witch trials in the colonial days. Truly, if there was any town in the whole country that looked as if it belonged to another age, it was Inswich. Nestled in long, low hills and thick woods, it is at once inviting for its quaint antiquity and forbidding in its somber suggestiveness. On this cold, tomb-gray day, the writhing empty trees and the tight-shuttered rooms of Inswich seemed anything but inviting. It was Sunday, and the streets were empty in the style of most small towns on the Sabbath. Scott felt suddenly forlorn as their lone car navigated the ghost streets of the village. The immediacy of their objective smote him, and he now felt the need for conversation.

"You going to stop and ask directions?" he inquired.

"Yeah, if I can find anybody to give them," Harry replied with exasperation. "Looks like one of those towns in the movies—you know, where everybody is dead during the daytime but rise during the night."

"I know what you mean, but I'll bet it's beautiful in the spring and summer. Fall too. It's like a picture postcard."

"Well, today it looks like Transylvania," Harry intoned solemnly.

"There's a gas station."

Harry pulled the Chevy into the gravel front road of

the gas station. At length a tall boy ambled slowly out of the station and up to the driver's side of the car. Harry rolled down the window. "Help yuh?" the boy asked.

"I hope so," replied Harry. "We're looking for two things: a place to stay for the night and Potter Road here in Inswich."

The boy paused and then smiled, a condescending smile of the type locals reserve for the tourists. "Well, let's see." He rubbed at his chin meditatively. "There's plenty of homes that take in tourists and the like—leastwise in the summer. Nearest motel is out on Route 133 a mile or two. Then there's one out on Route 6 too. That'd be about four miles. Nothin' here in town."

"Fine. Now how about Potter Road?"

"Potter Road? Well, that don't run through town. Runs out along the bay and up toward Newburyport. Cuts in and out. Kinda hard to follow. All rich folk're out on Potter Road."

"We're looking for 500 north Potter Road. The address I have says that it's in Inswich."

"Nope," replied the boy. "Mailin' address maybe."

"Well, can you tell us how to get out there—to Potter Road, I mean?"

"Sure. Just go on up the road here to the second road where you can turn right. Follow that for, oh, a mile or two 'til you come to a fork. Keep goin' left and before long you'll be on Potter Road. You'll have to find the exact address yourself."

"Thank you very much. You've been a big help."

"Great. You need any gas?"

"No, just filled up at the airport. Thanks again." Harry rolled up the window and began to pull away. The boy stood there looking after them. "That, my friend, is some of the local color." Harry looked at Scott and smiled appreciatively.

Scott looked back at him and said, "Like I said, a picture postcard."

Halfway up the block they saw a sign pointed toward a road marked Route 133. "You want to sample the local accommodations on 133?" Scott asked with no real interest.

"Might as well. I forgot to ask for the Duncan Hines rating," Harry chuckled.

He headed the car out of town down a long tree-lined road and past numerous small frame houses. Often, small plates or wooden placards were attached to the house on either side of the door bearing simple numbers like 1717 or 1734, indicative of their year of construction. They were mostly simple rectangular dwellings with no hint of wealth or pretense except for a few larger and obviously later buildings that were architecturally more impressive.

But soon the countryside flattened out and became more open, and it wasn't long before they found the motel the boy had mentioned. It was a drab, unelegant sort of place, but, then, their mission didn't call for plush quarters. Harry went in and registered for the both of them, then drove the car down to the unit on the far end of the building.

Once inside, Scott tested the bed and watched as Harry opened the black battered suitcase. He removed a dark pair of pants, a dark sweatshirt and a heavy black leather jacket. "Leftover from my days as a traffic cop," he joked. "I'll never get it zipped shut now, but it'll have to do."

Next he removed something bulky wrapped in soft fabric. It was a .38 caliber Smith and Wesson in a holster. He handed it to Scott saying, "I had a letter of authorization to carry mine on the plane, but you couldn't have gotten through the metal detector. Wear it in good health, as the saying goes, and don't use it unless you really have to."

Scott smiled but said nothing. He watched again as Harry removed a final article from the suitcase. It was also wrapped in fabric but was longer and bulkier. The detective began to unwrap the layers of cloth until Scott saw the gleam of highly polished silver metal. Suddenly he laughed out loud. "What are you going to do with that?"

Harry looked hurt and annoyed as he held up the large silver cross. "I got this from a priest. It's been blessed," he said defensively. "I figure, why take chances?"

"On what?" Scott continued to laugh.

"Well, hell! It works in those horror movies."

Scott stopped laughing, his face gone abruptly solemn. "I suppose I shouldn't be laughing. This whole thing is kind of like a horror movie, isn't it?"

"Yeah, and those movies are about the only precedent I've got to go on in this case. So, funny as it may seem, I brought along a cross."

"I'm sorry, I suppose that it's just kind of hard to believe all this is happening during the day. It's hard not to feel a little foolish."

Harry frowned a little, but his body, which had gone taut, relaxed a little. "That's okay. I felt a little foolish in asking Monsignor Kratschke for it too. I haven't been to church for ten years, and all of a sudden I'm asking him for a goddamn crucifix."

"Harry, I don't think. . .I mean, I really wonder if it will—"

"Do any good? So do I, but it's the best I could come up with one short notice. The desecration at St. Mark's implies that there might be some kind of religious motivation to all this. If I run into anything again like that thing I saw in the house that night—well, I doubt whether this will have much effect," he patted the slight bulge under the left arm of his suitcoat. "After all, you couldn't have missed from that range. Not with a full clip."

Scott felt suddenly uncomfortable. "I'm hungry," he said. "What do you say we have a bite to eat?"

"Good idea. It's cold out, and something to eat will help if we're going to be traipsing all over the countryside looking for Potter Road. You want to unpack first?"

Scott signalled toward the duffel bag. "Not much to unpack. I travel light."

They went out to the car and took 133 back into Inswich. It was quite a while before they found an open restaurant, but eventually they located a small diner that was open but nearly empty. Harry ate heartily, as befitting his bulk, but Scott had only coffee and a bowl of clam chowder. In minutes it had begun to bubble ominously in his belly, his stomach rising and falling in nervous expectation, but the detective seemed laconic and relaxed as he chattered sporadically about one thing or another.

Only once did the conversation turn to anything more serious or relevant to their present design. Harry started to talk about the murders in Oak Grove, about his gut certainty that there was some connection between the murders the huge Negro had committed and the rambling house on Fair Tree. That house and whoever had lived in it had been the key to those murders and, probably, the kidnappings too. A psychopath? He had originally thought so, but now he wasn't so sure. Now he was thinking along different lines, along a line similar to those witchcraft murders he had read about in New York a couple of years back. A group of doped-up kids had kidnapped and killed three children in the name of Satan or some such crap. God! It was unbelievable how warped and sick some people could get. But if he could crack this thing, if he could tie all the loose ends together in a nice, neat, tidy package—hell, he'd be able to write his own ticket in Oak Grove. Goddamn Frank Elliot wouldn't have a thing to say about it either.

Scott listened to Harry talk but said little. He liked something about this man. Maybe it was his basic simplicity and directness. He sensed that here was a man whom life had beaten down, whose dreams and pretensions to importance were mostly behind him but a man whose spirit was still essentially intact. He was harrassed and resigned, but he still enjoyed playing the game.

But Scott's mind was elsewhere. Harry sensed his preoccupation, so he ate quickly and they soon left the diner. Back in the heart of town, they passed the gas station where there was now no sign of the boy or anyone else. Harry turned the car at the second right, and they were soon proceeding down a narrow tree-lined road where the houses became fewer and farther between. They were moving presumably eastward toward the ocean, just a few miles away. Neither of them had talked at all since they had left the diner. Both were emotionally preparing for the unkown events ahead. It was a silence that both wanted and respected.

Soon they were in the midst of a densely wooded area, and the road dipped and gullied as the land became rougher and more hilly. Occasional houses were set back from the road, peeking out at them from wooded knolls and barren branches as they drove. They met no other cars. Finally, they came to the fork in the road and Harry turned left. A mile or so ahead they saw a clearing, and soon the roar of the surf made its way into their ears like some beckoning distant voice, low and mysterious and whispering great secrets of magic into their sullen, self-preoccupation.

They were coming to the bay area now, and they could already see great stretches of deserted beach before them. White-capped waves broke over the horizon, chasing the wind which clamored and cavorted before and in back of them. The sea looked cold and angry as they approached it, a deep ashen gray tinged with patches of somber green. Thick, leaden clouds moved ponderously overhead, and billowing, frothy whitecaps flung themselves skyward in a vain effort to reach the vaulted clouds and damply drag them back down into the covetous sea and into deep ocean caverns far beneath the murky, fathomless waters. But the vast swelling spread of vapors moved on unhindered, aimless in its eternal journey.

Now they had emerged from the dense blanket of trees into an area where the great empty beach on their right stood in stark, sandy contrast to the long, rolling line of hills which receded and grew ever higher on their left. The road curved and twisted before them, sometimes disappearing around a tree-lined curve and then appearing again at some distance ahead. Harry slowed the auto to compensate for the curvature of the road but continued on past the beach area without stopping, for it only resembled a bit of almost ghostly frigid desert. Quickly their world grew smaller and more confining again as they moved along the line of thickly forested hillside that loomed above them to their left, the beach giving way to the thick, dark veil of woods, the silent and empty limbs and gray light only reinforcing their grim solemnity. Two or three times they saw great houses set back from the road on hillsides or in protective thatches of trees—monstrous, rambling places that brooded over their woody landscapes and hovered close to the eternal moving sea. Clearly now they were in the haunts of the very rich.

As they proceeded along the road, they seemed to be heading inland and away from the ocean. The roar of the surf became softer, and the heaviness of the woods increased. They had yet to see any signs or markers to indicate whether they were on Potter Road or not, but twice they had seen mailboxes by the entrances to vast estates. There were numbers on them. Numbers in the 300 series.

Eventually, they came to a densely wooded spot where a long climbing road broke off from the main road. After a brief moment of indecision, Harry aimed the car up the steep incline, and they climbed steadily for a while only to end up on a hillside before large stone gates. Beyond the gates stood a large evergreen-shaded, white frame house with sea green shutters. It seemed to be silent and empty, probably the summer house of some wealthy Boston businessman. Scott spotted a mailbox, partially obscured behind a large outgrowth of ivy that clung decorously to the stone wall that encircled the property. The number on the box was 440.

"Well, if we're on Potter Road, we're getting close," he said hopefully.

Harry backed the car around, and drove back down

to the bottom of the hill and the main road. They continued to drive inland, and the forest continued to grow denser and more quiet around them. Both men sensed a change in the atmosphere, in the surrounding "vibrations," but neither said anything as the deep woods seemed to grow more watchful and waiting around them. Nerves could play funny tricks on your perceptions.

Suddenly, after rounding a bend, they saw it. A gravel road led off at right angles from the main paved road. Blocking it was a long, five-foot-high wooden gate connected to a weathered, sagging cyclone fence that ran in and out among the trees and undergrowth for as far ahead as their eyes could see. Beside the gate stood a rusted mailbox on a post. Though there was no name, the number 500 was drawn in black on one side.

"Looks like this is it," Harry said matter-of-factly and pulled the car off to the side of the road.

Scott looked back at the gate. "Yeah, if we're on Potter Road. Funny that there aren't any signposts."

"You've just learned something about the rich, my friend. They don't like anybody to know where they are. Makes 'em feel guilty, I suppose. But we followed directions, and the number on the mailbox is right. Let's take a look."

They both got out of the car and walked back to the gate. It was fastened shut with a long, stout chain secured by a padlock. Behind the gate the gravel road snaked its way downward and into a dense blanket of woods some hundred yards away. There was no sign of a house or building, only the impenetrable thick of trees.

Scott opened the mailbox which was empty. "Somebody either picks up the mail or nobody lives here," he said diffidently, not knowing at the moment which alternative he'd prefer. "What do we do now?"

"Good question," Harry replied. "We haven't exactly laid careful plans up to this point, have we? I was just planning on a little reconnoitering today, but it looks like that might be more difficult than I'd anticipated.

"How's your fence hopping?" Scott asked with a slight grin. "Or do we ram the gate with the car?"

"Very funny." Harry lamented.

"And how about the car? Are we just going to leave it here? Somebody might see it and suspect something."

"First thing I'm going to do when we get back to Oak Grove is enroll you in the police academy," said Harry with feigned sourness. "As long as we're here, we might as well see where this road goes, I guess, and we'll have to find some place to leave the car. Remember that little clearing about a quarter mile back? Let's try that."

It was twenty minutes later by the time they had parked the car and walked back again to the gate by the gravel road. Harry looked at his watch. It was almost three. "We'd better hurry. It will be dark in a couple of hours."

Scott nodded and looked up and down the road. There was no sign of life anywhere near them. "Okay, it's safe," he said and put his foot onto the lowest crossbar of the gate. Vaulting over easily, he turned around to face the dubious-looking detective.

"Uh, maybe there's a break in the fence somewhere," he said, glancing up the road.

Scott smiled. "C'mon, what about all that tough training you went through at the police academy?"

"Hell, I was lucky if I could do ten pushups even then."

"Don't worry. I'll help you over," Scott said, trying not to look amused.

Hesitantly, Harry put one foot on the wooden spar. After two abortive attempts to propel his weight up and over the barrier, he managed to tumble over the gate on his stomach. "Hell, we should have gone back and changed our clothes first," Harry said grumpily as he brushed the dirt and wood slivers from his white shirt. "This is my best goddamn suit."

"It'd be dark by then," Scott said, again trying to

disguise his vague amusement. Somehow the thought of this man worrying about his clothing or appearance seemed decidedly incongruous.

"We'd better hightail it out of sight," Harry said quickly. "Somebody might come down the road and see us standing here."

They set off then, the crunch of gravel against their feet. Moving swiftly at first, they covered the hundred yards or so of open road in a hurry. Now they would be invisible from the main road, but they had entered the long-ceilinged corridor of underbrush and trees that seemed to slope steadily downward, descending like some natural wooden and stone tunnel toward an uncertain destination ahead.

But they walked for fifteen minutes, and still they hadn't escaped the immense reach of towering elms, maples, lindens and other trees that marked their progress like silent, watchful sentinels. Gradually, they had come to the end of that first downward slope of road, only to find that it curved to the right and up again. As they continued to walk, the direction and the inclination of the road began to diversify, and the underbrush that grew in weedy and twisted among the lofty trunks of trees began to thicken and grow wilder. But still there was no sign of life or habitation. Now that they were on the property itself, not even a bird sang in a leafless branch; not so much as a squirrel or chipmunk peered at them from out of the leafy gloom to the sides of the road. These were not comfortable woods, not weekend hiking woods like Scott was used to trekking through. Something silent and impalpably heavy lay over them, a thick air of watchfulness that grew stronger the farther they penetrated into that hushed grove.

Harry was far more oblivious than Scott to the moods of the woods or the strange absence of small wildlife. He was no woodsman, and nearly all of his energy was taken up in the effort of their long hike. His face was flushed a deep red, and small beads of perspiration dropped from his forehead and neck, mingling there with the collar of his already soiled shirt. Whenever the road would begin to incline upwards, his body would hunch down a little and the breath would come faster, breaking in slight stifled gasps from his mouth. Once Scott suggested that they rest, but Harry had merely shaken his head vigorously. So they plodded on, walking for almost an hour before there was any sign of progress or change.

It came in the form of a slight breeze wafting its way through the thick tangle of barren trees. The woods had been so quiet and undisturbed that Scott had forgotten how the winds had been hungrily lapping the ocean on their way past the beach. These woods had been as quiet as a church, an inner sanctum of sorts, and they had walked on and on without ever stopping to measure their progress or question their way. But now the first touch of cold salt breeze told Scott that they were approaching the oceanfront again after their long sojurn inland.

Scott stopped suddenly. Harry walked on for a few yards before noticing that his partner had quit walking. Gratefully, Harry stopped and looked back. "What's up? Something the matter?" he said, puffing hard.

"Listen," Scott whispered putting a finger to his lips. "Ocean."

Harry listened for a moment before he heard it: the soft but powerful throb of the waves crashing against the islands of man. After the heavy, almost eerie silence of the woods it was a welcome sound. "Ocean?" Harry huffed. "Does that mean we're getting close?"

"Getting close to the ocean, yes. If you're asking whether we're getting close to our destination, I don't know. If there is a house, chances are it's near the ocean."

"Right about now any place will do." Harry continued to suck great quantities of air into his lungs. "We must have walked halfway to China by now."

Scott smiled. "No, more like about three miles at the most, I'd think. I'd say we're about twenty minutes more from the ocean itself."

"Oh, Lord. I've got to sit down," Harry groaned as he nearly fell to the ground at the side of the road. Leaning against a large, mossy tree trunk, he removed his shoes and rubbed the bottoms of his feet tenderly. "Shit. Blisters," he said angrily. "We should have gone back to town first. These damn shoes weren't made for all this walking."

Scott looked down at the detective's black Oxfords. "No, they weren't. But we've only got a little way to go before we hit the ocean."

"Yeah? Well, what if this road just keeps going right on past the ocean and all the way up to goddamn Alaska? I mean, we haven't seen so much as a sign of a house so far."

"I know, but there's not much sense in going back now. What do you say to walking down to the ocean? If there's nothing there, we'll go back."

"Christ," mumbled Harry as he rubbed his feet. "I suppose so. But I never bargained on all this walking, I'll tell you."

As Scott waited for Harry to put his shoes back on, he glanced down the road ahead. About three hundred yards in front of them, the road veered suddenly to the right, but just before that the gray dimness of the woods lightened. He started to walk slowly forward but soon stopped and waited for Harry to catch up with him. The detective looked a little less flushed, but the lines of weariness were clearly etched in his face. In truth, Scott too was tired. The last few weeks had been hard ones on him, and he was distressed to find his customery strength and vigor had apparently abandoned him. The ravages of doubt, fear, and sleeplessness. He was impelled onward now by his reserves and by a single thought: He might be close, so close, to Barb.

As they rounded the bend, the woods began to thin and slope noticeably downward again. Patches of rolling grays and greens could now be seen through the most distant trees, and he knew that they were back almost to the lip of the ocean, to the end of man's domain. A blast of salt air came gratefully to his face.

He inhaled it gladly, and for the first time that day felt a sense of renewal. Weeks of accumulated stress and fatigue had given way to a growing listlessness, an ambivalence and the seeds of potential despair. He realized now that he had been separated for too long from that revitalizing and sustaining force that he found only in nature. Too many weeks in dusty cities thinking dusty city thoughts weighed heavily upon him. He was growing dull and rusty, all sooted with the ultimate solitude of teeming masses. Here was his chance to gain a foothold again.

"Come on," he called behind him to the detective as he immediately began to leave the road and pick his way through the remaining trees that stood between him and the ocean. He virtually ran through that tangled labyrinth of bushes, creeping vines and fallen branches. Coming out of a small cluster of oaks, he ran directly onto a broad facing of mighty rock, hewn untold ages before out of the very bowels of primordeal universe. As if in sudden greeting, the wind rushed to embrace him, covering his face and hands with an icy draught. He inhaled again deeply and flung his arms outward, the breath of life and spirit come to him again like a baptism.

A great wall of water suddenly welled up before him and came crashing over the face of the rock, thundering and pealing like a vast, cavernous bell which rang gloriously in a soul suddenly come alive. The wave shot up before and all around him, then fell is seething rivers of bubbling foam about his exposed hands and face. He felt a sudden pull, and for an instant a tongue of wave licked at him and nearly pulled him back with it into the boundless sea. But he stood there anyway, his spirit feeling once again its innermost and unfailing source.

Abruptly all the dichotomies were resolved, all the blames forgotten. It was a tiny, fragile moment's mood, the inevitable swing of the pendulum away from the hopeless and despairing. But for that moment it was real and sustaining, and it made him whole.

It was a long while before he heard the rending of

small sticks and branches behind him, heard the voice calling him—the dismal croaking of reality. The joy, the mastery, the pride dimmed a little, and he turned around to where he saw Harry standing at the edge of the wood, a look of astonishment and concern on his face. A smile began to form around the edge of Scott's mouth, a gentle, tolerant smile. A smile that said much of wanting to tell the bedraggled detective about this strange, wonderful, inexplicable experience—this sense of elation and wholeness and pure, primal power. But it froze there, that smile, suddenly gone weak and sickly. A smile that congealed like plaster on his sea-drenched features as his eyes were drawn up against the high sloping line of hillside now open and exposed to his right.

There on a broad open knoll it stood, like some dreadful beast of wood and stone. It leered out obscenely from that gentle hillside at him, seeming to squat proudly in a cacophony of twisted lines, great asymetrical blocks of stone and crazily angling, leaping spires of deepest black. Gigantic black-shuttered windows set in huge iron hinges. They looked like nothing so much as hungering, soulless eyes that stared fixedly down at him, coveting him, reaching for him in hideous delight. A vast, ponderous blight on that hill. A grotesque abrogation of all the natural beauty around it.

Scott's eyes ran unbelievingly over these grim, absurd contours, over the hunched, fortress-like main body of the house which was comprised of a nameless yet discernable pattern of interlocking gray stones. The main entrance was double-doored—two vast sheets of wood that were fully twenty feet high. Flanking it were the seemingly innumerable black-shuttered windows that ran laterally across the face of the house on three levels. Above this third line of windows was a long balustrade of dark iron which bounded a parapet that ran around a smaller third or fourth story. Here the house formed again and stretched upward in a convoluted series of gables and flanking minarets which looked like so many needles aimed at the sky. In no sense was the house in bad taste; it was beyond all taste. In no sense was the house merely eclectic or even outlandish; it was impervious to any and all esthetic or architectural judgment.

But overwhelming all other features in that aimless confusion of wood and stone was the central tower that presided over this artistic chaos. It was a gray and forbidding finger of stone no wider than twenty feet across but as high, perhaps, as forty feet from its roof top to base. At the very top of this tower, just under the triangular shingled roof was a single great yawning round portal, an unfathomable blank eye that gazed forever out into the misty, unreasoning depths of the ocean. And above that eye, atop the conical roof, something hunched and squatted—something of deepest black stone veined in spidery red—something crafted by a diseased brain and uncanny fingers. At such a height and distance, its exact features were difficult to determine, but Scott could feel that its form was bestial and unholy, canine and glaring, an unhallowed avenger and a more than mortal enemy of all that was sane and good. It was the crowning glory of the anomalous, blasphemous house—its final horror.

30

By the time they reached the motel again, Harry had decided that he was through for the day. Originally, they had had a vague plan to reconnoiter their target and then go back into town until later that night when they would return to the grotesque house to do what needed to be done. But the combined trips to and from the car had been too much for the portly detective, and he fell with an exhausted and contented sigh on the bed immediately upon entering the motel room.

"You're going to be good company tonight—I can tell," Scott said grumpily but smiled.

"Son, put another twenty-five years and fifty pounds on you, and you'll be whistling another tune, I can assure you," Harry replied, his voice as tired as he looked.

Scott looked at his watch. It was almost seven. "You want to get some dinner?"

"Jesus, we just ate a couple of hours ago. What are you, a human garbage disposal?"

"No, *you* just ate a couple of hours ago. I just had soup and coffee. Come to think of it, it was more than a couple of hours ago too."

"I'm just giving you a hard time," grinned the detective. "But really, I think I'm too tired to move from this damn bed. My stomach might fall asleep in the middle of the meal, and I'd drown in my own juices. But if you want me to go along for company. . ."

"Naw, forget it. I'll just go out and get a burger or something."

"Good luck in this town on a Sunday night. You'll probably have to go all the way to Boston."

"Harry, where do we go from here?" Scott's voice was abruptly low and serious. "We've pretty much avoided talking about what we're going to have to do, though I think we've both known all along. Isn't it about time we talked about it?"

Harry looked earnestly at him for a moment before he spoke. "Yeah, Scott. I suppose it is." He motioned toward the black suitcase that was now resting on the floor by the small desk. "My magic bag," he said. "I 'borrowed' some tools from the evidence room, and what's more, I know how to use them. I spent a long time on the robbery detail and learned every trick in the book—well, almost every trick. We shouldn't have any problems getting into that. . .that building."

"I've never seen anything like it," Scott said. "I mean, it looked as big as one of those castles in Europe. I thought we had big houses in Oak Grove, but there isn't anything one tenth that size in Oak Grove."

"Yeah, Dracula's castle looked more inviting," Harry said, trying not to think too hard about the place. "Somebody sure had to have a lot of money to put that place up—a lot of money and awful bad taste."

"When I first saw it, Harry—well, it's crazy, but I could swear we were being watched. It was the same feeling I got that time at the old house on, on Fair Tree." He could hardly say these last words.

"Nobody could have seen us there. We were right at the edge of the woods and too far away."

"I know," Scott replied slowly. "Still, I could feel it. . .could feel the eyes on me. Somebody knew that we were there. We're coming to surprise them, and they already know that we're here."

Harry could see that his partner was beginning to withdraw again, to retreat inside himself. "Hey, it's just a big house," he said reassuringly. "Tomorrow we'll go into town and try to dig up some information about the place. We'll have to be cool, but we might discover something."

"Like what? We don't even know the name of the owner of the place."

"Well, yeah we do. The moving company keeps records, remember? The only problem is that that furniture and stuff was moved under the name of 'Ama Bloch'. That was your friend at the house right?"

"Yes, that was her name."

"Well, I already checked with long distance directory assistance when we were still back in Oak Grove. There was no listing, published or unpublished, for an Ama Bloch in Inswich or any of three other surrounding communities. Then I checked with Boston PD to find out if there was a listing for anyone at 500 North Potter Road in Inswich. The kid was wrong. Technically, 500 North Potter Road still is part of Inswich. But there was no telephone listing for anybody at that address. That goddamn place hasn't got a phone!"

"So what do you think we should do?"

"You're the detective," Harry grinned, "you tell me."

"Very funny," replied Scott.

"But seriously, I think tomorrow morning we should both go into town. I'll make some discreet inquiries, if only because I've got more practice than you. And maybe you could go to the library and look up the local newspapers and magazines. See if you can find anything in recent issues."

"What should I look under, 'houses designed by lunatics'?"

"No, but that's pretty close. You'll be doing some real detective work now: a lot of dull, repetitive leg work. You might find an article, for instance, that virtually tells you it's the house we're interested in—something like 'haunted house by ocean due for demolition.'"

"Are you serious?"

"Believe it or not, that's the way it works. That's the way eighty percent of all crimes are solved. Or you might make some very careful inquiries about the identity of the house, maybe from the librarian. Come up with some ploy about why you're interested in it, It shouldn't be too hard with that place. Any other questions?"

"No, I guess not. Not for now."

"God. Let me catch a half hour snooze. If you want to go out and eat then, I'll go with you." Harry settled back on the bed and shut his eyes, looking like some huge, contented child.

Scott sat down on the edge of his own bed. He felt like resting too, but the exquisite irony of his situation was more and more coming to dominate all his time and thoughts. Tonight was December nineteenth, a week before Christmas, and what was he doing? Decorating a tree? Buying presents for Barb and his friends? No. He was sitting in some little town in Massachusetts waiting to break into some insane looking house on a hill in the hopes of finding his missing girlfriend. . .a hope that was probably as useless as it was desperate.

Looking at the dozing detective, Scott felt a yawn overcoming him, and he lay back onto the bed. So tired. He hadn't really exercised in weeks, and his time in the hospital had made his muscles like rubber. But he was too busy being a second story man lately to have time for working out. He was becoming like some furtive, sneaking agent of the night. Everything involved stealth and secrecy. When would it all end? When would it be over?

He fell into a fitful sleep disturbed by hazy, ill-defined dreams. Worries and subconscious fears mingled with the history and the atmosphere of the old town to produce a collage of vaguely terrifying images which were all the more awful for their insubstantiality and the feeling of horror always lurking just out of sight or recognition. Twice he awoke, a clammy sweat clinging to his body and clothes. But his torpor was so deep that he hadn't the energy to even reach over to turn off the lamp. He jsut lay there trying to remember those formless nightmares. A small bit of the child's capacity for night terror had crept back into his heart.

He awoke finally feeling tired and edgy. The alarm

clock Harry had brought along and placed on the end table between them said it was only six o'clock, but he knew that he wouldn't be able to sleep again. He looked to the other bed. The lumpish form of the detective was curled under the covers, looking as if it didn't have a worry in the world. Scott got up slowly—it was cold in this damn room—and got dressed quietly. Going outside, he walked down to the small diner that had been closed the day before and had coffee and eggs. The coffee was reheated and the eggs were runny and undercooked. He was still cold.

He bought a Boston newspaper and perused it aimlessly for awhile over another cup of the bitter coffee but about seven decided to head back to the motel room. It was another stingingly cold day outside, and Scott pulled his heavy army fatigue jacket up close around his neck. The sky was thickly clouded like yesterday, a dull, sooty grey. The feel of snow still lingered in the air, but the biting wind of the previous day had died completely away. The day was cold and grim and silent around him.

On entering the room, Scott saw that Harry was still asleep. Deciding that twelve hours sleep was enough for any man, he shook the detective gently awake. "C'mon sleeping beauty, I want to go into town."

"Oh, hell," moaned the detective. "I tossed and turned all night. Take the car keys and drive in yourself."

"But what about you?"

"I'll call a cab or something. Meet me back here at four o'clock." With that he rolled over, burying his face in the covers as if to fall asleep again. Scott smiled with amusement and picked up the car keys from the table.

The first thing he noticed about the town this morning was the bustle of activity that had been so markedly absent the day before. Automobiles and pickup trucks were plentiful, and numerous people walked the streets. The town was certainly New England picturesque. A narrow winding river snaked through the heart of the business section whose halves were connected by a rustic looking old wooden bridge. An old mill complete with water wheel could be seen a little ways upstream as you crossed the bridge.

The town itself was replete with antique stores—a commercial enterprise that is apparently mandatory in all quaint New England towns. The local drug store still had an old-fashioned soda fountain, and the whole town in general had a rather archaic, sleepy quality that made it quite possible to imagine that you had been magically transported back into another time. Scott parked the car and walked around for awhile. It quickly occurred to him that the best and the worst of older times had been either consciously or unconsciously preserved.

Several large old homes had been carefully restored and maintained. For a small admission price one could tour most of them, including one Elizabethan cottage that dated back to the late 1600's, a spartan looking house where several colonial witchcraft trials had been conducted. There were also larger and more recently constructed homes that dated from the late 1700's and early 1800's. Shipbuilders' and traders' homes—built by people who had made fortunes in the maritime commerce of Boston and had come here to settle in all their pomp and glory. But most notable were the simple, well-maintained rectangular houses typical of the colonial period and still occupied today. Wooden placards by the door would announce the date of original construction, and the mind would boggle in this day of planned obsolescence that such structures were still even standing, much less functional.

But the commercial section of town was definitely decaying. The ubiquitous antique stores had more old door knobs and ice cream dishes than they did priceless Heppelwhites or Ming vases brought back from the China trade. A thick layer of dust seemed to permeate these places, and the merchandise was scattered in the most unorganized fashion. If there were any pearls hidden among the swine, they were well concealed.

But nearly all the commercial enterprises in town

seemed to have this same sort of lackluster, going-through-the-motions air about them. Inswich, it was plain to see, was the type of tourist town you pass through quickly, maybe stopping long enough to buy a souvenir or to see the "witch house." It clearly wasn't the type of town you stayed in for a week or even a night. The dearth of motels, tourist homes and fancy restaurants was testimony to that.

But Inswich did have a library. When eight-thirty rolled around and Scott had just about exhausted the town's immediate diversions, the Inswich Public Library opened its doors. And for no apparent reason. Only school children and elderly spinsters were accustomed to using it, and it was too early for either. But the library is an important cultural institution in any New England town, if only a symbolic one. Scott walked up the steps of the miniature Romanesque, slightly incongruous looking building and through the front doors. All was silent majesty inside. That peculiar hush reserved seemingly only for libraries hung over the interior in sanctifying grace. But Scott saw a pleasant-looking teenage girl of about sixteen or so standing behind the main desk.

"I was expecting somebody more typical looking," he said softly as he stepped up to the desk.

She looked up at him from a pile of books she was indexing, her freckled face crinkling into a look of puzzlement. She had open and warm, if somewhat bland, features, bright, expressive blue eyes and a small, pert mouth.

"Typical for a librarian, I mean," he continued. "You know, in her fifties, hawk nose, three-inch bifocals and a constant 'shhh' on her tongue."

The girl laughed with restrained delight. "That would fit Miss Roser all right, but she's sick today. They let me out of school so the library wouldn't have to close."

"Smart decision," Scott said. "I've come all the way from Chicago just to use your library."

"You're kidding!" she squealed with girlish enthusiasm. "Our library? Oh, you're kidding!"

"Well, a little. But it is important that I find some information. Does the town have any local newspapers or magazines that I could see?"

"Only the *Colonist*. It's the local gossip sheet. Comes out every Wednesday. We've got them going all the way back to 1955."

"Marvelous," Scott said miserably. "Well, I don't think I've got time to go through all of them."

"Well, if you tell me what type of information you're looking for, maybe I can find the right edition for you," the girl volunteered helpfully.

Scott looked at her thoughtfully. "No, I'd better not. I mean, it would be kind of difficult to explain just what I'm after. Maybe I could just start out with the issues for the past two or three months."

"You can't take them out of the library."

"That's okay, I'll read them here."

"Here." The girl smiled and handed him a card and pencil. "Fill out that withdrawal card while I go get them. They're in the basement." He watched her as she moved out from behind the desk toward a door in the back. Trim figure. Small, rounded rear. A sudden thought of Barb came to him. But all the softness, the gentleness, the everyday normality had gone out of his life. He fought down the other memories as they struggled to intrude.

He read enough *Colonists* to last him several lifetimes in the next two hours. It wasn't a badly done paper as far as small town tabloids go, but his brain churned with all the excruciating details of Betty Anderson's gall bladder surgery and Carol Ann Fargate's marriage to Jeffrey Holder of Hollywood, Florida. He grew to know intimately of the negotiations between the federal government and the state historical commission concerning the renovation of the old Altwell House on Windward Road and of the election of Clarence Thatcher to the post of new public school principal. He knew about every trivial detail in the town's sleepy life for the past three months, but he knew no more of the strange house on Potter Road.

Looking up from the pile of newspapers before him, Scott's gaze fell on the young girl again. She was wheeling a small book laden cart before her, stopping here and there to replace volumes on various shelves. He had been reluctant to confide about his interest in the house or its occupants to the girl because of the way news could travel in a small town, even just gossip. But he was getting nowhere fast, and the prospect of spending another two or three hours with the *Colonist* was more than he could bear.

"Miss? Miss, would you mind helping me for a minute?"

She walked briskly over to the table where he sat. "My name is Cathy, if you'd like to call me that. If you start calling me Miss, I might end up looking like one of those librarians you were talking about."

Scott smiled broadly. He could tell that this girl was precocious—and inquisitive. He'd have to be careful not to give too much away. "All right, Cathy it is. Listen, Cathy, I'm an architecture student and was visiting Boston to see some of the old colonial buildings. A friend of mine in Boston told me that there's a very interesting house here in Inswich, but he couldn't give me exact directions."

"Well, we've got lots of big old houses around here. There's the Fairfax House and the—"

"No, I'm not talking about an historical house, Cathy. This is a house on the ocean, somewhere on Potter Road."

Her eyes lit up like pumpkins. "Oh, you mean the spook house. The Glaeston place."

"Glaeston place?" Scott said, as if he had never heard the name before.

"Yeah, my dad is the town sheriff. He says he'd like to burn it to the ground. The kids are always tramping around out there, and sometimes they get hurt. Daddy had to check with the county to see who owned it. He said the name was Glaeston."

Scott couldn't believe his luck—for good and bad. On his first try he had stumbled into someone who knew about the house, but it did have to be the sheriff's daughter. He only hoped that she wouldn't go home that night bearing tales. "Cathy, you can't remember anything about this house ever having been printed in the *Colonist*, can you?"

"No, not really. You don't think that I read the *Colonist*, do you?". She laughed easily, the warmth spreading quickly about her face.

"It would really be a help if you could remember something."

She screwed up her pert little nose for a minute as if in deep thought. Scott guessed that she was Irish, like Barb. "Wait a minute," she said suddenly. "Last Halloween, not this very last one, but two years ago. Yeah, I remember. Daddy had to go out to the Glaeston place the next day because of something that had happened there."

"Was it in the paper?"

"I think so. Pretty much everything that happens around here is."

"Could you get me that issue?"

"I'll go see," she said and bounded away. Just watching her made Scott feel old. She was back in a couple of minutes with another issue of the *Colonist* saying, "Here, I can find it faster than you." She paged through the paper for a few moments and then let out a cry of satisfaction. Pointing to the top of the page, she put the paper down on the table in front of Scott.

LOCAL BOY IN SHOCK AFTER HALLOWEEN FRIGHT

Joseph A. Sparks, age thirteen, was admitted to County Hospital in Boston last night for observation. The son of Mr. and Mrs. Timothy Sparks of 728 Edgewood Lane, Inswich, young Joe was found bruised and unconscious in a ditch on Potter Road late last Halloween night.

While all details are not available at this time, Sheriff Kevin O'Donnell is investigating reports that the boy may have been attacked while on the enormous property at 500 North Potter Road, about half a mile from where Sparks was found.

This property is vast and of uncertain ownership or occupancy but has been the center of strange rumors and local controversy before.*

Apparently the accident or attack young Sparks suffered was due to a bet or dare with some of his young school mates, but information about the nature of that dare or how Sparks came to be found is not yet available from the sheriff's office.

Doctors at County Hospital have informed the parents that the boy is in no danger and is only being treated for minor shock and lacerations.

That was it except for the small asterisk at the bottom of the page. It referred to another article in an earlier issue of the *Colonist*, September 3, 1947. This article was surely a disappointment, having said nothing about the owner's identity or even the house itself.

Scott got up and walked over to the librarian's desk where Cathy was still idly talking in hushed tones to an elderly lady. "Excuse me, I hate to interrupt," he said while nodding courteously to the diminutive but heartylooking woman. "Cathy, you said you only have the *Colonist* back to 1955. Are you sure about that?"

"Oh, yes. Quite sure."

"Do you know where I could find an older edition— say a 1947?"

Cathy thought for a minute. "No I don't," she said doubtfully.

"But I do, young man." The tiny woman's voice was amazingly robust and resounding. "The Essex Institute in Salem has issues dating all the way back to 1823."

"The Essex Institute?" Scott asked while turning to face this old lady again.

"Of course! You haven't heard of the Essex Institute?" her voice was incredulous.

"No, I'm afraid not. I'm not from this part of the country."

"Eh? What's that?"

"He's from Chicago, Mrs. Upshodt," blurted Cathy.

"What? Chicago? Horrible place," she said with scathing conviction. "But you want the Essex Institute, young man. Less than an hour away. Cathy, give this young man directions." Saying that, she turned swiftly on her heel and marched primly through the front door.

"What the—" Scott began.

Cathy giggled joyfully. "Oh, I love her. That's dear old Mrs. Upshodt. We all call her the 'Mad Prussian.' "

"I can see why," he said and laughed. "If Hitler had had her, he might have won the war. But tell me Cathy, how do I get to Salem from here? Is it far?"

Cathy looked at him narrowly. "No, it's less than an hour easy, just as Mrs. Upshodt says." She paused.

"Well?" Scott finally inquired.

"Tell you what, I'll give you directions—but only if you tell me the real reason you want to know about the Glaeston place."

Scott groaned inside. The girl was precocious. He made a quick mental calculation. The other article might not be any more illuminating than the one he'd just read, and he'd have to go all the way to Salem. Maybe he'd just better forget the whole thing. All she'd have to do is go home and start talking to her father. "Oh, it's not that important. If you don't want to tell me. . ." He started to turn around as if to leave.

"Oh, all right," she said and her face wrinkled into a cute pout. "Here, I'll draw you a map."

31

Scott didn't get back to the motel until almost six o'clock. He found Harry anxious and angry, worried that he might have gone off and done something foolish by himself. But Scott hastily reassured him, throwing the spiral notebook he carried excitedly toward the detective.

"What's this?" Harry asked.

"Some notes I took at a place called the Essex Institute in Salem."

"Salem? What were you doing down there?"

"Looking up an old issue of the *Colonist*, the local newspaper. Harry, you should see this place. I thought I was in a medieval university. Anything that's old is automatically sanctified. It's a library of sorts with tons of old newspapers and books about local history. I couldn't take anything out with me, so I bought this notebook to copy down what I read."

Harry sat down on the edge of the bed and opened the notebook. "You write like a chicken scratches," he said. "Besides, don't you want to know what I found out?"

"What?"

"Well, it seems our place is sort of a mystery house. It's so far out of town and so removed from the road that nobody knows if anybody lives there. But I went over to the county land office—Christ, I spent a lot on cabs today—and looked up the owner of record. His name is—"

"Walter Glaeston," Scott interrupted, "Barb's grandfather." He cherished the look of shock and surprise that slowly dawned on the detective's face. "Maybe I will go to the police academy," he said smugly.

"Goddamn. I spent all day just finding that out. Who'd believe you could keep *that* place a secret. How in hell did you find out?"

Scott's smile was sphinx-like. "Elementary, my dear Watson."

Harry groaned. "Oh, shit. I'll never hear the end of this."

Scott smiled beatifically now, trying not to laugh. "Would you like to hear the results of my investigations?" he said.

Harry chuckled in spite of himself and waved his hand in disgust. "Go ahead, you bastard."

Scott was suddenly serious. "Okay, I'll read it first and explain it later. If nothing else, at least you won't be bored."

"Shoot," replied Harry, still a little amused.

Scott began to read from the notebook:

"The strange but little known saga of Walter Glaeston is continuing in our town, beknownst to few. His name will probably mean little if anything to the people of this town, but that is to be expected, for he covets privacy. Certainly there is nothing wrong or presumptuous in that; New Englanders have always relished keeping their affairs to themselves. But in the particular case of Walter Glaeston it is wise, perhaps, to ask why he so jealously guards his privacy.

"Why is it wise? I for one have my own reasons for feeling it to be so—reasons I dare not expose in print for fear of being subjected to ridicule or accusations of insanity. I trust, however, that I would have nothing to fear from Walter Glaeston in the form of a libel suit: His passion for seclusion extends, I am sure, even beyond the limits of his reputation.

"One thing is certain, however. It is an indisputable fact that Walter Glaeston has lived in the huge and grotesque castle-mansion he built near Cape's Neck in Inswich Bay for the past fifty-five years, since its construction in 1892. That fact is not entirely remarkable unless one is armed with the additional fact that Walter Garth Glaeston was exactly fifty-nine years of age when he moved here in 1892. This would make him precisely one hundred and fourteen years old, and all the readers of this paper may rest assured that this man is very much alive today.

"I have recently returned from a fact-finding mission to New York City which was even more successful than I had anticipated. The sole object of this trip was to gather information about the mysterious Mr. Glaeston. His very long history is not especially interesting in itself. He was born in Glasgow, Scotland in 1833 and came to this country under clouded circumstances in 1852. It is still uncertain whether he was fleeing criminal prosecution in Edinburgh at the time.

"As far as information was available, Glaeston apparently spent the next five years in working at whatever menial jobs he could find, but eventually his fortunes began to rise. He founded, along with two partners, an import firm that specialized in the importation of fine Scotch whiskies. Within three years this firm had become eminently successful, even to the point of taking away business from reputable firms that had been established long before Glaeston's. By 1860 Glaeston was already a wealthy man.

"He became even wealthier when his two partners sold him their shares in the company in 1862, apparently for minimal amounts. This sale was seemingly engineered under somewhat odd circumstances, and one of the former partners was noted for having said, 'I won't have anything more to do with that man for the promise of heaven itself.' In fact, the disgruntled ex-partner apparently began to make public statements to the effect that Glaeston was no 'God-fearing man' and that he 'hadn't a merciful bone in his whole body.'

"The partner's comments on the character of Walter Glaeston were silenced by his demise in November of

1862, three months after the dissolution of partnership. Cause of death was listed as a heart attack. Heart attacks were frequent killers even in those days, so it was no doubt just a coincidence when the other former partner also died from heart failure two weeks later.

"The next eleven years are uneventful excepting as they chronicle the steady accumulation of wealth by Walter Glaeston. He became involved in the importation of fine Scottish woolens and tweeds and in 1870 bought three of his own ships to transport his goods between Scotland and the States. It is interesting that never once during this whole time did he ever apparently return to his native land for either business or pleasure. All arrangements were made through business agents, lawyers and solicitors.

"It is only in 1873 that the name of Walter Glaeston again became somewhat controversial. Glaeston, who was described as 'a short and rather ineffectual looking man save for his piercing eyes', became engaged to a Miss Annabelle Redding, the daughter of state Supreme Court Judge Oliver Redding. Legend has it that Miss Redding was as beautiful as her father was wealthy (he was also the biggest shipper in New York).

"Despite Glaeston's apparent culture, breeding and love of historical tradition, the girl's parents were repelled by some of his opinions and attitudes and were puzzled by the attraction. Judge Redding eventually forbade the intended marriage, but it was only when he threatened to call in some favors and have Glaeston's more suspicious business dealings investigated that Glaeston cancelled the wedding plans. Annabelle was reputed to have been listless and pining for months, and her mother was known to have said that the girl acted as if she were 'bewitched.' Judge Redding died—from a heart attack—two months after the engagement was broken.

"For the next seventeen years, the public record relative to the life of Walter Glaeston is fairly silent except for references to his still increasing wealth and the accidental or coincidental deaths that always seemed to surround his movements. By 1887 he was accorded millionaire status by the Financial Registry, a New York City Who's Who of big-time money grubbers. But the man himself remained an enigma: He had a few apparent friends or even acquaintances outside of business. Even then he was already reclusive and turned down whatever few social invitations he received.

"But Walter Glaeston always managed to stay on the right side of the law despite some questionable business dealings and the long series of deaths to which his name was always somehow peripherally attached. Despite his estimable wealth and reputation, it seemed altogether worthwhile to stay on the good side of the man, even though no formal charges were ever placed against him.

"But his luck changed in October, 1890. It was then that the name of Walter Glaeston became involved in talk of witchcraft, deviltry and murder. A middle-aged, grossly fat woman of Armenian origin was arrested by police in conjunction with the horrible kidnapping, murder and mutilation of a seven-year-old boy in Brooklyn. The woman led police to several other conspirators, and it was a badly kept secret that the child had been used in some insane, unspeakable rite of witchcraft or similar perverted sickness. The woman also implicated one Walter Garth Glaeston who was promptly arrested and held for questioning. She contended that Glaeston was the mastermind behind the whole monstrous, despicable series of events and that she could prove it. Unfortunately, she died before she could—died in her jail cell while shrieking in fright. By the time the guards could reach her, she was dead. The doctor listed cause of death as heart failure. Eventually, Walter Glaeston was released for lack of evidence.

"But his reputation had, by then, grown fearsome, even in a city the size of New York. Glaeston's enterprises began to suffer, and several of his many businesses began to fail. So, Walter Glaeston quietly left New York in the summer of 1892. He had sold his businesses quickly and silently. He sold them for less than they were worth, but still at sums of many millions of dollars. And it was then that he moved to Inswich.

"He had bought more than eight hundred acres of forested land out near the bay from the Dodd family who owned nearly everything around here back then, and he imported hundreds of workers from Boston and more from Europe to build the grotesque house that can be seen only from Cape's Neck in one corner of Inswich Bay. Never was he seen in town once he was settled in that horrible house, and few have seen him anywhere since. In 1892 he was already fifty-nine years old—an extended age for that day. By now, certainly, he should be dead. Yet, he continues to live in the old house off Potter Road to this very day.

"But certainly it is no crime to live to one's one hundred and fourteenth year, even if it is unusual. Most people would probably consider it to be an amazing accomplishment, and indeed it is, though I suspect that it is more amazing than any of us realize. No, there is nothing seriously amiss there, and perhaps there is nothing especially newsworthy about rehashing the various stories and rumors that have come to surround the Glaeston property over the years: strange sounds and lights in the woods; the terrible fright of children who have trespassed into those vast, fenced-in acres of trees; and the odd reports of some local fishermen who have claimed to see strange things from their boats out at Cape's Neck.

"All this can be dismissed as conjecture, gossip or the making of a tall tale. But there are some things that cannot be covered up or ignored any longer. One of those things was the death last week of Allen Arnold, and if it is the last thing I do for this town and its people, I want them to realize that the same pattern of dark rumor and awful 'coincidence' that marked the life and career of Walter Glaeston in New York is even now insidiously affecting the lives of the people in this town. This article is tendered in the slim, almost despairing hope that something is done and done with all good speed to discover what mystery really lies behind the face of this very old and, in all probability, very evil man."

"Wow," Harry said softly. "Is this your typical small town journalism?"

"Hardly. I've read too many copies of the *Colonist* today to believe that for a minute. But this issue I've just read you part of caused quite a stir locally at the time. This article on Glaeston was written by the editor of the paper, a Michael Tarnoff, and Tarnoff was fired two days later according to an apology in the following week's edition. Apparently his poor taste and bad judgment in attacking one of the town's wealthiest citizens—even a reclusive, somewhat mysterious citizen—was judged by the paper's owners to be an unpardonable offence."

"But why did this, this Tarnoff rip into this guy like that?" Harry asked.

"Well, that took a little looking, and some of this is just supposition, but it seems that the Allen Arnold referred to in the article had been a good friend of Tarnoff's. There was some close personal tie, at any rate."

"So?"

"Well, Arnold was a local antique and curio dealer who had apparently had some business dealings with Glaeston—ordered him some rare things from overseas, or something like that. Well, Arnold and Glaeston seemed to have a falling out over some item that Arnold had promised to deliver but failed to or reneged on—presumably he changed his mind. At any rate, he told Tarnoff that Glaeston had threatened him, and a week later Arnold was dead from a sudden brain embolism. This made Tarnoff suspicious, and he made enough fuss that there was an inquest—and the records of the inquest are where I got most of this information."

"You got that at this Essex place too?"

"No, that was a detour, but as you said to me a couple of nights ago, if I take the time to tell you how I got all my information, you'd be here all night."

Harry looked exasperated. "I should have locked you up when I had the chance."

Scott grinned. "And lose your number one investigator? No way. But anyway, one of the reasons Tarnoff was so suspicious was because the only other time he had heard of this Glaeston was when some big time Boston lawyer who lived in Inswich had complained to him that his boy had been frightened near to death on the Potter Road property. When he had complained to local authorities, he hadn't gotten any satisfaction, so he had tried to pull some strings. He had told Tarnoff that he was expecting some results in a couple of weeks, but Tarnoff heard that he had died a week later—a heart seizure. This presumably struck Tarnoff as being a little too coincidental."

"I take it that Tarnoff was a witness at the inquest," said Harry.

"Oh, yeah. The chief witness. But when the inquest didn't turn up anything—Glaeston wasn't even called as a principal—Tarnoff apparently decided to dig around on his own. I imagine when he turned up as much as he did, he decided to go public with it."

"Yeah, but what has this all to do—"

"Wait a minute," Scott said and held up his hand. "On a whim I decided to go through all the *Colonists* for two months after Tarnoff's article just to see if anything had happened because of it. Two weeks after that article of his, he was dead."

"Oh, come on," Harry protested. "Don't tell me another heart attack."

"I don't know. It was just a small obituary column. There was no cause of death listed."

"Yeah, but Scott, what does this have to do with us? I mean, this Glaeston fellow would have to be—let's see. He'd have to be a hundred and forty-four years old now, and I *know* he didn't live that long."

"One hundred and forty-five," corrected Scott. "And I'd be inclined to agree with you, though with everything else that's been going on, nothing would surprise me any more. But Harry, there's one thing." He paused here, almost as if unable to go on. Harry watched him gulp and his eyes widen in an almost melodramatic expression of wonder and fright.

"What is it?" Harry asked softly.

"Well, I wondered how this Glaeston could have gotten away with so much. It seems that there were frequent complaints from people, mostly parents, through the years about the Potter Road property, but nothing was never really done about any of them. Glaeston wasn't even called to the inquest, like I said before."

"Okay. Go on." Harry encouraged him, sensing that it was difficult.

"It's hard to say how, but, well, I thought about the town itself and the article, and I got a hunch. The article had said that Glaeston was a sort of history buff, and the town is so chocked full of history and tradition. I looked up a list of all contributors to the local historical societies—you know, the ones that keep up these old houses—in Salem, Boston, Newburyport, Inswich and so on. Walter Glaeston had been a huge contributor over the years—I mean, hundreds of thousands of dollars. That might tend to give him a little local clout, don't you think?"

"Yes, I suppose," Harry replied.

"Enough clout no doubt to have the local cops brush aside any complaints that weren't really too important. But that's not my point."

"Hooray. I was beginning to wonder if there was any point." Harry said.

"The point is this." Scott said so low that Harry could hardly hear him at all. "The list of contributions is current through last May. According to that list it was only last April that a donation of $5,000 was made to the Salem Historical Society."

"So?" asked Harry wearily.

"It was made out in the name of Walter Garth Glaeston."

32

The sky was a brilliant flood of milky white moonlight as the two men once again climbed over the low gate leading onto the Glaeston property. Once in the woods, the luminescence paled and was filtered by the tangled, crowding boughs of the trees, but enough light penetrated to allow them to move without the aid of flashlights.

The air was cold but crisp, lacking that salty heaviness that sea air usually has. Perhaps it was only a thing of mood, their sense of expectation, but the night seemed charged with an almost electric potency, a feeling of energy that impelled them quickly onward along the rutted, winding, dimly lit road.

As they walked, they again felt the vague sense of watchfulness they had felt the day before. A subjective, barely perceptable feeling of presence or sentience. A slight change in the atmosphere the more they penetrated those deep, dark woods.

But it was not an alarming feeling and may have only been the result of their natural apprehension and uncertainty. They walked on resolutely and in less than an hour they could hear the sea murmuring against the rocks as it reached out to greet them. The light grew brighter as the trees thinned, and the nebulous watchfulness receded.

In another fifteen minutes they had come to the edge of the woods. Scott's pace began to pick up a little at the first glimmer of the ocean ahead, but he slowed himself as he noticed the other was falling behind. They came together to the end of the woods, and both of them looked out on the long, hilly, curiously barren plain before them. Inundated with a soft white light, it looked like some alien landscape of almost forbidding starkness. But Scott glanced to the right and pointed his finger at the long line of the bay. It seemed like nothing so much as a great shimmering pearl in the lunar light. . .a ghostly, alluring, luminescent map of shifting hues and gently rolling movements that beckoned and called with the gentle drumming voice of the waves. Both men stood there for awhile, mute and almost awed by the quiet, intriguing serenity of that scene. Visions of the past seemed to shape and float before them, and some of the fear departed.

But eventually they were wrenched back to the present with all of its imminent danger and doubt. Scott's gaze turned, moving up the slope of hillside until it came to rest on the squat bulk and the crazily twisting needle spires of the dark-shadowed monstrosity on the crest of the hill. There the pale reflection of the moon settled, sinking in a sinister, sallow glow onto the immense house until it became a forbidding phosphorus nightmare leering down at them from the heights above. Scott felt an involuntary shudder run through him and struggled to fight it down as dark memories welled up in him.

They stopped then and rested, Harry puffing vigorously on a cigarette a few yards back within the shelter of the woods. Scott propped himself against a sturdy oak that stood like a last lonely guardian between the woods and the rising hillside beyond. There he sat and gazed out onto the moonlit crests of waves as they rolled in their heedless abandon toward the rock strewn shore. Both sat apart for a while and thought their own private thoughts. Both sat and pondered, wondering what the course of the night might bring. Above them leered their destination and, perhaps, their destiny. Both had the feeling of imminence.

Reluctantly, they finally roused themselves and began the long, arduous climb up the hillside. Keeping just within the outer edge of the woods, they scuttled like frightened beetles up the precipitous incline of rocky, barely grassy ground. A little over half way up, they stopped and rested again, Harry's chest rising and falling spasmodically from the effort of climbing the steep slope. Then they were off again, running in a low crouch to counteract the seemingly inexorable pull of gravity as it conspired to tumble them back down to the base of the hill. And as they struggled against the hillside, the bulky, ominous shadow of the house loomed ever more darkly and threateningly above them and off to their right.

But finally the torturous climb came to an end. They were at the very top of the great hill, and here their covering of trees thinned but was still adequate. Scott stood hands on knees, sucking in the air greedily. Harry leaned against a Hawthorne tree, puffing and wheezing like a cardiac case. The house sat and waited in ominous silence.

There was one more run ahead of them, the forty or fifty yards from the edge of the tree line to the house itself. Here they would be vulnerable for as long as it took them to run up against the side of the immense stone building; here they would be fleetingly but highly visible figures scurrying in the bright moonlight. They could only trust to their luck.

But the vast, cyclopean house was all darkness. Black-shuttered windows stared out like fathomless eyes from those titanic walls of grey stone, but no hint of light broke through those dark barriers. They ran hastily, almost recklessly—two solitary, tiny figures— like bugs up against the cold, silent side of the great house. There gargantuan stretches of granite rose above them, like some mighty cliff, only to disappear into the deeper shades of night and shadow above.

Slowly, cautiously they began to move along the wall toward the back of the house, the baleful lunar light marking their way but also betraying their presence to any who were in a position to see them. Not a single bush or tree offered them the slightest cover. The hilltop around the house was a great bald pate of stubbly grass interspersed with protruding edges of rock like huge subterranean teeth slowly gnawing their way to the surface of the world. The hilltop was a virtual desert in the middle of the giant woods that surrounded the house.

As they came to the corner at the rear of the house, they could see the previously invisible slope of the hill as it ran for a full seventy or eighty yards downward, merging there with the dark ring of woods. Scott looked on that empty expanse of stark stone and parched grass disconsolately. Something about this rim of rough earth around the house, something about these woods themselves were strange and forbidding, as if nature had gone queer and rude and ugly in some indefinable, inexplicable way. Or was it just the immediate specter of the house, looming menacingly over them pervading and perverting even nature itself with its anomalous contours, its hidden breath of corruption?

The long, seemingly endless line of the rear of the house was a straight wall broken only by the frequent black-shuttered windows and the two large, exceptionally solid-looking oak doors that were set in giant iron hinges. Harry paused to examine both of these doors as they moved along the continuing line of the back of the house. Each door was graced by a large, ornate iron handle in place of a door knob, but it was the locks that apparently baffled the detective. Taking a ring of keys from his pocket, he tentatively fitted one key after another into the lock where they disappeared into the still gaping space around them. "Christ almighty," Harry muttered. "These locks must be at least a hundred years old. I've got nothing that'll even fit in the goddamn tumblers."

They moved on, finally coming to another corner of the building. Something low and dark projected at an angle away from the structure. Scott stopped, momentarily surveying it, then moved forward. Two large doors that swung upward then outward from a forty-five degree angle of stone attached to the vertical slope of the wall stood out conspicuously from the side of the house. It was an old-fashioned cellar entrance.

Harry moved a few feet from the side of the house in order to get a more expansive view of this side of the building. Stretching ahead of them was another long line of wall, a sheer face of stone marked only by the familiar black-shuttered windows which were set in the wall at least fifteen feet from the ground. Beyond this line of dim gray wall was another corner and then the front of the house—their least likely and most dangerous point of entry.

Harry walked back to the double doors, leaned over and gripped the handle of one. He pulled, leaning his bulk backward away from the door, but the stout wood didn't budge, Running his hand lightly over the surface of the door he said, "No lock. Must be bolted or barred from the inside."

Next he examined the edges of the doors as they were set in the stone around them. Dull iron hinges glinted slightly in the moonlight. "We can get these hinges off," he said with certainty. "What'ya think, is our spot?"

Scott paused and looked dubiously at the doors. "This probably leads into the basement, right?"

"Sure, but that's probably our safest entrance anyway." He stopped and looked at Scott whose face seemed pale even in the moonlight. "Oh, I see what you mean—that basement in the house on Fair Tree. Yeah, but that whole house was loony. Still, if you want to try another point of entry—"

Scott seemed to shake slightly. "No," he finally said after a long pause. "If this looks like the most logical place to you, let's do it."

Harry didn't answer. Opening his jacket, he fumbled with his belt and removed a large, clear plastic wrapper with loops attached to it. In the pale moonlight Scott could see that metallic gleam of the tools. Looking back at Scott, Harry smiled and said, "Don't worry. I'm a little handier than I look."

Scott stood behind him and waited as Harry deftly fitted a crescent wrench to the hinge, then another and a third until he got the proper fit. But years of rust and disuse lay on the hinges, and the work was slow and difficult. After about five minutes of unrewarding effort, Harry stopped and pulled a small tube from the plastic pouch. "Graphite," he whispered and smeared some of the contents around the two hinges of the door.

Scott alternated between nervously watching the man work and glancing from side to side. More and more, uncomfortable memories were beginning to surface in him; the more he attempted to repress them, the more they insisted on his recognition. Visions of that awful night in the house on Fair Tree began to swim in his head, and he could feel his hands go cold and clammy as he clenched and released them in an unconscious rhythm of growing trepidation. And one thought kept mercilessly repeating itself to him: If what had happened in the house on Fair Tree had been so hideous, so mind boggling, what could he expect to happen here in this monster monolith, twenty times as big and a thousand times as strange as the house in Oak Grove? What could he expect here, a thousand miles away from all that was known and familiar to him?

There was the sound of metal moving unwillingly against metal. He could see the detective's thick form bent over the door as other thoughts stole into his brain—thoughts about the shadowy, sinister Walter Glaeston whose house they were now forcibly entering. Thoughts of an intolerably old and wicked man who, if it could all be believed, was responsible for Barb's disappearance and the deaths of two of his closest friends.

"Got it," the voice came softly but triumphantly from in front of him. He looked down to see Harry grinning at him, half of the double doors upraised and pulled away from its foundation. Still, the doors seemed to be holding together in the middle, and the detective was having a difficult time in maneuvering the thick slab of wood by himself. Scott roused himself and moved quickly to his side, grabbing the end of the free side of the door.

"Push it upward," said Harry. They both raised the edge of the door up and away from the stone foundation, raised it until they heard a crack and the splinter of wood. It hung loudly about them for a second then was lost in the deep drone of the ocean as it crashed against the rocks somewhere below. They wiggled the heavy plate of wood several times, then something gave and the door fell in at the middle. Beneath lay a flight of stone steps leading down into utter blackness.

"Victory," said Harry. "Thank the Lord for those old-time external hinges."

"Yeah, the first battle is ours," Scott returned sardonically. He was thinking that maybe it wasn't their victory at all, that maybe somebody would want it this way.

They both removed small but powerful flashlights from their pockets. In his other hand, Harry gripped something cold and steel-blue. It was his snubnose .38. He turned and looked at Scott. "Good luck," he said and then moved down into the black recess below. With one last look up into the moon-dappled sky and one ear bent to the sound of the singing sea, Scott turned and followed the detective down into the depths of the house.

33

Eyes. Eternally questing and vigilant eyes. They looked out over the shimmering sea from their lofty perch high in the tower of the great, calamitous house on the hill. Eyes that drank deeply and gratefully of that eternal movement, that vast, cyclic power of motion driven water. The tides. The tides of sea and the tides of life. Those eyes knew all of such things, of how life takes its inexorable course, moves in its eternal rhythms, seeks its fathomless aims.

Eyes. Eyes that see with a sight beyond sight. Looking. . .looking into the great crystal globe of the sea. The seeing of strange images and currents as the mists of time and life ebb and sway.

At first those cold, ancient orbs see nothing, their deep power muted and far away. Images come and go, dancing aimlessly, the mind behind the eyes full of strange and languid thoughts, the mind like a resting cat.

But gradually some central thought, some more immediate desire or concern takes form, and the eyes become alive with a restless, sweeping power as they delve into the depths of the changing waters, as they listen more than ears can listen to the dim whispers of the waves.

And there are secrets to be had. Secrets that are carried on the wind, secrets that are written on the face of the moon, secrets that colossal rocks whisper to the sea. And the eyes watch and listen and drink of the secrets, the soft meandering messages of the earth.

And sometimes the eyes go out from that place and mingle with the waves and the woods, knowing them as they are. Sometimes they trod the waters themselves, then dive deep, deep under the rippled undulations of sea foam where they sport among the hidden life there and hear deeper secrets, primal unchanging secrets that were first whispered when the world was young and nothing yet crawled on the dark face of the land.

Other times the eyes rush up, moving faster and faster into the arid starlight until they reach past the thick ball of earth and out into star-plumbed depths of eternal night. Here the eyes search and roam and listen, moving rhythmically to inhuman melodies—the monstrous music of the spheres. There they sway above the bowl of dust and travail, mingling with the emptiness and things that surpass all recognition or understanding. . .things that whisper of greater secrets yet.

And sometimes those eyes are joyful with the unfathomable elation of discovery and rememberance. Drinking of delight—a thousand joys and wonders and delights. And again, sad and longing—the deep languor of melancholy floating fitfully against the stars and waves and night. Nature in her seasons. Joy and pain, life and death, seeing and unseeing—one and the same held fast by the unity that binds them. Oh, to know that unity! To feel the ultimatge feeling, to know the ultimate knowledge, to penetrate the impenetrable. The great wheel turns ever anew, and joy becomes pain, heaven becomes earth, and the sorrow for man becomes the ravening hate—hate, the eyes blazing with an unholy, ferile light as they sweep eagle-like to pick out the two tiny figures below. No surprise. The woods had whispered of their coming. The eyes rushed out to meet them, to search them, to know them.

Such pitiful prey. Such small and frightened quarry. Twin jumbled masses of impossible hopes and deep, sullen fears. So much potential there to realize; so little having been done. The reek of mediocrity. They moved and lived and thought like bugs, like the primal slime that mindlessly oozed and formed and became what they essentially were countless aeons before. Still the same. Still hoping but doing nothing. Still dreaming safe dreams and living drab lives that sanctify their mere existence.

The eyes grow dim again as the twin tiny figures move up the hillside. Dreams now so poignant and rich in that mind's capacity to relive them—to create them again—surged from the inner recesses, the untouchable inner limits of spirit. Spirit that swelled now with a majesty, a bounty that no other could know. . .the rich fabric, the splendid texture of life bent to purpose, of mind grown and flowered into something boundless and all-seeing. . .living life in its seasons and seeing beyond them. . .hungering still for the final prize.

And somewhere below there was the tiniest of sounds, the wrenching of wood. It hung in the air for a moment above the two small figures and was gone. But the wind whispered of it, the trees murmured and the eyes grew alive again, sprang to glinting awful life in a sudden glare of ultimate hate and fury.

The smile. The smile of carnivorous expectation. It spread gleefully across a face that was now full of two burning, red-rimmed orbs of lust and revenge.

34

They descended the eight long steps warily, the beams of their flashlights bouncing back from the narrow stone passageway around them. At the bottom of the last step was a blackened doorway that yawned before them. Harry was in the lead and directed the beam past the open door as his foot touched the bottom step.

"Oh, my God," he muttered.

"What is it?" Scott asked quickly.

"You tell me," the detective replied.

Harry moved closer to the side of the wall in order to let Scott gain the bottom step beside him. The twin beams of light reached out together into the surrounding blackness—into whast may have been an immense, cavernous chamber or a very small room, a room so clogged and gutted by great mountains of refuse that no speculations as to the area's dimensions were possible. Tremendous heaps and piles of stacked and fallen newspapers formed countless littered, almost impasssable corridors. Atop and around these veritable towers of yellowing newsprint could be seen a multitude of other discards: old tires, broken and battered pieces of furniture, empty bottles, gardening implements and a host of other worn or obsolete objects. Here and there the dim outlines of larger things could be seen too. There was a gigantic sofa missing one arm that was balanced precariously on its end against a particularly mighty stack of the ubiquitous newspapers. A large brass floor lamp lay on its side quite near to them, its dragon-chiseled contours acting as an unintended barrier across one of the dim and disordered passages of paper that stretched maze-like ahead of them. And from everything seeped the stale, stifling odor of age and decay, of dampness and rot.

"Jesus! It looks like the world's biggest indoor garbage dump," Harry whispered incredulously. His words were swallowed up by the seeming infinity of outworn and useless objects inside.

"I can see it now," Scott said. " 'Men die in avalanche of falling newspapers.' "

"I'd sure like to bring Luke Siemrow over here. He's the Oak Grove health and sanitation inspector. Christ. He'd have heart failure. This place could even make my wife look like a good housekeeper."

Scott laughed softly in spite of himself. It was partly a defense mechanism. He could feel the house drawing in on them already—patient, watchful, waiting. "Well, you're in charge, Harry. What do we do?"

"We go on, I guess. Unless you want to go outside and start all over again."

"Not hardly," Scott replied. "We might as well work our way through the wonderful world of junk."

"Okay, yonder is the promised land. What do you say we try that way?" Harry pointed toward one of the long, irregular corridors through the labyrinth of trash.

"Looks as good as any other way," Scott replied, shaking his head at the inglorious wonder of it all.

They began to step over and around the vast mountains of rubbish then. Sometimes the way would become clogged and impassable until they plowed through the heaps of fallen newspapers, old clothes or small items of furniture. Other times they would back up and find another way around, fearful that the whole uncertain structure might give way and collapse on them. After a while, they lost any sense of direction and just wandered slowly, laboriously and aimlessly through the great piles of waste.

"This is getting us nowhere," Scott finally said after

about thirty minutes of struggling through the basement.

"I know," Harry replied, "but let's go on a little further."

Eventually, they came to a slight bend in one of the makeshift paper passageways. Harry turned the light toward the ceiling and could just make out the joists and rafters above, though they were almost obscured by an inextricable jumble of furniture piled precariously on top of a seven-foot height of mouldering magazines. Scott leaned over and picked one up that had fallen away from the huge stack.

"Lord, it's a 1933 edition of 'National Geographic,'" Scott muttered in near awe.

"Yeah, probably valuable too. I'll bet there's a fortune in antiques down here," Harry said. "I saw an old spinning loom back aways, an oak wardrobe closet —lots of expensive looking pieces."

"I didn't know that you were an antique afficionado."

"Oh, I'm not. But my sister's got an antique store out in Woodstock. She'd give her soul to get some of this stuff."

"Bad choice of words," countered Scott with no apparent humor in his voice.

Just then they came to a spot where an immense grandfather clock with missing hands barred any further progress. It stood right in the middle of the narrow aisle they had been moving through for some time.

"Want to try and move it?" Scott asked.

"Not on your life. It's probably holding up the place." Harry moved forward and stood on tiptoe as he shone the light past the bulky clock. "Building equipment, bricks and bags—looks like plaster. I can't see anything beyond that. . .Ho, wait. Yeah, there's a wall. We've hit a dead end anyways."

They retraced their footsteps until they found another twisting, leaning tunnel through the blackness. Perhaps if there had been some kind of central light, their way wouldn't have been so slow and uncertain, but the feeble light of the flashlights did little but distort their perception of the shadowy spars of furniture, the seeming sameness of the ever-present newspapers and the general insane clutter of the huge basement. It was fully an hour before they came to the torn and canvas-rotted paintings hanging on the bare brick wall. Beyond that their lights fell on unpainted wooden stairs running upward against the wall.

Harry shone the light along and under the stairs. There was an old harpsichord or clavichord with a broken leg, a dusty crank-style phonograph, books piled on top of a battered wooden cabinet, and more. "Come on, let's get out of here," he said and withdrew the revolver that he had holstered during the treacherous journey through the basement.

The stairs gave way to a small landing and then turned sharply to the right. Another short flight up was a closed door, and like all closed doors in a spooky old house, it looked rather ominous. Harry put his hand forward and cautiously turned the knob. It gave, and the door swung outward into further blackness.

Then began an even stranger journey than the arduous trek through the junk littered basement, for the doorway opened on a very long, pitch-black passageway with a vaulted ceiling that was no more than eight feet high. Harry had to take several steps before the light from his flash would fall on anything other than the confining stone walls of the passage. Finally, there was a door, and Harry paused and waited for Scott who had gone a little ways along the other end of the long hallways.

"Nothing down there," Scott whispered. This dark seemed to call for silence. "A little alcove and a closet."

"Good," Harry replied. "Then this door must lead into the heart of the house. Now remember, it's easy to imagine things in the dark, so don't start popping with that cannon I gave you at the first shadow."

"Sergeant, I spent over a year in Viet Nam. I probably fired ten times as many rounds as you ever did. Don't worry, I'll be careful."

Harry opened the door and cautiously directed the light into the next room. Like the passageway, it was relatively low-ceilinged, many interlacing beams of rough hewn, unfinished wood running from side to side. The floor consisted of large blocks of rectangular stone, grayish with the consistency of granite. The walls were also fashioned from a stone of the same color but were coarser, almost like stucco. The room was singularly empty. There were no furnishings or decorations. Playing the flashlights about the walls and ceiling, neither of them could even see a light fixture. At the far end of the room was another door: large, heavy, sculpted.

They passed through that door into another long, low-roofed corridor in which there were many doors. Trying each, they found some locked and some open, the open ones giving way to small anterooms of indeterminate function or other passageways that threaded their way in different directions throughout the house. Making their way through the final door, they came into a long hall of rich dark panelling that contrasted sharply against the rough austerity of the previous room and passages. Far above them they could just see a great iron chandelier in the narrow beams of their lights. It was a black and simple wheel with many spokes and holders for candles—holders that seemed to be fashioned in the likeness of upraised and open human hands.

Scott flashed the light around the hall in aimless, sweeping arcs, but soon he just stopped and listened. Listened to nothing. There was no sound around them, not the creaking of a board, not the settling of the foundations, not even the dull throb of the ocean outside. All sounds were buried here in the great stone and iron heart of the house, and in their place was only the heaviness, the brooding, indifferent waiting that he felt growing slowly stronger all around them.

"I feel like a fly in a web," Harry muttered in sullen exasperation. He too was feeling the sentience of the house around them. "What time is it?"

Scott looked at his watch. "It's eleven forty-six."

"Christ. We've spent almost an hour and a half in this place already and got nowhere."

"What the hell *is* this room?" Scott asked in bafflement. "It's got to be seventy-five yards along and another thirty across. We can't even see the ceiling, and yet there's not a single stick of furniture in the whole damn place."

"This must be where m'lady receives her visitors," Harry said, trying to be funny. The constant silence and darkness was beginning to frazzle his nerves.

"Let's keep going," Scott suggested. "The more I stand around, the more I start to imagine things."

Finally, they came to a furnished room. Beyond the great hallway and down another blackened corridor was a set of high double doors crowned by a fanlight of prismatic, oddly fashioned glass. Inside was what must have once been a magnificent dining hall crowned by a monumental crystal chandelier of surpassing size and beauty. This collection of many-hued crystal baubles sat high over a long, elaborately carved mahogany table surrounded by sculptured, high-backed chairs of deep dark wood and upholstered in the richest burgundy velvet or velour. To one side, the dark lines of an elaborately carved Elizabethan buffet could be seen. It measured at least a full twelve feet and was redolent of images of gargoyles and mythical gods which balefully stared at them in silent reproach at the fitful beams of the flashlights. The walls were panelled in some dark, lusterless wood, and there were many tarnished brass candle holders set into the walls at intervening distances.

All the furnishings and appointments of that room spoke of great wealth and cultured, if somewhat gothic, taste. But great layers of dust and cobweb were discernible even in the near darkness. The rich woods of the table, walls, and chairs had grown dull and listless for a lack of polish and a huge rusty water spot bespoiled the ceiling to one side of the chandelier. Even the massive but faded oriental rug that covered the floor spewed forth little clouds of dust as Harry stomped lightly at one corner of it. If the room had ever been used at all, it certainly hadn't been used in years.

They passed on into other corridors and rooms. Some were empty, others were furnished. All suffered equally from the pall of dust and cobwebs and cracked plaster and all the other attendant signs of neglect. Still others were littered with junk, though none as badly as the awful basement. Eventually, they found a small library full of mouldering old volumes in Latin and Greek and even Arabic. The dust was a little less evident here, and there were even some papers scattered across the top of the rosewood desk. But still the room had the feeling of neglect and long disuse about it—a discomforting impression of age.

They found a large, empty ballroom with a magnificent terrazzo floor and another stately chandelier, cobweb bedecked and lonesome. From here they walked through a long balconied gallery that led to a series of small chambers or anterooms with connecting doors. Some were furnished while others were not, and one of the anterooms led to a small conservatory complete with stage and chairs. It was as if the whole house had been designed and built for some purpose that had never come to fruition. An almost melancholy feeling seized the two men as they continued to wander through the seemingly endless passageways and rooms of the silent, empty house.

After a long while, they came to a section of the house that seemed less dust laden and cobweb infested. The air too seemed less damp and more wholesome and made them realize that the house must be unheated, for it wasn't much warmer than it had been outside. But this section consisted mostly of large rooms connected by long halls, and in some of these rooms were things of great value. One room had been made into a museum of sorts and was given over entirely to the display of what appeared to be genuine Egyptian artifacts: gold and silver masks inlaid in precious stones, a gem encrusted ankh and a small mummy case of great antiquity among other things. In large glass cabinets there were bracelets and necklaces and scarabs of apparently incredible value, and yet they were left virtually unprotected, as if their owner had no fear of them being stolen. Another room contained several large curio cabinets devoted to beautifully crafted Chinese lacquerware and carvings of soapstone, ivory, and jade. The house was a museum, but it was also a treasure house of no small order.

At length, they came to a staircase, their first discovery of a passage to another level since the stairs leading up from the basement. It was a short stairway, however, consisting of a flight of only six broad steps leading to a massive closed door that was arched at the top. Carved right into the heart of the door was a figure: a representation of what at first appeared to be a lion.

But as they peered at it in the dimming light of the flashlights, both men could see that this was no ordinary lion. The contours of the animal's body were portrayed in such a way that the profiled beast seemed to be in the act of springing upward, heavy muscle groups exaggerated for artistic effect. But closer inspection of that figure betrayed the clawed feet and the protruding fangs that were quite uncharacteristic of any lion. But it was the one visible eye of the beast that destroyed any likeness to the great jungle cat of Africa, for the eye of the creature in the door was not soft and rounded like the lion's but was slanted and ferile, altogether purposeful and malignant. Scott felt a tiny rush of involuntary tremor at the sight of the thing.

But Harry showed no reluctance. He strode purposefully up the short flight of steps and grasped the long bronzed handle of the door, pushing downward. It didn't move. He tried it again. The door held fast against him. He turned around to face Scott who was still at the bottom of the stairs. "Looks important for some reason, eh? What do you say we, uh, 'effect an entry,' in the parlance of the heist game?"

Scott watched again as Harry bent to examine the lock with the flashlight. He was beginning to feel a little like a spectator. "Anything I can do?" he asked.

"Yeah. Next time find me a house where all the locks

aren't out of the Dark Ages. Nothing in this house must be newer than 1900, I swear."

"Well, maybe we shouldn't bother with it, Harry."

"Naw. People lock doors for a reason, and this looks like an important door for some other reason. I don't like being kept out anyways. I'm a natural busybody."

Scott looked at the carven monstrosity on the door. "Maybe it was intended to keep something *in*."

They stared at each other in the dim light, and a grim memory passed between them. Harry looked back to the door then to Scott again. "We knew the chances we might be taking when we came here," he said in a low voice.

"I know. Let's get on with it," Scott said resolutely.

Harry removed the packet of tools from his belt again. Working expertly, he fitted a long, thin metal shaft with a curved prong on the end into the keyhole. "A first-class second-story man gave me these," he said conversationally, sensing that both of them were steadily growing more apprehensive. "I mean, this guy was good. Specialized in apartments—thought they were safer because of all the people coming and going at all hours. He could steal you blind while you were asleep, and you'd never hear a thing."

"He gave them to you?"

"Well, in a manner of speaking. Somehow they got lost on their way to the evidence room. But they're being put to good use."

"I'll say. I'll bet you could have been a pretty good second-story man yourself."

"Naw. I could have never climbed over all those balconies. But with locks I'm not too bad."

There was a tiny click, and the detective reached up to grasp the handle with his other hand. Pressing it down, he felt it give. With a little push the door swung inward.

35

A soft cascade of light sprang to meet them. Their flashlight world suddenly ended as the suffocating black solitude of the house gave way to the milky, shifting, shimmering light that seeped through the partially opened door. Harry quickly snapped off his flashlight and reached to his side for the gun. Scott took two steps up the stairs and crouched down, the .38 drawn at his side. Even the soft white light hurt their eyes and startled them. They had become a little like night creatures in their short time in the house, and now they reacted with fright at the first onrush of light.

But no sound, no challenge or threat rose to meet them, and Harry rose up and peered through the door into the inner chamber. A tiny whistle escaped his lips, and he signalled Scott to join him as he opened the thick, massive door fully. Cautiously, they stepped over the portal and into the room itself, guns drawn, eyes darting from side to side—the mark of the hunter on both their faces.

They were in the heart of the house now. They knew it intuitively. Around them and far above them stretched a lofty circular stone tower fully a hundred feet high. From the very top of this deep well of stone and mortar, a pale light shone in, illuminating the gray, irregularly cut stone walls and the gleaming dark marble of the floor with a mystical fairy light, a melancholy glow of ghost vapor that seemed to expand and contract in a continual kaleidoscope of subtly changing hues and intensities as it played off of the tangible substance beneath it. It was Luna's light, the glimmering breath of the night, as it shown in and through the great diamond prism that crowned the deep inner tower where they now stood.

"It must be some kind of lens that reflects and distorts the moonlight," Harry's voice came to him sounding weak, awed, distracted.

Scott didn't reply, but remained mute as he gazed into the misty mass of changing colors that was at the center of the turning, wheeling vortex of light. Deepest crimsons and golds played there. Great splatterings of diamond light burst open suddenly like new-born flowers, and a blue deeper than the deepest blue bubbled and squirmed at the periphery of this cosmic carnival of colors. Over all, though, reigned the pale ghost light that was the source of the many-hued phantom brilliances: the eternally mysterious, ever baleful brooding frost glow of the moon itself. The other hints of color were only that—insinuations of a greater potency and a different principle than was apparent. In that instant, Scott knew that the light hid more than it revealed, and the deepest part of him—the most primal and unreasoning part—was stirred.

Five great doors were sunk into those thick walls of ancient stone. Five massive doors like the one they had just entered flanked them in the circle of the great tower. Each invited; each repelled. The great tower was an empty cylinder of cold, lifeless stone except for those five doors. They stood silent and closed against them, like guardians. Heavy and formidable looking. Forbidding, like some child's nightmare. Each was a choice.

Harry took another step away from the archway and into the heart of the tower room itself, and out of the great stone shaft a swirling vortex of colors rushed to embrace him. Swiftly, he was bathed in the shimmer of ghost beams that danced about that room, that rolled in sinuous waves against walls and dark marble flooring in streams of mottled, vibrant transluscence.

It was then that the voice spoke. . .long and low and

curiously hollow yet, somehow, familiar. . .a barely audible whisper that nonetheless reverberated over and over throughout the tower room in soft echoes that seemed as if they were carried on the currents of eddying light. A light, winsome voice but masked with something heavier and infinitely cruel.

"Welcome. You have come to the heart of my world, its eternal night. It is here that I may offer you my very best. It is here that I may reward you. You have choices. Choose well."

The words rolled off that invisible tongue like the slow hiss of a thousand adders, like a deathly, alluring hypnotic spell. Something in the quality of that voice was fetching, was irresistible in its very simplicity of want and evil, its poignancy of death wish and contempt.

"Come," the voice hissed to withering, scornful life again. "Each has come for a reason, though not the reason he expects. Each will find the prize he seeks, if only he will look."

The cascade of lights seemed to ebb and flow as the voice spoke. Scott began to feel that the voice was the light—he felt them to be one. He watched, silent and fascinated, as the light seemed to gather around the detective's body, until it became a glowing statue, a luminous tomb of flesh. Not a finger moved on that radiant body, and Scott slowly realized that everything was slowing down, that his thoughts were starting to come to him with singular languor, that it took aeons for the message to travel from his brain to his vocal chords. What came out was mush, a disjointed, indecipherable collage of slurred sounds.

Scott saw the detective's body begin to move with infinite slowness. He saw the light begin to drag him across the polished night of marble floor, and he saw the look of sickly dread, the awful fear as his body moved against its own accord, slowly toward the closed doors on the other side of the chamber.

And a darker shadow of night appeared in time, a crack in the glimmering grayness that grew longer and stretched out against the wall as one of the massive doors opened with silent, everlasting stealth. Even now, Scott could see the heavy outline there, the waiting figure.

He tried to yell this time, and slowly the sound gurgled along his throat and out through hapless vocal chords. It emerged as a strangled gasp, a croaking murmur of despair as it broke from his frozen lips. There was no volume, no power of sound to break the spell that held him, and still his friend, his only ally in this nightmare, was dragged on by the tentacles of milky white light that grew from the amorphous, ever-changing blob of incandescence that hovered and pulsed just ahead of him.

He was halfway across the floor by now, an eternity later. It was then that some free and unclouded part of Scott's mind remembered—remembered that this was the stuff of dreams—remembered that the infinity of slow motion terror was the primal material in many of the awful night visions of his childhood. Suddenly a cry broke from Scott's lips, harsh and free as he reached swiftly to his side for the holster where he had replaced the gun upon entering the room.

But for the other, it was already too late. Something swift despite its bulk flashed out of the distant doorway and toward the helpless detective. There was a glint of something bright and metalic drawn overhead in the witch light; it glowed there wickedly for a brief instant and then arced downward with abrupt, murderous intent.

The scream that rent the night, that everberated unceasingly throughout that spiraling, lofty tower of misty light was a pitiful cry of pain and terror—the lament of death. Scott's hand froze again just as it closed on the grip of the gun. Momentarily, all thoughts and resolutions gave way to panic and hopelessness and memories of the screams in a darkened house just a few short days ago. But then there was the glimmer of metal again: the upraised, cruelly tipped shaft of diamond light. Will returned, and the hand gripped wood and cold steel. Something instinctive guided it, or time became distorted again—bué this time in his favor. Halfway through the vicious downward stroke of the knife, he heard the explosion and saw the flash of fire. It was like being on the inside of a cannon as it was fired, and his ears pounded with the deafening roar of destruction amplified and repeated many times.

There was another flash, followed by an explosion, and another. Something inside of him made him pull the trigger many times, and the gentle, deadly witch light disappeared in the crescendo of echoing explosions that seemed to roll upward and away from him only to be lost in the gathering night. Swiftly the darkness came, and Scott only had time to see the last flicker of color in the great prism above, before he was swallowed into the gaping solitude of black.

Then his brain finally reacted to the sound, the slithering, dragging sound that was coming from somewhere closely in front of him. Close and getting closer. A small whimper broke from his throat as he tried to remember where he had put the flashlight. Something came at him from out of the blackness. Something animal and full of hate. His fist clenched involuntarily around the pistol; his other hand closed tighter around —the flashlight! It was still in his hand—it had been there all along!

He fumbled for the switch and felt a sudden blast of breath on his face. There was an awful grunting noise, a sound of fury and pain as the light went on. Directly in front of him was a woman's face—grim, bloodied and contorted in agony and hate. An insane death mask that knew only one final aim.

Dulled senses saw the arm reach up, the thin edge of light catching the contours of the long blade. And that heavy arm started immediately downward toward Scott's chest in the deadly sting of death. It was almost too late before he reacted. The hand bearing the flashlight swung up and outward swiftly in the last moment while turning the knife-yielding arm aside. But in that instinctive gesture of self-defense, the beam of the flashlight was turned momentarily away from the assailant, and Scott was left, if only for an instant, in the darkness again.

That moment was enough. Something sharp and cold skittled along his ribs and found a mooring place between flesh and bone. Letting out an instinctive screech of fright and pain, he twisted and felt the knife slip out of him like a pin yanked from a hat. As he frantically turned the light on the woman again, he saw another flash of steel, and he fell backwards trying to avoid the lethal blade.

There was a jarring thud as he hit the marble floor, but somehow he managed to keep hold of the flashlight. But the gun—he felt it slip out of his graps and clatter away somewhere off into the blackness to his right. There was no time or opportunity to search for it. The dim beam of the flashlight clearly outlined the bulky, bloodstained form of the woman—the woman from the house on Fair Tree—hovering menacingly over him. He had shot her four, maybe five times, and still she was on her feet. He flung his body to one side as she stooped and aimed a powerful horizontal slash at his body.

Somehow, he got to his feet, the thick figure of the knife yielding woman pursuing him all the while, stabbing and slashing with demonic wrath. Some detached, curiously ironic part of his mind thought it important enough to remind him that this was the second time his life depended on a flimsy flashlight, that without the light, he would be helpless to see and avoid the murderous efforts of the crazed woman who was screaming incoherently at him now as she pursued her frenzied attack.

But even though he could not see her well enough in the fleeting, swaying beam of the flashlight to attempt grappling with and disarming her, he knew that the tide of battle was gradually turning in his favor. With superior speed and agility, he managed to stay just out of the reach of the slicing blade, and whatever reserves of insane fury had enabled the woman to carry out her vicious attack were now failing. Twice she stumbled and nearly fell, her great bosom heaving mightily in an effort to draw air to her tortured lungs. Finally she fell against one of the stone walls of the tower room, leaning there for support.

It was then that Scott attacked. His adversary tried to move off the wall to meet him, but fatigue and the many bullets that had riddled her body had done her in. Scott lofted the heavy flashlight over his head, and it came down on the side of her skull with a sickening crush. He felt the woman's bulk give way beneath it, and even though the light went out after the collision between metal and bone, Scott could feel the lifeless body fall to the floor and against his knees. It was an ignominious end for Ama Bloch.

36

He made his way across the floor in darkness and nearly fell over the prostrate body of the detective. Scott knelt and searched the cold stone floor with his hands. Several yards away, he found the detective's flashlight. He switched it on and unsteadily moved back to Harry.

He lay there on his back, a great, gaping gash in one shoulder. But the heavy leather jacket he had worn had probably saved his life, partly slowing and deflecting the descent of the knife into the flesh and bone beneath. Scott turned the beam of light onto his face, the eyes flickering at the intrustion of light.

"Quit faking, you old reprobate," Scott said hopefully. "You're all right."

"I wouldn't be if you got that goddamn light out of my eyes." The reply was characteristically cantankerous but weak.

Scott turned the light back on the wound in Harry's shoulder. It was fairly deep and still bleeding, but he'd seen men live with far worse wounds while in the army. "How's it feel?" he asked, feeling ridiculous for having asked.

But no sarcasm was forthcoming. "Not too bad. Sort of numb."

"It seems to have missed any vital areas, but you're going to have one hell of a sore pectoral muscle for awhile."

"Great. I'm dying, and you give me a course in body building."

"Aha, back in form." Scott smiled in relief. "Now I know that it's not too serious."

"If only you were right," was the resigned, almost disconsolate reply.

"Listen, I should get you to a doctor right now." He knew that he should get himself one too. A growing pain was gnawing at his side where the knife had gone in, and he felt his shirt and undershirt both going wet and warm.

"Yeah, you should, but by the time we got back here again, everybody else would be gone."

"Not everybody," replied Scott tersely as he looked over his shoulder into the dark behind him.

"Jesus, Scott. What was that thing?" Harry's voice was a plea and a whine. "Something just took hold of me. . .kept dragging me—I couldn't do a damn thing to stop it."

The detective's body started to convulse slightly, and he coughed somewhere from deep inside. Scott knew the sound, had heard it many times before during his tour of duty in Viet Nam. It was the sound of lungs filling up with fluid—maybe blood. The wound was deeper and more serious than he had thought.

"I'm getting you out of here now."

Harry managed to lift a protesting hand. "No. We've come too far, and we'd have too much explaining to do to some damn country doctor. If I'm going to get burned on this one, I at least want something to show for it. Besides, think of your girl—we're so close now."

Scott's thoughts suddenly went out to Barb. He had almost forgotten about her in all of the apprehension and sudden action in the house. She could be somewhere in this demented tomb of a house even now, helpless, despairing.

"Hell, I don't even know if I could make it through this rockpile again," Harry continued. "Certainly not that basement. Do you realize we haven't seen one window or one outside door yet? We could wander around in here for hours just looking for a way out."

Scott knew that he was right. That coupled with his feeling—no, his certainty—that Barb was alive and close to him was enough to sway him. "Okay, but I'm not leaving you here. We'll get you to a safe place, and as soon as I find out anything, I'll be back for you."

"Sounds like one of those old westerns where they leave the prospector in the desert with a canteen and a promise," Harry chuckled weakly. A throaty, liquid cough welled up in him again, his body wrenching tightly on the floor.

Scott leaned over, trying to hide a grimace as a wave of pain shot through his side. Slowly, he helped the heavy man to his feet where Harry swayed uncertainly as he leaned against Scott's shoulder. "Help me over to the wall," he mumbled. "I'll be all right in a minute or two."

Harry leaned against the wall while Scott went back to the other side of the room to retrieve his revolver. He let the light fall briefly on the fallen form of Ama Bloch. It lay in a spreading pool of its own blood, and his gut heaved a little in response to the gruesome sight. But there was no remorse. She'd deserved it, and it had had to be done. Still, he couldn't be unaffected by the slaughter that had become so inextricably and completely woven into the fabric of his life. It was a ritual of death—a communion of destruction.

Coming back to Harry, he found that some of the deathly pallor had left the detective's cheeks and that he seemed to be breathing more regularly again. But he knew that the man was in no condition to continue the search. He would have to find him a suitable resting place right away.

From beyond the open door from which the hapless Ama Block had appeared on her mission of destruction, a dim hint of light issued. Cautiously, Scott moved over to the still open doorway where he saw a long flight of stone steps winding upward in a slight curve to the left. At the top of those stairs was an open archway through which a dim but altogether natural light poured forth.

He went back to Harry then, and together they climbed the long flight of barren stone steps, the narrow, low-ceilinged passageway pressing in around them while the feeling of watchful waiting grew stronger and more immediate. As they gained the landing just outside the dimly lit archway, Scott cast a nervous glance down the long corridor that stretched to either side of the open portal. Harry was breathing in quick, painful little gasps and leaning so heavily on Scott's shoulder that he feared he wouldn't be able to respond rapidly enough to another emergency. But the corridor was empty. Any dangers that lurked there were hidden dangers and beyond his ability to combat in any event. Together they stepped into the passageway.

Like the passage leading up from the great tower room, the walls of the corridor were comprised of stone, but a more regular, rectangular stone than that used in the outer walls of the building or the tower room below. At long but regular intervals there were fixtures extending from the wall: black iron sculptures that at a distance seemed to be representations of twisting, writhing human limbs. From each of these grotesque fixtures guttered and sputtered a single thick black candle—the sole ghostly illumination of that long, silent corridor.

Here and there there were single closed doors to either side of him, simple wooden barriers thrust into the dense, ponderous stone around them and set at irregular distances from one another as if the rooms they marked were of varying dimensions. Behind any of those panels another potential killer might lurk. Yet, those doors were also welcome: a small bit of relief from the tomblike masonry that apparently dominated the house.

Leaving Harry to rest against one wall, Scott drew his revolver and walked to the nearest door. After listening carefully for a moment, he tried it. It opened onto a small dusty room, windowless and empty save for a couple of old upholstered chairs and assorted boxes and old packing crates. Not exactly elegant but it would do.

He walked back to the top of the stairs. Harry was still leaning against the wall, his stout body perceptibly shivering., "Damn cold in this house," he said grumpily.

"I know. There can't be any heat at all, but you must be feeling it even worse with that wound." Scott carefully avoided mentioning his own wound, and the jacket hid the bloody stain beneath.

He guided Harry down the corridor and into the room where the detective immediately slumped into the dusty old leather armchair nearest the door. Scott trained the flashlight on his features again. They were pale, drawn and pained. Neither of them could stay here much longer. The detective needed medical attention badly.

"I'll make this quick," Scott promised.

"Wait a minute. Your gun. Did you reload?"

Scott felt embarrassed. Even now the detective was still thinking and planning for them. This whole business was going to be an even more dubious proposition without him. "No, I will," Scott said, reaching into his pocket for the cartridges.

Harry grunted as he reached into his jacket. "Here. Change your batteries too. That light is just about gone." Scott caught the cylinders as Harry lamely tossed them to him.

The detective could sense his partner's growing pessimism. "Hey, we're not far from the end now—I can feel it. They gave us their best shot, and we took it."

"You sound like a high school football coach," Scott said without a smile.

"Maybe I ought to leave the light with you. There's plenty of light in the hall."

"You don't know how long you'll have that. Candles. Ugh," he said sourly. "I feel like I've stepped into a bad Vincent Price movie."

Scott smiled at his ability to maintain some semblance of humor even in this situation. "Is there any other kind?" he asked in reply.

Harry grinned and shrugged slightly. "I don't know. I was always a sucker for that kind of stuff—until now." His tone of voice quickly changed, becoming more authoritative. "Now get going, and don't forget where I am. I don't want to be stuck in this crypt forever."

"You sure you'll be all right?"

"Sure. I got my gun, and the light from the hallway should be enough if I have to use it. Close the door behind you, and when you get back, signal before you come in. That door opens with no signal, and I start shooting."

Scott looked at him one more time. "Don't worry, I was voted Boy Scout most likely to get lost."

Harry smirked slightly. "I was right—I shoulda locked you up when I had the chance."

Scott winked in the dim light and turned to walk out of the room. Closing the door softly, he reemerged into the fluttering yellow-orange light of the long hallway. Looking swiftly up and down the corridor, he made a hasty decision and set off to his right.

Quickly but cautiously he opened each of the closed doors as he passed them, one hand gripping the pistol, the other the flashlight. He used the light intermittently to investigate the dark, littered and musty rooms along the hall. There was no time to be careful anymore; if somebody were waiting behind a closed door for him, he'd just have to hope he saw them in time. He began to pick up his pace and move swiftly through the rooms, some empty, others simply furnished or full of refuse like the basement. What was obvious from all of them were the fact that they were unused and had been for a long time.

Eventually, he came to a sharp leftward turn and again was faced with a long, narrow expanse of corridor fitfully lit by the solemn black candles projecting from the wall. His mind was just drifting back to the faded image of Barb when he saw the door open at the far end of the corridor. A stream of brighter light suddenly tumbled into the flickering orangeish glow of the passageway, and he stopped instantly, every muscle tensed, every nerve alert. No one emerged from the open doorway.

Only the adrenalin, only the sense of emergency prevented the nameless terror that had been growing in him for weeks from asserting itself and reducing him to helplessness. Slowly, with infinite caution, he placed the flashlight into the pocket of his jacket. Aiming the revolver ahead of him and toward the open door, he waited. Waited for some sign, some movement from the thin edge of doorway at the far end of the hall.

As he waited, a feeling rose up in him—an utter certainty. Someone was standing in the open doorway just out of his line of sight. Someone listening. Someone waiting as he waited. The flood of yellow light that illuminated the far end of that corridor seemed to pulse and ebb in a waxy, sinister glow. The whole house was deathly quiet, hungeringly still. And from that open door seemed to emanate a presence, a malignancy. Scott knew he was being observed, manipulated, toyed with by some invisible, merciless agent of despair.

The door slammed shut with almost tornadic fury, and from somewhere ahead of him and all around him came a long, high and hollow laugh—an unearthly howl that was both fragile and menacing, both trilling and harshly guttural. The thick stone walls of the great house muffled the sound, reduced its immediacy, but there was no mistaking it for what it was and no understanding for what it wasn't.

Scott stood as if paralyzed for he didn't know how long. It may have been seconds, perhaps minutes. The walls seemed dully to echo with the memory of that malign, alien sound. Finally, he roused himself and made his way to the closed doorway at a run. Turning the knob, he flung the door inward and stepped back against the wall, gun in hand.

Inside was a fairly large rectangular room, singularly empty excepting for the small table in the center of the room and the innumerable candles that were placed all along the walls in towering brass poles that flowered into candelabra at least six feet high. From each wall was suspended a length of heavy crimson material, probably velvet, which covered the wall from top to bottom. The floor was covered with a patternless rug of a coarser material of the same color, and even the ceiling had been painted in the same blooded hue. The effect was a solidly red room—a bloodlike, frenetic invasion of the senses that glowed weirdly in the candlelight. But of a living being there wasn't a sign.

Scott took a step into the heart of the room and felt something dark and oppressive fall upon him. Tangible. Heavy. Charged with a sullen energy. Little feelings of electricity ran down his spine and along his arms to his fingertips. The hand that held the gun seemed suddenly to glow with heat, and the weapon became very heavy in his hand. Minutes passed, and Scott stood mutely, his mind reeling with a thousand puzzles. A growing tension began to take root in him—the hard edge of anger and retribution. All his doubts and fears began to give way then, and something in his heart became hot and hard like the red of the room.

With a sudden movement inspired by intuition, he ran to the nearest wall and flung back the heavy crimson covering, there to discover only bare stone. Undeterred, he moved hastily to the wall opposite the doorway. Pulling back the heavy material again, his eyes fell on a small door set in the stone. Here was the route of escape the unseen figure in the door had used; here was the reason for that unholy laugh of mockery and triumph.

There was a small latch set into the wood of the door. He pulled at the door, and it opened with an audible click before him. The pale candlelight illuminated a small passage and stairs beyond. Looking back uncertainly into the room for a moment, Scott drew the flashlight from his pocket, lowered his head and stepped through the tiny doorway into the passage beyond. If anything, this passageway was even narrower and lower-ceilinged than the way up from the tower room. Shining the light on the walls, Scott saw the everpresent gray stone. It was damp, and from somewhere ahead he could hear the drip of water, an eerie, monotonous sound that intensified the sepulchural silence of the house and the winding steps that now curled forbiddingly above and beyond him.

The first step. A little of the seething anger and confidence dropped away from him. The dim illumination that infiltrated past the small open door to the red room became a bit less intense. He knew for certain that now was the time to be careful. Whoever had escaped from the red room had only this way to come.

Another step. Live flesh against dead, dull stone. There was a slight rustling sound from somewhere above him and beyond his sight. The first dark turn of the steps loomed above him in the fitful beam of the flashlight. Memories of another night in a dark house, another night alone in the grip of blackness, came unbidden and frightful.

Another step. Then another. Was that breathing? A rhythmic sound—barely perceivable but regular—pressed upon his ears. He began to round the first bend in the steps and was ready to confront any unseen adversary that might spring at him out of the darkness. There was a rustling sound again and—he thought the edge of the flashlight beam had caught the fleeting color, wispish and translucent. But above him now stretched an endless night.

He continued onward and upward. The cold was beginning to edge into his bones now, and he stifled the urge of his teeth to clatter one against another. The house was so damp, so cold. How could anyone actually live here? From his side there was now only a dull ache, the warm, lingering wetness having gone dry and binding. He felt his hand throb numbly as it gripped the revolver while the other holding the flashlight tingled from lack of circulation. Weeks of worry and neglect weighed heavily upon him now, and a deep inner part of him cursed his fatigue and the growing certainty that he wasn't as alert as he should be.

A noise. Perhaps the sound of some small furtive animal fleeing the light and his advance. Perhaps the house settling and shifting. Perhaps something else. It sound an almost human sound—a ghastly tittering?—a chuckle of horrible delight?

He climbed that curving stairway for what seemed like an eternity, weariness beginning to bunch his muscles into a complaining mass of stiffness. Still he tried to keep ready and alert. Still he tried to keep his mind only on his objective, to avoid the awful, implausible memories that sought to always intrude.

A slight droning sound became barely recognizable as he continued to climb, alluring him in soft whispers. But he tried to ignore it as he forced his body to trudge on. By now he was almost certain: Something or someone was somewhere close above him, always just out of sight, always lurking and waiting only to flee as he came near—as the light approached. He remembered the horrid thing in the house on Fair Tree and how it had shunned the light, all cold and dark and scuttling.

He tried to draw an image of Barb in his mind: Barb in her softness, her giving warmth. He loved her. He knew that. If they ever both escaped this business, if they ever both recovered from it—he would ask her to marry him, and she would be the light of his life for all the days that remained. They had often been somber up to now, and lately they had been more than grim. His worst and most unreasoning fears were being confirmed with every new step he took: Life was full of terror, and the black, nameless things were always lingering at the very edge of the light. He could either give into it—to hopelessness and despair—or he could try to surround himself with as much of the light as possible. Lithe, graceful, tender, bright Barbara—she was the best of what the light, what the good side of life had to offer.

Eventually, there came an end. The narrow beam of the flashlight took him around the last curve and shone on a massive arched door of some dark, heavy wood just a few steps above him. Another door. The reckless anger he had momentarily felt in the red room seemed only a dream or an illusion now, seemed to be another shadowed improbability in an aimless tapestry of growing confusion and fear. He stood before the door, silent and wondering.

But the time came when necessity and remaining reserves of inner fortitude impelled him forward. He moved up the few remaining steps and turned the cold iron knob. The door was ponderous, but it gave way before his pressure. Suddenly, he felt the rush of salt air greet him, and he heard the familiar throbbing roar of the sea—a roar that had only been a barely audible drone in the thick cocoon of the stone passageway. But now it came to him, fresh and new forever as it dashed against the land in timeless oblivion. At last he had emerged from the withered inner bosom of the house and was at its outer boundaries.

Pearl-white beams of moonlight glowed about small diamond pane cathedral windows, illuminating the passageway in soft rays of milky opalescence. Above him Scott could see naked rafters etched in sharp dark relief as moonbeams played about the corners of this tiny new room, perhaps thirty feet across. The dominance of the stone ended here, and the floor was comprised of great unpolished planks of rough virgin wood. Heavy beams stood out from the slats of dark shingled wood that were the walls. There was an almost nautical flavor about it, and the rudeness of the design and construction contrasted sharply against the other sections of the house, even those that had been austere and monolithic in their immense stone proportions.

But it was not the narrow room or hallway that faced him that drew Scott's eyes. Rather, they were inexorably focused forward to the closed double doors just a few feet ahead—another and a last set of wooden barriers behind which could lurk unknown terrors. He stood there for a moment listening and carefully watching those doors for any sign of movement.

Silently, he moved over to one of the four small arched windows that looked out on the moonlight. There he could see the brilliant cold disc of the moon hanging in an ice night-blue sky, a long rolling line of winter clouds moving under and behind the pale sphere toward the coast line.

Gazing down, he could see the rocky landscape of land and sea where they met in mutual cataclysm, the earth's eternal resistance pitted against the everlasting onslaught of the sea. A vision of primal power etched in winter's frosted light. His soul sighed a sigh of melancholy longing then, and a deep part of him regained some of what had been lost in the deeper recesses of the house.

He turned from the window and made his way softly to the double doors to his right. He placed the hand holding the flashlight on the door knob, switching off the light with his thumb. This would make him less of a target, and he could only hope that there would be light, however feeble, in the room beyond.

He stopped one last time to listen and prepare himself. No sound reached him except the mournful drone of the sea. No thin edge of light protruded from under the door. But this was it. Upon looking out the window, he had realized that he had come to the top of the great needle-like tower at the very crown of the grotesque house. There was no other place to go.

He turned the knob slowly. It gave. He pushed the door forward, and it swung silently on its hinges. Every nerve alert, every muscle tensed. He knew instantly that this was it.

The moon winked balefully at him through the great expanse of rounded window that was set in the opposite wall of the room. Long drapes had been pulled back, and a robed figure was silhouetted against the silver surface of glass as it gazed out into the night. Scott felt his stomach rise and his spine contract at that sight. His brain took in volumes of information in microseconds: the raftered ceiling, the long expanse of oak-planked floor, the canopied bed and brass kerosene lamp beside it, the book cases and writing desk. But never once did his eyes really leave that robed figure that stood with its back to him, its eyes directed out the spherical window. He felt as if the house had just taken a breath around him and was preparing itself like some living sentient being for the final awful climax to his life. It was all here and now.

"Turn around. Very carefully." His voice was low and menacing as he aimed the revolver at the dim figure in the moonlight.

Slowly the robed figure swung around, the glow of moonbeams etching the contours of face and hands in specter light. His hand tightened slightly on the trigger. Then he let out a gasp as eye met eye. A light glimmered there in the moon-dappled orbs of the other: recognition!

37

"Barb!" he called out in sudden amazement and joy.

Time stood still as he saw the look of mingled astonishment, relief and wonder that passed over her face, then the sudden sweep of joy. Instinctively, her arms went out, and she took a faltering step toward him, nearly falling as she did. He ran to her then, covering the floor in long, loping strides, and he held her before she could tumble to the floor. The touch and he felt the rush of concern and protectiveness course like a fire through his veins. She moaned softly, weakly as she laid her head against his shoulder, her body sagging heavily in his arms.

"Oh, Scott," she mewed it like a hurt kitten. "Oh, Scott. Thank God."

She seemed to collapse in his arms then, and he picked her up and carried her to the large canopied bed where he laid her down with infinite care. Finding a match in his pocket, he lit the crystal bulbed kerosene lamp that rested on an end table next to the bed. It sprang into a dim, flickering life that filled the room with a light golden-orange glow. Some of the ghostliness fled the room then, and Scott looked down at Barb as she lay on the bed.

She was pale, as pale as the moonlight that she had been standing in. She looked up at him searchingly and in her eyes he saw a listlessness, a vacuous ennui that was uncharacteristic of her. Fatigue and doubt and fear were all drawn around the edges of those soft brown eyes, but at their core was a look of resignation, of hopelessness.

He took her hand lightly into his own, and her thumb began a light, instinctive carressing motion on the broad back of his hand. "How did you find me?" she said weakly, gratefully.

He stared at her for a moment without answering. She looked so drawn, so spent. Burnt out. "My God, haven't they fed you?" It was the only response he could think of or, at least, the only one he was willing to entertain.

She smiled wanly. "Not much. Just enough to survive on."

He looked up and down her robed body. Even under the folds of cloth he could see that she looked thinner, gaunter. She had always been marvelously full of body before without the slightest hint of being fat. But now she looked emaciated, almost sickly. He fought to keep his voice even. "Who did this to you?" he said in a deliberate tone of voice.

She looked up at him, a hint of wetness forming in the corners of her eyes. "The woman. Her and the other, the other one," her voice quivered.

Scott froze. It couldn't be! "The other one?" he began diffidently. "Do you mean Glaeston?"

A look of surprise seemed to flit about the corners of her eyes but quickly disappeared back into her mask of languor. "I—I think that's his name. Old. So very old," she half-whispered.

"But why?" he pleaded. "Why did they want you?"

She turned her face away quickly and seemed to stifle a sob. He felt something deep within wrench in compassion and pity for her. A flood of tenderness mixed with his icy anger.

"Barb, what has this all been about?" he insisted again after she seemed reluctant to answer him. "I found out about your mother's father, this man Glaeston—"

She gazed up at him again, her limpid brown eyes

now clouded completely by tears. Her whole face seemed to convulse as she tried to speak. "Oh, Scott," she finally began, "I don't know. . .not exactly. For something evil. . .something unspeakably evil. It's him. He used me—violated me. He comes here every night. Comes to—oh, I can't bear to tell you!"

She stopped then and another wrenching sob of despair overtook her. Scott leaned closer and cradled her protectively in his arms, cursing this devil of a man who had caused her such pain. He kissed her cheek lightly and tasted the salt tear of fear and abandonment, like the salt of the great ocean outside but issuing from a source so much more fragile and tiny. How he loved and cherished her.

The house creaked ominously from somewhere out in the passageway, and he stiffened in sudden alertness. He had almost forgotten their danger in his sudden joy upon seeing Barb again. And then he remembered. Remembered the feeling of presence on the stairs, the sounds that had been just above and ahead of him. The slight, ghastly tittering.

He gripped her wrist a little tighter and whispered, "Are there any other rooms or passageways up here besides the area just outside the door? Quick."

"I don't think so." She looked up at him in puzzlement. "Why?"

"Because I think somebody was coming up here ahead of me. No. Someone *had* to be. The only entranceway to this tower is through a hidden door in a room below—well, you must know that. But there might be some other hidden passageway or little room off the corridor outside. It would be expected in this place. There's got to be. Somebody had to come up here."

"Oh, no!" she paled even more. "Then it must be him. Him or the woman. She brings my food. They're the only ones I ever see."

"It's not her, I can guarantee you that," he said with quiet finality, his finger edging toward the gun which he had lain down on the end of the bed.

They both listened into the night that surrounded their little oasis of light and comfort. But only the rolling waves and the occasional groaning of the wooden beams and joists in the tower came to their ears. Unlike the lower sections of the house, sound penetrated here freely, and they found themselves listening to a scattered litany of irregular noises. Scott was prepared to move instantly at the first suspicious sound, but all was normal around them, and he found his mind going finally to another matter of urgency.

"Listen, I've got a friend below who's hurt and in need of medical attention. We came here to find you and whoever was responsible for taking you...for that and other things," he said grimly. "Right now I'll settle for finding you. Maybe I can come back and settle accounts later if anybody decides to stick around. But the important thing now is to get you out of here."

She just looked up at him, saying nothing. There was gratitude and still a little fear in her eyes.

"Can you walk? I can help you if you want me to."

"No. I can make it." Her voice was soft and wispy.

"How about clothes? It's mighty cold outside." He realized as he said it that it wasn't much warmer in here. No fire or heat. No wonder she looked so pale and weak.

"No, I've got nothing but this," she said softly, her hand touching the floor-length, coarse robe. "But it's heavy—really it is," she said to reassure him.

He looked around the room and saw the huge old wooden wardrobe in one corner. It was one of those antiques Harry would like. "Have you checked in there?" he said and pointed.

"No."

"Do it while I check the hallway outside again," he said quietly but urgently.

He started to get up from the bed. A hand reached out and held him back. He looked down at her again and saw the look of doubt and need carven into her drawn features. Softly she pulled him to her lips, and they met in a lingering embrace. Their lips meshed, and he ached for her—not the ache of desire but the ache of sympathy and shared pain. He tried to shut out the thought of what she had gone through—the darker, more vile thought of what the old man had used her for. She hadn't been able fully to disguise that fact, even though she had tried.

Suddenly her lips, her cheek felt somehow different, almost alien, to him. No longer fresh and innocent. Spoiled. Sullied. Like the rape victim must feel to her husband. Or. . .was it something else?

He pulled himself away somewhat abruptly and stood up. "Look for something to wear, Barb," he said perfunctorily and moved away toward the door. The kerosene lamp shed some light into the moon brightened passage, but he still used the flashlight to examine the walls of the hallway. There had to be something.

He ran his hands over the rough wooden contours of the unfinished walls and shone the light into whatever crevices or crannies he could find in the wood. He went from one end of the corridor and back again, then directed the light up into the rafters and beams above him. A strange thought came to him unsought.

Carefully, he played the light across the floor. It was comprised of broad, tightly sealed planks of thick oak. He could find no seams except for these that joined the long lengths of wood together. Quickly, he moved over to one of the diamond paned windows again and looked out into the night. Below him he could see the vast bulk of the house spreading outward into the moonglow. He went swiftly to another window. Beneath him he could just see some of those incongruous needle spires projecting upward from a flat rooflike section of the house beneath him. Like giant black spikes thrusting upward into the sky. This strange, awful house, and he was in its highest, most inaccessible point—a point to and from which there was only one conceivable entrance and escape. The full import of his own realization suddenly smote him like a thunderbolt. Why hadn't he seen it before? Was he that tired and confused?

But he knew the answer. Whatever his mind might have been trying to tell him, his emotions wouldn't let him hear. There had been too much excitement, too much relief and joy. It had all seemed so natural, and he had only been too willing to forget the fear. But *someone* had opened the door in the red room below and had laughed madly. *Someone* had run up here at their own will, taunting and teasing him all the way. Who else—God forgive him—could it have been?!

Something awful happened then. A dismal, clutching fear far worse than any he had known began to grab deep within him, and he felt his knees actually tremble and go weak with the hell of it. Not this. After all he'd been through, not this.

One thing had kept him going. One hope. One desire. Then to find that slimmest of hopes suddenly fulfilled only to be brutally, inexplicably yanked away from him in something too mystifying, too inconceivable to be understood or even believed.

The glow of the lamp went out in the bedroom, and he was left again in the virtual darkness. It would have been altogether reasonable then to call out, to ask why she had extinguished the light. But he didn't. That subterranean, instinctive part of him was working again, and, despairingly, he knew that he already knew the answer.

Slowly, resignedly he trudged toward the open doorway. Thin shafts of moonbeam reached out to greet him in a baleful embrace. His hand worked falteringly to his belt where the .38 was lodged in its holster. He came into view of the open door. The interior of the room was once again illuminated only by the ghostly gleam of the moon as its vaporous essence streamed through the great round portal in the far wall. But this time no silent figure stood before it.

His eyes maneuvered quickly around the room and finally onto the bed where the long, motionless figure lay under the coverlet like some recumbent corpse. Pale, cadaverous features shone even whiter under that moonlight until they seemed to almost glow with an eerie light. That smooth skin gleamed like white bone ivory, fragile and hollow looking.

He took one step into the room—half knowing and half uncomprehending. He could see her thin, still lovely features framed in tresses of long, chestnut brown hair as she lay against the pillow. Cautiously, he crept forward, his mind and eyes ablaze with his despair. Her eyes were closed, and her breathing was deep and regular as marked by the swell of her bosom against the coverlet. The white opalescent light danced and played about the bed, twining in sinuous cords around the canopy posts. Everything was still, so silent, save for the gentle murmur of the sea below.

As he looked down at her, his eye was drawn to the nightstand where the now darkened kerosene lamp rested. Next to it was a small brass bound box, perhaps for jewelry or trinkets. Beside it lay a woman's hair brush and comb. Hadn't he noticed something else there before as he had lit the lamp?

He looked back to Barb. Her wan features were passive in apparent slumber. Almost blank and empty. She looked different—something beyond the pale, drawn aspect of her face. Why hadn't he noticed it before: the slight change about the eyes: They were more cat-like and ferile. Still, it was undoubtedly her— her features, her hair, her body, however thin it might be.

His eyes once again went back to the nightstand. What had been there? He had seen something before. He had barely noticed it but, nonetheless, he *had* noticed it. The mottled, moving lights continued to swarm softly about him; his brain swam with a thousand half-formed images and thoughts as he stood uncomprehendingly by the side of the bed. Was he really going mad? Was all this driving him beyond the point of endurance? If so, other people were in the same boat, including the detective downstairs. Damnation! He wished it could be all over. He wished he was back in Oak Grove and all this had never—

Something moved quickly to his right. His head turned instinctively in mid-thought and caught a glimpse of what he had vaguely feared and expected. Sitting bolt upright in the bed was Barb, the soft indifference of her eyes now transferred into a look of cunning, gleeful expectation, her still beautiful features twisted into a mask of hate. He turned the gun toward her then, but his will was not in it. It was locked in those eyes—eyes grown suddenly and inexplicably grim and unendurably powerful. They blazed like some dark, unholy fire, capturing him in their overwhelming will and purpose.

One slim hand was drawn out from beneath the quilted cover. It gripped something dark and heavy. A tendril of moonbeam touched it and bore it to illuminated life. Scott's memory opened then, and he remembered what was missing from the nightstand. It was a small carven statue, about eight or nine inches high, thick and heavy looking. A representation of some grotesque mythical creature or god. A round, thick, blunted base. The pale, slim hand gripping it by the carven creature's frightful head.

He reacted too late. Something moved swiftly like a shadow, and he was smote heavily upon the side of the head. Reeling, spinning, the force of the blow carried him backward and down to the ground, the sound of triumphant, maniacal laughter still ringing in his ears.

But that was not all. She was on top of him almost instantly, clawing, tearing, tremendously strong. Once he managed to grab a slim arm as he struggled on the verge of unconsciousness. He fought on while he tried frantically to gather up his senses. There was something...he must use it...the gun...couldn't be Barb...too wicked...too strong...must find it.

But the gun was not in his hand, and that thin arm was yanked away with enormous strength—a strength that her frail body should never have possessed. Two cold, thin hands found his throat, and his lungs convulsed as their supply of oxygen was suddenly, ruthlessly cut off. He reached up and gripped her by the wrists. Pulled. Pushed. Fought and struggled for his life. Became dimly aware that the side of his head was swelling up with pain and fluid. Felt the pain in his side come in hot, stabbing flashes. Remembered the pain and hopelessness of the night in the house on Fair Tree—the thing that scuttled horribly in the blackness. The dark well of unconsciousness sought to swallow him then, and his struggling, thrashing body began to relax.

With his last reserves of will and strength, he tried to pull her forward by her elbows. He felt the grip on his throat relax a little, and hope mingled with the blackness of despair. Suddenly, a great peal of laughter rang out. It was high, lilting, full of the unbounded energy of youth. But underneath there was something leaden and grim, something infinitely cunning and ancient. It trilled then in a wild ululation of triumph and ultimate doom. And the voice spoke, now low and menacing, yet still familiar—partly Barb's and partly not—the voice that had whispered in the great tower room.

"I lied not! I lied not! You have sought her and you have found her. You have found what you have come for. Here it is. I am your prize! I am your victory!" She spat out the words in a torrent of fury and ecstasy, her body swaying and undulating suggestively above him in an instinctual rhythm of triumph.

"Fool!" she hissed at him with utter scorn. "I deceived even you! You who are like all the others! You who can see only the shell! Did you come here thinking to really see her again, to rescue her? Do you really think that justice triumphs, that love prevails?" Her grip on his throat tightened, and she lifted his head up a few inches, only to drive it back down into the floor.

"Ah, to be young again! To feel the energy, the lust

run through a body again!" she trilled and growled at the same time. "Oh, the process is not yet quite complete. I am still adjusting to this new shell, but soon it will be right. Soon I will be all healthy and rosy looking for you again, my sweet." She purred now as she said these last words, and the fingers gripping his throat caressed the flesh of his neck in a vile pawing motion.

She looked down at him, saw the incredulity and disbelief in his face, and she scowled darkly. "Could it be? Could it be that you still don't understand, my pet? Do you still have some puny hope that it is her—perhaps gone mad or drugged or hypnotized?" She seemed to raise up now as she spit out her awful message at him, to extend and grow taller until she was glowering down at him from some great height above. "Fool!" she yelled in a deep growl. "She has been gone since the night of the Varleth! She made the choice freely—to accept me or that Other which no mind or spirit can withstand. *I* am her! I am perpetuated and shall live on until the Great Work is completed! It was the only way, for the shell could no longer sustain me. It was the only way! And now we are one. One throughout the ages to come. One seeking the unknowable, the limitless, the ultimate. You should be proud of her destiny, for it was more than such as you will ever know!"

Again the wild laughter rang out. Scott inched his hands down the slender arms, preparing for a final effort to dislodge the fingers that still mercilessly gripped his throat. His eyes were flooded with tears now as his body spasmed and arched in pain. His mind reeled down the long corridor to oblivion. The air would come soon now, or it would never come at all.

The voice spoke again—it hissed and intoned at him. But he didn't hear the words anymore. All effort, all concentration was contained in his body's desperate need to save itself. He was not aware of the other anymore, not aware of the movements that bespoke the growing abandonment and lust that seized her as her body moved and writhed above him.

He felt his hands once again come into contact with her wrists. Little time left. Seconds. A moment's memory of her as she had once been intruded, but he banished it. Must think now only of the enemy she had become.

He thrust his pelvis up off the floor and drove it down again, his back slamming against the hard wood underneath. A ripple of energy coursed up his spine, and he willed it to his arms and hands. With a tremendous wrench, he pulled the hands that held him apart, and the grip on his throat loosened and fell free. He saw her body lose balance and tumble from him then as he lay there making hoarse sucking sounds at the air.

But she was on her feet instantly, looking down at him. A slow, vulpine smile passed across those hate-contorted features, and she stilled the rage spasms of her body with a visible effort. The voice came again, low and slow and neutral in inflection, and this time he understood it. "Ah, for a moment...for a brief moment you understood...you knew the gift of life for what it is. But that's what it takes with your kind: You must be facing your own death to appreciate your puny life." Her face twisted into a look of disdain.

"Sheep! Ant! Cow!" she spat at him. "For the brief flicker of a momentary flame, you struggled, and your life became something more than a mere waking sleep, a vast lassitude. Do you regret it? Do you regret grinding the delicate pearl of life into muck? Ah, I wish I was not so young in this new body. It is here now, yet it is not. Time. A little time is still needed before my consciousness is fully absorbed."

He coughed, still grasping with tortured lungs for air, and her wicked smile grew. "Yes, I'm afraid I'm not up to some of the treats I would have had in store for you in another week or so. I regret having to be so mundane as to resort to physical violence, but, after all, you were rather resourceful in getting past my moon tower—that and the late lamented Mrs. Bloch."

He tried to raise up on his elbow, to scream his unbelieving hate and fear at her. Finally, the air was having an effect. Her uncertain form was beginning to substantialize in front of tear filled eyes, and his thoughts were beginning to respond to the insistent panic in him. The moment of decision was close, and he'd only have one chance to be ready for it.

"Do you abhor me? Do you condemn me? You who value the thought of merely existing more than the quality of your life. Do you judge me? It is like an ant judging a man. It is a cry of dumb pain that makes no difference." Her voice was like the poison of a thousand snakes.

"No!" he shouted, finally able to speak again. "I—I don't understand. I don't know if I can even believe it. All I do know is that you are not my Barb. And if what you say is true all it proves is that you needed her. . . needed one of we puny ordinary human beings. That doesn't make you so special, does it?"

Her smile was condescending now, her voice low and solemn. "Like the human needs the cow: to feed off of. To live on, that is all." He wanted to speak, to say something to give himself time, but she raised her hand in an imperious gesture. "No, I will not argue with a gnat. This little encounter—it was the prelude to your destiny, as pitiful as it is." She stopped, and he could see those eyes begin to swell and flame again.

Two small but preternaturally powerful hands were thrust overhead. Once gentle features were transformed into a mask of power, hate and delight, and the voice was as a growl. "Now is the moment itself. Enjoy it as you can." A crouch. Coiled power. Demon hate. He struggled with his fear—the certainty of death.

She was in mid-air, a scream of ultimate hate tearing out of her throat when he heard the sound from somewhere behind him. It was the same sound he'd heard exploding from his own hand in the tower room below. It repeated. Again and again. Time slowed to a crawl. The room pulsed and ebbed with a dim orangeish glow.

Her great leap stopped short, the lithe robed body falling to the floor in a jumbled heap of sudden agony, writhing. A great wail of surprise and pain. Self-doubt unknown for a century of power and dominion. The body twisted in the moon's dim glow, in the agony of torn flesh and spent blood. Haltingly, he gained his knee, struggling to stand.

The other's voice behind him. Now familiar, it sought him in fear and concern. The voice of his ally. The voice of one who had overcome his own pain and fear out of a greater concern for another. The voice of another of those puny, weak humans this woman-demon despised. Suddenly that voice sounded like the deep merciful chords of a god to him—the voice of the one who had saved him yet again.

But his attention snapped back to the one before him now. She was on her feet again, this time unsteadily. He could see her etched in the moonlight, and he knew then that it was a witch glow of icy fire and hostility to man. The moon and her: like one—great and powerful but cold and hostile to the life of man. He could see the great splotches of red covering the robe she wore even in the dim and silvery light of Luna's baleful eye; he could see the awful eyes, still full of power and hate; and lastly, he could see the gun that he had dropped in the battle before.

It was raised now, pointed somewhere behind him with a wavering but still potent hand. The hiss of death. Metallic fire. "Come in, detective," the awful voice rasped, "My mind had forgotten you."

A click from behind him. Another. The sound of hammer and empty cylinder, and a moan of despair. It was then that he knew. The smile of victory had just began to spread in silver luminescence across her face when he launched himself at her. He could hear her pull back the hammer just as his shoulder drove into her chest. Three long strides of fury, and he felt her give way before his charge—back, back, moving back. He wrapped his arms around her torso, and kept churning his legs forward, a vision of Barb beckoning to him in her distant purity ahead. She wailed, and fingers sought his throat—to rend and destroy.

There was as great fury in him now, a righteous and powerful wrath. In a shard of time he thought of Barb, and he thought of the pale, hideous counterfeit before him. This awful creature who had no right to live but he could feel her body beginning to slow down now, the unnatural power of her reacting in surprise to the quick strength of his attack. Oh, God. It has to be now, he thought.

Drawing back one hand, he drove it forward, into her belly—a belly riddled by many leaden holes. He heard the cry of pain and felt the hand at his throat slacken but still hold. He could feel her body tumble and begin to fall.

Fall, fall, fall. . .there was the sound of diamonds exploding around them, great glints of brilliant light bursting all about as they emerged from the rounded portal and out into the silvery night. Falling, falling. . . locked in a deadly embrace as the icy night hurtled to embrace them forever in their last journey. Something in him went free at that last sound—that great, inhuman cry of loss and grief.

38

Somehow he found his way through the great cavernous house again, chancing upon the two huge double doors that he figured must be the front entrance to the monstrous house. He turned the great key, slid back the huge iron bolt and pulled open one of those doors with a groan as his injured shoulder became a flame within him.

Moonlight, the long swell of grass stubbled hillside and the distant diamond-capped throb of the sea greeted him. It was cold now, bitterly so, and snowflakes were beginning to fall lazily from the sky. Above him he could make out the dark forms of the clouds as they moved swiftly to embrace the moon, but they had not touched yet. The full round orb shone spectrally like some huge lamp above the ocean, illuminating the slow, weaving course of his way.

Painfully he made his way down the hillside, the throb in his shoulder becoming an angry fire. His breath was ragged, and his chest heaved, but he struggled downward until he came to them. Torn and wrecked they lay there in a lover's final embrace.

He knelt and bent over the young man then, his eyes gone suddenly wet. Little known. Much shared in a short time. His face was neutral looking as it lay in the bloody bosom of the girl now, the lines of worry and anger suddenly erased. His life was gone, but his soul was at rest.

He looked at the other one. The neck was splayed out at a funny angle, probably broken in that long fall. The inside of her body a mush of broken bone and splattered tissue. What about her? In death had she become herself again, only to console him with her final breath?

Of course not. He had heard her great vulture scream of fear and hate, and he knew that death had had to be instantaneous as frail flesh hit solid rock and ground. Still, he wondered. He hadn't known her at all: not before all this insantiy had begun and not after she had become whatever she had become.

He sighed and looked out to the sea. It swelled and roared at him in barely muted power. Could it decide to heave itself up and wash over the land? Could it just suck that monstrous thing on the hill up and wash it away, down into some inky forgotten corner of forever sea? He wished it could be so, wished to have the knowledge and the memory blotted out of his mind.

Turning, he looked up at the vast looming carcass of the house. High atop its peak crouched the carven form of the winged thing, gleaming ghost-like in the baleful sheen of the moon. Suddenly, it seemed to twitch and move, two black wings unfolding and stiffly flapping against the sky. Awkwardly, it rose off its resting place and moved up into the heavens, there to flap a short while in ever widening circles above the hilltop. He watched silently and then heard its unearthly cry of revenge as it suddenly swooped in an immense looping arch, talons spread in destruction, to carry him into the sea.

He sighed and waved his hand in tired mockery, too soul weary for imagination or dread. With a grunt of pain and weariness, he took the first step back up the hill, knowing what he had to do. Something in him burned brighter than fatigue or fear for the moment: that age-old reverence for the dead. He was a slumped and solitary figure as he crawled ant-like up the side of that cancerous mound, thinking somewhere in that ridiculous house there had to be a shovel with which he could bury his friend. Above him the sky was cold and pure and empty except for droplets of crystalline white that only now were beginning to spread a slender blanket over the lonely earth.

ASSAULT ON BORDEAUX   LB570DK $1.50
B. J. Hurwood   War

Allied shipping in the North Atlantic was plagued by German submarines, based in the captured city of Bordeaux. They couldn't be attacked by air or sea. Or so the invaders thought! Four men set out to prove them wrong.

THE FREE AND THE BRAVE   LB591RK $2.25
John Cornwell   War

Not since CATCH-22 has there been a book that captures the war so well. Doomed to boring inactivity on the obsolete destroyer *Goddard,* George Kelly thought World War II would pass him by. Before long, he learned there was plenty of action—and danger—in the Caribbean!

DAWN COMMAND   LB600KK $1.75
Roland K. Jordon   War

The Pacific Fleet had been all but destroyed at Pearl Harbor, and there was nothing to threaten Japan's control of the seas. Nothing except the men whose bombers had survived the savage assault.

THE BATTERED BASTARDS   LB631 $1.75
Gordon French   War

In the middle of the heaviest action of the Battle of the Bulge, Sergeant Alan Bishop and his platoon of Screaming Eagles took what relief they could after six months in the front lines. Each one of them had his dreams—but they'd all settle for survival!
Setting: Bastogne, Belgium 1944

SGT. HAWK
Patrick Clay

LB640 $1.75
War

It was just another island in the Pacific to James Hawk and his Marines, another landing and another chance to kill Japanese—or be killed by them. But the Dutchman's plantation should have been a safe post for them, and, one by one, the Marines were being picked off!
Setting: the Pacific, 1943

HOLD SAIPAN!
William Herber

LB614 $2.25
War

Lieutenant Mike Andreas, U.S.M.C., had two jobs in front of him. The first one was tough—he had to convince his platoon of veterans that a green officer could lead them. The second job was impossible—he had to lead his men to the top of Mount Tapotchau on Japanese-held Saipan, and capture and hold the mountain!
Setting: Hawaii and Saipan, World War II

ACE OF SPIES
Robin Bruce Lockhart

LB650 $1.75
Adventure

Most espionage is done by anonymous men and women who work in back rooms of obscure ministries. The superspy who tracks down and stops the enemy singlehandedly is mostly a myth—except for Sidney Reilly, the British spy who changed the course of history!
Setting: Europe, World War I

THE HYDRA CONSPIRACY
Philip Kirk

LB655 $1.75
Adventure

Introducing Butler, the renegade ex-CIA agent who joins the fight to keep the U.S. out of the hands of the CIA and the military. In his first adventure, Butler confronts the super-secret and incredibly powerful organization known as Hydra!

SHARK HUNTER
Capt. William E. Young
LB563DK $1.50
Non-Fiction

The shark is the most feared creature in the oceans, and for good reason. It is also the most fascinating, attracting writers—and readers—from Zane Grey to Peter Benchley. No man knew them better than Captain William E. Young, who lived to kill them.

THE TUNGUS EVENT
Rupert Furneaux
LB619 $1.50
Non-Fiction

Thirty-three years before the atomic bomb, *something* streaked across the sky and exploded with a force 1500 times more powerful than the bomb that destroyed Hiroshima. No one knows what caused the explosion—only that it came from outer space. Now all the evidence is brought together in one book for the first time!

SEX WITHOUT ANXIETY
Nathan A. Shiff, M.D.
LB581VK $2.50
Non-Fiction

Dr. Shiff's experiences in the Pacific theatre during World War II awakened his realization that there was more to medicine than healing ordinary ailments. He found that many of his patients' problems, real and imaginary, were based on sexual dysfunction. In private practice at Broadway and 81st Street, a colorful New York crossroads of the world, Shiff spent thirty-five years treating everyone who came to his office—from Broadway stars to street prostitutes, male and female homosexuals, nuns, priests, and businessmen. SEX WITHOUT ANXIETY is the vivid account of Dr. Shiff's unusual practices and experience in treating complicated *sexual hangups* with medical knowledge and common sense.

SEND TO: LEISURE BOOKS
P.O. Box 270
Norwalk, Connecticut 06852

Please send me the following titles:

Quantity	Book Number	Price
_____	_____	_____
_____	_____	_____
_____	_____	_____
_____	_____	_____
_____	_____	_____

In the event we are out of stock on any of your selections, please list alternate titles below.

_____	_____	_____
_____	_____	_____
_____	_____	_____
_____	_____	_____

Postage/Handling _____

I enclose..... _____

FOR U.S. ORDERS, add 50¢ for the first book and 10¢ for each additional book to cover cost of postage and handling. Buy five or more copies and we will pay for shipping. Sorry, no C.O.D.'s.

FOR ORDERS SENT OUTSIDE THE U.S.A.
Add $1.00 for the first book and 25¢ for each additional book. PAY BY foreign draft or money order drawn on a U.S. bank, payable in U.S. ($) dollars.

☐ Please send me a free catalog.

NAME _____
(Please print)

ADDRESS _____

CITY _____ **STATE** _____ **ZIP** _____

Allow Four Weeks for Delivery